SCARLET DEVIL

MATT TOMERLIN

ISBN-13: 978-0-692-88765-3

Flintlock pistol by Bragin Alexey/Shutterstock.com.
Island map by Anna Trueman
Kate Warlowe hand print and Scarlet Devil jolly roger by Brendon Mroz

thedevilsfire.com | mtomerlin.com
Twitter: @MattTomerlin

For Dad.

A dude who conjured imaginative stories out of thin-air
with mere seconds of preparation.

① Cenote
② Spaniard Landing
③ World Tree
④ Cave Entrance
⑤ King Stela
⑥ Broken Stela
⑦ Persephone's Landing
⑧ Mangrove Forest

"Barbarism is the natural state of mankind. Civilization is unnatural. It is the whim of circumstance. And barbarism must always ultimately triumph."

— Robert E. Howard, *Beyond the Black River*

IX CHAK SAHKIL

The three men could only watch in despair as the masthead slipped beneath the water, leaving nothing but the tattered foretopsail floating in the waves, a red cross emblazoned on roiling white canvas. They knew no one else would emerge, but they did not permit sorrow, for the weight of so many lives could not yet be contemplated. The guilt of survival would come later, but for now they were happy to be alive, and they would not think about comrades trapped below decks in dwindling pockets of air, bracing their lungs to take in the same briny water that had concealed the sharp reef that had gutted the keel of their ship.

Their longboat was gone too, ruptured upon one of the many clusters of sharp rocks littering the treacherous shoals, forcing them to swim to shore. There had been five aboard when the boat eased into the waves, but they lost two to the sharks along the way.

The three survivors stood in the warm shallow water as little bubbles caressed their legs, rising from submerged fumaroles venting gas through cracks in the sea floor. They faced their new home, which was green and lush and quiet, with three dark grey volcanic peaks teasing the heavens. The white sands of the beach blistered their heels as they hopped across. They collapsed in the shady perimeter of the dense jungle, backs unguarded against that strange place where each would meet his end, estranged and terrified.

It seemed less than a few turns of the glass before the sun vanished behind the tallest peak. A pyramidal shadow extended before them, parting the sapphire of the sea and piercing the foretopsail floating in the water. The red cross became indistinguishable from darkening canvas, until the sail was finally absorbed by the ocean.

"El imperio en el que nunca se pone el sol," the carpenter remarked with an ironic chuckle, and then he was overtaken by a swell of grief, sooner than expected. He fell forward, setting his hands in the cool, shaded sand. A wave washed over the beach, and the other two men scattered before it could touch them. The carpenter laughed at their irrational fear. The water rushed over his hands and soaked his breeches, carving away the earth beneath him. He went on laughing and laughing until tears watered his cheeks and his belly seemed to be collapsing in on itself. A hand squeezed his shoulder. The hand had been branded on the backside with a cross. It was the young steward he had rescued from the hold, whose name escaped him. The lad had been pinned by a barrel, and the carpenter had leveraged him free with an oar as water cascaded in on all sides.

The steward helped the carpenter up and into the jungle, but not too far in, and they sat in a soft patch of sand the sea could not reach. Two iguanas, one bright green and the other light grey, scampered off. Signs of life lifted the carpenter's spirits a little, enough for him to gaze upward and thank his maker for sparing him, though he could not imagine what he had done to deserve God's grace. The steward joined in. The third man, an old cook, turned and spat in the sand to make plain his thoughts on God.

The jungle came alive with the sounds of animals, squawking birds, buzzing insects, and chattering monkeys. The carpenter wasn't certain if the animals had been keeping quiet until now or if his ears had finally cleared of water. Small shapes dashed through the trees, lithe and dark.

The cook, a grimy fellow with deep creases in his cheeks and a salt-and-pepper beard, was the first to hazard the jungle in search of food, hoping to find some fruit or catch a monkey. And that was the last they saw of him.

In the hours that followed, the carpenter was too tired to lament the cook's absence, even as it became clear the man would never return. He hadn't known the cook all that well, and he'd never cared for his meals.

The swim to shore had stolen the carpenter's energy. He marveled at the steward's wide-eyed alertness. He asked his name, the boy told him, and he promptly forgot it. He inquired about the brand on the steward's hand, and the boy told him he was a blasphemer. He offered no further explanation.

Through breaches in the jungle canopy the sky was dark and alive with starlight by the time the carpenter closed his eyes.

When he awoke, a muted violet gave the jungle a ghostly

illumination, and the air was warm and wet. He was alone. He spotted an imprint in the sand where the steward had been resting his ass, but no other sign of him. The carpenter licked his chapped lips and swallowed, wincing. He needed water. He stood on uncertain legs, setting his hand on a tree to steady himself, and trekked into the jungle without delay. His head throbbed in the sweltering humidity. His stomach seemed to be feeding off itself and drawing inward. He needed something, anything, in his belly. The sky grew brighter through the trees, but the canopy was growing thicker. Soon he was stumbling through fat palm fronds and thorny bushes. A plump hummingbird with dark feathers and a vibrant green crest almost slapped him in the face, hovering before him and tilting its head inquisitively before zipping off to attend to whatever business hummingbirds attend to.

The flora swirled about him in a colorful blur as he tried to take in everything at once. When the colors threatened to make him sick, he looked down and watched his bare feet marching one after the other. Dried blood encrusted his left foot. Had a shark bitten him? He couldn't remember. And what had happened to his boots? Had he lost them during the swim? It didn't matter. He would have removed them anyway, thanks to the heat. He unlaced his shirt and tore it free, tossing it away. It landed on a fern and settled there. He would retrieve it if he came back this way.

He wouldn't come back this way.

Some animal loosed a guttural, predatory growl. The carpenter's heels left the ground, his heart stopped mid-flight, and he settled in the sand an impressive distance away, knees bent and hands splayed. He pirouetted in place, but he found nothing of danger to fend against. Another growl, much closer, much louder. It was so close he felt it in his gut. And then, with a relieved laugh, he realized it *was* his gut. He ran the back of his hand over his damp forehead. The heat made him feel heavy, lost in a sweltering fog. He trudged forward, determined to find relief. This was an island. There was vegetation. There were birds. There had to be water.

Time slipped away. He might have walked for minutes, he might have walked for hours. The sky began to surrender its vibrancy through the canopy above. Bright blue yielded to light purple. He swallowed, and the walls of his esophagus stuck together. He choked, forcing air through. He pushed onward, no longer watching his step, slapping at plants. Giant leaves offered casual vengeance, rebounding on springy stems to strike him in the arms and face.

The ground inclined but he refused to let it slow his pace. He scaled the hill with his eyes on the ground and the crown of his head aimed forward like a missile, and he almost cracked his skull on the trunk of the great ceiba tree standing at the top. Thick, gnarled branches curled upward, reaching for the heavens, or supporting them. He stood between the massive buttress roots unfurling from the trunk's base, plunging to untold depths. Slick green vines entangled the roots, veins that fed the tree with the blood of the Earth. The ground was a vast web of smaller roots, spongy underfoot like a rotting deck threatening to give way. He imagined horrible little creatures with too many legs nestled in the dark crevices, watching him. This tree was old. Very old. Perhaps it had been here since the beginning of time. He circled it, stepping around the roots, some of which were taller than him.

His fascination with the monstrous thing was short-lived.

On the opposite side he discovered a severed hand pinned to the trunk, its palm flat against the bark, lopped at the wrist. Black blood oozed a path down the tree, indistinguishable in the darkening shade from the many streams of sap. A thin, bleached stingray spine served as a nail, driven through the center of the cross branded into the hand. Dread and sorrow crept into the carpenter's gut, chilling the sweat on his brow and prickling the flesh of his arms. He backed away, almost sticking his foot in a human-sized hole. He stared into the void, wondering how far down it went. He shouted a greeting, expecting to hear his voice in return, but there was only silence. Until, after a prolonged moment, a voice answered . . . but not his own. It croaked something in English, which he did not understand. And then, something moved in the black. At first he thought he was looking at a crab or a very large spider, but he'd never seen a spider with pink flesh.

Fingers, he realized. Trembling fingers, dirty and bloody, reaching for him.

He caught his heel on a root and tumbled backwards down the hill. It was a small miracle that he avoided rolling over any large rocks on his way down, suffering little more than welts and scratches. When he reached to the bottom he sprang to his feet and ran. He felt eyes upon his back, but he would not stop to confirm his paranoia. Whatever he had glimpsed in that black abyss had crawled free, and it was coming after him. He ran until his clothes were soaked and his heart threatened to burst.

He ran out into a big green field, through tall green grass bending in the wind. He skirted a little stream that zigzagged its way through the field. A gut-curdling howl sounded somewhere behind him and rolled across the grass like thunder. Some demonic thing giving chase . . . or a howler monkey. He would not stop to find out. He reached the end of the field and returned to the dark sanctity of the jungle.

He was not in the jungle long. The end came without warning. His toes caught on something, bending his knees, and he flew forward, raking his shins on a hard, washboarded surface. The jungle had opened upon a clearing where the ground was nothing more than a large round plate of dark grey rock, unbroken by trees or weeds, with a towering stone pillar standing at the center, casting a long shadow from the setting sun in the west. He moved around the pillar, framing it within the three peaks, which stood as shadows in the distance, further than they had appeared from the beach. It was nearly forty feet tall, carved of the same dark rock, casting its shadow over him. The carpenter had seen these monuments before, but usually made of sandstone, and never had he seen one so tall. The figure of a proud man, likely a king, was engraved in the stone. His eyes were large blank orbs, his mouth half-open. He wore a crown of three stacked skulls topped with an elaborate headdress. His attire was a labyrinth of indecipherable patterns and glyphs. Before him, stretching from foot to chin, was a long, thin tree. Large serpents with feathers emerging from their yawning mouths flanked the king. He was perched atop a plinth engraved with a fat, dreadful face, also wearing a crown. At the foot of the monument sat an unremarkable rectangular stone block topped with a flat stone slab, almost as long as a bed. Perhaps it was an altar for offerings to the king.

Nothing alerted him to the woman behind him. He turned without knowing why, and there she was, standing exactly where he had emerged from the jungle. Her age was a mystery. She might have been less than twenty, but she carried herself with the knowledge and careless grace of a woman twice that age. Her skin was a rich medium-brown, much like the natives he had glimpsed during his time at Tulum. Heavily-lidded brown eyes studied him skeptically with a hint of curiosity. She was very pretty, with plump cheeks, a broad nose, and full lips. Her face sloped into the proud oval of her chin. A band of blood-red paint ran across her eyes, from one temple to the other. Her posture was straight and regal, her body robust and curvaceous. She was slightly taller than the carpenter, and he was not a short man. A lofty headdress of quetzal feathers sprouted from her skull and fountained about her. A white shift dress embroidered with red and orange beads clung to her majestic form, tucked into a waistband. A gigantic medallion covered her navel, etched with the face of a proud man who wore the upper half of a jaguar's head for a hat, its fangs piercing his brow. A brown skirt sheltered her dress, woven with red stripes that descended from her hips and met between her legs in a sharp V. Beaded metallic cuffs shackled her thick wrists and ankles. She walked barefoot toward him, intoxicating him with the easy movement of her strong legs. She spoke strange, alien words with an inquisitive tilt of her head. "Ka páahtal in natz'ik imbah?"

He shrugged.

She came closer, eyeing his clothing. "Tu'ux a taal?"

Perhaps she was asking his name. He opened his mouth to tell her, but the name caught in his throat. He held it there as long as he was able, and then it fell away, lost somewhere inside him. How could he have forgotten his own name? Had he hit his head?

She pressed an index finger to her nose and said, "In k'aaba Chak Sahkil." She placed the same finger on his nose. "Ba'ax a k'aaba'?"

He shied from her delicate touch and told her he needed water. She did not seem to understand the word. "Bixi'?" she said. He bowled his hands and brought them toward his mouth. She seemed to understand that. "An! Uk'aheech? A k'áat ha'?"

He nodded eagerly. She took his arm and led him toward the altar. Her touch was gentle. Warmth streamed through her fingertips like blood through a vein, and for whatever reason he thought of the vines entwining the branches of the huge tree he had encountered earlier. He didn't see any jugs or goblets of water at the altar, but he let her guide him. His legs were wobbly, the gashes in his knees trickling blood down his shins. When he reached the altar, he collapsed atop the stone slab and rolled onto his back. The dark pillar loomed overhead, aimed at the center of the sky, and there he saw a faint pinprick of white light. She leaned forward and whispered in his ear in a deeper, seductive voice. "Tun yée'ho'ch'e'ental."

He did not protest when she unlaced his breeches. She peeled the sweat-soaked cloth from his waist and slid his breeches down his legs. A light, cool breeze caressed his damp, naked skin. She hiked up her skirt and mounted him. His thirst was not forgotten, but it became a distant concern he assured himself he would address later. She was heavier than he expected, weighting down his pelvis. Her strong legs held him in place. In his exhausted state, he would not have been able to escape even if he wished to. She set one palm on his chest, above his thudding heart, and curled her fingers. Her movements were slow, as though she had all the

9

time in the world, and she murmured in her strange language what he assumed were sweet-nothings. He cupped her breasts, felt nipples hardening against his palms through the fabric of her dress. She took hold of his wrists and slid his hands down to her waist. He tugged at her dress, drawing it up through the waistband so he could feel her smooth, sun-kissed skin.

It had been too long since he'd felt a woman's touch, though he couldn't remember exactly how long. Months? A year? He knew he had a wife waiting in . . . wherever he had come from. What was her name? Did they have children together? Yes, he was certain they did. At least one. A boy. Shiny black hair. His mother's hair. A round, jovial face split down the center. Innocence to the left, mischief to the right, neither mingling with the other. The boy was a nuisance, but his father had never been able to stay angry at him. They'd embraced before he left. A long, tight embrace. Take me with you. I can't. Next time. When you're older. He could still feel the boy's pudgy little fingers digging into his shoulders, hoping to root him in place. The boy knew his father would not return.

The woman slid her index finger up the side of the carpenter's face and massaged his temple. His son's features eased into the black, lost forever. The specifics of his life seemed a troublesome triviality. He wasn't sure why he had ever cared. His thirst had robbed him of all concern.

It didn't matter.

She was all that mattered now.

He seized her waist as he neared climax, digging his fingers in. The face in the huge medallion at the front of her waistband seemed to be reproaching him, so he slapped a hand upon the cold metal, yet still he felt a judgmental impression against his palm. She moaned in ecstasy as he struggled to hold back his seed for as long as possible. He was dimly aware of movement out of the corner of his eyes. A shadow moving around the monument, watching, but keeping its distance. The thing that had materialized from the pit beneath the tree had followed him all the way here. He ignored the interloper in favor of the woman's beautiful, alien face. Her dark eyes arrested his through the band of red paint smeared across her face.

He did not know there was a dagger in her hand until the tip of the blade pierced his flesh, below the sternum, and then it was too late. She leaned into the hilt, inserting the jagged obsidian blade underneath his ribcage and up into his chest. A searing bolt clinched every muscle in his body, none harder than the one between her thighs. He wanted to strangle her, but his hands slid from her hips. He managed to lift his head. He felt every notch of the blade as she withdrew it. She set the dagger on the slab in a growing pool of blood. She extended four fingers, tucked her thumb into her palm, and drove her hand into the open wound. She did not halt until half of her forearm was in his torso. He heard himself shrieking like some mangled animal as his seed coursed upward in concussive surges. Her belly constricted as if to lock him within. She arched her back. The last sliver of the sun flared as it slid below the jungle, and the brilliant light swallowed the young king's features for an instant. The quetzal feathers of the woman's headdress flashed of dazzling iridescence, from green to blue to gold. When the light dimmed, the king's face remained indifferent to the carpenter's terror. Perhaps those vacant orbs saw everything the carpenter had forgotten. Perhaps they saw nothing. Neither was a comfort.

Her fingers probed beneath his ribcage, wriggling through the network of his interior like a tarantula scouting for a secret place to build her nest. Foul odors assaulted his nostrils, tinged with the stench of his own shit. The woman's sweet face showed no revulsion, only determination. She grinned when she found what she needed. Her fingers clutched firmly and she twisted her wrist.

Lightning struck the top of the monument. A red bolt from a cloudless sky, originating from somewhere beyond his sight. There was no sound. The trees slid from his peripheral vision as he fell skyward. The world blackened. Stars blinked into existence, one after another, and then hundreds at a time, and then too many to count. He let his head fall sideways, and he glimpsed the stone pillar and the blood-covered slab far below, tumbling into the darkness. Soon there was nothing but the pair of them penetrating one another on a curved highway of stars. The starry road stretched for more leagues than his mind could comprehend, connecting to some impossibly bright orb that framed her body. There were other highways spiraling outward from the light, turning slowly. And in the blackness far beyond, he saw more orbs, each birthing their own spiraled highways.

She removed his heart and showed it to him. Thousands of stars danced like mad fireflies in its red sheen. Severed valves spurted hot blood across his face and into his eyes. The stars burned crimson. Each pulse of the heart echoed in the cavity from which the organ had been extracted. It beat three times, no more. He withered inside her.

As the red universe forfeited its luminance, a nagging voice from a long-forgotten past urged him to make peace with God. He knew very little, and soon he would know less.

He only knew there was no God. There never had been. There was only her.

I

THE MAP

PREY

"Snow should never fall so near the sea," the captain murmured to herself as soft flakes trailed from a darkening grey sky and dotted her cheeks with icy freckles. A light dusting had collected on the furled sails above, and the tall trees lining the broad river were already topped with snow, luminous even in the deepest blues of twilight.

As she gazed at the frosted trees from the main deck, she thumbed one of the silver death's head buttons of her maroon coat. Overcome with a sudden, involuntary shiver, she tugged the flaps close to her chest, binding herself in it, but it was a poor blanket. Not since London had she watched her breath freeze before her face. Long ago, before all this. The garbled skin of her severed right ear ached in the cold, even beneath her dense shroud of red hair.

She had ordered most of the crew to return for the night, to sleep below decks where they might keep some semblance of warmth. The men had made camp on the northern bank of the river, huddled about small fires that would not attract much attention, but they were not prepared for this kind of weather. They had few jackets and fewer blankets, and only so much canvas left to drape a tent after patching the sails. They had ferried back to the ship earlier that afternoon. It was hard to believe so many men were lingering beneath her feet. She couldn't hear a sound. The cold had pilfered their energy, and the only thing they wanted to do was drink until they passed out. She felt inclined to do the same, but she needed to remain alert.

Her fingertips grazed the splintered starboard rail where a cannonball had skimmed past, killing a young deckhand named Timmons in the process. A few inches lower and the cannonball would only have damaged the bulwark, and Timmons would be breathing still. When she closed her eyes, she could still see the remains of his head, the twisted mockery of a once handsome face sinking into a pink stew of shattered bone and brain matter.

Her trailing index finger halted on something sticky. The deckhands had cleaned most of the blood, but they had missed a spot. She wondered how many red spots were hidden in the grain of her ship, tarred over and forgotten between the creases of new planking inlaid beside the old. The many repairs and careens over the years had temporarily renewed her, but the *Scarlet Devil* was old, as ships go, her age accelerated by constant travel and frequent combat. She was an eighty-foot long brigantine of one-hundred-and-fifty tons. Clean sails, new masts, and spars would not sustain her forever. Teredo worms, which thrived in the warm Caribbe-

18

an waters, had eaten away at the hull over the years. The captain kept a clean ship, but the aftermath of the battle had left her deck affright, littered with heaps of cordage and empty bottles that collected near the scuppers. She hadn't the heart to order the men to clean it up, not now, not after her blunder. And she wasn't sure it mattered. The ship had another year left in her, maybe two. She creaked and groaned even in still waters. A ship that frequented the Caribbean could not last more than ten years, even under constant care. Like the bones of an elderly woman, her ache ran deeper than surface damage.

The captain's regret ran just as deep. She had lingered too long in the Atlantic, preying on merchant ship after merchant ship. "No prey, no pay!" she had shouted to her men, again and again. They chanted it in turn, with an insatiable hunger brightening their eyes, though their pockets were already weighted with coin. She had ignored the uncertainty that crept into her belly as the men continued to chant, "No prey, no pay!" long after she had stopped. She could have swayed them against further greed, if she had so desired. She could have called for a vote after leveraging key members of the crew in her favor, but the anticipation of one more plunder took priority.

"No prey, no pay! No prey, no pay!" The chant echoed in her mind, distant and haunting, but loud enough to serve as a mocking reminder of the fortitude she no longer felt. Scouring the Atlantic was dangerous work, and she longed to return to the Caribbean, but greed had pressed her and her men ever onward as they pretended not to notice the mounting chill in the wind. Their final prey had been a simple British merchantman, or so she had thought. That mistake had cost her twenty-four lives. After sighting the ship fine on the starboard bow, the pirates had pursued their quarry for the better part of a day, firing chase guns when in range, shattering windows of the stern gallery and punching holes in the mizzen's course and topsail. This went on at some length until they were within view of the Virginia coast. The captain ordered her colors hoisted, a black flag with a horned crimson skull suspended above a pair of crossed humerus bones. More often than not, the sight of her banner put a fright in any merchant captain with an inkling of good sense, either spurring him into flight or jarring him to a halt. This vessel did not halt for the *Scarlet Devil's* jolly roger, nor did it increase its pace, except when the pirate ship gained speed. She should have known then what the enemy was up to, because it was a trick she had employed more than once.

The ship lured them into a secluded bay, and she ordered her ship within range of a broadside. The fight seemed to be over, for the prey had struck their colors and topgallants. She readied a boarding party, which she would happily lead, and called to the other vessel in a cordial but firm voice, "Lower arms, furl sails, open all hatches, and we shall grant good quarter."

But the merchantman was more heavily armed than any of her scouts had been able to discern through a spyglass. In fact, it was a warship. Her armament had been carefully concealed, the many gunports covered with undetectable paneling. The volley that followed pulverized *Scarlet Devil's* mainmast and hull, leaving twelve dead. The ensuing cannon and musket fire that originated from the shore killed seven more. Five died of their wounds after *Scarlet Devil* put the enemy to her rudder before suffering another crippling attack.

"It was a trap," the boatswain, Hawkes, had needlessly remarked. "They lured us into a trap. Why do that? Why go to all the trouble?"

The captain had a theory, but she wasn't prepared to share it with her crew. The year was seventeen-twenty-seven. Eight years had passed since she purchased her ship. In that time, most pirates with a name had been captured and executed. She was among the last, and the Crown did not suffer pirates to live. Her audacity had been noted. She had been too successful where others had failed. Somewhere in England someone was scheming to put an end to her once and for all. Woodes Rogers, former governor of the Bahamas, was the first name that came to mind. She had slighted him one too many times, and his failure to apprehend her had festered until he could think of nothing else.

"How many times must I tell you to trim that hair?" came a wry voice from behind, wrenching her into the present. She didn't have to turn to know it was Breton, the surgeon.

"Never," she replied. She ran a hand through the crimson mane that spilled halfway down her back, streaked orange here and there by the Caribbean sun. She had braided red silk ribbons into random locks, lining them with shells that lightly clacked when she turned her head.

"Suppose you'll get it caught in a block before you heed my warning."

"Good thing I don't work before the mast. What do you want?"

"Lost another," he answered.

Twenty-five, she thought as she plucked at a loose splinter along the bulwark. "What was his name?"

"Kelvin."

She twisted the splinter until it came loose, flicking it

over the side. There was no sense pretending she recognized the dead crewman's name. She knew more than half of her crew, but it was impossible to memorize every face. "Who was he?"

"Just a deckhand," Breton replied casually.

She turned to face him, setting her rear against the rail. "How old?"

"I wager he couldn't have been more'n sixteen." If there was any judgment in the surgeon's face, he hid it behind a weathered mask of indifference. His skin was dark and cracked, with scabby red patches on his cheeks and forehead. His hair was light blonde with only a few hints of grey, is mustache equally golden. His white shirt, which had been clean and new not so long ago, was rusty with dried blood. He seemed to have aged two years in the past week from lack of sleep as he tended to the wounded.

"One of the lads who enlisted from the *Diligent*?"

Breton nodded. "Aye."

A snowflake infiltrated her vision, touching the tip of her nose. She resisted a shiver and wiped it away. The gold and silver bracelets sang like wind chimes, drawing attention to the casual motion. She cursed her affinity for shiny things, which had grown worse over the years. The large golden hoop that dangled from her remaining ear was her most hazardous piece of jewelry. She'd been fortunate to not yet have it torn off in combat. "Don't suppose he went in his sleep?"

"He went in violent throes. Slapped me in the face twice, the little rotter." Breton never softened his prickly disposition, not even when delivering news of a death. She would never tell him, but she admired that about him. She had hoped so much time in the company of death would harden her to it, but it never had. Not when it came to her crew, anyway. "He said something about God cursing him for a traitor, and then he was gone."

"God didn't curse him." *I did*, she almost said.

The surgeon stroked his mustache as he looked past her, into the distance. "You may not recall the boy, but I do. He was awfully eager to sign our papers."

"We didn't exactly give him a choice," she reminded him.

"Aye, but you're not exactly known for murdering a man who refuses the offer. You cannot take credit for every death, much as you'd fancy the blame."

Had the perpetually grouchy surgeon offered a kindness? She decided not to ask, for fear the answer would disappoint. "He was a boy," she reminded him. "Not a man."

He waved a dismissive hand flaked with dried blood. "He wanted to be a man. And now he is."

The surgeon's glib tone irritated her. "I think you should get some sleep."

His face reddened in offense. "I what?"

She pointed at his dirty fingers, knotted and twitchy from constant use. "Those are no good to anyone right now."

He locked his hands behind his back, as if that would solve the problem. "Still have to bury the dead."

"Not tonight. Tomorrow we'll have a funeral." She pointed at the trees of the northern bank. "We'll bury him out there. Far enough inland so the water can't touch him."

The surgeon looked puzzled. "Dirt is no kind of grave for a sailor."

"The sea brought him nothing but death," she said. "The least we can do, with land so near, is spare him an eternity in its depths."

Breton relented with an incline of his head. "And where

would you see yourself buried, Captain?"

The irrelevance of the question gave her an involuntary chuckle. "Do you think I'll be given a choice?"

"Nay, but if you were?"

She hadn't thought about it. It was pointless to dwell on the inevitable. "I won't be alive to care, but I hope whoever buries me puts a great deal of thought into what I might have wanted."

The surgeon barked a bitter laugh and took his leave, disappearing below deck.

The captain turned around and placed a fist against the shattered rail, grinding her knuckles into the splintered wood until pain spiked through her hand. She hissed through her teeth as a small stream of blood seeped into the grain. This was as much open lament as she could afford, at least until she was behind closed doors.

"To hell with this," she cursed at the falling snow. It would do no good to linger here. Mourning and regret would not bring the dead back to life.

She started toward the bow. There was a full moon somewhere beyond the thick cloud cover, providing eerie illumination. The snow increased, tumbling silently. Most of the flakes dissolved in the planking after hitting the deck, but the larger flakes remained, clumping together. Not a week prior the deck had been slick with blood. Soon it would be slick with ice. When she reached the bow, she watched the dim ripples of the river glide past. It gave the illusion of movement, but the stillness of the snow-topped trees was a reminder that the ship was anchored firmly in place.

Only a few lookouts were posted on deck. Killian and Slim were gambling beneath the amber glow of the mainmast lantern, and Gangly John played a garish tune on his old fiddle while belting lyrics that always culminated in, "Betwixt the swells, that's where she dwells, and ne'er shall you take her!" His bald pate was turning white beneath the snowfall, but he seemed oblivious. She considered telling him to stop playing and go below, but John was the oldest of the crew, and useless apart from his fiddle. The men liked him. She liked him. So she would let him play his annoying tune, even though its morbid lyrics only darkened her already unsalvageable mood.

There were no chores left for these men tonight. Aside from Gangly John, the efficiency of her crew never ceased to impress her. After retreating to the safety of the estuary and sailing upriver, they had wasted no time repairing the mainmast and patching the many breaches in the starboard hull. They had gathered water in barrels and wood for the galley stove and campfires. A hunting party had gone into the woods and returned the next day with fat hogs and the meat of black cattle, and later that night the smell of roast hog had wafted down the river, and the crew slumbered with full bellies, forgetting their troubles despite the cold.

She was proud of her men, and disgusted with herself for allowing them to get into this situation, but she never let them glimpse her shame. She was still their captain, and she had afforded them too many victories to let one failure taint her leadership.

A lookout had spotted the enemy ship only once since the battle. It had sailed past but had not entered the river. This position was hardly defenseless, with a narrow entrance and little room for maneuverability. The enemy wouldn't have aid of an ambush this time, as they had in the bay. Still, that wouldn't be enough to stop a ship of that size from getting through and finishing her off. It was only a matter of time. *They were prepared for this*, she reminded herself. She looked again to the darkening sky. The white flakes fell like stars that had grown too weary to remain aloft. As efficient as her crew was, she wondered how much longer they could withstand this weather. It was only the beginning of winter, and it would get worse before it got better.

She guessed the enemy had moored their ship some-where nearby, waiting for her to emerge. She had dispatched two scouting parties—one led by Quartermaster Corso, and the other by her unofficial first mate, Gabe Jenkins—into the woods earlier in the day to determine just that. They were currently investigating the bay where the ambush had taken place. It was an obvious spot to linger in, but too often she had found the obvious answer to be the correct one. She had instructed her scouts to be careful and quiet, and take no action should they secret upon the enemy.

She was sick of waiting. She wanted out of here. The trees on either bank of the river felt like walls closing in. And now the sky conspired against her, raining ice upon her deck. The exit to sea beckoned in the distance. The gap was so inviting, so open, begging her to slip through to freedom. And maybe she could. Maybe she would get lucky. But her enemy would endure, even follow her all the way to the Caribbean. She would not take that chance. And she would not let twenty-four—twenty-*five*, now—deaths be for nothing.

She had told herself she wouldn't find sleep until her scouts returned, but her body did not share her mind's resolve. The snowfall grew dense, weighting her hair. She ran a hand over her scalp, and her fingers came away glisten-ing with ice. After three hours of pacing the deck, with the cold biting at the raw skin of her lost ear and seeping through her coat, her eyelids grew too heavy to ignore. "I'm going to get some rest," she announced to the lookouts, and started for her cabin.

"Captain," one of the men shouted from aloft, halting her.

"What?" She massaged the rubbery skin of her absent ear. *I just want to sleep. Is that too much to ask?* She glanced around until she found a shape perched in the main cross-trees. She squinted through half-blurred sight until she could make him out. It was Charlie. The young man seemed impervious to sleep, and never lacked for energy. He pointed to the northern bank.

It was hard to see through the falling flakes, but she glimpsed movement near the boat on the bank. Three dark shapes climbed aboard and started rowing for the ship.

He's back.

She maintained a stolid expression when Gabe finally climbed over the gunwale. He wasn't smiling—he never smiled—but she knew him well enough to know when his pulse was racing. He swept a loose curl of thick black hair out of his eyes while catching his breath. Though he was the same age as the captain, he appeared to have overtaken her by at least five years. The pinch in his brow had lengthened since first they met. She had always warned him not to scowl so much. He remained incredibly fetching, in a grizzled sort of way. He didn't shave as often as he used to. He had let his curly hair grow out. Aside from a blue sash around his waist, he dressed all in black, as usual. The jeweled hilt of a curved Ottoman dagger protruded from his sash. It was his favorite weapon, and she didn't want to guess how many lives it had claimed. "You found something," she said, forgoing a greeting.

"How did you know?" he asked between heavy breaths as the other two members of his party, the Castillo twins, climbed over the gunwale to join him. Their black hair was wet with perspiration. They greeted her with their customary stupid grins, despite looking exhausted and cold.

She folded her arms. "You were in a hurry to get back."

"We just missed them," Gabe answered with a sigh. "We found the leavings of campfires and the stakes of tents." He hesitated, glancing at her uncertainly.

"And?" She didn't appreciate being kept in suspense.

The Castillos exchanged wary glances.

"And this." Gabe reached down the cleft of his shirt and produced a rolled parchment. "Pinned to the largest tree, so we wouldn't miss it."

She snatched the parchment out of his hand and unrolled it. It was stiff from weather and sticky with sap, stained with golden spots. The words were few, but bold and large, spread across the entire page:

No Pyrate shall
escape The Gallows
Not even
Bloodshot Kate

The note didn't frighten her as much as the author had hoped, but it did put a murderous fury in her gut. "Bloodshot," she grated as she looked over the parchment. Of all the colorful monikers, she hated that one most.

She crumpled the parchment in a fist, until her knuckles turned white as bone, and tossed the bunched wad away. She swiveled on her heels, marching aft. Gabe followed her across the deck, all the way up to the quarterdeck. She stared at the exit of the estuary, not a mile down river. Her right eye strained through the falling snow, and she ignored the throbbing behind it. She would find no sleep tonight, and tomorrow she would have a splitting headache. That was the least of her worries.

"What's our move, Captain?" Gabe asked.

The formality curled her lips into an involuntary smile, while the pleasing image of him slumbering naked in her bed flashed through her mind. She wished she could find the time for him tonight, but that wasn't going to happen. So she kept her back to him, because if she looked at him, she might forget her resolve in those wayward strands of curly hair. And if she made the mistake of locking eyes with him for too long, she might lose herself entirely. "They're out there," she said. "Patrolling. Moving camp each night."

"They will attack at night," he said.

"I had hoped to catch them unaware at their camp, swarm down on them with all our might."

"It would seem they anticipated that. They won't stop until they've scuttled this ship."

"The ship is of no consequence." Her raspy voice sounded distant to her, as though someone else spoke the words emerging from her lips. "It's me they want."

"Well, they'll have to come through the rest of us first."

She angled her head uncertainly. "Hawkes would happily hand me over to them."

He laughed. "The crew would never back Hawkes."

"Hawkes is a fool," said Domingo Suárez del Castillo as he reached the quarterdeck with his brother, Salvador, in tow. The only reason she could tell the twins apart was the scar running down the center of Domingo's chin. Somehow, she thought that gave him the edge in looks. She had never asked their age, but they couldn't have been more than twenty-five. They were short and small of frame, but dangerous in a fight. Their expressions were ever-mischievous, with thin black mustaches that curled up at the ends, accentuating their smiles.

"Some of them would," she insisted.

"How many?" Gabe wondered. "A dozen?"

She shook her head. "More like a score."

"Not enough in a vote," said Salvador.

The captain sighed. "This little misstep may have cost me numerous votes, should I require their favor. One failure soils a thousand victories."

Domingo twisted a handle of his mustache between thumb and forefinger. "Only if failing is the last thing you ever do."

His words brought her no comfort. "Failing is the last thing anyone ever does."

"A captain is allowed a misstep," said Gabe.

Not a pirate captain, she wanted to say, but she didn't feel like a pirate or a captain right now. She felt like prey. *No prey, no pay.* Was the enemy captain shouting that very phrase at his men right now, in preparation for a final attack? Only one crew would get paid before this was over.

"It's not a misstep if it ends in victory," Gabe said, and the Castillos nodded their agreement.

She faced them. She was tired of deliberating. She was tired of waiting for the inevitable. She hated waiting. She would rather die swiftly than wait here one more day to die a slow, cold death, as the ice froze her ship in place. And she doubted the enemy captain would wait much longer either. The man fought without honor. The man fought like a pirate.

"He's a pirate," she said aloud as the realization struck her.

"Who?" asked Gabe.

"Their captain. He uses subterfuge. Dirty tactics. Concealing his gunports. Playing the part of prey. Have you ever seen royal navy try that? Why would they need to?"

The crease in Gabe's brow lengthened as he tried to work it out. "Maybe he's working for the Crown. Maybe they hired him."

She bit her lower lip. "We anticipated everything but ourselves. Rogers is getting smart. There will be no staying here."

"Woodes Rogers?" said Domingo. "You think he's behind this?"

She nodded slowly. "I know he is. And whomever he's hired will be coming for us very soon. Pirates aren't a patient lot, are they?"

Gabe straightened his back. "Then they will meet our guns."

Any other day she would have welcomed his confidence, but she knew he was only humoring her. "Our guns will be of little consequence unless we use them smartly." She turned back to the rail and gazed down into the black water. The larger snowflakes did not dissolve immediately when they hit the water, but lingered atop the surface for a few seconds, flowing downstream before they dissolved. "There's only one way out of this. We have to give them what they want."

"And what is that?" Gabe wondered.

No prey, no pay. The words echoed. Captain Kate Warlowe heard her own voice, louder than all the rest. "Me."

RENEWED

"I hereby surrender myself to your captain," Kate announced after being helped over the bulwark onto the well-lit main deck of the enemy ship by two burly deckhands.

The shirtless, bearded man on the left was hairy as an ox everywhere except his bald head, and the cold air did nothing to quell his sweating. He stunk like an animal that slept in its own filth. He had fumbled at her inner thighs with feigned clumsiness as he helped her up, licking his chapped lips. After she was aboard, the far less smelly but equally large deckhand on the right kept a massive hand on the small of her back longer than was appropriate, until she asked, "Is this a courtship?"

The crew gathered around to stare at her, as though they'd never seen such a strange creature. And maybe they hadn't. She must have painted quite the picture, with her provocatively low shirt, long red coat, shiny ornaments, and casual stance. She gazed confidently over their dirty faces. Above them, a frosted British flag hung limp and motionless.

It hadn't taken long for the warship to make its presence known after two of *Scarlet Devil's* men rowed out in a longboat with torches for beacons, waving a white flag. She had waited for a strong wind to kick up before dispatching them. The wind swirled in from the east, angling the snowfall. The warship had closed with haste, presenting a towering silhouette at full sail. Kate had boarded a longboat to meet them halfway. The warship dropped anchor and doused canvas in the middle of the river, its crew moving about their various tasks with practiced efficiency. Its fat hull broke the glassy black water that ran toward it like liquefied obsidian. The long bowsprit targeted *Scarlet Devil* in the distance, promising a spear of vengeance should the pirates try anything foolish.

It was now two hours before dawn. The wind had died down in the last hour, but the snowfall persisted, each flake weaving a haphazard course through the night, unconcerned with the petty dealings of those it settled upon. The banks of the river were now thick with snow, the trees weighted by heavy clumps that bowed the branches.

"You do have a captain, don't you?" she said, after a long silence from stunned faces. Many were young, but here and there she spotted the weathered face of a seasoned sailor. Cracked lips and sun-marbled skin. Earlobes stretched by oversized hoops. Rusty cutlasses and trusty old pistols. None were wanting for food, however. There were no sunken cheeks or bony limbs. Their eyes weren't as orange as most would be after a long voyage without fruit. Their ship was in good condition as well, aside from the chewed-up bulwark on the port side, courtesy of *Scarlet Devil*. The deck was clean and the sails were bright even by night, smelling of fresh hemp. These men had been well-funded and provisioned, but that did not fool her. Though they weren't starving, the hunger in their eyes was unmistakable.

Pirates, all.

Her wandering gaze halted on a very young face with a dainty nose, full lips, and narrow jaw, the upper half hidden under the low brim of a broad straw hat. Crudely-sheared blonde hair shined golden in the lantern light. The frumpy brown clothes were meant to hide this one's slight build, but it wasn't enough. Kate knew a woman when she saw one.

The crew parted to reveal a small man. He was almost a foot shorter than Kate, and he had a face that was neither handsome nor ugly. His hair was long and black and neatly combed. His eyes were possibly hazel, though the glow of the lanterns made it difficult to tell. He wore an orange vest over a white shirt tucked into brown breeches. He had thin eyebrows and thin lips. His skin was smooth and pale, as though he avoided sunlight. He approached with determined haste, and came to an abrupt halt before Kate. He thrust out a tiny, creamy hand. "Captain Lindsay."

"Warlowe."

"Ah yes, of course." His voice was surprisingly loud for so slight a man. "Your maiden name?"

Kate offered no elaboration. The less strangers knew about her the better. Her true maiden name was Marlowe, but a "WANTED!" poster had capsized the M. She was content to let the name catch wind.

"Welcome aboard the *Fortune Renewed*. I am first mate,

Sterling." He enunciated every syllable, yet Kate did not sense any condescension.

After a moment of consideration, she shook his hand. His grip was firmer than she expected. "Pleased to meet you, Sterling."

"We thank you for your surrender," he continued in his laborious tone, "and I needn't convince you that any effort toward deception would go ill for you and your crew."

"You needn't," she agreed with a smile that appeared innocuous, but concealed a private musing.

"If you'll follow me," he said, "I will take you to my captain."

"Lead the way," she replied, and followed the little man through the ogling crew, who leaned in as she passed by. She ignored their eyes and their stench. She was well-accustomed to the smell of sweat. This was nothing new.

A particularly grimy young man reached out to grab her ass, giving her left cheek a squeeze fierce enough to stiffen her back. That was nothing new, either. He retracted his hand when she angled an evil look his way, hardened by years of practice. "What?" she heard the young man tell a friend. "It was there."

Laughter.

And then came another hand, clutching her right cheek and squeezing so painfully that she let out a tiny squeal. The entire crew burst into fits of howling laughter, save Sterling, who halted to scold the offender with no more than a disappointed scowl.

The fingers gripped harder, refusing to let go, sure to bruise her. Kate spun. She wasted no time with the particulars of this man's face. She had eyes only for the rusty cutlass dangling from a rope around his waist. She slapped his hand aside, slipped her hand through the brass knuckle-guard to get her fingers around the roped hilt, and pulled it free. She saw a flash of surprise on the old man's red face as she swung the weapon downward. The blade caught his wrist and smashed his arm against the top of a nearby barrel, severing his hand on impact. The hand flopped away, dancing through the air, and slapped the deck with fingers curled upward like a dead spider's legs. His violent shrieks replaced the crew's laughter. He grasped at the stump where his hand had been, blood spurting through his fingers in a steady stream. A splintered bone protruded from his wrist. The ruddy hue fled his face. Kate tossed the cutlass aside. Two pirates skittered out of the way as it clattered near their feet, the knuckle-guard clanging noisily.

Sterling turned his scowl of disappointment on Kate. "You have maimed our carpenter."

She shrugged. "He maimed himself when he laid his hand upon me."

Sterling looked to the old man on the ground, writhing in agony against the barrel. "Someone fetch the surgeon."

A young deckhand scurried off.

The little man beckoned for her to follow, and she did, while the crew backed away from her and chattered amongst one another in shock. "Just like a woman to make something o' nothing."

"Aye. Seems a tad excessive, it does."

"Could have been settled with words."

"Punishment didn't really fit the crime, did it?"

A long-necked man with a large head frowned at her as she passed by. "Me night is ruined."

Sterling led her inside the captain's quarters and closed the door behind them. The cabin was expansive and dimly lit. It took her eyes a moment to adjust, especially after the bright lanterns of the main deck. The stern gallery was the largest she had ever seen, with long windows that made her more than a little envious. Snow lined the sills and frosted the murky panes.

Before the gallery, behind a wide desk, stood a tall man in a crimson damask waistcoat emblazoned with golden swirls. A red feather sprouted from his black tricorn hat, and a red scarf shrouded his thick neck. Beneath the scarf dangled a heavy gold chain, weighted by a large cross mounted with fat diamonds. His long, combed hair might have been blonde once, but was now a light brown, with silver streaks running from either temple. His complexion was tan and unblemished, his chin smooth with no hint of stubble. He had a tapered jawline and a long, straight nose. His face reminded her of a beautiful Roman bust she had seen in the house of her late husband's family friend, Lord Edward Harley. Narrow eyes glinted emerald in the flickering light, fixed on Kate, and unlike most men, they did not descend to her bosom. The heels of his shiny, gold-buckled boots gave hardly a clack as he stepped around his desk to the center of the room. Rolled charts had been piled upon the desk. A batch of large candles flickered at one edge.

"I have ill news," Sterling began as he approached his captain. "The woman severed Mr. Gregory's arm on her way in. I daresay he instigated the retaliation."

The tall man offered a shrug of one shoulder, but said nothing.

"Who are you?" Kate demanded.

The captain's lips parted, and then he blinked and looked to Sterling, who made haste to his side. The contrast in their respective sizes was impossible to ignore. The captain placed a hand on the smaller man's shoulder and gave it a light squeeze, which seemed to goad him into speaking. "Captain Roberts lost his powers of speech some time ago, I'm afraid," Sterling explained in a strenuous drawl.

"Captain Roberts?" She chuckled. There must have been a hundred captains named Roberts.

Sterling's thin lips curved into a polite smile. "You have the awful pleasure of meeting Bartholomew Roberts."

Kate couldn't have prevented her eyes from rolling if she'd wanted to. "The pleasure is all his, I'm sure."

The small man feigned shock, placing a hand over his heart and curling his fingers with a slight shudder. "If a man come back from the grave does not impress, I'm not sure what would."

"I've crawled from a few graves myself, sir, and I'm not the only pirate to do so." Her bracelets clinked as she flung a hand at the voiceless captain. "But I see no reason to believe a man dressed as Bart Roberts, calling himself Bart Roberts, is in fact Bart Roberts. Not without proof, mind you."

Sterling glanced uncertainly at his captain, whose eyes flittered his way in return. "The proof stands before you," Sterling insisted, at a loss.

She snorted. "Roberts was killed in seventeen-twenty-two. Buried at sea by his crew."

"A body was cast over the side shrouded in a sail, aye," said Sterling.

Roberts' eyes rarely left Kate as the smaller man spoke for him. She wasn't sure who to look at. "I read an account of his death in a very thorough book."

"Was this book called 'A General History of the Robberies and Murders of the Most Notorious Pyrates'? Written by one Charles Johnson, who calls himself a captain?"

"It was." She knew where he was going with this. "I chanced upon it in a British captain's quarters."

Roberts' gaze fell on Sterling, his glare full of meaning, though only Sterling seemed to understand. "Have a care how much stock you place in that book, Captain Warlowe. After all, last I looked, you were left out of it. Don't you find that curious?"

"I find it fortunate," she replied. "And hardly surprising. I am a woman."

Roberts spread his hands, and Sterling spoke. "Yet Anne Bonny and Mary Read are accounted for."

"I never met Mary Read before she died in prison. I did have the privilege of knowing Anne *Cormac*. She annulled from her husband, and was like to stab any man who called her Bonny. As I recall, she was never a *captain*. If she had been, I doubt her tale would be recounted in that book."

Roberts nodded. He might have even smiled, but his strict mouth scarcely accommodated it.

"Aye," said Sterling. "A woman pirate captain eluding the His Majesty's Navy for so many years is a scandal that must not be permitted."

She started around the room, circumventing the two men, and made her way toward the desk. "Happily, I have no desire to see my name in a book. The regard of history is a man's concern."

Roberts and Sterling swiveled as she moved around them. The captain took a single step forward, and Sterling fell in line. The golden accents permeating the blood-red field of Roberts' waistcoat twisted like snakes as he moved. "Yet you have no doubt seen the names of comrades," Sterling said.

"I'd not call them comrades. I crossed paths with Charles Vane more than once, and I might have enjoyed his company had he not tried to murder me. Jack Rackham treated me well enough, probably because he wanted me."

"And Edward Teach? I've heard you—"

"Contrary to gossip, I never met Teach up-close."

Sterling and Roberts looked confused. "But you did scuttle the *Queen Anne's Revenge*?"

Kate smiled. "I might have lit a fire in his hold. In truth, gentlemen, the only famed pirate I was truly fond of was Anne. She fell in with my crew for a time after she so cleverly eluded the gallows by pleading her belly."

Roberts gestured at Kate's hair, and Sterling nodded knowingly. "I heard a rumor you were sisters."

"In another life, perhaps," Kate allowed with a protracted sigh, growing weary of this. "We shared a common temperament, although Anne's Irish tongue was a tad crude even for my liking."

"You have not entirely discarded British propriety," Sterling noted approvingly, as if to imply there was hope for her yet.

"Oh, fuck off," she blurted with a frivolous gesture. She made her way to the desk and looked over the open charts. There were no weapons on the desk. *Smart men.* But that was fine. She wouldn't need weapons to win this game. There was, she was happy to see, a half-full goblet of wine. She drained it in a single swig and wiped her lips with the back of her hand. It went down smoothly, but she could no longer discern an expensive vintage from a cheap one. Rum had dulled her taste for the finer spirits.

"If you knew some of these infamous pirates," Sterling persisted, "you no doubt noticed discrepancies in Johnson's text, yes?"

She leaned in close to the topmost chart, which detailed the Southern Caribbean. She yearned to swim in those warm waters again. "I paid tribute to Charles Vane's supposed corpse when I was passing through on . . . other business. The birds hadn't pecked away everything yet. The man in that gibbet was *not* Charles Vane."

"Are you saying Vane is still alive?"

"No, because I killed Charles Vane well before his 'capture.'"

"That should come as no surprise," Sterling said in a conclusive tone, now that she had finally let him come to his point. His direct and passionless voice was beginning to grate on her nerves. "The chapter on Benjamin Hornigold was most kind. Contrary to what was written, I'd heard he returned to piracy only to be drowned by a vengeful Captain Teach."

Kate grimaced. "I'd heard that as well."

"The book tells a fairer tale of a man redeemed, only to tragically perish in a storm. The deaths of Vane, Blackbeard, and my captain are but a few of many fictions spread by the Crown."

Kate had long ago concluded that Woodes Rogers had been inventing fictitious endings for each notorious pirate. Still, that did not prove this man was Bartholomew Roberts. "Grapeshot in the gullet is a difficult thing to survive."

"Says a woman who has repeatedly eluded certain death. Is it true you lost an ear?"

"Come near and have a look," she replied sweetly.

"I can see from here."

She tossed her hair over her right shoulder, offering them a glimpse. "Satisfied?"

Sterling gasped, raising a creamy hand to his little mouth. "That must have been painful."

"Not quite so painful as grapeshot. I got a taste of one once. Merely a graze across the shoulder, fortuitously, but it was hot enough to melt the skin and leave a scar." She turned around, placed both palms on the desk and hitched herself onto it, crumpling an open map and knocking two rolled parchments off the edge. The sudden pressure made her rear throb where One-Hand had left his five-fingered mark. She looked at Roberts. "Your captain might as well be dead. He can't even talk."

The sculpted face of Bartholomew Roberts, if that was truly his name, remained stolid as he unbound the scarf about his neck to reveal a grotesque gaping maw in the center of his throat. It resembled a second mouth, raw and slick around the rim, and she could swear she heard a low whisper of breath escape the void. She didn't want to think about how deep it went. "How could you live through that?" she wondered in awe.

Sterling's passionless gaze faltered for but a moment, and Kate glimpsed regret. "Captain Roberts would have begged us to end his suffering, had he the voice to do so. We selfishly kept him alive, by every means necessary. He hated us for a time. He killed some of us, when his energy was restored. And that was his right as captain. He is too strong a man to take his own life, and we robbed him of relief. That is all I will say on the matter."

"So you're his voice?" Kate said, winking.

"I speak for him now," Sterling said, while Roberts refastened the scarf.

"How does that work?" she wondered. "He shoves his hand up your ass and words come out?"

"You cannot offend me, Captain," Sterling assured her without a trace of anger darkening his blank face. "I am offended only when my captain is offended."

"What good is a captain without his voice? He cannot command his crew."

Roberts touched Sterling's shoulder again, stroking it with two fingers. "He commands them through me," Sterling dutifully answered. "The sooner you accept the oddity of our relationship, the sooner we can proceed with the business at hand."

She loosed a wild, musical laugh. "I absolutely do not accept it. This is some elaborate trick, nothing more. You needn't waste precious time convincing me otherwise. I honestly don't care if you're Roberts' puppet or he's yours. Whoever's hand is up whomever's ass is of no consequence to me."

A frantic rap on the door gave Sterling a start, but Roberts did not budge. "Excuse me," Sterling said. He crossed the room, cracked the door and peeked through the gap.

A heavyset bald man cleaved his way in and bellowed, "Mr. Gregory is dead! He bled out! He's dead! DEAD!"

The long-necked man Kate had spotted earlier poked his large head in and scanned the room until he found her. He frowned accusingly. "Me night is ruined."

Sterling looked at Roberts. The captain returned a sharp glare. "Get out!" Sterling snapped at both men.

"But what will we do?" demanded the bald man. "We need a carpenter."

"Me night is ruined."

"The carpenter's mate has been promoted," barked Sterling. "Now leave us to our business."

The men backed out just before Sterling slammed the

door shut.

"Right," Kate said, sliding off the desk onto her feet. She couldn't believe how alert she felt, despite a long night without rest. "To that business you mentioned. Who hired you to capture me?"

"You don't know?"

"I have a wager," she offered. "It was Woodes Rogers. He wants nothing more than to see my neck stretched. Go on, you can tell me. I'm going to find out eventually anyway."

Sterling hesitated, looking to Roberts. Roberts nodded curtly. "Tell me, where did you get that coat?"

Kate looked down at her coat. She had been absently fingering one of the death's head buttons without realizing it. What possible value could Calico Jack's old coat have to Roberts? "What does it matter where I got it?"

"You stole it from Jack Rackham, didn't you?"

"He let me take it, more like."

"Rackham did not know the value of his gift."

"Value?" She doubted it was worth more than a bale of silk.

"Sentimental," said Sterling with a little smile. Roberts' eyes were set on the coat. "It was not Rackham's to give."

Kate shrugged. "I gave him little choice in the matter. I've taken everything I've ever wanted."

Roberts clutched Sterling's shoulder, digging his fingers in and causing the smaller man to wince. "And now you will lose everything you've taken."

She looked to the stern gallery. Beyond the warbled glass, the ghostly ambiance was growing brighter. Dawn was approaching. Kate bit her lip and continued to stroke one of the death's head buttons. She looked at Roberts, ignoring Sterling. "No. I'll be keeping my coat. And you'll be releasing me to my crew, and you're going to release me before dawn."

Sterling actually laughed. It was short and barely audible, but she got the impression he didn't laugh much. "Why would my captain release you?"

She halted two paces short of both men, smiling at each. "Because when you sailed so boldly up this river, your bow caught on a rope. It's not so much the rope that should concern you as what is attached to said rope: Twelve powder kegs, well-sealed, tarred black as the night's water, so none of your scouts would spot them unless they knew where to look. My men, stationed on either side of the river, severed each end of the rope when your ship passed by, and the kegs collected along your hull, where they remain presently, waiting to be fired upon."

Sterling showed no sign of concern. "You're fortunate there was a wind. If not, we would have cruised in on sweeps, and the tips of our oars would have snagged on your rope."

"I left nothing to chance," said Kate. "I bided a moment for the wind, and had one not kicked up, I would not have sent men to signal our surrender."

It was Roberts' turn to laugh, though no sound emerged.

"Do you take Captain Roberts for a fool?" Sterling asked with genuine curiosity. "He has not lived this long by being stupid."

She shook her head scornfully at Roberts. "You're alive because you compromised yourself to the Crown."

"This is pointless," Sterling interjected with a raised hand. "No musket can ignite a powder keg, and that's all there is to it. Not from that distance and certainly not bobbing up and down in the water. You are a silly woman."

45

"No musket, true enough. That's why, before I instructed my men to signal you, I positioned sixteen-pounders on either bank of the river, concealed in the brush, manned by my finest gunners." Roberts' eyes enlarged. She permitted herself a moment to relish Sterling's stunned silence. "I shouldn't have to tell you that any attempt to remove the kegs will result in my men firing all at once. Their aim is precise. And even if it isn't, there are twelve kegs."

Roberts shook his head and pitched Sterling a dubious frown.

"No," said Sterling, in apparent agreement with his captain's silent words. "No, I don't believe they will. Your men won't fire on their own captain."

Her heart was thumping rapidly now. She lived for these moments, and it had been too long since the last. "I wouldn't be so sure of that. Captaining a pirate ship is precarious business, notably for a woman. Some of them don't even like me very much, seeing as I haven't let them defile me."

Sterling was fervently shaking his head. "You're lying. My captain knows a bluff when he sees one."

She hazarded another step forward. Sterling tossed one of the flaps of his coat aside, revealing a dagger tucked in his breeches. He slapped a hand to the hilt. She ignored him and peered deep into Bartholomew Roberts' green eyes. He was not hard to look at, as long as she didn't think about what was beneath that red scarf. She wasn't necessarily attracted to him, but his face was far more interesting than the man who spoke for him. "Your voice is gravely mistaken, Captain. My men have strict orders to fire, should you not release me to them by sunrise."

"You must know you will perish in such an attack," Sterling hissed in her ear. "That many powder kegs will scuttle us faster than we can escape."

"That's the idea. If I allow you to take me prisoner, I'm a dead woman anyway." She lifted a nonthreatening hand to the golden cross dangling from Roberts' neck and caressed one of the large diamonds with her index finger. "So why not end it here, on my own terms, and take the whole bloody lot of you with me?"

"There's one little problem with your plan," said Sterling, standing on his tiptoes and leaning into her line of sight.

"Do explain." She continued not to look at the little man, favoring only Roberts.

"Your crew might feel they have no choice but to destroy us, seeing as there's no conceivable way my captain can convince you he won't circle back once freed of your trap. That puts us in a bit of a stalemate. This plan was ill-conceived. Unless you hail your men with orders to stand down, we shall all of us perish in flames."

She nodded. "Which is why I will have to take your captain hostage. He will be released on a longboat once we are safely out to sea. You have my word on that."

Roberts did not so much as blink.

"That is unacceptable!" Sterling protested, a little too forcefully.

"You're right," she said, showing Roberts her teeth. "I will not take *Roberts* hostage. I will take something he cannot live without. I will take his voice."

PLANS

The same deckhands who had groped her while ushering her aboard *Fortune Renewed* an hour prior kept their hands on their oars as they rowed her and Sterling to the northern bank of the river. The hairy ox on her left grumbled to himself, while his fairer companion glowered at her whenever he thought she wouldn't notice.

She felt the eyes of Roberts' entire crew on her back. Sterling had ordered them to stand down and lower their arms for the time being. There was still a slim chance that one undisciplined fool with a steady musket and an itchy finger might not be able to resist taking a shot at her. It was a chance she'd been willing to take. If she was fatally struck, at least she would take Bartholomew Roberts and his crew with her. And her men would kindly deal with Sterling in her absence.

A thin mist crept up the river from the sea, encircling the longboat with phantom arms amplified by the soft purple ambiance of approaching dawn. The air was cold and crisp, spearing her sinuses whenever she inhaled too sharply. The skin of her missing ear ached worse than before, nearly as raw as it had been in the weeks after it had been bitten off. It had taken so long to heal, and she had scratched it too many times. The wound might have looked less horrid had it received the attention of a proper surgeon, but she had been too busy at the time for such trivial concerns. It didn't occur to her until later how fortunate she was that it had not become infected and eaten through her skull. *So much of youth is luck,* she realized, as dozens of familiar young faces sifted through the mist, long dead, but no less muddled by time.

The last snowflake of the waning night tumbled lazily through her vision and settled atop one of the fat diamonds embedded in the golden cross she held in her lap. The flake crystallized against the carved gem, virtually camouflaged. She set her thumb upon the star and felt it melt beneath. "You wouldn't let a lady leave without a parting gift, would you?" she had quipped as she snatched the necklace from Roberts' neck, snapping the chain and smiling as golden ringlets rolled down his crimson waistcoat and collected about his boots. Flame had consumed his eyes, but there was little he could do, and less he could say.

"This is unnatural," said Sterling. He sat ahead of her in the longboat, facing the shore, still as a plank.

"What?" Kate asked. One word was enough to form an icy cloud before her face. It dissipated swiftly.

"This cold. It's as unnatural as a woman captaining a

ship."

She laughed. "Which is more unnatural, do you think? A captain with no voice, or a captain with tits?"

"A *captain* with tits," the ox growled.

"It be an abomination," said the fairer man. "Bad luck to boot."

The longboat slid over the shore, splitting the snow. Sterling needed no incentive to disembark. He knew what was at stake. She helped herself out after him, hopping over the rail and dipping her boots into the river. Water streamed in and nibbled at her toes with icy teeth. Behind her, the ox grunted. "Good riddance, bitch."

Over twenty men materialized from the shadows offered by the dense woods, slipping from between the tall trunks. She looked around until she found Joseph. He was the darkest-skinned man she had ever encountered, and the others had named him "Shadow." She despised nicknames, but Joseph didn't seem to mind his. Joseph wasn't his true name either. She'd taken him from a slave ship bound for Louisiana, its entire "cargo" imported from Senegambia. His former captain, who had separated him from his fellow slaves and put him to work as a cook after the old one died, had given him a "proper Christian name." Joseph had been across the Atlantic three times now. Kate had asked him for his true name when she welcomed him aboard, but he refused to tell her, though she never understood why.

"Joseph," she called. He stepped forward. "Hail the others across the river. Captain Roberts and I have come to an accord."

"Aye, Captain." Joseph rushed up the river, where he would light a torch to give the signal. She considered herself lucky to have him on her side. He was well respected among the blacks, who presently numbered eighteen. The whites allowed them no say in votes, but if it came to a scuffle, Joseph would make sure they took Kate's side. She suspected many of the whites were intimidated by them, though they would never admit it.

Quartermaster Corso stepped forward with a perplexed look twisting his bullish yet paradoxically kind features. He was a big man with bulging muscles, stubbles of thick brown hair that he shaved once a month, and a resonant voice. He wore an untucked tan shirt with the sleeves torn off at the shoulders to bare his massive biceps. Two large flintlock pistols hung from either hip on a thick black belt. Corso did not like swords, as he had cut himself too many times. He preferred his hands, which were deadlier than most blades. "Roberts, you say?"

"Aye," she said. "Bartholomew Roberts, or so he claims."

The quartermaster's huge chest trembled as he laughed. "That's a stretch."

Kate shuffled out of the freezing water, shoving Sterling forward when he slowed. Sterling flailed his arms as his heels slid in the ice that lined the shore, where snow met water. Corso caught the little man by the collar before he could land on his ass. "Who's this, then?" he wondered with a raised eyebrow.

"A hostage of some import," Kate replied.

Corso's sharp eyes narrowed, his brows descending. "He's not much to look at, is he?"

Sterling tried to shove Corso away, but he only managed to topple himself, legs flailing. "I don't need to remind you what should happen if I'm not returned in one piece!" His breath drew out in a cloud before him.

"We'll return one piece alright," quipped Corso.

Kate turned to wave at her former captors as they rowed back to their ship. "Do me a favor, my good lads, and remind your captain that we are watching. Your ship does not move until I give it leave to do so."

"Devil take you," the ox spat back. His curse ricocheted off the trees.

"Do as she says!" Sterling shouted at them.

Corso gave Sterling a reassuring clap on the shoulder. "You make yourself a compliant little man, and we won't have to set matches under your fingernails."

Kate handed Corso the golden cross and said, "That will buy us three months' worth of supplies, maybe more."

A lopsided smile softened the quartermaster's broad jaw. "I'm not saying I doubted you, but—"

"You doubted me," she finished for him under her breath. "I won't hold it against you."

He handed the cross back to her. "Looks genuine enough. Doesn't mean Roberts is."

She opened one of the flaps of her coat and stuffed the cross in a large pocket. "No matter. Whoever he is, he's agreed to leave without a fight."

"And you believe him? What if he circles back? He won't fall for the same trick twice, will he?"

"I have more than one trick up my sleeve." The exhaustion from earlier was creeping into her bones again, aided by the icy water sloshing around in her boots. She wanted nothing more than a few hours' sleep, naked and tangled in soft dry sheets with Gabe to warm her.

She looked to her gathering crew. She couldn't find Gabe among them, but she knew he was there somewhere, in the dark. "There are a lot of men on that ship." *And one woman.* "Pirates, all. Our brethren. Let us be the better pirates.

There is no need for more bloodshed."

They returned dubious scowls and grunts. All except the Castillo twins, who would have happily leapt off a cliff if she'd so ordered.

"Let us be the *dead* pirates, more like," came an alluring voice she knew all too well. He approached from the right, skirting the bank of the river on light feet that did not crack the ice, and he was within five paces before she knew it. Instinctively her hand jerked toward her waist, but then she remembered that she had removed her weapons before boarding Roberts' ship.

Hawkes' long blonde hair shone silver in the purple gloom. He was thin of frame, with narrow shoulders beneath a plain white shirt, but he was stronger than he looked. His reedy limbs were corded in muscle, and his stomach was flat and notched. He brandished dual cutlasses, one on each hip, with a pistol shoved down the center of a garish orange sash. He smiled a charming, perfectly even smile, and she wondered, not for the first time, how he kept his teeth so white. She wagered he would have been the dashing hero of any woman's dreams, but she thought his grey eyes were set too far apart, his free-flowing hair too feminine, and his clean-shaven jaw too smooth. Most of all she didn't care for the gleam in those eyes when he fixed them on her. She knew he was envisioning his fingers unlacing her shirt. "We have them right where we want them. There will never be a finer opp—"

She sliced the air with a curt sweep of her hand. "Your captain has spoken, Hawkes. I'll hear not another word."

"Do you speak for us all?" he wondered with aggravating nonchalance.

Ives, a skinny gunner with stringy black hair and a tremendous underbite, shivered violently. He had rolled the long sleeves of his blue shirt down over his hands in a futile attempt to keep them warm. "Meaning no disrespect, Captain, but seeing as we've been made to wait in this dreadful cold for hours on hours after all the trouble of trap-setting, seems a powerful waste to let it all go to . . . waste."

"Aye," Ives' friend, Roche, agreed through chattering teeth. "Can't even feel me bloody cock."

"Neither could all those strumpets," quipped Ives.

"Oh, hardy har."

"Enough!" Corso barked. "Captain's orders stand."

Hawkes stepped between the captain and her crew, spreading his thin arms to them in an amicable gesture. "Then what say we put it to a vote?"

She shook her head. "Votes hold no sway in matters of combat, Hawkes."

Hawkes raised a finger. "In the *midst* of combat, aye. But we are not yet in combat, are we? The air is still and that ship has not fired upon us, unless I've grown deaf and blind in the last five minutes."

"True," she agreed. "So why fill a peaceful air with murder? We are free. We have a valuable hostage who will not be released until we are a safe distance clear of the enemy."

"He don't look valuable," said Ives through chattering teeth.

"He looks like a worm," said Roche.

"He's the most valuable man on that ship," Kate informed them. "Their captain is nothing without him, isn't that right Mr. Sterling?"

Sterling said nothing.

She seized the little man's collar and drew him near. "This is not the wisest time for silence."

Sterling chuckled sardonically. "A brash woman instructs me on wisdom."

She flung him away. He managed to turn around before toppling to his knees and sliding in the snow, leaving a long trail. Before he could get to his feet, the ginger-haired Tommy Killian burst from the bushes and came bounding up to gleefully kick him in the ribs. Sterling let out a high-pitched yelp not unlike an injured dog. Killian laughed until his freckled face turned red. He was the second-youngest of Kate's crew. Two months prior he had walked in on her as she was getting dressed, and he got a good long look at her. From the lustful expression that dulled his youthful face, she suspected he had creamed his breeches right then and there.

"Leave him be, Killian," ordered Corso. "We'll need him alive."

"I weren't killing him," Killian shot back defensively.

"Wretched though he looks," Kate said, "that ship is nothing without this man. Roberts is captain in name only. He has lost his powers of speech and Sterling speaks for him. He may not carry the title, but for all intents and purposes he is the acting captain on that ship." She approached Sterling. "Admit it, sir. If you do not, you will be of no further value to me, and I'll be forced to oblige my boatswain and fire on your ship."

Still on his knees, Sterling lowered his head. "The woman speaks truth."

"Well of course he'd say that," Hawkes guffawed. "The little coward would say anything to save his own skin."

"I don't think this man fears for his life," Kate said. Sterling had been shocked by her request to take him prisoner, but he hadn't put up as much of a fight as she'd expected. "He fears for the lives of his crew, as any good captain should. Not that I expect you to understand, Hawkes."

Ives tittered at that. Hawkes threw an evil glare over his shoulder, silencing him.

Corso folded his arms and stared at Sterling, his frown growing. He was as skeptical as the rest, though he would never say it. *He doubts me,* Kate realized. *One failure soils a thousand victories.* Never mind that she had already turned her lone failure into another victory. These fools were too blind to see it. Or maybe they didn't want to. Maybe failure and victory were no longer of consequence. Maybe the only thing that truly mattered was the heat of battle. It was all they knew. There was no higher endgame. They were no richer now than when they had started. Eight lifetimes of fortune had been squandered over as many years. If these men desired freedom and peace, they would have taken each at will, as easily as they plundered a ship's hold. What better end could a pirate hope for than a glorious, bloody death? *What better end could I hope for?* she wondered. She had always known, even when she first stepped foot aboard the *Scarlet Devil* and grasped the wheel, that she couldn't do this forever. In that moment, as the sun-cooked helm channeled the warmth of the Caribbean through her palms, she had glimpsed her death cresting the rippled horizon, like the sail of a ship at the edge of the ocean. She didn't care. Fate was a small and distant thing waiting somewhere beyond a life of adventure and bounty. So, she set her gaze to the glistening sapphire rolling beneath ship and sky, knowing all the while where the tide would lead her. It didn't matter, because the water was so impossibly luminous, fracturing the sun into a million knife-like slivers that writhed in an elegant yet aimless dance. Nothing mattered compared to that. Yet now there were no blinding slivers from which to shield her eyes. Now there was only a black river cutting through a cold white land.

"We must finish this," Hawkes pleaded to the crew with a clenched fist. "Elsewise they will hunt us to the ends of the earth. This slight will not go unchecked."

Kate shook her head. "There's no profit in blowing up that ship."

"You grow soft, Captain."

"Watch yourself, Hawkes," warned Corso. His right hand fell casually to the flintlock on that hip.

"I'm merely conversing with our captain, Corso." Hawkes returned his attention to Kate. "We're all murderers and so are you. You've plunged your blade into more bellies than I. How is this any different?"

"I've killed men who aimed to kill me, but never have I killed an innocent man, save to pluck him from his misery."

Hawkes approached with a friendly smile. His corded arms hung loose at his sides, fingers of each hand brushing his cutlasses. His teeth were whiter than the snow. "Why should you care if Roberts and his crew live or die? They are not your crew. We are your crew."

"We are not animals." Her raspy voice made a whisper of the words. She studied his pretty face, wondering how often he shaved to keep his jaw so smooth. She sensed him tensing beneath his cool exterior. "Back down," she told him. "You are too bold for your own good."

Hawkes shook his head. "Nay, Captain. I must not back down, because, as you made plain, we are not animals. Animals are too easily shepherded into a holding pen. Animals are simple. Animals do not vote."

"What's he saying?" Ives asked Roche.

"I don't follow," Roche admitted with a heavy sigh. "This

is a lot of talk."

Killian stepped forward with a raised hand. "What he's saying is . . . is animals be simple, and we isn't animals." He looked to Hawkes for confirmation.

Ives wrinkled his gaunt face. "That goes without saying, don't it?"

"I'm saying the captain doesn't think for us," Hawkes informed them.

On any other ship, these would be words of mutiny, but *Scarlet Devil* was a pirate ship, and Hawkes had every right to contest Kate's intended course. She knew he had her, and if she fought too dearly for the enemy's lives, the crew would consider her weak. She turned away from them and looked to *Fortune Renewed*. The two deckhands who had boated her to shore were just now making their way up the ratlines that had been tossed down to them to serve as a crude ladder to the main deck. *So many of them. Too many. And somewhere among them . . . a girl.*

"It's the only way to be certain." Hawkes was suddenly beside her. He moved on feathered feet, it seemed.

The word spilled out before she considered moving her lips. "No."

He cocked his head, as a dog does when it hears a curious sound. "No, Captain?"

She turned to him, leaning close enough to smell the dried flakes of soap still clinging to his oh-so-clean face. "We will not murder an entire ship without good cause. 'It's the only way to be certain' is not good enough. You do not have my vote, and not enough crew is present to call for a consensus here." Many were on the other side of the river, and a good number were still aboard *Scarlet Devil*.

"Fine," he said at once, undaunted. "That ship isn't going

anywhere. I'll make the rounds and tally the number. It will take an hour, maybe two. I think you know what the outcome will be. These men hunger for revenge." He stretched a lanky arm to the crew. "Should we let our kindhearted captain deny us retribution for comrades lost?"

"Nay," said Ives, and frost tumbled from his stringy hair as he shook his head.

"Nay," said Killian, and he gave Sterling another kick in the ribs for emphasis.

"Captain knows what she's doing," said Domingo, and his brother agreed. Both were glaring dangerously at Hawkes, but he paid them no mind.

"I don't care," said Roche. "I'm tired."

Kate was laughing to herself. "I've been called many things, but never kindhearted. I'm flattered, Hawkes."

"Captain's given her order," said Corso. "Quartermaster tallies votes, so you won't have any sway over the crew, apart from the friends you keep below. That won't be enough."

"The majority favors me here. You heard it yourself, Corso. Why should it be any different when the question is put to the rest?"

Kate's bracelets jingled as she ran both hands through her thick, wet hair in frustration. "Maybe we'll get lucky and we'll destroy that ship in one blow, but what if we don't?"

"We will cut down anyone who survives," Hawkes answered swiftly.

"We have all we need right here." She aimed a finger at Sterling. "We can resolve this without further bloodshed and be on our way."

"This was *your* idea, Captain," Hawkes replied. He favored the men with a smile. "The mist is closing fast, lads. Soon we won't be able to see the kegs in the water, and our captain's brilliant plan will be for naught. And then they'll have us."

And then, out of nowhere, Gabe was advancing on Hawkes, hand clenching the hilt of his curved dagger. Kate darted between them, slamming a fist to Gabe's chest, halting him. "No." She wouldn't allow him to make a martyr of Hawkes. If she killed a man for voting against her, a new captain would be elected before the week was out.

"Were you intending to murder me, Gabe?" wondered Hawkes. His tone was frivolous, inviting.

"The intent has yet to pass," replied Gabe.

"Is our captain's arm so strong that it holds you in place?"

Corso advanced on Hawkes. Everything about him dwarfed the other man. "Watch yourself, little man."

"There's another way," Kate said.

Before she could conjure "another way," Sterling made the decision for them. The little man sprang to his feet, catapulting himself headfirst into Tommy Killian and knocking him off his feet. He landed on top of the lad, wrestled the gun from his sash, aimed it skyward, and fired. "TO ARMS, MEN!" he bellowed. His voice was unexpectedly forceful, echoing off the trees. "THEY MEAN TO FIRE ON US! THEY MEAN TO FIRE ON US!"

BATTLE

Sterling was the first to die, and Kate couldn't have saved him if she'd wanted to. Killian drew a dagger from his boot and plunged it so far into Sterling's throat that the tip poked from the opposite end. When he pulled it free, he was doused in a geyser of blood. Sterling's face paled to the color of the snow and his little body went limp atop his killer. Killian shoved the dead man away and spent the next minute furiously wiping blood from his eyes.

Three flashes lit *Fortune Renewed's* deck a split-second before thunder cracked along the tree trunks. Cannonballs hurtled forward. Kate's hair whipped away from her good ear when one streaked past to impact a tree behind her, scattering bark. The second cannonball struck Roche in the face, bursting his skull like a melon and splattering his brains all over Ives.

"To cover!" cried Corso.

"Light up those kegs!" Kate shouted to the gunners. She had hoped to avoid this, but Sterling had left her no choice. *You stubborn fool, you've killed your men as well as yourself.* She could have talked her crew out of an attack if only she'd had more time, but that was no longer an option. *Not with Roche's head scattered all over Virginia.*

Four gunners returned to their positions in the brush, where the cannons had been concealed. Corso followed to make certain they did their jobs right. A few heartbeats later, four blasts lit the bushes, and cannonballs flew toward *Fortune Renewed*. The water ignited, illuminating the river for an instant. The explosion swelled horizontally as each keg was triggered one by one. A massive fireball crawled up the hull, rolling over the bulwark and spraying the furled sails with embers. A black cloud roiled into the sky. Kate could hear men shrieking from beyond the impenetrable wall of fire as the ship lurched violently to its port. And then she heard the cannons firing from the opposite side of the river in four consecutive booms, and the ship jolted starboard, its masts angling toward Kate's side of the river as fire slithered up the mainmast toward the frozen flag. Men were scrambling about the decks, sliding toward their doom. They tumbled through the blaze, their limbs flailing in midair, fire clinging to their backs. Crates and barrels toppled out of the hold, breaking open and scattering their various contents. Chickens flapped their useless wings to avoid the inevitable. A goat skittered on its hooves, bleating madly as it caught fire and tumbled into the water. It raised its head above the surface a few seconds later, half its face scorched black, and loosed a wail disturbingly reminiscent of a human child.

A bulkhead fell away and powder kegs tumbled toward the fire. Kate was too slow to shield her eyes, and then she saw only white. The sound arrived an instant later, along with a blast of searing air that whipped the flaps of her coat and pressed her shirt flat against her chest. When her sight returned, the entire ship was ablaze, and the British flag was no longer frozen, but reaching for the heavens on its tether as the fire chewed away at it. Soon there was nothing left but a flaming tuft of cloth that tore loose and sailed over the river like an angel of death.

Unrecognizable charred lumps floated downriver, toward the Atlantic. Many of those who emerged alive were taken apart by musket fire. Some dove beneath the water rather than face the muskets. *They'll find no refuge there,* Kate thought.

"Give me a blade," she told Hawkes, who was admiring the chaos, his comely yet off-putting features bathed in the warm glow. "Hawkes!" she pressed.

"Where's yours?"

"I took no weapons aboard that ship."

"Ah yes." He handed her one of his two polished swords. "I want this back."

"Careful what you wish for."

She looked to the forest, where the men had retreated for cover, crouched with their pistols and cutlasses at the ready. "On me, lads! Hold pistols and cutlasses ready. We've no more fear of cannon fire. Our hand has been forced." She threw an accusatory glare at Hawkes. "But we will see this job done. Grant their surrenders if they seek it, for we need the men, but do not hesitate to cut down any man fool enough to cross blades with you." They joined her along the shore, waiting for survivors to emerge from the water. Embers rained down all around them, stinging their arms and sizzling in the snow. The sky was black again, muted by the intense blaze in the center of the river, where the ship was listing to its starboard and already sinking. It was as if the sun had met its match and thought better of rising.

The first man to emerge shivering from the water held up his hands . . . and was shot in the crotch by Ives. He curled forward, gripping himself and screaming through clenched teeth, until he collapsed into the water and stopped moving.

"Goddammit, Ives," Kate snapped. "What did I just say?"

Ives gazed at her through a mask of blood. "That was for Roche."

She snatched the pistol from his grip, twirled it in the air, caught the hot barrel, and cracked him over the skull with the pommel. His knees gave out and he plopped his ass in the snow with a stupid look on his face. She dropped the gun in his lap. "You're lucky I don't maroon you with naught but that pistol for company."

"Doesn't matter," Hawkes said with a little smirk. "They won't surrender now."

She whirled on him. "And you, Hawkes, shall not have the comfort of a pistol if you question me again. By thunder, I'll scout the smallest key in the Caribbean, and if there's a single tree, I swear to God I will have it hacked down to deny you shade. Is that understood?"

"Aye, Captain." The smirk remained.

The next man surfaced from the water. He was large and muscular, with an open blouse that was too tight across his chest, and a long braid of fair hair whipping about. He might have descended from the Vikings. This one had his cutlass drawn as he burst into a sprint, howling at the top of his lungs.

An older deckhand whose name Kate didn't know took aim and fired, but missed. The Viking continued his charge, sidestepping a very young, very skinny, and very blonde lad nicknamed Harry Harmless. Harry took a swing at him with his cutlass, but the bigger man easily avoided the blade. The Viking continued toward the older deckhand who had fired at him, opening his torso with one heave of his cutlass. The deckhand fell to his knees and looked down at his exposed ribs with a curious expression. "I fired," was all he said, before falling on his face.

"You killed Jack!" Harry Harmless screamed, chasing after the Viking with his sword held high. He motioned for the others to follow. "He killed Jack!"

Jack, Kate thought. *An easy name.* So why hadn't she remembered it?

The Viking spun on his heels. Harry skidded to a halt and nearly fell as he narrowly avoided his opponent's sweeping cutlass. Three more men joined him to encircle the Viking as he swung wildly at them. They laughed at his fervor, and that only seemed to make him angrier. His face was red with fury and his neck throttled with veins. "I will kill every last one of you," he promised. "And I'll finish with your red bitch of a captain."

"Red bitch," Kate said as she approached. This was the second time she'd been called that in one night. "A fine name for my next ship."

"There won't be a next ship for you. There won't even be a tomorrow. You'll watch every man here die, and then I will kill you."

Kate set her cutlass on her shoulder. "You're big, but we are many. Drop your weapon and we'll let you walk away."

"Drop your breeches and I'll make certain you never walk again," he returned.

Kate pinched the bridge of her nose. "I set myself up for that." She looked to her men. "You may kill him now."

The Viking looked around until he found his next target. "I'll start with you."

"Kill him!" cried Harry Harmless, who had drawn the large man's ire.

Before the Viking could get very far, a shadow leapt onto his back. The Viking paused and raised an eyebrow. "Who is this man who wants to die first?"

"You," whispered the shadow. The polished blade of a curved dagger traced a red line across the man's throat. The Viking clutched himself. Blood washed over his hands. He gurgled an unintelligible curse and collapsed. Gabe placed a heel on his victim's back. "Thanks for the distraction," he told Harry.

Harry's face was whiter than usual. "Aye. That weren't what I was trying to do, but aye."

Thirteen more made the swim to the bank. Like the dead Viking, these men had no intent of surrender. They charged with their blades in the air, bellowing war cries. "Fire!" Kate ordered, even though she admired her enemy's fortitude. They had escaped fire and ice only to die by sword and pistol. Kate's men fired, taking down three. Blades clashed as the remaining ten persisted onward. The snow was painted in streaks of blood.

Hawkes and Gabe threw themselves into the fray, striking a tall black man at once from opposite sides. Gabe attacked low and from behind, slashing his prey's Achilles heel and dropping him to one knee, allowing Hawkes to impale his chest. The black man gripped the blade that had

66

killed him and stared dumbly at Hawkes, until Hawkes slipped the blade free. Hawkes and Gabe went separate ways as they honed in on their next targets. Both were skilled, and Kate had often wondered which would win in a contest. She feared for Gabe's chances in a straight duel, stripped of subterfuge and stealth. He rarely gave his enemy a chance to see him coming, and that was why he was still alive. As she watched Hawkes engage his next target, it was clear that he was better than Gabe. *And me,* she begrudgingly admitted to herself.

Hawkes was light on his feet, like a dancer, swirling about his irritated opponent, who was far too young to put up with this sort of nonsense for long. Hawkes darted away whenever the other man lunged at him, allowing the blade to come close but never close enough, occasionally parrying him with a lazy flick of his wrist. Normally he wielded both cutlasses at once, but he seemed no less of a fighter with just the one. Hawkes circled the young man, letting no one else get close, and continued to elude his opponent's wild thrusts while never attempting one of his own. After a dozen lunges, the young man's frustration overwhelmed him, stealing his senses, and he raised his blade high and charged. Hawkes dropped and rolled in the snow, letting his opponent pass him. The swipe of his sword was so fast that Kate didn't even see it. The young man didn't realize his side had been struck until he tried to turn around. Half his waist opened, curtaining blood down his leg. His arms dropped lamely at his sides, his sword slipped from his fingers, and he fell.

Kate did not witness the rest of the battle. A man had risen from the water, splashing toward her. At first she didn't recognize him in the gloom. And then she realized he was the turtle-necked "Me night is ruined" man from earlier, and he was aiming two pistols. She faced him and pointed to the center of her chest, instructing him where to aim. Half of his face was slick with blood, pouring from a gaping crevice in his scalp. "I would not be opposed to surrender," he informed her.

"Then drop your pistols, sir."

He kept both barrels level. "How would I know you'd keep your word?"

"You wouldn't."

"Then I must decline."

Kate frowned. "Wait, what?"

Both hammers clacked at once, useless after the swim to shore. Turtleneck stared at the weapons while Kate laughed at his stupidity. He dropped the pistols and drew a stunted cutlass. The blade had been severed two thirds of the way up, and he had allowed the jagged tip to rust. He wasted no time, rushing at her with a high-pitched cry from an obscenely stretched maw. As comical as Turtleneck appeared, Kate doubted she could afford a single cut from his rusty blade. She stepped aside, letting him charge past, and raised her cutlass to clash with his. He spun around, threw out a foot to steady himself, and drove forward. One, two, and three strikes, each harder than the last. She parried them easily with one hand, but her arm trembled under his surprising power. Before he could deliver a fourth blow, she grasped the hilt with her other hand. Hawkes' cutlass had not been designed for two hands, but this man was strong with fury. He delivered five more blows, chipping away at the blade. As he prepared for a sixth, raising his sword and drawing in a deep breath, she kicked him in the gut. He stumbled back, stunned and gasping. She plunged her blade into his stomach and jerked upward, catching it on his sternum.

Something dark snagged her peripheral vision. She glanced sideways to see a shadow ascending from the water. She squinted to make out his features, but he was hurtling toward her too swiftly, shuffling through the water with startling speed, framed by the fire beyond. She ripped the blade out of Turtleneck and heard him crumble. The shadow made it to shore and bore down on her with a long and broad cutlass held high, poised for a cleaving stroke. She raised her cutlass instinctively, halting his blade inches from her face, and the tremendous force of his momentum rattled her entire body. He leaned into the blow, and as the edge bit into her forehead, the sculpted features of Bartholomew Roberts filtered through the gloom. Blood trickled into her right eye, darkening half of her vision. She braced herself against his weight, but her feet slid backwards in the ice. His green eyes looked to the corpse of Sterling. "Lose your voice?" she asked as cheerily as possible as she strained against his sword. She couldn't resist.

He looked at her. She saw no anger or sorrow, only a promise. There was only one thing left for Bartholomew Roberts to do: murder the woman who had taken what little remained to him. She couldn't blame him. She would have done the same.

She freed one hand and gripped his wrist, which was as icy as the river he had emerged from. She bent her knees and sprang forward like a cat, shoving his blade away with all her might. She backed up before he could strike again. When he raised his sword, she saw her opening, and raked her blade across his stomach in a horizontal swipe, then backed away. A cascade of blood darkened his waistcoat, but he was oblivious. He marched at her, not fast, not slow, but as sure and deliberate as death itself. Her back slammed against a tree before she realized how far she had retreated, rattling her teeth in her skull. Dazed, she thrust her sword blindly. He parried it with a hard swipe that knocked the cutlass from her hand. She didn't see where it landed. He tossed his own cutlass away and seized her by the neck, squeezing and lifting her up with one arm, grinding her back along the bark of the tree. In the distance, she saw her pirates fighting Roberts' crew, too far to help her and too occupied to notice her dilemma. Her eyes rolled skyward, and she saw a network of sharp branches. She pried at Roberts' constricting fingers with both hands, to no avail. Her vision blurred and darkened. She released his hand and reached for one of those sharp branches, but it was further up than she realized. She reached back and grasped frantically at the cold tree, but her fingers found nothing except coarse bark. She heard herself gagging as he slowly crushed her throat. She reached for his eyes, trying to gouge them with her jagged nails. He closed his eyes and angled his head away, relinquishing his grip somewhat, but not enough to allow her any air. She managed to get her fingers around his throat, but she didn't have the strength to squeeze. One of her fingers ran over the hole in his neck, beneath his scarf. She jammed both thumbs into the old wound, puncturing his scarf. He opened his mouth for a wail, but nothing came out. And just before her vision could darken entirely, he opened his hand, and she slid down the tree.

She breathed deep the sweet, icy air, letting it fill her lungs. She found her cutlass in the snow. Blood oozed from the hole in Roberts' red scarf. He reached for her, clutching the folds of her jacket, and lifted her to her feet. She managed to close her hand around the hilt of her cutlass and bring it up with her. She pressed the tip into his open wound. "Do you surrender?"

He shook his head.

She plunged the blade into the wound, and his fingers splayed in pain, releasing her again. He punched her in the chest, smashing her against the tree, and slapped her cutlass away. This time it landed too far for retrieval. Kate's throat was on fire and her lungs seemed to have collapsed. Roberts reached for her with red hands. She dropped to her knees and plunged her hand into the crevice in his gut. She wriggled her fingers through the slimy cords of his belly, gripped a handful, and wrenched loose his bowels. Wet entrails slithered out of his belly, piling into the snow in a steaming heap of glistening tendrils. A noxious fume groaned from the yawning wound, blasting her full in the face. She struggled to her feet and pulled away, but the foul stench lingered in her nostrils, turning her saliva to rust, and she felt the contents of her stomach rushing into her throat. Vomit exploded from her mouth before she could stop it. Roberts stood for several moments longer than she would have thought possible, until his eyes rolled up in their sockets, his knees buckled, and he collapsed atop his own intestines.

Kate wiped the blood from her eyes and gathered a clump of snow, pressing it to her forehead. The ice stung as she ground it into the cut, but only for a moment. Head wounds always bled worse than any other, even the small ones. She would need stitches, which would mean putting up with Breton's grumbling.

When she returned to her men, only four of *Fortune Renewed's* crew had surrendered, begging for mercy on their knees. The bodies of their comrades were scattered about them. Salvador and Domingo were watching them closely.

"The rest fled into the forest," said Hawkes.

"Where they will freeze to death," said Kate.

"You look terrible," Gabe told her.

"Roberts looks worse," she replied, aiming a thumb over her shoulder.

"Some men won't be bargained with," said Hawkes. "Unlike women."

She slapped the cutlass into Hawkes' hand. "The only women you've bargained with, Hawkes, are those you pay to spread their legs." Gabe and a few others chuckled. Hawkes laughed with them, but one of his eyelids twitched.

"No one else need die tonight," Kate told the survivors.

"Oh, thank you, Cap'n Bloodshot," said the youngest man through chattering teeth. "Thank you. Thank you."

"You can thank me by signing our papers, or you can remain here and freeze. And don't call me by that name again."

"I will sign!" he cried, and so did two others.

"I am b-b-but a humble m-m-mercer," sputtered a squat man with short black hair, a double chin, and a large belly.

"A mercer you say?" Kate pulled at her shirt, showing it to him. "I could use a new shirt. Your captain's intestines made a tragedy of this one."

The mercer's eyes bulged, flickering to her shirt, then away, as though looking too long would earn him a similar fate. "Yes, but he w-w-wasn't my captain."

She took no small amount of satisfaction in the man's palpable fear. The battle with Roberts had earned her that much. "How's that?"

"I was p-p-pressganged into Roberts' crew, you see."

She shrugged. She'd heard this excuse more times than

she could count. Most of the time it was a lie, although something told her this man was telling the truth. Not that it mattered. "Then he was not the captain of your choosing, but he was your captain nonetheless. And now *I* am your captain."

"As you s-say, Captain."

She caught a hint of something in his tone. Resentment? Defiance? Perhaps his sudden lack of stammer. Whatever it was, she didn't care for it. She took a step forward and raised her voice. "Preferable to freezing, yes?"

The gravity of the situation dawned. Color fled the mercer's pudgy cheeks. "Yes, I s-s-suppose it is."

Kate moved on without bothering to let the man know he was off the hook, for now.

A lanky young man with trim blonde hair sat rigid in the snow with his pointy chin held high. He met her gaze with surprising confidence in his bold blue eyes. He raised one arm, presenting her with a little black book imprinted with a cross. "You would not murder a man of God?"

"I would if he aimed anything more than a book at me."

"The Book can be a weapon too, Captain."

She plucked the book from his hands, turned it over, shook her head. "Not this one. It's too small." She dropped it in the snow.

He fell to his hands, scrambling to retrieve it. "I shall pray for your soul," he blurted.

"Good. You'll be closer to God working the topmasts. I'd suggest you pray not to fall."

There was one more who hadn't spoken, a blonde man who kept his head low. "Looks like this one prefers the cold," said Hawkes with a laugh. "Might be kinder to slit his throat now and be done with it."

She approached the silent man. "You don't accept my offer, lad? Would you rather die here in the cold? That's no way for a sailor to go." She slipped a finger under his chin, and when she lifted his head, she saw the face of a girl. Her soft cheeks were frosted with tears. It was the girl she had spotted aboard *Fortune Renewed*, now absent her straw hat.

"A lass!" Ives licked blood from his lips as he stepped forward. His eyes were obsidian beads gleaming of firelight in a grotesque crimson mask. "I'm starved for some proper entertainment."

"No one touches this girl," Kate said.

"A pirate has a right to his prize," protested Harry Harmless.

"A girl is not a prize," she said.

"Since when?" wondered Ives.

She ignored their grumbles of disapproval and set a hand on the girl's shoulder. "Are you injured?" The girl gave a timid shake of her head. "I'll put you in a safe place."

"Where's that?" She made a joke of the question, but her chin was trembling.

"How old are you, girl?"

"Seventeen, I think."

Jesus. "You shouldn't be out here."

"Didn't have no choice." She was trying so hard to appear casual, uncaring, but the frozen tears betrayed her. "He was my father."

"Who?"

The girl nodded to the distant tree where Roberts was sprawled in his own guts. Corso stood over the corpse, giving it a nudge with his boot. "The captain."

Kate was not surprised. This explained how such a pretty thing had survived so long among miscreants. She had been under Roberts' protection. "He came at me with zeal to murder, and I could only defend myself. I fear he was devoted to destruction."

"I know that better than anyone," the girl replied in a chipper tone. "He got what he deserved. I always knew this was coming."

"You'll be safe." Kate was aware her voice was harsh and toneless, offering no weight to the vague promise.

"It don't matter." The girl pointed her button of a nose down at the snow, so Kate could only see the top of her head. Her hair was so thick that it must have been a wondrous thing when fully grown. Her father's hair had likely been just as radiant when he was his daughter's age. "You can't protect me any better than he did."

Another sad story, thought Kate. She'd heard them all. Nothing was anyone's fault. Everyone was a victim of someone worse.

"Let me cut off her tongue," said Harry Harmless.

"Nay," Ives protested with a raised hand. And then he grinned through his red mask. "She'll be needing that."

"Put her in my cabin," Kate told Gabe. "I won't have her below." The girl needed time to comprehend what had happened. Kate would speak with her later.

Gabe was clearly unhappy about the order, and she knew why. He'd gone too long without a night's pleasure. A guest would complicate things. "Aye," he grumbled.

"Soon as we get back," she told the rest, "we're getting underway. When we're to open sea, we'll crowd on all sail and make for the Caribbean as swift as the wind will carry us. I'm done with this bloody cold."

They cheered, but not as loudly as they might have if they'd had a good night's sleep. Today would be sluggish, and she wouldn't press them.

She faced the flaming scaffold in the river. Distant, warbled shrieks trickled from somewhere within.

"Is it not beautiful, Captain?" Hawkes was suddenly at her side with a prideful expression.

When water quenched the last of the fire, only a blackened mast remained to mark the ship's passing, like the rotting headstone above an ancient grave. Already it seemed it had been there an eternity.

UNDERWAY

When Kate returned to the captain's cabin with two plump pieces of chicken and a warm biscuit, the girl offered a polite smile and shook her head. "I'm not hungry."

"You'll have to eat eventually." The cook had over-charred the skin and dried out the meat, yet it still made her stomach growl. Kate couldn't remember the last time she had eaten. She hadn't been particularly hungry after the ordeal with Roberts, but it seemed her appetite was return-ing. She was thankful the cook hadn't been killed, even though his skills in the kitchen were debatable.

"Kind of you to offer," the girl said. Her gratitude seemed strained, as though she thought Kate might eject her from the cabin if she offered anything less. "I fear me stomach won't stand for it."

Kate set the plate before the girl and slid it toward her. "At least tell me your name."

The girl looked at the food for a moment. She made a face and pushed the plate away. "Eira. Me name is Eira."

"That's a pretty name."

"Means 'snow.'"

Appropriate. That's where I found you. She moved to her dresser and shuffled around the bottom drawer until she found a small tin container. She opened it, dabbed two fingers inside, and liberally applied kohl about her eyelids. It had become a habit every morning, but her supply was running low. She hoped she would happen across more in the coming year. "You'll be safe in here, Eira. Don't wander out."

"I already been sullied, if that's what you mean. My father killed the man who done it, but he couldn't take it back." She held her sad, artificial smile.

Kate closed the tin and wiped her fingers on a handkerchief. She returned to Eira and looked into her eyes, which disclosed a hint of emerald in the lantern light. They were much darker than her father's. "I do not permit rape on my ship, but that doesn't mean they won't try."

"They don't care what you permit!" The girl slapped a palm over her mouth. "I'm sorry for me outburst, miss."

Kate smiled reassuringly. "I don't begrudge your bitterness. I would expect nothing less, given your circumstance."

"I don't hate you."

"Of course you do," Kate said. "I scuttled your ship. I killed your friends. I killed your father. And now you're surrounded by my pirates."

The girl shrugged a bony shoulder, or maybe she turned a shiver into a casual motion. "I'm used to pirates."

"Good." Kate touched the girl's chin, lifted her head and locked eyes with her. "Then you know what they're capable of."

The girl pulled her chin away. Defiance flashed in her eyes. "You talk like you're not one of them."

"I am one of them," Kate replied, "but I'm the only one who can keep you alive, if you do as I say. You mustn't forget what waits outside this cabin. Monsters are ever-starved. In here they cannot touch you."

Eira couldn't mask her skepticism, even as she smiled submissively for her fearsome captor. "If you say so."

Kate pinched the bridge of her nose and closed her eyes. She still hadn't found time to sleep, and probably wouldn't until day's end. "I'm too tired to lie."

Kate locked up any loose weapons in her cabin and left the girl to her misery.

The day was long and the men were particularly sluggish after their long night. It would be another day or two before they returned to their prior efficiency. She found Stubbs and Cross playing dice amidst a batch of crates near the mainmast.

"Fancy a game of passage, Captain?" asked Stubbs. He was the cooper, and he begrudgingly answered to Hawkes, but he was one of the few who cared less for the boatswain than Kate did.

"I think not," she replied. "I've caught wind of your abnormal fortuity."

He adjusted his monmouth cap and chuckled. "I'm a lucky man. We ain't playing for coin, of course."

"I should think not, unless our articles have been amended without my knowing."

Cross grunted. He wore black like Gabe, except Cross

sported a red sash instead of blue, and his hair was brown instead of black. If she didn't know better, she might have mistaken him for Gabe's less attractive younger brother. Cross didn't seem to care for women, least of all his captain. "Silly rule, you ask me."

"More ships have been lost to games of passage than to storms."

"Aye, Captain," Cross muttered, and looked down at the three dice cupped in his hand. They clicked as he gave them a vigorous shake, and then he tossed them before Stubbs. "Bollocks."

Kate leaned over to have a look at the results. "A pair of twos and a five." Doubles meant the game was over, and combined with the third die any sum less than ten was a loss. She smirked at Cross. "You see? It's a good thing you aren't playing for coin."

"I disagree," said Stubbs with a satisfied smile. "I enjoy that sour look he gets when he loses."

"These is rigged," said Cross, snatching the dice that had come up double and inspecting them. "Weighted, aye?"

Kate gave Cross a sharp pat on the back. "No reason to rig dice on a ship which does not permit gambling. When you boys are done, patch up the number two jib."

Early in the afternoon she approached Granger, the helmsman, who looked particularly weary. He was older than Breton, and he spent his nights drinking rather than sleeping. "The wind, she's turning on us," he said.

"Perhaps a storm messing things about. Wants to keep us from our home."

Granger grunted. "Good luck."

Kate looked forward and called to the men below, "Close-haul that jib." Normally she would be annoyed to

80

have to order the obvious, but her men were tired. She set a hand on Granger's shoulder and said, "Down with your helm, sir. Easily, now."

He obliged with a weary nod. "Full and by, Captain."

After a few minutes, Kate relieved the old man and allowed herself a two-hour trick at the wheel. The handles never warmed beneath her fingers and the air remained bracingly cold, biting at her cheeks. When she closed her eyes, it was difficult to picture warm turquoise waters. Around two in the afternoon, Gangly John struck up his fiddle, but he was unable to coerce the crew into a song, and after fifteen minutes he quit.

When the helmsman returned to his post, looking refreshed from a nap, there was little for Kate to do but wander the deck and speak to some of the men. As exhausted as she was, she didn't want to go back to her cabin and deal with that annoying girl. She conversed lightly with the crew, careful not to mention the lives lost in the battle. Pirates did not dwell on the past, and it would not be prudent to remind them what had been lost. They were no longer in combat, nor were they in pursuit of potential prey, so she was their equal again.

Breton stitched up her forehead on the quarterdeck late in the afternoon, but only after he had attended to the more grievous wounds some of the men had suffered on the river banks. No one else died. When Breton finally attended to her, he told her the wound wasn't anything to gripe about, though she hadn't offered a word of protest. The sting of a stitching needle no longer made her wince. "Probably leave a scar," he warned, but that wasn't a concern. Her swollen throat was more of a bother. Roberts' fingers were imprinted blue on her neck. He advised her to soothe it with rum, but she feared she would pass out if she partook of spirits.

By dusk she was painfully hungry. Her stomach felt as though it had been hollowed out with a rusty spoon, and her temples started throbbing. She filled her belly with a tasteless porridge the cook had brought up to the main deck, boasting that it was better than turtle soup. When he enthusiastically asked if she liked it, she evaded with a smile and said, "Nothing's better than turtle soup." Still, it went down easily enough, which was more than she could say for most of the cook's enigmatic concoctions.

The air grew even chillier when the sun ducked beyond the New World. The sky dimmed to reveal bright stars twinkling against an inky canvas through breaches in the clouds. Kate managed another hour on deck before she retired to her cabin, with Corso in pursuit, detailing the remaining supplies and what plunder they'd been able to recover from *Fortune Renewed*. "So we're not going to starve and our purses are overflowing," she summed up.

"Aye," he continued on, "but—"

She stopped outside her cabin. "Quit your bellyaching and have a drink with me, Corso."

"Aye."

She unlatched the door and swung it wide, letting it clang against the bulkhead. "Gabe, I am ready to drink!"

There was no answer.

"Think I last saw him below," said Corso, "wrestling with that unruly goat, Lily. Found her way to the main deck again. Climbers, them."

She shrugged. "He'll catch up."

Eira was asleep, or pretending to be asleep, atop a mound of spare canvas in the starboard corner nearest the door, which some of the men had used for tents overnight in

Virginia. She was shrouded in the many blankets Kate had provided for her. Half of her head was visible, her eye squeezed shut with the iris darting back and forth beneath the lid. One of her bare feet was poking out from under the blankets. Only thin chicken bones remained on the plate Kate had left her. Kate wondered how the girl could sleep so soundly after her life had been uprooted. This girl was either very strong or very complacent.

Kate moved to the round oak table that occupied the forward half of the cabin and kicked out one of the four rose-cushioned chairs for Corso. He took it and helped himself to the rum punch from the large glass bowl sitting atop a map of the Atlantic, beside a three-pronged brass candelabra of which only the middle candle was still burning. "How old is this?" he wondered as he produced a battered tin cup from his breeches and dipped it into the brown solution.

"Gabe made it yesterday."

Corso closed his eyes and smiled as he took a swig. "Good blend."

Kate snatched a pewter cup from one of the four corners of the map from amidst a clutter of shiny reales, gueneas, Louis d'ors, an empty rum jug, and an old pistol that didn't work. She dipped her cup, took a seat opposite Corso, and sipped liberally, savoring the sweet blend of rum, lime juice, and sugar.

The cabin was a claustrophobic mess of eccentricities, with few areas spared of clutter. Barrels of tobacco were crammed in the corner opposite the sleeping girl, overpowering the smell of wood and salt with a sweet aroma that reminded Kate of raisins. In one corner was an old globe with tan oceans and dark brown continents. Crates were stacked along the hull as high as the upper deck, and sacks of fruit and bales of silk hung in nets from above. A large armoire barely contained her wardrobe, which was bursting out of open drawers. Four tricorn hats rested atop it, and many pairs of boots were scattered about the base. Beside the armoire was a locked chest that held guns, grenadoes, cutlasses, and knives. Flags of major nations were piled between the armoire and the chest. Among them was Kate's old Jolly Roger, embroidered with a white cutlass crossing a red rose. A year into her piratical career, she had decided on a more fearsome flag that befit the name of her ship.

"So what's next, Red?" Corso asked as Kate settled into the seat opposite him.

"Quartermaster is the real boss," she reminded him. "You tell me."

"I look to you for a grand scheme, as ever."

"My grand scheme is to pass out drunk on a beach."

"A fine goal, but I wager there's more in your head than you're letting on."

She glanced down at her coat, the silver buttons glinting in the dim light. "My head is presently unoccupied."

"It's been a long year."

"We are bursting with swag, are we not?"

"We are, true enough."

"Then let us enjoy it," she said, and took another drink.

"Aye," Corso said, following her lead. He finished his cup and dipped it again. "And after we've spent it all?"

"We start over." The rum suddenly tasted bitter.

"You're liking that notion less and less every year, I think."

She picked at a lime seed wedged in her teeth, the source of the bitterness. "It's astonishing we've come this far."

"It is," he agreed, toasting her cup.

She flicked the lime seed across the table. "Yet as bountiful as our plunder is, we are no richer than when we started."

"You look to an end?"

"It ends when we die."

"Does it not get to you?"

"What?"

"The company of death?"

She pondered the question, swirling what remained in her mug. "You remember that plague ship we encountered on our way up the coast last year?"

Corso looked down at his drink. "I try to forget."

Kate nodded. Some nights she dreamed about what they found aboard that ship. The bodies and the strange way they had rotted. Pieces had fallen off. Hair. Ears. Limbs. The ship had come to a rest in the doldrums, and there was nothing left but the stench of death. She tried not to dwell on what their final days must have been like. They had not been pirates. They had not been slavers. They had been simple Dutch merchants. As far as Kate could tell, they had done nothing to earn God's wrath. "Everyone is in the company of death," she muttered darkly.

"Most do not make it their trade."

"Am I in danger of losing you, Corso?"

He smiled, but she worried he was merely favoring her. "Nowhere for me to go. Land won't have me."

"No safer there anyways," came a young female voice, and Corso nearly dropped his drink.

Kate glanced down at the mound of blankets and noticed the girl's eyes open and watching her. "Care to join us?" Kate said.

Eira sat up and stretched. Her shirt lifted to reveal her

midsection. She was painfully skinny. "You're a noisy lot."

"A thousand apologies for disturbing your slumber, your highness," quipped Corso.

The girl took her time emerging from the blankets, like a bear recovering from hibernation. Eventually she shuffled over and fell into a chair. Kate dipped her cup into the rum punch and handed it to Eira. The girl downed half the cup. "It's sweet, ain't it?" she observed, licking her lips with an uncertain scowl. "Seems a waste of good spirits, sugaring it up like that."

Corso grinned. "I might like this one."

Eira shot him a nervous look. "What you mean by that?"

Corso raised his hands innocently. "Nothing sordid, I promise."

"We'll see about that," the girl replied skeptically, but one lip curled suggestively.

Corso looked down into his cup and changed the subject. "Works fast, this. Haven't eaten enough today. Think I'll turn in for the night."

"Good night," said Kate.

Eira looked after him as he hastily took his leave. "He's handsome," she said when the door closed. "In a doggish sort of way."

"Don't do that," Kate snapped.

"What?"

"You're bracing yourself for what you think is inevitable. You needn't concern yourself with Corso."

"That what you did when I was took by a pirate? Braced yourself?"

"I killed him."

"How'd you do it?"

"I shot him in the face."

"Why'd you do that?"

"He killed my husband."

The girl's eyes narrowed. "That ain't why you killed him."

"No."

"He handsome?"

"I don't know. I can't remember."

Eira shook her head and sniffed. "You ain't forgot nothing."

"Fine, he was handsome."

"Shame."

"It was him or me."

"What were his name?"

"He doesn't have a name. He's dead and no one remembers him. Captain Johnson makes no mention of him in his fiction."

"Makes no mention of you neither."

"You read the book?"

"I can't read, but I'll wager you was left out."

"Your wager is correct."

"That make you mad?"

"No."

"You won't have no name."

"Names get you killed."

"Well you got one, even if it ain't in no book. They got a big ledger o' names, and a few of 'em still need crossing out."

"They can try."

"Maybe someone else will do it first, eh?"

"Are you plotting revenge, girl?"

"Might be."

"You're trying to hate me, but you can't. I know hate. Your eyes are clear of it."

"Well, I ain't got nothing against you, If I'm being truthful."

"I killed your father."

"He ain't never done nothing for me I couldn't a done for meself. You done more in a day than he done me whole life."

"I'm sorry."

"What you sorry for?"

"Nothing," Kate admitted. "It was merely a kindness."

The girl fell silent. She handed the cup back to Kate. "All that sugar is angering me head," she said.

Kate stood. "It's late. Sleep well, girl. And don't leave the cabin."

Eira nodded and returned to her blankets, sitting atop them and contemplating the door.

Kate removed her coat and tossed it over one of the chairs before the table, pausing to regard the old garment for a moment. She couldn't figure why Sterling and Roberts would want it. There was no sense going through the pockets. If there had been anything valuable within, she would have discovered it long ago. The silver skulls taunted her with their hollowed eyes and morbid grins. "We know things you don't," they seemed to be saying. "We've always known." She wasn't sure she liked this coat anymore.

She unhooked one of the two lanterns on either side of the door and circumvented the table. She slipped through the red drapes that partitioned off the back half of the quarters, where the bed was laid out before the stern gallery. Books lined the shelves on either side, most slanting or tipped. It was pointless to straighten them, as the endless rocking of the ship would only knock them over again. She had read them all many times over, from Homer's epics to

Shakespeare to the journals of famed sailors. While her crew pillaged the hold of a merchant vessel, Kate would plunder the books, if they had any. Though captaining a ship could be busy work, there were always long stretches at sea.

She was fading fast, and the messy mound of plump sheets and blankets atop her bed looked so inviting. She took off her necklace and her bracelets, tossing the jewelry onto the little bedside table next to Gabe's blackened tobacco pipe. Some bracelets fell off the edge and clinked against the deck, but she was too tired to retrieve them. She was more careful in removing the hoop earring, which Breton claimed would keep her eyesight sharp due to the healing powers found in gold. She rarely removed the seashells and trinkets from her hair, and tonight was no exception. She slid her breeches down her legs and kicked them away, leaving only her dirty, blood-stained shirt, which was just long enough to cover her modesty. She snuffed out the lantern and set it on the ledge before the stern windows, amidst dozens of old candles. She collapsed into the bed with the grace of a wooden plank and wrapped herself in the sheets, moaning pleasurably. She didn't care if the girl heard.

She woke to the girl standing beside the bed, staring down at her. It scared her, but she managed not to start. Kate wondered how long she'd been asleep, how long the girl had been standing there. "What are you doing?"

"Nothing."

The girl's eyes were icy, like a predator's, and Kate reached for her pistol.

"You don't have to do that," the girl said.

"I hope not," Kate replied, hand hovering over the weapon. "What do you want?"

"Could sleep with you, if you like."

"No."

"Keep you warm."

"Gabe will be back soon. He'll keep me warm."

"He won't mind unless you tell him to mind."

"He might."

"You trained him good."

Kate let her hand fall to the gun. "Go back to your blankets."

"You don't fancy a woman grasping at you?"

"As tempting as you make that sound," Kate flatly replied, "it's not my persuasion."

"How you know if you ain't tried it?"

"Some things you just know." Kate pointed. "Go to sleep."

When she woke again, the garbled pink skin of her severed ear was cold and aching. The soft violet of dawn filtered in through the stern gallery, spilling over the bed.

She propped her back against the oak headboard and looked down at Gabe. He must have come in after she fell asleep. He was sleeping on his chest, as usual. She ran a finger along the bulky muscles and scar tissue of his bare back. His head was angled toward her, half of his face mashed in a pillow. The lid of one eye parted to glance up at her, then closed. She spread her hand through his hair, twirling a thick lock around her index finger. She gave it a gentle tug, and he offered a lopsided smile without opening his eyes.

"Wakeup," she whispered. "Gabe? Wakeup." Her voice sounded raspier than usual, and her throat was still raw.

He made a low sound that might have been a word, or a grunt.

"Gabe?" She poked at him repeatedly, like she used to do

when she was a young girl trying to wake her mother too early in the morning. "Gabe. Gabe. Gabe. Gabe. Gaaaaaaabe." When he didn't respond, she shoved him. He rolled onto his back. He was wearing only his breeches, half unlaced. He must have been too tired to get them off. "Wakeup."

"No."

Kate whipped the sheet away, revealing her bare legs. The air prickled her skin. She snuggled close to Gabe and entwined his nearest leg in her own. "Get up."

"No," he groaned.

She slid her hand down rows of abs that were nearly as hard as rocks, and continued onward, delving into his breeches. She tore open the remaining laces and teased him with her fingers. She felt the heat of blood stiffening his cock. "They're going to mutiny."

He stubbornly refused to open his eyes. "Let them."

She crawled on top of him, sitting on his stomach. One edge of his lip curled upward as she rubbed herself against his abs. "It's not a request."

"Leave me alone, you bitch," he murmured halfheartedly, with only one eye open.

She slid up his body until she was smothering his face. He kissed her inner thighs, working his mouth closer and closer, licking her here and there. His tongue parted her lips and curled up and down, slight licks at first, building in intensity. She leaned back to stroke him. His tongue worked diligently for what seemed an eternity. A contented gleam brightened his sleepy eyes.

"We slept in . . . too long." The words came out in breathless quivers as she started to sweat inside and out, despite the cold.

He freed his mouth long enough to say, "Yes."

"Need to get up . . . and about."

His tongue retracted for an instant. "No."

"Yes."

"No."

"Devil take you," she half-snapped, half-moaned. She lifted her shirt up over her face and lingered in that pose for a moment, with her arms above her head, hair gathered in the shirt. She saw him watching her through heavily-lidded eyes, his nose nuzzled in the curly red patch between her legs. Her stomach constricted with pleasure as she struggled to hold in a breath, until it finally shuddered out of her. She tossed the shirt away, and her hair tumbled down, seashells and trinkets drumming her back.

She slithered down his waist and straddled him with thighs made strong by years of hard work on deck and in battle. She eased him inside and leaned forward to mash a breast against his wet lips. She felt his mouth open and his tongue swirl about the nipple, before he gently bit down. She spread her hands through his hair and held him close, while he clutched her ass and thrust upward with increasing force. Her entire body seemed to be constricting, from her midsection upward. The muscles of her thighs were so tightly clenched about him, she feared she would crush him. She slapped a palm to his chest and pushed upward, arching her back. His hands found her breasts. She curled her fingers, digging the nails into his skin, drawing blood. He grit his teeth and groaned, and she felt him explode inside her, warmth spreading into her abdomen, sweat burning along her skin, all tension loosing from her muscles in a glorious wave. "Don't ever die," she gasped as she fell back down to him.

"Nffr drf."

"What?" She almost laughed, and then realized she was smothering him with a breast. She lifted up. "Sorry, what?"

"Never do," he said.

They stayed there for longer than she planned, ten minutes maybe, slick with sweat, skin gleaming. It was the warmest she'd been in weeks. He ran his hand beneath her damp hair, down her backside, until he found her rear and lingered there, fingers teasing. When the tip of his cock nudged her thigh, she sprang from the bed. "You're inexhaustible," she informed him with mock surprise.

He shrugged and pulled the covers over his waist. "Mind of its own."

She searched for the breeches she had haphazardly discarded in her eagerness to snuggle into bed. "It's freezing," she said as she hopped up and down to get the breeches up to her waist.

He propped himself on one elbow and admired her. "Have I ever told you how much I love watching your tits jiggle when you jump?"

"You're a poet, Gabe."

"And never a quill and paper," he said with a sigh, plopping back down.

"There's a quill on the desk, and plenty of parchment."

A reflective look darkened his face for an instant. "You can kill a man with a quill, did you know that?"

"I can kill a man with just about anything." She pulled her shirt over her head, struggling to get her hair through it. She adjusted the sleeves and half-laced the collar, and then she set about retrieving each piece of jewelry, which proved a maddening scavenger hunt. She found the hoop earring first, which was the most important piece. She found most of her bracelets, but gave up on the necklace. Her pelvis was sore from lovemaking, and she didn't want to bend over until the ache subsided. "I really don't understand where all my shiny shit scuttles off to in the middle of the night," she muttered while glancing about, perplexed and annoyed.

"Night crabs," Gabe murmured, closing his eyes. "They steal your shiny shit while you sleep."

"Don't go back to sleep," she warned.

"I'm not. I'm awake." His eyes didn't open.

"You're asleep."

"I might be, if your lips ever stopped moving."

She grinned. She liked him when he was crotchety. "You seemed to be enjoying my lips a minute ago."

"I was expecting reciprocation." He sighed.

"Cry me an ocean."

She opened the curtain to the forward half of the room. The girl—*Eira*, she reminded herself, *her name is Eira*—was still sleeping, shrouded in her blankets.

Somewhere outside Kate heard a gull screeching obnoxiously, probably circling the ship and scouting for food. They were still close enough to shore.

She slid out one of the chairs and sat before the round table, unrolling a map of the Caribbean and weighting the corners. "Where to start?" she murmured to herself, trailing a finger down past Florida and weaving through the Bahaman island chain. Her finger halted at Nassau. She could only imagine how the once tranquil, rustic port looked now, overrun with British ships and a suffocating air of propriety. She hadn't returned since escaping the clutches of Woodes Rogers so many years ago. She was a loose end, and as long as Rogers lived, she would feel his breath on her neck.

She shivered at the thought and reached for her coat. But

the coat wasn't there. She stood and searched around the table, expecting to find it crumpled on the floor. It was gone.

She looked to the girl. The blankets were piled high, and Eira was buried somewhere within. Or was she? Kate plunged her hands in, tossing blankets aside with increasing haste. Eira Roberts was gone.

And that's when she realized the screeching bird outside was not a bird. The chair toppled in her haste to get to the door.

TRIAL

"Wily little wench gutted me," Breton growled.

Over a third of the crew had bunched together amidships at the starboard, where the surgeon lay sprawled with one arm slung over a cannon. The blood had drained from his face, and it was obvious he was less than a minute from death, but he seemed only mildly put out. "Tried to talk some sense into her, got a rusty dirk in the belly for my trouble."

Kate forced a laugh. Breton wouldn't appreciate her fawning over him in his final moments. "You should have stuck to your prickly disposition."

"Oh, I was mighty prickly. Wager that's what earned me this."

She crouched before him and lifted his arm. An intestine

glistened in the sun before he shoved her away and slapped his hand over it, hissing in pain. Blood swirled in the seawater that sloshed about him as the deck swayed. He ran his fingers over his scalp and streaked his blonde hair in red. "I'm done," he said.

"Damn you, Breton," she said. "Couldn't you go and get your throat slit? I've had my fill of guts."

He laughed. "Happy to be a bother one last time."

Granger paced nearby with a palm over his mouth, barely able to look at Breton. He would never have admitted how fond he was of the surgeon, but the agony in his red eyes said more than words. The two old men had been friends since long before Kate met them, though they had never been heavy conversationalists.

There was no sense lying to the surgeon about his chances. Kate leaned in close, whispering in his ear so the others wouldn't hear. "Where would you see yourself buried? On sea or on land?"

He tried for another laugh, but his cheeks turned red, and blood dribbled down his pale chin. "You were right," he groaned.

"I was?" She was shocked. He had never allowed her any leeway in an argument. "About what?"

"It doesn't ma—" He died before he could finish, mouth ajar on the final word. Kate placed two fingers beneath his jaw and closed his mouth. She had seen too many men go midsentence, trying to get out some final words of portent. A rare few went silently, without protest, but too often a dying man fought for more words than his fleeting breath would permit.

Granger fell to his knees beside Breton and grabbed his friend's arm, shaking him and wailing. Now that it was too late, he permitted himself a show of affection. *Men are fools,* thought Kate.

She stood and looked to the crew. "Where's the girl?"

A sandy-haired lad pointed to the bow without removing his haunted eyes from the dead surgeon.

She shoved through the crew to find the girl bent over the gunwale on the port side of the forecastle, squirming terribly while Ives fumbled at her breeches. Even through the mask of dried blood, which he hadn't bothered to rinse from his narrow face since the battle, his drunkenness was evident. She was trying to scramble away, but her only way out would be over the gunwale. The slim green line of the coast was within sight, but too far a swim. Ives wasn't going to let her off so easily. Every time she made a mad scramble for freedom, he pulled her back.

"Ives!" Kate shouted. "Keep it in your breeches!" He didn't seem to hear her, so she stole the pistol from the nearest man, aimed between two jib sails and fired into the murky grey sky. Everyone quieted at once, turning their heads toward her. She tossed the spent pistol away, and one of the pirates snatched it out of the air instinctively.

Ives froze for a moment, then started giggling like a little boy caught in the act of stealing. Eira raised her head, glancing desperately at the only person she thought could save her. A thread of spittle ran across one cheek, tinged in red. She mouthed the words, "help me," at Kate, before Ives gripped her short hair and ground her face against the rail. "This ain't no reprieve, girly."

"It's too early for rape," Kate said.

Ives' upper jaw nearly eclipsed his sloping lower jaw as he gnashed his teeth and struggled to make sense of Kate's words.

"It's *never* too early for rape!" someone said. The voice wasn't familiar, and Kate didn't look to see who it belonged to.

"She killed the surgeon," said Ives, finding his voice at last.

The crew looked from Ives to Kate. "Seeing as you didn't bother to watch him die, I don't think that concerns you terribly."

"She must be dealt with."

Kate looked at the girl. "Did you murder my surgeon, girl?"

"They all saw it!" Ives protested.

Kate thumbed her temple, hoping to avoid another headache. "I wasn't asking you, Ives. I want to hear it from her mouth."

"Plenty of uses for her mouth."

"He wouldn't get out of me way," Eira said, guilt plain on her face. "He wouldn't get out of me way."

Kate felt the pressure building behind her eyes. She grit her teeth too much. Breton had warned her about that. Who would gripe at her about her bad habits now? Good surgeons were too hard to come by. "That was a mistake, girl. I could have let you die, but I gave you my quarters. This is how you repay me?"

"You shouldn't never have took me." Eira's voice remained disturbingly low and calm. "You should've left me in the snow."

"You're right about that," said Kate. "I should have let you freeze."

"I weren't yours to take. I just wanted a boat. I just wanted to get away. That's all. I just wanted a boat." The girl's eyes lined with water.

"You didn't take a boat," Kate reminded her. "You took my surgeon's life."

"That's not all she took," said Ives, and he gestured to someone in the crowd. "Show her!"

Young Tommy Killian approached with a bunched garment, and judging by its deep red, Kate knew what it was. "She were wearing this." He shook the garment loose of its folds, holding it by the shoulders. None of the silver skull buttons were missing, which were the only pieces of real value.

"And why didn't any of you come to me immediately?" She snatched the coat from Killian, hastily refolded it and tucked it under one arm.

"We didn't want to wake you," offered Morven. He was an older pirate with a barrel chest, curly red hair, and a thick Scottish accent. He and Breton had come to blows years back, nearly killed one another, and hadn't spoken since. She imagined he was quite pleased with this outcome.

"Yet you saw fit to dispense punishment before consulting your captain?"

Morven shrugged. "She's a murderer and a thief, Cap'n."

"We're all murderers and thieves last I looked."

She would never forget the Dutch merchant ship she had taken in the first year of her career. The surrender had gone well enough, with no deaths. The captain had been polite and obedient. She should have known then that he had something to hide. The captain had concealed his daughter in a crate in the hold, and six of Kate's men kept the discovery to themselves, for all of four hours. When she finally delved below to find her missing men, the girl could no longer stand. Kate could show no sympathy to the girl or her father, for that would only weaken her in her crew's

100

eyes. She left behind a shivering, bleeding girl who, in all likelihood, had succumbed to her injuries, and a man she imagined had plunged into drunken shambles shortly thereafter. *Maybe he put a pistol in his mouth,* she had considered more than once. *Who would blame him?*

"We didn't know consulting were needed," said Duncan with a challenging glower in his one beady eye. Amusing coming from a fat little man who was at least a foot shorter than her.

"Of the two of us," Kate said, "which is captain?"

Duncan's eye darted about for a moment, as if he suspected some form of trickery. Finally, he looked at her and said, "You is."

"I *am*."

"You am."

She would've laughed under lighter circumstances. "'You are.'"

"I are?" Duncan looked around. "Since when?"

"No, *I* am. I say 'I am,' you say, 'you are.'"

Duncan frowned. "You are."

"Aye."

"You what?"

"I'm confounded," said Morven. "Who's captain now?"

Duncan turned to Morven, aiming a thumb at Kate over his shoulder. "She are."

She gave up on the grammar lesson. "And while I'm captain, there will be no raping on my deck, above or below. Ives? Are you hearing me?"

Ives was not hearing her. He was groping Eira's ass while licking his red lips.

"IVES!"

"Whut?"

"Back away."

"Or you'll what?" It wasn't so much a challenge as a fanciful musing, as though there was nothing she could possibly do to him, but it was amusing to entertain the notion. "You'll kill me, will you? For taking my rightful spoils?"

Kate smiled. "No. I won't kill you."

"Damn right you won't," he boasted, before she could finish. "Even if you got me from behind, Hawkes would have something to say about that."

She felt an eyelid twitching and wondered if anyone else could see it. "I'll feed your guppy's cock to a clownfish."

Tommy Killian chortled, and started choking on his own saliva. Others laughed, even Duncan. Ives cast an evil glare about. "Haul your wind, the lot of you!" he roared, and that made them laugh all the harder. It was impossible to tell, but Kate knew his face was turning the same shade as his crimson mask. After a moment of twitchy hesitation, he took two steps away from Eira. Kate moved between them, keeping her front to Ives. "Get your breeches up," she instructed Eira, who hastily obeyed.

"I weren't finished with her," Ives protested.

"You have to start before you can finish," Kate replied. "Touch her again, and I'll make certain you never finish anything."

"That she would," came an alluring voice.

She turned to see Hawkes emerging casually from the crowd. It was unnerving that she never knew he was about until he decided to announce his presence. "Here to back your man, Hawkes?"

"Nay, Captain," he insisted, opening his hands to show her he had no weapons. "I would only dissuade him from a foolish course."

She met his misplaced grey eyes. "Would you?"

Hawkes reached out to Ives. "Now is not the time."

"Nor will it ever be," Kate reminded them both.

Ives' cheeks quaked, his fist tightened, and blue veins bulged from his temples. "You're going to let this murderer roam free among us?"

Before she could answer, Corso shoved through the crowd and said, "What's all this?" His shirt was off, massive chest glistening sweat, as though he had been hard at work below decks.

Hawkes wasted no time. "Our captain's hostage killed Breton and tried to make off with one of our boats."

Corso looked at Kate. Kate closed her eyes and nodded confirmation. Corso sighed. "Then put her in the brig and we'll maroon her first island we come to."

"That's not what we agreed to," said Ives. "I signed articles when I came aboard this ship, and them articles said any man what kills another man unjustly gets the same treatment."

"If you could read," Corso said, "you'd know that the punishment is marooning with a pistol and a single shot."

Not a direct execution, thought Kate, *but an execution nonetheless.* Still, it would give the girl a slim chance.

Hawkes shook his head. "And in the meantime we must suffer a woman—no offense, Captain—bringing ill fortune upon us."

Kate laughed. "You've enjoyed eight years of good fortune under my colors, Hawkes."

"You are an exception to the rule," Hawkes allowed with an inclined head.

"How kind."

"Don't matter what the papers say," said Ives. "We'll vote

103

for it."

Kate closed her eyes. Those were the words she dreaded to hear.

Ives moved to Corso and grasped his arm. "Go on. Put it to a vote, quartermaster."

Corso stared at Ives' hand until he removed it. "What exactly am I putting to a vote?"

"We kill her now, as we see fit, as slowly as we want."

Kate stepped forward. "You're not raping this girl."

"That's not up to you, Captain," said Hawkes.

"That's not up to you, Captain," parroted Ives.

Corso folded his arms. "I won't tally such a vote. That's barbarism, plain and simple."

"Then must I submit myself for the position of quartermaster," said Hawkes with a sigh of feigned resignation.

"Put it to a vote, Corso," Kate said. Her hand was forced. The thought of Hawkes as quartermaster unnerved her, and the girl was dead either way.

"I'll have no part of this," Corso muttered, and stormed off while Kate stared after him in disbelief.

Hawkes pirouetted with the grace of a twirling dancer, facing the crew with his arms spread wide. "Then I'm afraid I must accept the quartermaster's duties. All in favor of executing this young woman, say aye."

"Ayes" sounded here and there, sparsely at first, and then Ives reminded them all, "She done in our doctor! Any of you what's injured has no one to turn to now."

And then the "ayes" formed a deafening roar.

"I trust the vote doesn't need to be tallied," said Hawkes.

Ives grinned through his mask of blood. Kate approached him slowly, and his grin faded. She reached to his waist and slipped free his pistol while he watched uncertainly. "I should use this on you," she said.

Ives was nervous, but not for himself. "You're not going to kill her yet, are you?"

"Isn't that what you just voted?"

"I didn't mean right away. I meant . . . you know . . . after."

Eira drifted toward the front of the bow on wobbly legs as the wind beat against the jibs above her. She set her small hands on the rail and collected herself with long, deep breaths. Maybe she knew what was coming. *Now's your chance, you idiot. Jump.* She wouldn't make it to shore, but at least Kate wouldn't have to do the deed. Yet, now that she had the chance, Eira didn't leap. Perhaps she thought Kate could save her. And there was a time when Kate might have tried, before she realized the price of good deeds.

"Where did you think you could go?" Kate asked.

Tufts of golden hair fluttered in the wind. "Anywhere."

"Why did you steal my coat?" She felt the hard lump of Roberts' golden cross within the coat tucked under her arm. "Surely not for a bit of shine. You could have stolen that without taking the coat. It would have been easier to conceal."

Eira's dirty brown shirt had fallen away from a creamy shoulder. The sun had done her no favors, probably because she had tried so hard to keep her gender hidden beneath frumpy clothes and broad hats for so long. Her shoulders began to quake, and for a moment Kate thought she might be crying, but then she realized the girl was laughing. "What's so funny?"

"You won't get a trifle out of me." She faced Kate and stubbornly pursed her lips to emphasize the point.

"We could make her talk," said Ives. The bulge in his

breeches was returning. "It's silly to kill her so soon."

Kate wanted nothing more than to put a shot in Ives' crotch. In a world without consequences, she would have done just that. But she'd be killing herself in the process.

"You'll kill me either way," said Eira, pointing at the pistol in Kate's hand. "Get on with it."

"I'm not going to kill you," Kate replied under her breath, hoping no one else could hear.

"What?" someone said. "What's that?"

"I think she said she weren't going to kill her."

"What?!"

"Someone will." This was from Hawkes, not a promise so much as a calming gesture.

"Just a matter who gets at her first." Ives. He would make sure no one but him got to her first. And killing wasn't what he had in mind. Not right away.

Kate ignored the chatter.

Eira scoffed, surrendering all former pretenses. "I don't use long words like you, Captain, but that don't make me stupid."

Kate looked over the girl's shoulder, to the distant coast of North America. *Maybe she's a good swimmer*, she thought. But she knew better. No one could swim that distance, and Kate knew the torture of drowning better than most. "Turn around, girl."

Eira hesitated a moment, scrutinizing Kate with eyes that belonged to someone much older, and it occurred to Kate that the girl held no hatred for her. There was something worse than loathing in her gaze: exasperation. Her eyes surrendered all tension as she looked past Kate to the monsters gathered at her back. "What's the point?"

Kate urged her to turn around. "Look to the horizon and

tell me what you see."

After a moment, Eira turned to have a look. Her bony shoulders sagged. "I see land," she said. "I see the—"

The hammer struck the frizzen and the pistol recoiled, jolting Kate's arm. The shot cracked along the canvas like thunder. The girl's head snapped forward and a red mist sprayed from the front, suspended against the blue horizon for a split-second before it dispersed. Her slender body slumped over the gunwale. A cloud of smoke lingered before Kate. She dropped the gun and kneeled to grasp the girl's legs, which were shockingly thin, like twigs. It took minimal effort to heave her over the rail. Her feet scraped the hull on the way down and sent her into a spin, head over heels, and Kate glimpsed a red cavity where the girl's right eye had been. Her back slapped the water, limbs awkwardly sprawled, before a whitecap rolled over her and swept her underneath the ship.

Kate ignored the groans of disappointment from the men at her back as she gazed across to the New World, a thin green line barely visible through the coiling tendrils of smoke that danced like milky-white snakes before her.

DIEGO

Ives was appalled, barely restraining himself from lunging at her in a murderous fury. "You know how long it's been since I had a woman?"

"You can wait a little longer," she replied, while thinking, *One day it will be your corpse I push over the rail, and I will smile as I do it.*

He was oblivious to her thoughts, however plain the dark promise written upon her face. Ives had never been good at reading people. "That girl deserved everything I were going to do to her."

Kate tried to rub the gunpowder from her fingers, but only smudged it. "She murdered one of ours and paid with her life. There is no greater price."

Hawkes raised a helpful hand. "I respectfully disagree,

Captain. I call that a kind death. Breton went slow. The girl went fast. If there be equity in the dealing of the punishment, it eludes me."

A handful of deaths were etched in her memory, like paintings that too closely resembled reality. Most had been illustrated by her hand. Eira's death would find a place in that morbid gallery, tiny red droplets spattered across a blue canvas, lingering beyond short golden locks and a scrawny neck. "There's no such thing as a kind death," Kate informed the boatswain. "Only a quick death and a slow death."

"You might have left a body," Hawkes suggested, ever helpful. "Don't give me that look, Captain. It's not my persuasion, but I doubt Ives would have minded. And it's not like the girl has any cares, if that sort of thing unnerves you."

"Very little unnerves me anymore," Kate lied, inwardly shuddering at the thought of Ives pumping away at a young woman's corpse. She called to the others. "But I do understand there are some thirsts only a woman can cure. A fortnight's rest in fairer company will do you all good, aye?"

There was a general pause as the men considered the implications of "fairer company," and then their faces brightened with comprehension, and they cried "AYE!" in unison.

"Then man your sheets, before this dreary weather drives us all mad."

Hawkes hesitated after most had started toward their duties, as though wrestling with hard thoughts, but Kate suspected calculation. He confirmed it by raising his voice for those that remained. "You'll understand if I tally a vote for a new quartermaster?"

Heads swiveled, followed by nods of approval. "Corso can't be relied on no more," someone said.

Goddamn you, Corso.

"He left you to his duty, Captain," said Hawkes with a gentle smile. He was enjoying this. He looked like he might burst into song at any moment.

"Aye," she agreed, with no choice. It was the truth. She'd already pressed her luck enough today. "It appears he no longer wants the job. Tally your vote. Who did you have in mind?"

Hawkes' smile broadened.

"I thought as much." She leaned in close so no one else would hear. "Unlike Corso, I *do* value my duty. If you get in my way, I will kill you in your sleep."

The threat did nothing to distress Hawkes' delicate features. "Fair enough, Captain." He dropped the smile for a moment. "I was hoping we might be allies. Perhaps friends."

She snorted so hard it shot a fierce jolt through her sinuses. "And maybe I'll let you put your little prick in my ass, hmm?"

He blinked and looked at the deck, then chuckled a little, plainly flustered and trying not to show it. Ives stepped between them before Hawkes could muster a reply. "What was it she were after? What's so special about that coat." He reached for it.

Kate pulled away. She unfolded the coat, reached inside and retrieved the golden cross she had taken from Roberts. A piece of jewelry would have been much easier to smuggle than a coat, so why take both? *There must be something else.*

"What's that?" Ives demanded, eyes glinting of gold.

She slapped the cross into his palm. "Buy yourself a strumpet, since I've robbed you of your pleasure. Any woman brave enough to take *you* into her bed deserves a shiny reward."

He licked his red lips. "That's right," he said with a sharp, entitled nod. "That's right." And whatever slow, gruesome death he had been planning for his captain vanished in that moment. Hawkes favored Kate with a strange look that might have betrayed respect, but she couldn't be sure, and she didn't care.

"And wash your face," she told Ives. "You look like a man who spent a month too long betwixt a strumpet's thighs."

Hawkes slapped Ives on the back, laughing heartily as he towed him away, showing everyone how amicable and jovial he was, and what a great quartermaster he would make, and hell, maybe even a captain one day. Kate glared at the back of the boatswain's head as he left, wondering how best to kill him.

On her way back to her cabin, she found Granger where she'd left him, beside his dead friend. "Think you can get him cleaned up?"

"Aye, Captain," Granger sputtered through dramatic sobs.

"Good. We'll put him to sea at dusk. Seems right, somehow. He was always griping about the sun, up and about after hours. I gather he liked the stars." *Or maybe he simply hated them less than sunlight.*

Granger stopped sniffing for a moment as he gave it some thought. "I suppose he did." He nodded, looking at her. The whites of his eyes were shot with red. "Aye."

Kate returned to her cabin without a glance back. She slammed the door behind her. Corso was leaning against her armoire, safely on the other side of the table. His shirt was on, dark with sweat. "Captain."

"What the fuck was that?" she demanded.

"My resignation," Corso replied.

"No finer time," she hissed.

"The girl was too young."

"The girl forced my hand."

"There was another way."

"Was there? You might have enlightened me *before* I scattered her wits across the Atlantic."

Corso looked down at his feet, his mouth distorting as he wrestled with his thoughts. He shook his head. "She reminded me of someone, is all."

"You didn't know her."

"Didn't need to. It was the look of her."

Kate waited for him to explain, but he kept his head down. She thought he might cry. Her fearless quartermaster, who had killed men with his bare hands, was on the verge of tears. "You plan on telling me who she reminded you of?"

"Nay."

"A lover. Is that it?"

"Nay."

"Your mother? Do you miss suckling at your mother's teat, Corso?"

"Guard your words, Red."

Kate laughed. "Why? I know you're too craven to lay hands on a woman."

He raised his head, glaring. His eyes were red, lined with water. "I may find exception."

Gabe slipped through the curtain. His pipe filled the room with a light vapor. "What was the commotion?" He stifled a yawn. "I thought I heard a shot."

Kate glared at him. "The girl killed Breton, so I killed the girl."

Gabe lowered his pipe. He looked mildly surprised. "Oh. I see."

"You didn't see, because you were abed."

He brought the pipe to his lips, inhaled deeply, held it, and exhaled a massive cloud. "Looks like you handled it."

She blinked, her eyes stinging from the light haze that had already filled the room. "Do you really have to do that?"

"What?"

"That!" she exclaimed, jabbing a finger at his pipe.

He removed the pipe from his mouth, looked at it. "No."

"Then would you put it out?"

"No." He placed the pipe back in his mouth.

She tried to take a deep breath to calm herself, and nearly choked on the smoke. "It's an order," she rasped.

Corso smirked at Gabe.

Gabe lowered the pipe, but didn't put it out. "We're not in battle, Captain."

"Are we not?"

He stared at her for a long time, as if trying to determine if she was serious, and finally snuffed out the pipe with his fingers.

"Thank you," she said. She opened her hand and stared at her palm. It was stained black with gunpowder. She licked a thumb and furiously rubbed at the powder, but it wouldn't come off.

"Well," Corso concluded. "This was a fun little talk, but I must be off."

Kate smiled at him as he passed. "You can toss yourself off the ship, if you like."

"Maybe tomorrow," he said, suddenly cheery. "I think I'll find myself a nice hammock. I'm due for a nap."

"Try not to wake up with a slit throat."

113

He paused at the door. "I'm sure I won't."

"Sleep well," she hissed.

"I'm sure I will." He left the cabin, gently closing the door behind him.

Gabe set the pipe on the table and wiped his hands on his breeches. "Sounds to me like the girl killed herself."

"Eira."

"What?"

"Her name was Eira, and she didn't kill herself." She felt anger rising again, bitterness tinging her words.

"Didn't know her," said Gabe. "I *did* know Breton. Good surgeons are hard to come by."

She wanted to hit him. "Are you trying to make me feel better?"

He tried to disarm her with that wolfish grin. "Aye. Is it working?"

"No it isn't," she muttered sourly. "They are electing a new quartermaster right now, you know."

He didn't pause to consider the news. "Corso met his limit."

"Do you understand what just happened?" She was almost yelling now, because he clearly didn't understand the gravity of the situation. "They're going to elect Hawkes in Corso's stead. One more step toward captain."

"The man had a daughter," Gabe calmly explained.

"What?"

"Corso. He had a daughter. Did you know that?"

"No. Who cares?"

"He cares. That's what I'm trying to tell you. He let her stow aboard his merchant ship. She was killed outside Port Royal when his ship was mistaken for pirates by the British navy. Corso was compensated for his loss, but also chastised for putting a fright in the navy with his run-down boat. After that, he turned genuine pirate."

Kate was stunned. "He never told me that."

"He was drunk, otherwise he probably wouldn't have told me."

"That's a very sad story," Kate said, resting her hands on a chair. She couldn't dwell on Corso right now, though she knew she would eventually come to regret being cross with him. She suddenly despised the irritating part of herself that felt sympathy, and she might have strangled it if she knew how. "If we don't solve this problem, we will become another sad story, you and I."

"Mostly you. I can slip into the shadows when they mutiny."

"They know you share my bed. They'll kill you out of caution."

He considered that. "Could pretend we had a fight and I don't like you anymore."

"That would never work. You're a terrible liar."

He chuckled. "It doesn't need to come to mutiny."

"Does it not?"

"Can I ask you a question?"

"You just did."

"A second question, then?"

"It will be the third at this rate, but why stop now?"

"I can solve all this, you know."

"That wasn't a question."

"Let me kill Hawkes for you."

"Lovely gesture."

"I'd enjoy it."

"Thought you didn't enjoy killing women?"

"Thought you didn't either."

Her cheeks burned as she glared at him, wishing him dead in that moment. "I'll kill Hawkes myself when the time comes."

"Was a time you would've saved that girl."

"She was beyond saving."

"You would've found a way. Wouldn't have let anyone make the decision for you."

"Things aren't that simple anymore," she replied, softening her tone. She didn't want to fight. Not with him. They were fighting too easily of late, too gleefully.

The sympathy fled his eyes in favor of a cold comprehension. "Maybe you enjoyed it."

She stared back at him. He had intended the insult to sting, to jar her from apathy, but she felt nothing. Perhaps she was too tired, or perhaps she truly didn't care. "It's done now," was all she could say. "No sense going on about it."

"I agree," he said. "Glad that's settled."

She spread the coat flat on the table, the interior facing up. The lining was light brown, worn over the years. "Give me your dagger," she instructed without looking at him.

"What?"

She held out a hand. "Give. Me. Your. Dagger."

He eyed her suspiciously as he set the hilt in her hand. She dug the pointy tip into the seam of her coat, where the exterior met the lining, near the left collar, and drew it downward. When she finished, she stripped away the lining and exposed the stained wool interlining beneath. She tore the wool away to reveal the interior of the outer fabric. She tried to smooth out the creases, but some were too stubborn and too old. There were thirteen dark stains scattered across the back, all roughly the same size.

Gabe brushed his knuckles over the black stubble of his

chin as he studied the coat. The line in his brow grew. He pointed at the creases. "These spots are queer."

"It's an old coat."

"This is ink," he said, placing the tip of his index finger upon one of the spots near the center.

"Look like stains to me."

He shook his head. "I would have seen them on the backside."

"You spend entirely too much time gazing at my backside." She didn't care for the sound of her own voice. There was no playfulness in her tone, only a drawling rasp. It was ugly, and she wasn't sure how Gabe could stand it. *Would that I could begin this day anew, and wake before that stupid girl snuck off.*

Gabe was running his finger over one of the dark blotches. "These aren't random."

"How do you know?" She knew what he meant, but she didn't feel like admitting it. The spots were generally spaced the same distance apart, as if strategically placed.

"This one is red." He moved his finger to the upper left corner, very near the sleeve, and tapped a red dot.

She waved a hand. "That's just a spot of blood."

"Your blood?" He sounded more amused than concerned.

She had been stabbed a few times, but never there, and the coat would have had a hole in it. And she was good about tending to her more serious wounds, so she doubted she had bled on it after the fact. "Rackham probably got stabbed or shot and put the coat on without tending to his wound." When he didn't reply, she looked up to find him scowling at her. "What?" she asked self-consciously.

"Sometimes I forget how many times you've cracked

your skull."

She recoiled with what she prayed was the ugliest face she'd ever made. "Don't. Not today."

He grinned, which only made her angrier. "This is too red for blood," he explained quickly, before she could strike. "It's ink."

She wanted to plant a fist in his pretty jaw. It wouldn't have been the first time she'd assaulted him. Instead of respecting her when she was in a dark mood, he antagonized her. After a full minute of trying to bore a hole in his forehead with a glare, she gave up and looked for herself. She leaned over the map, studying the blotch closely. He was right, but she didn't want to admit it. "Why would someone spill ink there?"

He searched around the coat with his hand. "I don't see any other red drops, do you?"

"No, but—"

"What's this?" He moved his hand into the sleeve, opened it. There was writing at the edge. All she could see was:

eard

The rest was hidden within the sleeve. Gabe thrust his hand in, as though he was going to try on the coat. His fingers emerged, curled round the cuff, and he drew the sleeve inside out. He flattened the cloth on the table, revealing the short passage scrawled within, in thick black ink and a sloppy, nearly illegible hand:

Hay trece ataúdes.
Número trece es la clave

118

en el cementerio de Blackbeard
-Diego

"There are . . . thirteen . . . coffins," Gabe translated uncertainly. "Number thirteen holds the key, in Blackbeard's cemetery." He stood up and clapped his hands. "I don't even want to know what that means."

Kate tapped the red dot near the sleeve. "It means this one has something we want."

Gabe tried to walk away, but he was pulled back to the coat like a magnet. "What are these, then? Graves? Blackbeard is buried here?"

A chill prickled the flesh of her arms as something occurred to her. "This isn't where Blackbeard's buried. It's where he buried everyone else."

Gabe laughed to mask the dread she knew had flooded his gut, same as hers. "So this is a map to what? Everybody he killed?"

"Only the ones he truly despised." She rounded the table and approached the old globe. She spun the globe, then slapped it to a stop with her palm, and knelt to focus on the Caribbean. "If Edward Teach buried his victims, they're either in Carolina or somewhere in the Caribbean."

"And you think something else is buried with them?"

She shrugged. "I don't know what to think."

"You know as well as I that some pirates hide their fortune, but there's no sensible reason for a pirate to draw up a helpful map guiding some imbecile straight to it." Gabe sat down before the coat, leaning in close. After a moment, he shook his head, baffled. "And even if it is treasure, what good is it? There's no latitude."

Kate found a small mark she had placed on the globe, just

a few leagues east of the lower tip of Florida. "I know someone who might help us with that."

Gabe thought for a moment, scowled. "You don't mean—"

"The men are starved for sex. Ives in particular."

"Ives is a hungry dog," Gabe finished. "Feed him and he's your best friend."

"Exactly. The dogs need feeding. And while we're there, I can find out what, if anything, *she* knows about this. Two whales, one harpoon."

He eyed her apprehensively. "You haven't seen her in how many years?"

"A long time."

"Long enough?"

"Likely not."

She knew from Gabe's half-smirk, half-grimace that he wanted no part of this. "And what if she doesn't know anything? Worse yet, what if she *does* know something?"

Kate gave the globe a sharp spin, and the continents blurred together as they sped past. It all looked the same, sea and land, land and sea. "You have somewhere else to be?"

He sat back, sliding his hands off the coat and into his lap. He gave her a very serious face, which she had to chuckle at, because it did not fit him at all. He persisted through her amusement. "You can't trust that woman, Kate."

"I trust women even less than men, Gabe." She opened her hand and stared at it. The powder had seeped into the lines of her palm, little black rivers winding through calloused skin. "But they're no harder to kill."

"You're taking a risk, and for what? You don't even know."

"For the hunt," she said, sounding out all three words as

though talking to a child. "The hunt is where we thrive."

Gabe grunted. "How much longer, I wonder?"

She was tired of this. She made for the door. "Caution earns us an empty stomach, nothing more."

"One day our luck will run dry."

She halted before the door. "The first time my luck ran dry, I learned who I was."

"And you need a reminder?"

There was a vaguely feminine form in the swirling patterns of the door, slender and delicate. The image faded as she scrutinized the individual lines. "Maybe I do," she admitted.

"Then you'll go looking for trouble."

She opened the door. "I will rescind neither pleasure nor pain if it means leaving a path unexplored."

He frowned, pretending he didn't understand, but she knew he did. "There's more than one path, Kate."

"I only see the one."

"You're only looking at the one."

She lingered there in the doorway, hand on the latch. "You want to quit," she concluded, still not looking back at him.

She heard the legs of the chair groan as he stood. "Is it so terrible a thought?"

"How many have succeeded?"

He laughed. "None we'll ever read about."

She tilted her head, and the shells in her hair clicked and clacked. "Woodes Rogers already knows my name. You know why he didn't put me in Captain Johnson's book? Because he wants me for himself. He'll keep me from history if he can."

"Use that to your advantage." Gabe's heels thumped the

deck as he started toward her. "We have enough to vanish forever. Change our identities. Buy land. A small plantation."

"A *plantation*." The man who had killed her husband and taken her for himself had imagined her sitting pretty and silent in a big house on his plantation. She had put a shot through his face instead. She hadn't favored him with reminiscence over the past few years, until now. He deserved to be forgotten.

"Or whatever," Gabe said, realizing his error. His heels made no sound now. He had stopped halfway. "Whatever we want."

"You can do as you like," she said, abruptly moving forward and closing the door behind her.

The remainder of the day was long and eventless, and the crew was uncharacteristically quiet. She spoke only to Tolliver, the navigator, to inform him of their new heading. She didn't feel like dealing with Granger's melodrama, so she told Tolliver to tell him for her and adjust course. Tolliver seemed to glimpse something dark behind her eyes; the thing that Gabe had gleefully ignored. The old man, who doted on her as though she were his daughter, didn't question the instructions.

With little else to be done, she retired early that night, and joined Gabe in bed, where he had the gall to be waiting as though nothing had happened. They did nothing more than sleep, and she nudged him away in the night whenever his hand touched her thigh.

It took her a while to fall asleep. The wind was whining through a seam in the sill of one of the aft windows. It sounded like a miniature woman screaming her little lungs out. The hull creaked in the gently rolling tide. Gabe started to breathe heavily, and mumbled, "No, no, grasp the *shards*, not the ratlines." Evidently he was instructing a green deckhand on the nuances of scaling the rigging.

And then she was lost in a dreamless sleep for most of the night.

She woke in the early watches of the morning to angrily kick off the blankets, but they were hopelessly tangled in her legs. Her skin was hot all over, and her scalp felt wet beneath matted hair. The warm air seeping through the seam in the window was thick with humidity. White rays spilled onto the bed through the stern gallery, moisture swirling in spectral light. With a final kick, the blankets tumbled over the foot of the bed, and there she saw a slender shape standing in the shadowed recesses just beyond the moonlight's reach. She watched the figure impassively, for it was surely a manifestation of her dreams. Though her eyes were open, she was only half-awake, and it was not the first time she had glimpsed something in the dark that wasn't there.

She heard water drip-drip-dripping, lightly pattering the deck, as though draining from a faucet. Her eyes followed the slender figure upward. It had legs, it had a waist, it had arms, and it had a head framed with short, scraggly hair. The edges of its jaw were moving rapidly, and she thought she heard a soft chatter beneath the whine of the wind, barely there. It might have been a voice, whispering urgently, desperate to be heard, but deprived of the vocals. If she did indeed perceive words, most were too quiet and too quick to make out. At least twice she thought she heard the word "cave."

Kate set a hand on Gabe's shoulder. "Gabe."

"Yes?" His voice was sharp, alert, with no trace of dreariness. Had he been awake all this time? "What is it?"

She squinted into the darkness, straining to see beyond the foot of the bed. After a moment, she gave up. "Nothing."

II

THE SCARLET DEVIL

PERSEPHONE

The warm winds lashed at the flames in the night, and she glared into the searing white heat until her eyes were dry and she could withstand no more. Her eyelids fluttered shut of their own accord, and she rubbed at them with her knuckles as she turned away from the torch.

When she opened her eyes, she saw a tall man limping up the long pier, his features muddled from this distance. She shifted uncomfortably in her coat as beads of sweat trickled down her armpits. She would have preferred not to wear it, but what better way to conceal a treasure map without drawing attention to it?

A three-masted ship, *Persephone*, was moored at the end of the pier, seductive crimson sails furled and deck blazing with lanterns and torches. The hull had been painted red to match the sails, though much of the paint was chipped near the draft. The ship had many oar-ports, which meant, with enough crew manning the sweeps, she could travel without wind. Three ornamented lanterns stood at her stern. At the top of the mainmast, a black flag danced in the low wind, with the red outline of a voluptuous woman aiming a spear at a heart. Kate heard laughter and music, and she saw lithe figures moving through the orange aura. The ship was presided over by Madame Jacqueline Teach, a woman Kate had known as Calloway, before she changed her surname to gain notoriety. How and when Edward Teach's daughter obtained a galley after the death of her father was a mystery better left unsolved. Kate assumed she enlisted the aid of Blackbeard's old crew, but she never understood why they remained loyal to their dead captain's daughter. Rumors of a luxurious "Pleasure Galley" had spread swiftly over the last few years, and soon its route and itinerary became common knowledge. Jacqueline entertained all manner of merchants, pirates, and, when she visited larger ports such as Kingston and New Orleans, British and French navy. Ten Shells was too small an island to be of much concern to the royal navy, and they rarely interfered with Teach's business.

A third of *Scarlet Devil's* crew had already rushed over to the ship. A night aboard Jacqueline's ship would do Ives some good. *A dagger in the gut would serve him better.* Before departing, he had informed her he would seek out the youngest and blondest strumpet and have his way with her. "Be careful," she had warned him. "Teach keeps her ladies well protected." In truth, she prayed Ives *would* try something stupid, so one of Jacqueline's bodyguards would open his throat and return his corpse to her in a sack. These things had been known to happen.

The platform seemed to wobble beneath Kate's feet as the surrounding trees swayed in the wind. She glanced up, but the palm-thatched roof blocked the stars. She looked down instead, and through the slatted planking she glimpsed the sand ten feet below, striped orange from the torchlight shining through. The tavern was suspended on stilts to prevent it from succumbing to a high tide, but the sea was calm and there were no waves washing over the isle tonight. Ten Shells was a quarter mile mound of sand twelve miles southeast of the southern tip of Florida, emerging from the sea in an oval, like the back of some great white-shelled turtle. A dozen platforms were connected by rope bridges lined in netting, to prevent drunkards from tumbling off and breaking their necks. Most of the platforms supported crude merchant huts that sold fish, fruit, and supplies by day. The merchants were enjoying their time off, sitting around drinking and smoking. Some were fishing from the long pier that stretched out over the northern beach. *Scarlet Devil* was moored in the shoals west of the pier.

As the tall man limped closer, his features were brightened by the torches of the tavern. He was lithe yet broad of shoulder. His long brown hair was bound in ratty dreadlocks threaded with orange and red strips of silk. A short but frazzled beard covered his sharp jaw. His nose was long and slightly hooked, dented midway, as though he'd been struck with a pistol and it hadn't healed properly. His cheeks were bright red and scabbing from too much sun. He wore a dark blue coat, white grilled shirt, and tall black boots. At his hip was a Spanish cup-hilt rapier. "I am Israel Hands," he informed her when he was within five paces. He stopped before her, and his vivid green eyes held hers.

"I've heard of you," Kate said. She'd heard Israel Hands had eluded the gallows by testifying against fellow pirates in Williamsburg, Virginia. Not a man to be trusted, but then, what pirate was? "You worked with Teach on occasion?"

He patted his bad leg and scowled. "Until he shot me to make a point." He offered a scarred hand. "Jacqueline has instructed me to bid you welcome to her island." His grip was a little too firm, and she squeezed harder to match it. They held each other's gaze while both grips tightened in an unspoken contest, until Kate released and allowed him to win. "I have overheard many elaborate and, if you don't mind my saying, difficult to believe tales concerning you, Captain Warlowe."

"Kate," she corrected, clenching and unclenching her sore hand. "And I assure you most of the tales are a touch hyperbolic."

"What now?"

"Hyperbolic. Exaggerated."

A breeze swayed his dreadlocks. "I know what it means, I just didn't catch the word. You mumbled."

"I did not."

His eyes fell briefly to appraise her body. "Your man, Hawkes, tells us you desire council."

"You work for Jacqueline?" Hands didn't have the look of a man who took orders.

"You could say that," was his lethargic reply. "I captain the *Persephone*."

"You're a captain yet you take orders from a woman?"

"Orders? No. I assist her and she keeps me well compensated. She is shrewd, mind you, but rare is the woman who can command a ship, if you'll pardon the generalization."

"No need," Kate assured him. "Jacqueline had no

knowledge of ships when I knew her. I doubt much has changed."

"Yes. And what is a ship without her captain?" He smiled, but she detected disdain in the green glint of his eyes. "Shall we?" He gestured at *Persephone*.

Kate glanced behind her. Gabe and Joseph were seated at a long table. Gabe was watching her. She'd refused his request to accompany her. His presence would only anger Jacqueline. He raised a tankard of ale to her in a salute, took a massive swig, and slammed it down too hard. His jaw was so firmly set she feared his teeth would crack. She'd sent Cross and Stubbs ahead of her, mostly to make Gabe feel better.

She gave Gabe a reassuring nod, to which he returned his best "you're making a mistake" glare. She sighed and faced Hands. "Permit me a moment."

Hands smiled politely, but was unable to suppress an impatient fluster. "Jacqueline is waiting."

"It wasn't a question." Kate left him standing there and approached Gabe, keeping the long table between them. "If I'm killed, don't let Hawkes have my ship."

Gabe's jaw tightened. "Meaning I should kill him."

"Meaning don't let Hawkes have my ship."

"Who can have it?"

She knew what he wanted her to say. "I don't care. Not Hawkes."

Gabe looked away and sullenly worked his jaw. "I might say 'aye' now, but as for what I do after you're dead, well, you won't really have any say in it, will you?"

"Don't pretend you wouldn't enjoy it."

"Hawkes' mortality is tied to yours." Gabe looked at her. "Any other requests, your highness?"

She imagined a shard of glass jutting from his neck. "Aye. Take a lengthy stroll off a stunted dock."

He slammed down his mug, splashing ale over his hand. "I think maybe I hate you."

She knew he believed it, for the moment anyway, but she hadn't the time nor the inclination to change his mind. "I hate you quite often."

She returned to Israel Hands before Gabe could offer retort. Halfway up the pier, her cheeks cooled and she wondered why she had allowed him to get her worked up. Gabe was the only man alive whose jabs could crawl beneath her skin and linger there like worms. Naturally, she had decided to spend her life with him. She allowed herself a small, private chuckle.

The sand beneath the pier descended into the water. Hands tilted his head and said, "Wise of you to send your men ahead of you, though I assure you entirely unnecessary. Never has a patron come to harm on Madame Teach's galley, unless he brought harm upon himself by first attempting harm on another."

"My men were eager for sordid congress, that's all," Kate said. "And why should Jacqueline try anything? Our debts are settled, by my account."

"She has spoken of you in excessive detail."

"Does she hate me still?" Kate hadn't given Jacqueline much thought over the past few years. Captaining a pirate ship was tireless work, and she hadn't the time to dwell on the past. She liked it that way.

"No. I don't think so." He seemed perfectly sincere. "I believe she laments your absence."

Kate laughed. "We'll see about that. I promised to throttle her with her own entrails if I ever saw her again."

Hands twitched his head, flinging dreadlocks over his shoulder. "She has mentioned that incident once or twice."

Something occurred to her. "You two are . . . ?"

"Jesus!" He stumbled on a plank, and she thought he might tumble off the pier. He turned to her, cutting the air with a sweep of his hand. "No."

Kate resisted a giggle. "Never?"

"No! No. Why would you even ask . . ." He frowned. "Wait. What were you asking?"

"You never shared a bed?"

"Oh, that." He paused contemplatively. "Well, yes. Just the once. That's why I don't drink anymore."

She followed him the rest of the way in silence, watching him limp with impressive agility. When they reached the gangplank, he held out a hand to help her up. She refused and urged him forward. The heat of torches rolled over the bulwark. Two muscular men, one black and one white, guarded the breach in the gunwale where the gangplank led to the main deck. Their shirtless chests had been completely shaved and their oiled pecs gleamed in the early light. Their breeches were clean and white, bound in red and gold silk ribbons that crisscrossed down powerful legs. They moved to help Kate onto the ship but she curtly waved them off.

"This is Captain Warlowe," Hands informed them.

The guards stepped back.

"I welcome you aboard the *Persephone*," Hands announced.

Nearly four dozen strumpets and as many pirates filled the main deck, lounging in hammocks or sprawled across crates. Tables were arranged in two rows starboard and port, stretching nearly the length of the main deck. Three eight pound cannons jutted from gunports on either side.

Kate's pirates were guzzling ale and fondling women. Three strumpets were dancing at the foot of the mainmast while a pale, skinny lad played a pochette, a mousy woman with scraggly blonde hair thumped at kettle drums, and a pretty brunette sang her lungs out.

"Oh there was a lofty ship that sailed across the sea. And the name of the ship was the Golden Vanity." The singer winked at an approaching pirate, who raised his tankard in toast to her beauty. *"And we feared she'd be taken by the Spanish enemy. And they'd sink her in the lowland, lo. They'd sink her in the lowland sea. Sink her in the lowland, lo!"*

One of Kate's pirate's joined in, bellowing "lowland, lo," at inopportune moments, and the pretty singer looked a little flustered as she struggled to accommodate him.

"Then up stepped the cabin boy and boldly outspoke he, and he said to the captain, what would you give to me, if I swim alongside the Spanish enemy, and sink her in the lowland sea?"

Below the deck Kate heard muffled screams of pleasure.

"A treasure chest of gold I will give to thee," the singer belted on. *"And my own fairest daughter, thy bonnie bride shall be, if you'll swim alongside the Spanish enemy. And sink her in the lowland, lowland lo! If you'll sink her in the lowland sea!"*

Other than her crew, Kate spotted only four men lingering on the opposite side of the ship, watching the proceedings. Guards, she wagered. Not enough to overwhelm her men if it came to a fight. The women looked more formidable. Aside from the tiny woman thumping away at the kettle drums, most were tall and lithe, as though Jacqueline had selected from only the healthiest stock. Not a single strumpet was under or overweight. Their legs were long and toned. They had sharp, vigilant eyes, not the sweet, vacant expressions Kate expected from women of leisure.

Makes sense, she thought. Average strumpets could not endure long at sea with only a handful of men to protect them. These women knew how to defend themselves. She was impressed with what Jacqueline had accomplished in so little time. She had her father's ambition. Kate hoped that was where the similarities ended.

"*So, the boy he made ready, and overboard sprang he. And he swam to the side of the Spanish enemy.*" Kate squinted to get a clearer look at the singer. The singer misunderstood and winked at her. "*And with his brace and auger, in her side he bored holes three. And sank her in the lowland, lowland lo. He sank her in the lowland sea!*"

Kate found Stubbs and Cross perched atop crates at the forecastle. They were sipping liberally from mugs of ale, keeping a sharp eye on their surroundings. When Stubbs spotted Kate, he placed a hand atop his soiled monmouth cap, signaling that all was normal.

Cross merely glanced at her and looked away.

"*Then the boy swam back to the cheering of the crew. But the captain would not heed him, for his promise he did rue. He scorned his sad entreaties, though loudly he did suit. And he left him in the lowland, lowland lo. He left him in the lowland sea!*"

Israel Hands spun round on his good leg and held up a hand. "I almost forgot. All weapons must be surrendered to the quartermaster before coming aboard."

"Fine," she said. "Where is he?"

"*. . . up unto his messmates, so bitterly he cried, 'Messmates, pull me up for I'm drifting with the tide.'*"

Hands frowned. "Who?"

"*And I'm sinking in the lowland, lowland lo!*"

"The quartermaster," said Kate. "Where is he?"

"*I'm sinking in the lowland sea!*" The singer caught her

135

breath here, allowing the pochette and drums to take over.

Hands came to his senses, stepped aside, and up walked a very tall, very muscular black man she recognized instantly. Kate had journeyed with him before she became a captain. As always he wore no shirt, allowing everyone to see the deep trenches carved in his chest from his time aboard a particularly cruel slaver's ship. His crisp, white breeches, however, were far cleaner than the hemp rags Kate recalled. The cutlass that hung from his leather belt was new and polished, as opposed to the rusty horror he used to carry.

"Dumaka," Kate greeted warmly as he approached, wondering if he would remember her as well.

"Well his messmates pulled him up but on the deck he died," the singer started up again.

Dumaka might have smiled, or maybe he flinched in the glare of the torches. "You remember."

". . . And they placed him in his hammock, which was so fair and wide."

"How could I forget? I thought you left Jacqueline's employ."

He glanced over his shoulder. "I returned when she offered something shinier than friendship."

". . . And they lowered him down, and over the port side."

Kate, though happy to see Dumaka, couldn't help but be distracted by the singer. "Jacqueline seems to be doing well for herself."

Dumaka grunted. "For now."

"And he sank into the lowland, lo. He sank into the lowland sea! Oh he sank into the lowland, lowland lo. Sank into the lowland sea!" The song ended, and the pretty singer smiled gratefully as the pirates cheered. She fell into the lap of a particularly burly pirate whose name Kate was fairly certain

was Garrett, and she slapped half-heartedly at his hands as they slid up beneath her dress to caress her smooth thighs.

Kate handed Dumaka her pistol and cutlass before he could ask. His huge hands were gentle as he patted her waist and legs. He seemed surprised not to find any other weapons. "I trust you're not hiding anything anywhere uncomfortable?"

She smiled. "When I want a weapon, I will take one."

He wagged a knowing finger. "Ah yes, I remember. Strength is always in reach."

She frowned. "What?"

"You said this many times."

"I did?"

He bowed his head in a forgiving manner. "It was a long time ago."

Hands cleared his throat. "Jacqueline is waiting."

"Good to see you again, Dumaka," Kate said.

Hands led her through clamoring pirates and sweet-smelling strumpets lounging on barrels covered in red satin and lace. The heat from the torches and bodies was stifling, and she couldn't wait to get her coat off. Hands opened the cabin door and motioned for her to go inside. She let her eyes pass over his, while casually scanning the deck behind him, until she found Stubbs and Cross again. They were standing now, feigning interest in a strumpet, but their eyes were on Kate. She gave a little nod to let them know she didn't need them, and they returned the nod. She went inside, and heard the door close behind her.

CAULDRON

The room was swathed in red, smoky with some kind of incense that smelled of grass and dirt after a heavy rainfall. And maybe, beneath that pleasant aroma, there was something else . . . another scent, sweet yet vaguely foul, a scent that no amount of incense could subdue. Or maybe it was Kate's imagination. Nevertheless, she reached back to make sure the precautionary dagger hadn't slipped from her breeches. Dumaka had been too courteous to search her there. She'd always liked Dumaka.

What little she could see through the smoke was blurred by her right eye. A table here, a bed there. And then the tall woman materialized before her in the haze, and Kate's legs went rigid.

She was wrapped in a black silk mantua interwoven with

a deep blue floral brocade. The dress matched the long raven hair running in a straight line down her back. A black corset, which she wore as a decorative outer-garment, was laced up the front, accentuating her small breasts. She had always been tall, but her long legs seemed to have sprouted another inch or two. Or perhaps she was wearing boots with long heels, but her feet were hidden beneath the dress. Her broad shoulders were bare, revealing skin as pale as her lean face. Her eyes were heavily shadowed in eyeliner, yet steely blue irises beamed through the darkness. Most of her freckles seemed to have faded, and her lips were nearly as pale as her cheeks. A silver necklace dangled from her long neck, with a jewel nestled in the nook of her cleavage, glinting sapphire and complimenting her eyes.

The woman who stood before her now was a shadow of the girl Kate had known. The desperation had left her eyes, and only a survivor remained. "I'm shocked to see you, Katherine. Your circumstance must be dire."

Kate smiled casually to let her know there was nothing dire about her circumstance. "There are few brothels of quality left to pirates, and so, I bring them to you."

Jacqueline's lips curled. "And if their lust be not slaked, they might turn eyes on their lovely captain."

"You look to be doing well for yourself."

"My purse is heavy, if such is your meaning." Traces of a French accent gave her voice a musical flow that contrasted her stark face.

"What else could I mean?"

There was something terrible behind Jacqueline's haunted smile, and Kate had no desire to find out what it was. She'd learned the price of sympathizing with this woman. "Wealth and happiness are two different things."

Kate laughed carelessly. "Yet the shine of coin never fails to bring a smile."

"That's because you've never lost anything," Jacqueline snapped, and then composed herself with a false smile.

"I lost a husband." Kate could spare no further sorrow for Thomas, but the fact remained.

"And gained your freedom. A husband is a small price to pay."

Kate slowly maneuvered her way across the cabin, as casually as possible, while Jacqueline's steely eyes trailed her. The woman was a wraith in a red haze, but her eyes seemed illuminated by some otherworldly light. Just as her father's had.

"You look good, Kate. You've kept yourself thin, but not too thin."

Kate frowned. "Thank you?"

Jacqueline smiled thinly through the smoke.

Kate turned her back to her old friend as she neared a bed in one corner of the cabin, pressed against the bulkhead. Above it, a young girl's face materialized, large and brooding, steely eyes piercing the mist and locking with Kate's. Long black locks framed her beautiful, pale face. A dense smattering of freckles dirtied her cheeks. She was not smiling. She couldn't have been older than five. The paint was thick and crusty upon the canvas and the divergent white and black was vivid even in the dingy red glow.

"Is this you?" Kate asked. It was not hard to imagine Jacqueline as a girl, for she had scarcely been a woman when Kate last saw her.

"She is my daughter," Jacqueline replied in a measured monotone.

"She's beautiful." The portrait cut off just above her

chest, but her shoulders had already started to broaden like her mother's. "Where is she now?"

"She's here."

Kate turned to look, but saw no smaller form beside the indistinct shadow of Jacqueline Teach. "I don't—" Kate started, but stopped herself short, recalling the oddities of Jacqueline's personality. This was a woman who believed the sea had magical healing powers, and that tokens of the dead, such as a severed toe, brought fortune.

"Don't look at me like I'm crazy." Jacqueline's brow furrowed with more lines than a woman of twenty-three should carry. "I know she's . . . I know she's passed. But the dead never really leave us, do they?"

"I'm sorry, Jacqueline." The condolence was hollow. The girl was just a painting. Kate had never known her. She had been born and died within the years since they'd parted. Jacqueline's mother had raised her daughter in a brothel, and that cycle had continued.

"Sweet of you to say," Jacqueline replied flatly, clearly not convinced.

"Whose was she?" The question was little more than a formality.

"She was forced into my belly on that dreadful island, where you left me. I don't even know which man was responsible. For a time there were many. Few chivalrous. But I loved her nonetheless."

"How did she die?"

"The disease was cruel. It was slow. It might never have killed her. It might have kept her alive forever, with nothing but a shell of a body to inhabit." Her eyes were dry, her tone cold, flat.

You killed your own daughter, Kate realized. She wondered if she would have had the courage to do the same. She was temporarily thankful she was incapable of having children. "You did what you had to do."

Jacqueline's expression turned sour. "It's nice of you to feign concern, but let's waste no more of the other's time. Why are you here?"

Finally, Kate thought, and stripped off her coat. "Is there a desk around here? I can't see a thing."

"Use the bed."

Kate avoided the portrait's blue eyes as she placed the coat on the bed and turned it inside out. "I happened upon something. A map, I think."

There was a moment of silence, and then, without so much as the pitter-patter of her heels, Jacqueline was at her side, staring down at the coat. "Blackbeard's Cemetery. This is your coat? The one you took from Jack Rackham?"

"You remember it?"

"I remember everything, Kate."

Kate indicated the black spots. "Do you know where this is? Did your father say anything about it before he died?"

"Before Gabe Jenkins killed him, you mean?"

"Gabe saved your life."

Jacqueline looked at Kate. Her face was very close now, delicate and smooth, though the lines of her brow were more evident up-close. Kate saw an ocean in her eyes, infinite, calm, and cold. For a moment, she thought Jacqueline might try to kiss her. "Everyone thinks it was you. No matter how many times I tell them it was just some scoundrel who owed me a debt, they go on believing Kate Warlowe killed Blackbeard."

"That's not a myth I embellish, Jacqueline, I assure you."

"No, of course not. But you did scuttle his ship. And the

fire did lead to my father's weakened state."

"Fortunately for you," Kate reminded her. "Gabe told me your father was trying to strangle the life out of you."

"Well, I *was* trying to kill my father *first*," Teach admitted with a light smile. "Is Jenkins with you? I would love to speak with him." She offered a thin-lipped smile that Kate didn't care for. "For old times."

"Slit his throat, more like," Kate blurted. She was tired of mincing words. "For old times."

"A horrifying thing to say." Jacqueline didn't seem particularly horrified.

"Not here to dredge up the past. Do you know where Blackbeard's Cemetery is or not?"

"Always cutting to the point." Jacqueline sighed, relinquishing her hard gaze and turning away from the bed. "I don't know what that is, let alone *where* it is."

Kate nodded and promptly started folding the coat. She was eager to be out of this place. "Sorry to waste your time. My men will make it worth your while."

Teach spun round. Her thin smile had returned. "It's been years since you and I shared words and already you wish to leave? Do I make you so uncomfortable?"

"No," Kate said. "There are better things I could be doing." *Like drinking myself into oblivion on a beach.*

"You promised to kill me if you ever saw me again."

"I was angry at the time. I was your prisoner, as I recall."

Teach's smile faded, replaced by something that might have been regret. "You misread my intent. I tried to help you all those years ago, by having you sent back to your family, where you would have been safe."

"And you would have claimed a lofty reward in the process." Kate smiled.

"Is that so dreadful? I could have bought myself off that island, and in doing so I would have sent you away from this. Both of us would have been better off, but you . . . you desire nothing so much as death."

Tufts of smoke remained, but the red haze was dispersing. Most of the incense had burned out, and that implacable, vaguely foul aroma intensified. "Yet here we are, Jacqueline. I am alive, and you are prosperous. Let us leave it at that."

Jacqueline looked at the portrait of her daughter, then turned her cold eyes on the coat, half-folded on the bed. "Do you not believe you'll be made to account for your sins?"

"I've naught to account for. I take what I desire, I slay fools who would block my path, and I am free. If there is a god, then he wished me upon this world, and that is his sin, not mine. I will savor every breath and every last drop of wine and every shiny thing in my grasp and I will not concern myself with judgment from above or below. I am here, now."

For nearly a minute Jacqueline seemed to lose herself in deliberation. Just when Kate was about to take her leave, the woman spoke up. "I've never heard of any cemetery, but I know someone who might tell us where it is." She looked to the door. "Israel! I know you're out there."

The door opened immediately, and Israel Hands limped in. "Maybe I was, maybe I wasn't."

"Clearly you were."

Hands gave that some thought while fingering one of his dreadlocks. "This time you were right, but just as easily you might have been wrong. Partitioned by a solid barrier, you can't know a thing exists until you see the thing with your own two eyes. Not really."

"Fetch the old man," barked Jacqueline, losing patience.

"Not sure I appreciate your hyperbolic tone." He closed the door.

They waited in silence. Jacqueline drifted to a corner, her feet seeming to barely shuffle beneath her black skirts. She used a long candle to light more incense. The vaguely foul low stench—*maybe a rat*—lingered. When the silence became unbearable, Kate asked, "Is Hands fetching the old man?"

"He does as he's told."

"He seems a tad . . ." Kate hesitated, struggling for the right word.

"Touched?" Teach finished for her. "He was British navy. His crew mutinied and marooned him. Pirates found him months later."

"Why did they mutiny?"

Teach shrugged. "He was indecisive."

"And you've employed him as captain of your ship?"

"It's his ship. We have a mutually beneficial arrangement."

"How did that come about?" There were too many scenarios to contemplate, most beginning with Jacqueline and Hands fumbling desperately beneath the sheets, slathering one another's nether regions with drunken passion. Kate shuddered.

"Are you cold, Kate?"

"No. No. My mind is a silly cunt sometimes, that's all."

Jacqueline placated her with an understanding nod, while eyeing her as one would a naked woman running through a village. "Well, we met rather simply."

"Have you told him what happened to the last captain

you won over?"

The remarkable sapphire circling Teach's pupils dimmed as her eyes narrowed. "It's been many years, Kate. I've won over many captains."

The door creaked open and an old man ducked into the cabin. He was nearly seven feet tall, his head practically touching the deckhead, and his eyes were creamy voids with no hint of irises or pupils. His beard was a dense thicket of silver coils. His bald pate was littered with brown spots and a crater where he must have been struck with a musket shot. He wore a long grey coat that looked as old as time, pocked with holes. "I smell a woman I haven't smelled before," he wheezed.

"Kate Warlowe," Kate replied, offering her hand.

He did not shake her hand, nor did he offer any vague sort of courtesy. "What be the meaning of this?" he demanded of Jacqueline. "My days wane. I would prefer to go in my sleep." His voice was barely a whisper, escaping his throat in a phlegm-wracked hiss, like a dying snake.

"I'd prefer to spend my final days alert," said Kate.

The old man might have rolled his eyes, if he had any irises to roll. "Tell me how you feel after you've lived eighty years worth o' days."

Kate chuckled. "I'll be lucky if I reach thirty."

"Every young lad thinks so."

"I'm no lad."

"You might as well be." He took a deep breath, and Kate heard gurgling sounds in his chest, rolling liquid fighting to accommodate oxygen. "I can't see you. You've a rough pitch for a lass."

"This is Ash," said Jacqueline, stepping between them. "My father's brother."

"Your uncle, then," said Kate.

Anger, unmistakable and raw, flushed Jacqueline's pale face. "Ash was little help when—" She cut herself short, smiled. "Nevermind. Ash, the captain here—"

"Captain?" wheezed the old man. "A she?"

"Yes," said Teach.

"How is this woman still breathing?"

Kate had to laugh. She liked this old man, despite his frightening visage. He reminded her of Breton. "Your wager is as good as mine."

"She has stumbled on some sort of map hidden in a coat," Jacqueline explained. "Did my father say anything about a cemetery?"

Ash's face was indecipherable, and Kate realized how greatly she relied on a man's eyes to tell her what was going on inside his head. He might have been frowning, trying to sort through years of memories, but his cheeks were so wrinkled it was hard to tell. "A graveyard, aye. Where he buried those he despised most."

"Where?" said Kate, stepping beside Jacqueline. "An island?"

"Not land," gasped the old man. Words seemed to pain him terribly. Kate got the impression this was the most he had spoken in years. "Nay. Tis in the depths, not many fathoms. Just enough for a man to glimpse the surface above as his life fades. Air so close, taunting him. That be Edward's way, to show you what you can't have. Made coffins for 'em, he did. Special coffins, you see. The kind that keep water out, for a time anyways. The water never stays out for long, does it?"

As stuffy as the cabin was, Kate suddenly felt cold. "A man could swim down there?"

"A *man* could."

"Do you still know where it is?" Jacqueline asked her uncle. "An underwater grave would be hard to find without precise coordinates."

"Aye, I know it," said Ash. He tapped his spotted temple with a knobby index finger. "Records, I keep up here. I keep it all. That's what I was. The keeper of records. My brother burned all the maps to the places what mattered most, to the secrets. It's all here. I try to forget. I try to forget the murder. I try to forget the screams. I try to forget all he done. I try, but it never goes. Not till I go."

Jacqueline Teach moved closer and whispered in the old man's ear. "I need you alive just a little longer. One more task, and then you can go."

"Anything for me brother's daughter," he said, but his ancient voice revealed no doting love for his niece. This was an obligation.

LONGBOAT

"There be a prince down there somewhere," said Ash, "if you can believe that."

The longboat swayed right and left as sunlight refracted off the gently rolling waves. Kate sat on a thwart at the stern alongside Ash, with her folded coat tucked under her arm, while Stubbs and Cross rowed silently before her amidships. She wasn't sure Ash's memory could be relied upon, but she was willing to sacrifice a day to find out. Besides, it was a beautiful, clear, warm day, with nary a cloud in sight. Unbroken horizon stretched in all directions, blue challenged only by darker blue. Jacqueline Teach sat silently at the bow beside Dumaka, staring over the water without so much as squinting, her thoughts as distant as her eyes. The *Scarlet Devil* looked small behind her. It had only been half a day's journey east of Ten Shells. A quarter of the crew had come along, while the rest had stayed with Teach's strumpets.

"A prince of what?" Kate asked as she settled against the starboard rail and peered down into the water, not really expecting to see anything other than fish, and certainly not a prince. It was clear and shallow here, six fathoms at most. Webs of light danced along the rippled white sands at the bottom, broken here and there by coral and seaweed teeming with colorful fish, big and small.

Ash's milky eyes seemed to be watching her as he told the tale. "A queer people. A people of a darker complexion, if you catch my meaning, but not so dark as Negroes. They be descendants of the natives the Spaniards quarreled with at Tulum, some two-hundred years back. Found themselves on an island somewhere 'twixt Yucatan and Jamaica. Isla de la Niebla Roja, the Spaniards call it. Island of Red Mist."

Kate leaned back, letting her hair spill over the rail, and opened her shirt nearly to her nipples, sunning as much of her chest as she could. The shirt fell over one shoulder, and she left it there, but pinched the laces below her breasts so she wouldn't reveal all. Not that Ash would notice.

"A buccaneer by name of Armitage happened across the island. He and his crew settled there after his ship went down in them evil waters. Sharp rocks hiding under the waves, eager to slice open any ship what got too close. Great big reefs, pretty to look at, deadly to approach. And rough waters, too. Naught but a third of the pirates survived. Weren't long before they ventured into the jungle for food, and at the heart of the island they found a village and a pyramid. Have you ever seen the like?"

"I haven't," said Kate. She had only seen illustrations. It was hard to believe such wonders existed. She had hoped to see one someday, but the odds were shrinking.

"Most of the natives were addled with plague, scarcely breathing. Armitage and his men met their leader, a queen. She spoke in a queer tongue like none you've ever heard. As you might wager, Armitage didn't know what to make of this. Feared for his mortality, he did, but he was a keen man with fast wits. He had his doctor see to the dying villagers. Nursed 'em back from the brink. The queen were grateful, but she were also the greedy sort, and she wouldn't let Armitage or his men leave. She forced them to teach her our ways, our language."

"A queen?" Kate leaned forward. This story was finally getting interesting.

"Aye. She had herself two sons with a Spaniard who arrived many years before. Twins. One would be king, but the other were a weaker man who harbored no desire for the throne. The weak prince lived on the outskirts of the village. Exiled, mayhap. It were never clear to me why. The prince favored his Spanish half, and he wanted to know more of the outside world, but his brother would not let him leave. It were Armitage's treacherous first mate, Diego, who befriended the prince. After the queen died and the stronger son became king—"

"How?"

"What?"

"How did the queen die?"

Ash shrugged. "I never got the details of that. Anyways, the weaker prince and Diego conspired behind the king's back and built a boat. Worked on it every night, they did. Diego and the prince stole away in the night, leaving Armitage and the rest to their prison.

"Diego promised the prince he would bring him to Spain.

But Diego were a pirate through and through, and he brought him to Nassau instead. The prince pleaded with him, and Diego assured him they would get to Spain, just be patient. Well, that weren't in the cards. Diego got hisself drunk one night and told a tavern full of pirates where he come from. He spoke of a lost city, and, as you can wager, all the eyes in that room lit up with notions of jewels and gold. My brother, Edward, got wind o' this, and he urged Diego to surrender the bearings, but Diego said drunkenness had muddied up his memory, and if you know Diego, you know that be true. He weren't the reliable sort."

Kate couldn't help but interject the obvious in a droll monotone. "So, Diego gave Blackbeard the prince."

"That's what Diego did, aye. Alas, pain held no sway over the prince. He might have been weaker than his twin brother, but he were stronger than any other man you've ever seen. I can't say as I saw it, on account of me eyes not working, but I heard it. I smelled the matches burning the flesh under his fingernails, but he didn't scream. On it went for more turns of the glass than I care to say. So, finally, Edward sent the prince down to the depths to join the others who annoyed him best."

Kate peered over the boat into the water. "You're telling me a half-native, half-Spanish prince is down there somewhere?"

"Aye."

"And what happened to Diego?"

"Edward made him watch the whole affair, promising he'd be next unless his memory got unmuddified. 'Look what you done to your friend,' Edward told him. 'The pair of you will be together again soon.' Edward gave him some time to think on his fate. That were a mistake. Diego stole away in a longboat soon after. I wager he scribbled that little riddle in his coat to remind hisself where the prince were buried, on account of him being so forgetful. He were a fool to return to Nassau. Rogers showed up soon after, proclaimed hisself governor of everything. Someone must have told him Diego's tale, and Rogers put redcoats on his stern. Maybe Rogers wanted a piece of that fortune for hisself. That must be when Diego gave his coat to Calico Jack, figuring he'd retrieve it after Rogers had him searched."

Kate chucked her hands skyward in frustration. "So this is a waste of time. What can a dead man tell us?"

Ash leaned in close, narrowing one eye, as if he could see her. "If Diego needed to remember where the prince were buried, that means princey down there is holding onto something, seeing as he can't speak so good now."

Kate sighed. She wondered how much of Ash's tale was true, if any of it. "How much further?"

"Not far now," said Ash.

"You never had much patience, Kate," said Jacqueline. She never swayed with the boat, remaining straight as a plank, with her hands neatly placed in her lap, knees pinched together. Her eyes were abstracted.

Kate sat up and tightened the laces of her shirt just enough to make sure a breast or two wouldn't slip free. "I grow anxious when removed from my ship."

Jacqueline glanced over her shoulder at the ship. "Oh dear. I do hope they don't depart without us."

"Never have."

"Surely there is an ambitious man among them."

"One or twelve."

Jacqueline's light freckles, which were far more perceptible in broad daylight, bunched together. She hastily returned her gaze to the sea. "Wise of you to string Jenkins along all these years. I'm impressed you've kept him sated."

Kate had instructed Gabe to remain on Ten Shells for the day, to "keep an eye on the men." In reality, she didn't want him anywhere near Jacqueline. "I make no demands of him."

A smile, calculated and mirthless, played at the edges of the younger woman's pale lips. "I doubt that."

"We are here," said Ash.

Kate looked over the rail, and her breath caught in her throat. She saw the dark objects below the boat, resting at the bottom in a dense bed of seaweed. Black columns, several still standing upright, lurked within tall strands of dark green.

"Stop rowing," Jacqueline instructed the shirtless men, and they retracted their oars, laying them flat in the boat.

Dumaka peered over the rail and scratched his broad chin. "What are those?"

"Coffins," said Kate. "And there are more than thirteen." She counted twenty-three, although there may have been more beneath the boat. "This isn't going to be easy."

Stubbs and Cross exchanged nervous glances. "Don't worry," Kate assured them, "I didn't bring you here for that."

Dumaka stood and pulled his shirt over his head, revealing his scarred chest and a stomach that resembled a stack of flattened rocks. "I will go."

"Not alone, you won't," said Kate.

"You don't trust Dumaka?" asked Jacqueline.

"I trust him to do whatever you pay him to do," Kate replied. "We'll go together."

"You almost drowned once," Jacqueline reminded her.

"To save you," Kate said. *Would have spared myself some trouble if I'd let you drown,* she thought.

Jacqueline's eyes went distant. "And a fine job of saving you did."

"Maybe I shouldn't have."

"Maybe you shouldn't have."

She unfolded the coat and handed it to the two rowers. They spread it out between them while she perused it. Kate looked at her shadow, and then at the sun. She pointed larboard. "That's North."

"Aye," said Dumaka.

"I'm going to assume this is also North," she said, touching the collar of the coat. She moved her finger to the red mark in the upper left corner. "So this is the northwest corner."

"There are three more coffins there," said Jacqueline. She had rested her hands on the rail and was looking over the side. "You're certain this is the correct spot, Ash?"

"There be only one," Ash grimly replied. "Edward was sentimental about these things. He buried Ben Hornigold down there."

Kate was stunned. "Always wondered where he'd gotten off to."

"T'was not a good death," said Ash.

"I expect not." Kate tried to picture being locked in a coffin, sinking to the bottom, while the water seeped in. She decided now wasn't the best time to let her imagination run rampant.

"They be special coffins," said Ash. "With portholes. So a man could see—"

"I'll see for myself soon enough." She had another look over the side, comparing the black spots in the coat to the black things in the water below, like lining up a constellation to a star chart. "Yes. These thirteen marks seem to coincide, except for one or two. It must be one of those four in that corner."

"I will take the two on the right," said Dumaka. He unhooked his belt, which holstered his pistol and cutlass. He hefted two pairs of nine pound cannonballs that were linked by chains. "This may require more than one dive. What are we looking for?"

Kate slipped out of her boots and kicked them aside. "Don't really know. Piece of jewelry, maybe?" She removed the pistol from her belt and folded it into her coat. She placed the coat atop a thwart.

"If it's a tattoo or something, there won't be anything left," said Jacqueline. "This trip might be for naught."

"The pleasure of your company is reward enough." Kate took deep breaths, preparing herself. She closed her eyes and conjured soothing thoughts to slow her heart-rate. She didn't want to hyperventilate when she got to the bottom. She imagined swimming with giant turtles, bathing naked, taking a shower under a warm waterfall. A tremendous splash interrupted her thoughts, and her eyes opened to see Dumaka's hulking form descending into the depths.

She glanced at Jacqueline, who was appraising her skeptically. "You don't have to go, Kate. Whatever Dumaka finds, whatever it leads to, this is a two-way split."

"I've got nothing better to do." And she didn't trust Dumaka to share whatever he might find.

Kate lifted two pairs of cannonballs connected by chains, grasping a chain in each hand. She placed a foot on the rail and dropped into the warm water. A cerulean world enveloped her, clear and eerily beautiful. Schools of colorful fish darted from their intended course to avoid her as she descended, and the blue ambiance grew thicker. A bed of coffins waited peacefully below. *Hornigold is down here somewhere.* She hadn't cared for the man. He had tried to force himself on her. She wasn't sorry he was dead, but nobody deserved this.

She swished her legs when she was two fathoms down, increasing her descent. Dumaka was already two thirds of the way down, a stream of white bubbles trailing his feet. The bottom seemed deeper than it had from the surface. Kate continued downward, arms stretched by the weight of the cannonballs. Her ears began to sing, and it seemed as though someone had wrapped their arms around her chest in a loving embrace, squeezing tighter and tighter, until the embrace was no longer welcome.

She put the discomfort out of her mind and focused on the beautiful horror below. The particulars of the coffins came into view. When she reached what she wagered to be four fathoms, she noticed one had broken open, and a skeleton was suspended above it, legs bound to a chain. She wasn't out of breath just yet, but she suddenly wanted to ascend. More than anything.

Dumaka reached his destination and latched onto a coffin. He used it to right himself, deftly swirling around and planting his large feet on the seabed. A billowing cloud of sand obscured him from view.

Kate swam for her two coffins, holding the cannonball chains with one hand while swishing her other arm. One coffin was upright and the other was on its side, broken. Her jaw began to ache, and she wiggled it this way and that, hoping to loosen it up, but that sent a stab of pain through her skull.

The cloud of sand Dumaka had stirred wafted over Kate's coffins. She released one chained pair of cannonballs as she dove into the cloud. Less weight was needed the deeper she went. She thrust out her free hand, grasped the edge of the coffin that was standing vertically, and tried to pull herself down to it, and then she saw something terrible. It did indeed have a little porthole. The glass had long since shattered, with two little shards remaining. She couldn't see anything within, just darkness. The coffin's lid snapped open when Kate tried to right herself, and she dropped the other pair of cannonballs as bubbles and sand and things that were long and thin and yellow poured out of it. The yellow things coiled and then shot toward her, like snakes. She almost screamed, but managed to hold her breath. The eels slithered over her legs and arms. One went up through her shirt, slithered around her breast, and then worked its way up her neck and over her face. It turned an evil, gold-ringed eye on her as it ascended.

She closed her eyes for a moment, struggling to calm herself. Seaweed caressed her body, and that might have been soothing, except she couldn't help but wonder if some of it wasn't seaweed. Her head was aching and her ears were ringing, suppressing any soothing thought she tried to conjure. She tried to imagine Gabe in bed, the sheets barely pulled to his waist, but he was too far away, somewhere warm, above water, and she was down here for some silly reason, and Jacqueline Teach's words echoed in her skull. "You desire nothing so much as death." That wasn't true. In these moments, when she was closest to death, she desired nothing so much as life.

She opened her eyes. It was impossible to see through the murky cloud that roiled like smoke all about her. She flailed until her hands slapped the coffin lid. She tugged on it, tossing it aside. It broke into flinders, stirring more sand.

A white blur materialized before her in the cloud. She instinctively reached out to touch it, or push it away if need be, and her fingers slipped between what felt like the thin branches of a tree, hard and brittle. She leaned forward, and nearly inhaled when she saw a skeletal hand with fingers splayed, as though waving to her. And then a skull appeared beyond the hand, its grinning teeth inlaid with jade rocks. The head cocked sideways, like a dog hearing a high-pitched noise. Sharp fingers brushed her cheek in a gentle, loving caress. The skeleton leaned forward, its jaw opening slightly.

My prince wants a kiss.

The morbidly amusing thought kept her from screaming and expelling the air in her lungs. Instead, she seized the hand and gave it a sharp tug, easily drawing the entire skeleton out of the cloud. Seaweed and moss and other things clung to its bones. What little remained of its clothes dangled from it in grey tatters. She had no time for fear. Already she needed a breath, and when she looked up, the glimmering surface seemed dauntingly distant, a translucent ceiling that she could never reach. She quickly inspected the fingers, but there were no rings. She felt the scant bits of clothing, but there were no pockets left to conceal anything. And surely Blackbeard would have searched the man's clothing before throwing him to the sea. She curled forward, grasped one side of the coffin, and reached further down, fumbling about the skeleton's legs and feet. Her fingers brushed something hard, cold, and round. *A cannonball,* she realized. There was more than one, and they were big. Possibly twenty-four pounders. No wonder so many of these coffins were standing upright. But she found nothing else, other than rocks and something with a spiny shell and far too many long legs. She heard a muffled, pathetic little sound in her throat, like a child squealing in distant room. She needed air, and she was starting to panic. Her head seemed to be filling with tar. She prepared to kick herself off, but she didn't want to come down here again, and there was yet another coffin to inspect. She hesitated, glancing around. The sandy cloud was beginning to disperse. Her eyes locked with the grinning skull. The hollows of its eyes were an infinite, impossible black. The jade insets glinted in the faint glimmers of sunlight shining down from above.

And then the waters darkened. Kate turned, wondering if a cloud had passed overhead, though there had been no clouds in the sky when she left the boat. She saw something moving toward her, but the veil of her hair drifted over her face, and she swept it out of the way. The thing was seven feet long, sleek, and grey. And it was swimming toward her from above, its mouth yawning, a bleak void rimmed with white, triangular teeth with serrated edges. Its pectoral fins dipped aggressively.

Kate reached back instinctively, grasping the skull and twisting it free of the spine. The snap was dull but distinct. She swung the skull around, brandishing it like a rock, and smashed the shark in its broad snout as it came within two feet of her face. Blood spurted from its mouth. It angled away, slapping Kate with a sickle-shaped dorsal fin. The impact sent her crashing into the coffin, which tumbled onto one side, breaking apart. A larger cloud of sand erupted. Kate buckled her legs and thrust herself upward, brushing the shark on the way up. She kicked at the creature, scraping her toes on its grainy skin. She expelled what little breath was left, bellowing underwater. Bubbles rolled up her cheeks, too many to count. Her upper torso seemed to be falling in on itself, shying away from tiny knives pricking at her from all sides.

It seemed to take hours to reach the surface, but it was only a few seconds. She exploded to the top, near the boat that was calmly bobbing in the water. She gasped hoarsely and vowed to never, ever do that again. Cross reached for her.

Something clasped her ankle and jerked her beneath the surface mid-gasp, and she sucked water into her throat. Something sharp dug into her belly, raking her skin. It tugged on her breeches, pulling her down. She briefly got her head above the water, hacked seawater and flailed her arms, before she was jerked under again. She kicked at the whatever-it-was. Her boot hit something hard, and her head popped above the water again. She heaved violently, until she saw bright stars and thought her head might burst. And then she inhaled sharply, gagging on the rough grains of salt that were lodged in her throat.

A shadow surfaced inches from her face. She opened her mouth, but the salt made a travesty of her scream.

"Sorry," Dumaka said. "You were in my way."

Cross helped Kate aboard the boat. She rolled over the gunwale like an over-sized fish and crumpled between two thwarts. She stayed there for a moment, catching her breath, while Cross stared down at her. When she met his eyes, he blinked and pretended to be distracted by something else.

"What is that?" Jacqueline asked, while Ash leaned forward as though he could see.

Kate realized she was still holding the skull. She pulled herself up onto a thwart in the middle of the boat. "A prince's head, maybe," she croaked. "You know what,

Jacqueline? Your father was an asshole."

Jacqueline's blank face showed no offense.

Dumaka was helped up next. "I found nothing. Just bones." He collapsed on the thwart at the stern, beside Ash, and shook himself off like a dog, splattering the old man.

"There's one coffin left," Kate said. "I befriended a shark. That was fun, but I'm not going down there again."

"Giving up already?" asked Jacqueline.

Kate shoved the skull at her as she pointed. "*You* can go next."

Stubbs and Cross moved around Teach and perched themselves at the triangle of the bow on opposite rails. Stubbs reached up to wipe his wet hands in the fur of his cap. Cross glanced at Kate again, saw her watching him, and looked away.

"It was only a reef shark," Dumaka replied between heavy gasps. "You are fortunate it was not a tiger shark. Much worse."

"Lucky me," Kate drawled as she inspected the skull. She pressed her thumb to an incisor, rubbing away grime from the jade. She stuck two fingers in the skull's mouth, carefully unhinging the mandible. The jaw easily snapped off and fell to the deck. It had probably loosened after she'd bashed the shark in the face with it. She recovered it and inspected the backside of the teeth, and nearly dropped it out of shock. "I think I've found what we didn't know we were looking for."

Jacqueline leaned forward, jutting her chin and looking down her nose. "And what didn't we know we were looking for?"

"If I'm not terribly mistaken," Kate said, handing Jacqueline the jawbone, "Those are coordinates, carved in the back of the teeth."

162

"That doesn't make sense." Jacqueline stared at it for a long time, turning it over, rubbing the brittle bone with her thumb. The lower halves of her irises were reduced to slivers in half-lidded eyes. "Why would anyone do that?"

"Apparently our prince was sentimental," Kate offered.

"Elaborately so," Jacqueline replied.

"He must have carved the numbers sometime after leaving the island. I can only assume he enjoyed pain. Whatever the reason, we may never—"

A cannon sounded, distant but unmistakable. Kate leaned sideways to have a look over Jacqueline's shoulder. She saw nothing other than her ship, which sat motionless in the gentle water, shadowed against the bright blues of ocean and sky.

Cross and Stubbs shifted on their thwart, swiveling their heads like ducks. "That wasn't ours," said Stubbs. "Too far, and muffled."

"No it was not," said Jacqueline.

Kate glimpsed movement on the deck, men running about. They were clustering at the starboard bow to have a look at something. She heard shouting. Something about guns. They scattered from there, rushing to their various stations. She saw a second mast and sails through the gaps of *Scarlet Devil's* sails, moving independently. The enemy ship emerged across *Scarlet Devil's* bow, moving swiftly at full sail. Its crimson sails were plump with the wind. A voluptuous woman danced in the throes of the black flag. *Persephone* hardly seemed a pleasure galley now. She was a warship, and men lined her decks in place of strumpets. "Israel Hands," Kate said. The enemy ship unleashed a volley, smoke billowing from the mouths of its cannons, punching holes in *Scarlet Devil's* sails well before Kate heard the reports. It sped past and easily came about, dwarfing Kate's ship.

For a split second, before her wits took hold, Kate considered diving into the water and swimming. It was too far. The battle would be over before she got there, assuming she could make the swim. Instead, she scooped up her coat, letting the pistol roll out of it as it unfolded. She caught the weapon in her opposite hand and aimed it at Jacqueline. "Call them off!"

Jacqueline Teach was smiling, clenching each end of the mandible in trembling fists. "Have you so little faith in your crew, Captain?"

"No. I instructed them to clap a spring upon the cable in event of an attack."

"A what?"

"You never bothered to learn anything of ships, did you? A hawser rigged through an aft gunport for clout, bent to the cable and hauled to the mainmast. The ship will pivot on its stern when the anchor cable is veered, allowing her to bring a broadside to bear. Oh, why bother explaining? Show don't tell. Here, let's watch it together. It will be good theater, if nothing else. My crew will endure until your scuppers drain red and your men are naught but pulp."

"Your ship is old, Kate."

"And yours is a galley. A galley! What are you going to do, poke at us with your oars? She's heavy, even for her size. Ribs too closely spaced. Don't think I didn't notice. She's built for combat, aye, but she's not exactly fast." In truth, Kate was a bit surprised how fast *Persephone* could move, but she wasn't about to let Jacqueline know. "I hope Israel Hands killed the slavers he took that thing from. They're likely to return with something worse, assuming they care to retrieve it."

"We have more than oars. We have thirty-four guns. She'll make fourteen knots."

"Fourteen knots? Did Israel tell you that? This is pointless, Jacqueline. We're women with no cocks to measure. We're wasting men and ammunition, over what?"

"Nothing to you," said Jacqueline. "Everything to me."

Something slid through Kate's hair. A cold ring pressed against her skull. "I am sorry, Kate," said Dumaka.

"Stubbs, Cross," she snapped, "train your guns on the man behind me, if you please."

Stubbs drew the pistol from his belt, aimed it across the boat at Dumaka.

Cross aimed his pistol at Stubbs. "Teach pays good," he explained.

"What's happening?" said Ash, looking around, as if that would help.

"I am betrayed," Kate answered.

"Ah, yes, that," Ash said. "I dozed off, I think."

Kate straightened her arm, bringing the gun closer to Jacqueline's forehead. "Care to wager who dies first?"

"Not I," Jacqueline said. "Not with that pistol."

Kate glanced at the priming pan, but found nothing amiss. Either the shot had been removed while she was underwater, or Jacqueline was bluffing. "Are you sure?"

Jacqueline did not blink. "I am."

Kate squeezed the trigger. The hammer struck the frizzen, igniting the powder, and there was a tremendous report. When the smoke cleared, Jacqueline remained, blinking in surprise. The mandible fell from her open hands, clacking the deck. "Settles that," Kate said, lowering the weapon.

During the commotion, Stubbs had shifted his gun to Cross. Cross noticed and gasped. "We're friends!" he protested.

"You pointed yours at me first, didn't you, *friend*?"

"For gold!"

"Oh, that makes it all right?"

"Gold and strumpets! Anyway, I weren't really going to shoot."

Jacqueline had heard enough. "Dumaka, shoot Stubbs."

"Which is Stubbs?"

"The one to my right."

The barrel left Kate's hair, and she heard a hammer cock.

Stubbs looked from Cross to Dumaka and back again. "Wait!" he said, raising a finger.

"I work for Teach," Dumaka replied, voice devoid of emotion.

Cross looked pained. "I'm sorry, friend."

"I don't believe you," Stubbs said, nudging Cross's belly with his pistol, like a child poking his friend with a stick.

"I never been more sincere," said Cross. He emphasized the point by lowering his gun just a little.

"You have to be sincere 'fore you can be more sincere than you were, which you wasn't ever."

Cross considered that. "That's not true. Why, just the other day I—"

"SHOOT THEM BOTH, DUMAKA!"

Perhaps it was the startling intensity of Jacqueline Teach's outburst that caused Stubbs' finger to twitch. Perhaps he truly didn't want to shoot his friend, traitor or not. Perhaps bloodshed could have been avoided, but all that mattered was what happened next.

The shot punched a small hole in Cross's red sash, and

he clutched himself as he toppled out of the boat, but not before he got a shot off, which strafed a lock of Kate's hair as it zipped past, striking Ash in the throat and prompting the old man to thrust out a hand and seize Dumaka's arm, which may or may not have factored into Dumaka squeezing his trigger, blasting Kate's eardrum and catching Stubbs in the shoulder, hurtling him from his seat.

Dumaka shook loose of Ash's grasp, pitched his gun aside, took up his cutlass, and drove past Kate, heavy feet drumming the boat. Jacqueline slid sideways to get out of his path. Huddled up in the nook of the bow, Stubbs tried to shield himself with his hands as the huge man fell on him. Most of his fingers were lopped off before the blade bit into his face. He opened his mouth to scream, and the blade sliced through his tongue. Blood bubbled out of him as Dumaka methodically hacked away. His lips split open, teeth fell out, and his nose was diced and flattened into a black pulp. Stubbs groaned pathetically, unable to scream, until the blade split his monmouth cap and wedged so deep in his skull that Dumaka couldn't remove it. He tugged and tugged at the hilt, twisted it this way and that, and finally placed his heel on Stubbs' mutilated face for leverage.

Kate had fallen to her side, bracing herself with one hand. Her fingers brushed the mandible. She picked it up and stuffed it down her shirt. It tumbled down and collected at her lower belly, where her shirt was tucked into her breeches.

Ignoring the ringing in her ear, she righted herself and charged Jacqueline, who was momentarily distracted, maybe a little excited, by the gore filling the boat. Kate knocked her from her thwart and straddled her. Jacqueline tried to claw at Kate's face with her nails, but Kate slapped her hands away and walloped her with the butt of the otherwise useless pistol. She got five solid blows in, turning Jacqueline's face beet red, before she realized Jacqueline was no longer fighting her, because her hands had delved into her black skirts, fishing for something. Kate was blinded by a flash of sunlight reflected in a thin, polished blade. She curled forward, crushing her forehead into Jacqueline's. The dagger fell. The hilt was some sort of bone, engraved with wavy patterns and little fish.

Kate squeezed until Jacqueline's tongue lolled from a gaping mouth. She brought Jacqueline toward her, like a husband reeling his new wife in for a kiss, and flung her down, and she felt a tremor beneath her knees as Jacqueline's skull impacted. Jacqueline's eyes bulged and rolled up in their sockets, and for an instant Kate thought she had done her in, but then Jacqueline blinked herself back to life, and her hand fumbled for the dagger.

Dumaka got to Kate before she could finish. He grabbed a handful of her hair first, whipping her head back, and then wrapped an arm around her neck, and she was lifted into the heavens as Jacqueline, who was holding her throat and struggling to cough as her bruised cheeks worsened to a deep shade of purple, fell away from her. She saw the forward half of the boat in all its brutal clarity beneath her. Blood everywhere. Stubbs was unrecognizable, and the cutlass was still wedged in the remains of his face. Cross was floating in the water to the starboard, dead eyes taking in the sky, the lower half of his body vanishing into a red cloud. She looked up and saw the *Persephone* passing between the boat and *Scarlet Devil*. Both ships fired broadsides at the same moment. There was no sound, just ringing. She saw men torn apart, two somersaulting over the side, and there was Israel Hands near the helm, gazing in the direction of the boat, probably wondering if his employer still lived, and if this elaborate distraction was worth it. Cannon-shot perforated the enemy canvas. Kate prayed one of the strays would strike the longboat and send Jacqueline and Dumaka to Hell with her, but they sailed harmlessly overhead, leaving the acrid scent of gunpowder in their wake. And then Dumaka turned her aft, where there was nothing to see but a dying old man, and he hurled her to the deck. The impact almost buckled her arms, but she held steady, and then toppled to her side next to Ash. The boat was rocking in the waves stirred by the warring ships. Smoke from cannon fire started to waft overhead, like a marine fog tinged yellow. Her ears were still ringing, but she thought maybe she heard yelling in the distance. The old man was rigid as a plank, clasping his throat as blood gushed between his fingers. His milky white eyes seemed to be fixed reproachfully on her. She knew he couldn't see her, but he was *trying*, and Kate thought, *Don't look at me like that, old man. You lived more years than I.*

BONES

Thick strands brushed her cheeks as the shears slid together. Rusty blades shrieked in her ears and deep red blurs took focus as the strands fell away, landing softly on the deck. Dumaka held her neck in place, the full weight of him bearing down on her, keeping her hands and knees rooted. The shears opened and closed, opened and closed, opened and closed. It didn't take as long as she would have thought. When it was over, there was a dense wreath of red curls beneath her, like the nest of some giant bird. She stared not at the hair, but the void within, where her face should have been. It took all her strength just to lift a hand and retrieve one of the locks. She balled it into a fist. *Persephone* tilted starboard, and water and blood washed over her hands. She watched as her hair was swept toward the scuppers.

Jacqueline had perched herself on a cannon, no longer wincing as she pressed a blood-soaked wad of cloth against the back of her head. She was smiling now. Pain was a distant thing to satisfaction. She'd hardly blinked during the entire process, as though she did not want to miss a single severed strand.

Dumaka grasped Kate's arms and put her upright on her knees. She was behind the mainmast, facing aft, and Dumaka allowed her to see nothing forward. She heard commotion off the starboard. Somewhere in the distance *Scarlet Devil* was circling for another pass. Jacqueline's men were scrambling to reload the guns while Israel Hands watched confidently from the quarterdeck above.

"What now?" Kate asked. The voice she heard emerging from her throat was low, hoarse, and guttural. She'd heard that voice only a few times before. A promise of death always fulfilled, until now.

Jacqueline's smile widened. "We're not done, if that's what you're hoping."

"You're right. My crew will retaliate."

Jacqueline glanced starboard. "I don't think their heart is in it. That last volley was pathetic. They don't want to harm their dear captain, do they? They didn't fire once as we took you onboard. I must say, I'm a bit surprised. I didn't think they would care."

Dumaka released Kate's head to flex his hand, and she took the opportunity to look sharply to the right, catching glimpse of *Scarlet Devil* drifting off the starboard bow. It was odd not feeling her hair drag over her shoulder as it always had. Her head felt light and cool. Dumaka seized whatever hair remained and painfully returned her gaze to Jacqueline. "If they suspect I've been killed—"

"They'll get you back soon enough," Jacqueline promised. "This won't take long."

"How much of me will be returned?"

"Most." Jacqueline slid off the cannon and moved close. She ran a hand over Kate's head, sharp nails sliding along her scalp. "For a barber, Dumaka makes a fine sailor." She tittered at her own joke.

"That is very funny," Dumaka replied flatly.

Jacqueline was enjoying herself. Through the puffy mess of her battered face, the youthful girl Kate had met so long ago had returned in an awful way. Her index finger caressed the garbled skin of Kate's lost ear. "I always knew how ugly you were underneath that pretty mane, Kate."

"You should kill me."

"Probably I should."

"Don't make the same mistake I did."

"Do you want to die?"

"Not as much as I want to kill you."

Jacqueline bit her bruised lower lip. "But I would not be here if not for you. Alive."

"To my great regret."

"Nevertheless, you did save me." Jacqueline shook her head. "No, I can't kill you. I've suffered all these years since you left me on that island with no means of escape."

"Still blaming me for every ill course your life has taken?"

"You never so much as asked her name."

"Who?"

Jacqueline snapped her fingers. Two deckhands hurried off. She stood quietly before Kate, watching her, until the deckhands returned carrying an oak chest with gold latches. They set it down carefully between Jacqueline and Kate. The wood was so dark brown it was nearly black, polished

172

and shiny. Kate glimpsed her silhouette in the gloss, the outline of her new haircut, short and scraggly, no more than a few inches long.

Jacqueline hunched, flipped up both latches of the chest and flung open the lid. She reached inside and withdrew something white and brittle, setting it before Kate on the deck. At first she thought it was a crab, long dead, but as the details came into focus, she realized she was looking at a skeletal human hand, albeit a very small one. Jacqueline reached into the chest again, this time withdrawing a rib-cage, also small, and then two arms, a femur, legs, feet, and finally a tiny skull. She closed the chest and arranged the little skeleton before Kate, until it was in full form, feet pointed at Kate. It couldn't have been longer than three feet. "Your daughter," Kate concluded.

"My daughter," Jacqueline confirmed. "And you never asked her name."

"I don't care," Kate replied. The truth came too easily. "Would you have me pretend otherwise?"

"You will care. You will know my loss. You will know *her* losses."

Whatever food she had eaten earlier that morning, which already felt a lifetime ago, seemed to be expanding like a sponge in her belly. She willed it down. She would not be sick all over herself in front of Jacqueline. Not unless the bitch was near enough for her to be sick upon. "What's next then? Fingers? Toes? I only have so much to offer."

Jacqueline slammed the chest closed and set her palms on the lid. "I've waited years, Kate. Years. I knew you would come to me eventually."

"I hadn't given you a second thought."

Jacqueline's teeth clacked. "For the rest of your life you

will think of nothing else, I promise you."

Kate avoided looking at the tiny skeleton. She would not allow it to become anything more than bones. They could have belonged to anybody. For all she knew, Jacqueline had stolen someone's child and convinced herself it was hers. "You can do whatever you like, but I'm not responsible for this."

She felt the sting of nails raking her cheek before she realized Jacqueline's hand had lashed out. "She was forced on me!"

Blood trickled down her cheek, cool in the breeze. "I'm sure she would appreciate the sentiment."

"You left me there."

"I heard you the first time."

"You'll hear me as many times as I care to say it."

"So it's torture by reprise, then?"

"No," Jacqueline replied, wagging a finger. "No, I have something else for you. Something more permanent. You are a woman of instinct. You have neither a mind for plans nor reflection. You live in the present. The wind in your hair, that's all that matters. Well, your hair will grow back."

Kate laughed. "I'm glad you said it. I didn't want to point out the obvious."

"Keep with the jests, Kate. As long as you are able."

"You're not cutting out my tongue, are you?"

"I wouldn't take your voice. You need it."

"What don't I need?" She intended to keep Jacqueline conversational, until her crew could intervene. She hadn't come this far to be taken down by Jacqueline Teach of all people. Still, a small, infuriating part of her was beginning to consider the dreadful possibility. She pushed it down, refusing to accept it.

"I'm not going to take anything from you, Kate. I'm going to give you something."

"You took my hair."

"A practicality. You'll see why."

Kate frowned. This woman wasn't making any sense, but then again, she never really had.

Jacqueline grinned, reveling in Kate's confusion. "Always the pirate, thinking in piratical terms. Unlike you, I am not a thief. I am not my father. But I intend to remind you of what you are."

"I know what I am."

"Does it gnaw at you? The weight of everything you've taken? Every life you've ruined?"

"No," Kate said. "I sleep well."

Jacqueline seized Kate's chin and held it aloft, glaring into her eyes. "Not always, I think."

"Well, some nights Gabe keeps me awake." Kate braced herself, expecting to be struck again.

Jacqueline released her chin and smiled, kindly this time. "His desire might wane after I'm done with you." She pointed at Dumaka. "Remove her shirt."

Dumaka's huge arms encircled her from behind. He hastily unlaced her shirt and tore it over her head. The mandible tumbled out, landing on the deck before her. She retrieved it, held it tightly. She wasn't sure why.

Jacqueline laughed. "You hold onto that as long as you can, dear."

Dumaka crushed her painfully to the deck before she could respond. The cheek Jacqueline had scratched was mashed into the grain, her bare breasts pressed flat. Dumaka ground a knee into her back, pinning her there, and she fought to fill her compressed lungs with air. A strand of red hair fluttered across her vision, snagged on a splinter in the wood and uplifted by a light draft. It was two inches from her eyes, blurred by close proximity. She fixated on the strand, but it wavered before she could bring it into focus.

"Bring the barrel."

Kate felt the reverberation of heels upon the deck, large men off to their task. She tried not to think about whatever Jacqueline had planned for her, and the time for questions was over. She would remain silent. She would not give her the satisfaction of her voice, let alone her cries. They dropped the barrel close to her head, rattling her skull. Streaks of tar had hardened along the exterior, oozing from the seams.

"It's my own special concoction," Jacqueline said. "Laced with gunpowder."

She reached out to one of her men. "Give me that." She was handed a white paintbrush. She dipped it into the barrel and smiled at Kate as she let the tar soak into the bristle. "I'm just going to draw the outline. The men will fill in the rest."

"The rest of what?" Kate asked.

Jacqueline's expression turned earnest. "If you live long enough, there will come a day when you try to forget who you are and what you've done. I can't allow that." She aimed the brush at her daughter's skeleton, splattering the bones with black droplets of tar. "For her sake."

Kate returned her eyes to the single strand of hair. "Get on with it, then."

"You don't want to know more?" Jacqueline tried to hide her confusion behind a little laugh, but it only made her sound all the more flustered.

"You're insane, like your father. There's no point."

Kate watched the crimson thread twisting in the breeze as Jacqueline painted her back with hot tar while Dumaka and another man held her arms outward. Their hands were sweaty, but their grips firm as steel shackles. The long teeth of the mandible bit into her palm as she clutched it, and no one cared to take it from her. Jacqueline remained silent and took her time, pausing every so often to stand and dip her brush in the barrel. Her strokes were delicate and precise. Kate never asked what exactly she was drawing, because Jacqueline wanted her to ask, wanted her to care. Gradually, as Jacqueline traced the lines, the shape became elusively familiar. And when she withdrew the brush and drew a much simpler pattern onto her lower back, below the larger shape she had drawn above, Kate knew what it was.

The breeze dwindled. The strand of hair curled in on itself, before the wind kicked up again, straightening it to its full length. It quivered frantically, performing a mad, awkward dance, and Kate felt a bubble of fear expanding in her gut. She knew what was coming next. After about ten minutes, Jacqueline's brushstrokes became less frequent, and she would reapply the brush only to touchup some detail before drawing back to surmise her work. Her shadow extended over Kate as she stood. She set the brush atop a cannon and snapped her fingers at another man Kate could not see. "Fill it in. Don't break the line."

The man heaped globs of tar onto much of her back, and the stinging heat quickly seeped into her core. Beads of sweat formed at her temples and armpits. Her cheeks sweltered with blossoming fury. She closed her eyes and inhaled slowly. Rage would serve no purpose here, other than delight Jacqueline Teach.

The man spread the tar evenly, filling in the shape. He

was more precise with the edges, but his hands shook. Perhaps he feared for his life. She closed her eyes and could see the grinning horned skull and crossbones, black as night, peppered with gunpowder stars. It would not be black for long.

"It's done," said Jacqueline. "Fetch the torch." Kate felt footsteps thumping away, only to return a few moments later. "Give it to me."

Dumaka offered Kate a chunk of wood. "You will want to bite down on this," he said, forcing it into her mouth. Her teeth sank into the wet grain. It tasted briny and old. She closed her eyes.

Light feet approached. Jacqueline's slender, tall shadow passed over her. She held a long torch in one hand. The outline of her head flickered in pulsing swells of heat as she lowered the fire toward Kate. The heat rolled over Kate's back in blistering waves, a famished beast promising to devour her, if only it could free itself of its master's chain. Sweat rolled down her cheeks, pattering the deck. What little hair she had left was damp and matted to the edges of her face. She opened her mouth to gasp for breath, and the chunk of wood fell out. She squeezed the mandible in a trembling hand until the teeth broke the skin of her palm and her blood trickled over the jade insets.

"Katherine." Jacqueline's voice was suddenly gentle. Soothing. Had all this been a game, to see how far she could push Kate before she broke? Had she no intention of going through with it? The girl Kate had known, as bizarre as she had been, could never have been capable of something like this. "If you'd like to beg—"

"Fuck you," Kate spat. "And fuck your daughter."

Jacqueline's wrist twitched. A tendril of flame scarcely

178

licked Kate's back, but that was enough to ignite the tar.

AWAY

Beads of sweat refracted prismatic light from foreign skin as the blood simmered in her veins. Her arms were darker and thicker than they had ever been, forearms shackled in copper rings. Spread chaotically on the woven reed mat before her was a half-eaten maize cake, an upturned bowl of splattered stew, and a toppled ceramic gourd oozing a dense purple liquid. Silver light sifted through thin windows set in white plaster walls on either side of the door in a rectangular room, illuminating churning mist. The air was thick with humidity and an overpowering animalic odor. A chevron-patterned curtain hung over the door, rippling violently in heavy gusts. Screams of pain and howls of rage sounded from without.

She was on her knees, one hand at her chest clutching the

fabric of a red and white shift dress, the other caressing the jaw of a man who was lost in a dreamlike blur, just beyond her diminished vision's reach. Something heavy weighted her head, some sort of hat with a tight band preventing sweat from trickling down her temples. She glimpsed green feathers out of the corners of her eyes. A headdress, perhaps. The numbness in her throat was filtering downward. She prayed it would draw out the pain.

The man stepped forward through the haze. She lifted one knee, slapped a bare heel to the wet rug, and awkwardly rose to meet him on quivering stalks. He stood no taller than she, though only because he hunched forward with the posture of an older man. He clasped a hand over hers, pressing her palm against his smooth jaw. Despite his enfeebled poise, he was very young, possibly a teenager. His face was pleasantly slender, with an elongated skull sloping proudly from brow to crown. Straight eyebrows hovered far above large, sympathetic brown eyes. His full lips parted in distress, revealing jade insets.

He was beautiful. But of course he was. He was her son. One of two. She didn't know how she knew this, but there was no doubt in her mind. Sorrow, remorse, and fear warped his pretty face. He said something in a bizarre tongue. The words were unintelligible, but somehow she knew what they meant. "I had no choice."

His apologetic tone did nothing to appease the heat blistering through her. She curled her fingers and raked them across his jaw, tracing three angry red lines. She shoved him away and swept her arms about the room in a rage, beseeching the fire within to burst forth and consume the room, her son, the world.

But the fire remained within, horribly confined with no-

181

where to go. She managed only to topple an alabaster vase that had been perched on an outcropping of the far wall. Yellow shards danced across the floor. Fire swirled in her chest, desperate for an exit. Her knees lost the power to sustain her weight, and before she knew what was happening she hit the floor, spread-eagled on her front. She rolled onto her back and fought for air, clawing at her neck. Her arms felt loose and rubbery, and her fingers lost their rigidity. Every breath was shallow and insufficient. Her son kneeled beside her and removed her hands from her neck, setting them at her sides. She could not find the strength to muster her arms again. She felt nothing in her limbs, only the searing fire in her core. She would have killed herself to snuff out the fire if she could have. She would have taken up one of the alabaster shards and driven it into her jugular, offering her blood to the gods. There was power in blood.

White light washed over her body. She angled her gaze toward the doorway. The curtain had been pushed aside, framing the silhouette of a tall man. His shadow fell over her as he stepped into the room. The curtain fell back into place, and his shadow faded into the darkness between the two columns of light on either side of the room. "Tz'uul." The curse rumbled through her like lava through the subterranean channels of a volcano threatening eruption. *White man.* "You did this," she snarled in rough, unpracticed English. "You did . . . all of this."

"No. You did. Long ago." His cadence was dreadfully measured and unburdened of emotion. His jaw scarcely moved with each syllable.

"I wanted only to . . ."—she struggled for the word—"*strengthen* my people!"

She had no control over the words coming out of her

mouth. She might as well have been watching the memory of another from within. She didn't want to be this person anymore. She wanted to return, but something told her she would find no solace in her true form.

"You weakened them." The man moved closer, standing beside her son. His features gradually took form, but there was little of consequence. The details only emerged when fixated upon. At a glance he was little more than a shadow with a face. Pale white skin and close-cropped, neatly-trimmed dark hair. A bold, ugly face with a broad jaw and protruding brow. A deep crevice ran from forehead to cheek, cutting through his right eye, which was sealed shut. The remaining eye saw enough for two, with an amber iris reduced to a thin wreath eclipsed by the pupil. He stood awash in black, draped in a long coat with gold buttons. A cutlass hung from one hip and a pistol from the other. "I will help strengthen them in your stead. I will guide your sons."

"They . . . are . . . weak."

Her son stared sullenly at his feet, suffering the truth of her words. The man in black placed a huge, reassuring hand on his shoulder. "They are torn between two worlds, through no fault of their own."

"Your brother will take the throne," she promised her son, whom she had always considered the weaker of two. Yet, this son managed to look his mother in the eyes after plotting her demise. At least he was here to watch her fade. Perhaps she had underestimated him. "He will kill you if you try."

"I do not wish the throne," he replied. "I wish to leave this island."

"And you shall," said the man in black.

"His brother will not . . . let him leave." The white man's

words were difficult, and her throat seemed to be closing in on itself. Her heart flew into a rhythmic frenzy of panic, pounding violently against her ribcage.

"I will see to his departure," said the man in black. "I will teach the young king what his mother would never allow, because she fears what she has created. I will teach him to lead."

"And where is he now?" she asked. "He cannot even watch me die. He is . . . weak. He is not . . . worthy of . . ."

"His hands remain clean," said the man in black. "He will bury you as a queen. That is more than you deserve."

Her son spared her a final look, but he could bear no more than a glance. His temporary courage had fled. "You will . . . die," she promised him, and she knew it was true. "The world of the whites . . . will swallow you."

"Goodbye." He spoke the word in the white man's language. A final insult. He spun on one heel and departed hastily, dashing the curtain aside with an angry hand.

The crowd's howls reached a crescendo. She heard him calling to them for silence in the foreign tongue of his people. After a few seconds, their cries faded. "My mother, the queen, is dead."

The silence was short-lived. Their collective roar was a thunderous swell of elation that washed into the room through the windows like water bursting forth from a crumbling dam.

The man in black towered over her, looking down on her with a placid expression. "He says you're dead. You're wondering why you're not. I'm afraid that's my fault." His hand delved into his coat to produce a tiny berry. He bent forward and held it before her face between thumb and forefinger. It was mostly black and shiny, dotted with purple. He squeezed until it popped, dribbling juices down his fingers. "When we first arrived, we found these in a meadow on southern stretch of the island. We were starving. Three of my men ate these. They were incapacitated in minutes, as you are now. We thought they had perished. As fortune would have it, we were too exhausted to dig graves. A day later one man was dead, but we were surprised to find two alive and able to move their limbs again. That won't be enough time for you. Your sons do not know. I assured them this would be swift and absent pain." His brow fell over his eyes as he squinted, appearing conflicted for an instant. Despite his somber poise, he said, "I want you to know, I take great pleasure in this moment."

He waited there until the numbness had overtaken her entire body and she couldn't so much as wiggle her toes, let alone speak or move her eyes from side to side. Her breathing became shallow, her chest barely moving. The fire in her torso dwindled to a smoldering warmth. She wasn't sure what happened to the man in black after that. He faded from view, probably to linger in a dark corner, as he always had. That was his way.

Four women poured in through the doorway, one after another, carrying large ceramic jars and cloth and other items she couldn't quite see. Their aggravating little faces registered no sorrow, yet whenever one passed through her field of vision, she felt an unmistakable familiarity. She knew these women, and they knew her. They set about their task immediately. They carefully removed her clothes, raising her flaccid arms and gently lifting her up to ease the dress over her head. They slid the skirt from her waist. The moist air caressed her brown skin, prickling her flesh, but none of the women seemed to notice. They left the bracelets on her arms. With delicate, deft fingers they removed her head-dress and bound her hair. They slipped jade rings on all ten fingers, and they raised her head and adorned her with necklaces weighted heavily by tubular jade beads that collected at the chest.

She tried to swivel her eyes, but they remained stubbornly locked on the nondescript ceiling. No matter how hard she fought to move any part of her body, even a finger or a toe, nothing would budge. Surely one of them had noticed the shallow rise and fall of her chest? Sweat trickled from her armpits and back, softly tapping the floor. *A dead woman does not sweat, you fools!* Perhaps they knew she was alive and didn't care.

They pried open her hands and placed cold jade trinkets within, closing her fingers around them. A feathered serpent in her left hand, a plump round woman with massive breasts in her right. They straightened her body, positioning her arms at her hips and pressing her feet together. Over the next hour they wrapped her in cotton winding-sheets, layer upon meticulous layer, until she was completely cocooned save her head, and she sweltered in the suffocating heat.

She suffered a rage of maddening stillness. She wanted to shriek at them, to claw free of her binds and shower them in fire and blood, but her body was as stagnant as a stone monument. Finally, a slender hand fell over her face, thumb and middle finger delicately drawing shut her eyelids, but she managed to open the lids ever so slightly, viewing the world through thin slits.

When they were finished, she felt the plodding footsteps of two men entering the room. They set down a wooden litter and retreated. The women flanked her. Eight hands scooped her from beneath, lifted her a foot from the ground, and deposited her upon the litter. She ascended suddenly. She felt the curtain slide over her as they carried her through the doorway into the sweltering midday sun. A hot, humid breeze seeped through the cotton sheets.

The crowd's roar quickly dwindled in favor of gasps and hushed chatter, and soon all were deathly silent. The litter shook her from side to side as the pallbearers navigated the steps down to the main plaza, and her constricted gaze swept over piteous and judgmental faces. They carried her down the long stretch through the middle of the city. Pungent copal smoke streamed out of the mouths and eye-sockets of stone heads lining the procession, creating ghostly walls of twining haze on either side. Her narrow peripheral vision offered a vague impression of her surroundings, like the mottled yet colorful backdrop of a painting. The city was nestled within three sharp volcanic mountains. On her left were dozens of red and orange structures, spread far and wide across an ascending plain. On the right were huts nestled among the trees along the much steeper slope of the eastern mountain. She heard a river running alongside the main stretch, through the city.

The view ahead was much clearer. The tallest of the three mountains towered at the northern end of the city, while the shorter two flanked either side. At its base were three pyramids rising above the jungle, which encroached lovingly on all sides except for the long white stucco courtyard laid out before them. The pyramids mirrored the mountains in their size relative one another, with the shorter two on the east and western ends of the courtyard, and the tallest in the center, narrower than the others. Each consisted of a simple stepped platform with a stairway carved up the middle, and a vaulted temple standing proudly at the top. The temples were sheltered by mansard roofs crowned with two combed plaster walls leaning in on one another and displaying intricate murals. The western and northern pyramids were bright white with red accents. The eastern pyramid was entirely stained in red, as though some prehistoric god had impaled himself upon it and rinsed the entire structure in his blood before lumbering away to die in the jungle.

A low, ominous hum emanated from the crowd as the pallbearers reached the end of the plaza and carried the litter through twin columns bearing stone jaguar statues with comically large eyes and long fangs. Thick incense streamed from their gaping jaws, rolling over their hideous faces. The crowds progressed no further, and she was glad to leave them behind. The center pyramid seemed to increase exponentially in height as she was brought down a series of steps into the sunken courtyard. The midday sun irradiated smooth white stucco, brightening the blank faces of the women bearing her. Above it all, a man in elaborate garb stood framed in the entrance to the temple of the center pyramid. The other son. Already he had assumed his place as king. She knew he would not descend the stairs to pay his respects. She could not see his face, for he was too far and too high, but even from this distance she could see that there was something wrong with his skin. It was cracked and too pale for his people. He remained still as a monument, even as her pallbearers veered off to the right.

They were taking her to the red pyramid. They were taking her to her final resting place. She thrashed against paralysis, but her mind had no power over her body. If only she could move one part of her body, enough for her pallbearers and her son above to see she wasn't dead, surely they would cease the procession? Surely they would not bury her alive? She implored her arms from apathy. Nothing. She projected a mental shriek skyward, but it was lost in the cold sapphire of the heavens.

The women carried her litter up the steps of the pyramid, never pausing to take a breath, all the way to the top of the stepped platform, where smoke roiled out of the dark entrance to the temple. Dread consumed her as they carried her through the portico and into the central chamber, where the world vanished in shadow and smoke. They set down her litter, and she heard the soft pattering of their little feet. A moment later, heavy footsteps thudded the stone floor. Fire flared suddenly in the mist. Hundreds of hieroglyphs covering the walls came into view, a dense network of lineage and mythology and time. A large shadow passed by, a man moving with purpose. He handed one of the women a burning torch and retreated quickly, as though he didn't want to be in here any longer than he needed to be.

Two of the women returned to her litter, lifting it from either end, and they carried her through a large opening in the floor, down a narrow stairway, with the torchbearer in the lead and the fourth woman lingering behind. Firelight danced along the stone walls, illuminating rows of confounding hieroglyphs that descended with the stairs. The women rotated the litter sharply to the right as the stairs reached a wider passage, changing course halfway down, slanting inward toward the center of the pyramid.

The stairway ended and the litter levelled out as the women carried her into a small chamber. They angled left, into a much larger thirty-foot-long chamber. She could see little of the tomb other than the corbelled arch of the ceiling and the black glyphs and red murals covering the white slanted walls. The largest mural depicted a dynasty of three imposing kings, ending with a nude woman wearing an extravagant headdress and sitting on a throne of feathered serpents, with two children before her, one pursuing the other, as she looked on in disapproval. The mural on the opposite side depicted the same woman crawling on her hands and knees through a tunnel of serpents in the underworld.

The walls lightly trembled from a distant, raucous current running somewhere beneath the chamber. A river, perhaps. A highway to guide her to the underworld. The air was cool and damp on her cheeks. The rest of her body sweltered in its thick cocoon.

They carried her to the end of the room, where a twelve-foot long monolithic sarcophagus awaited, open and eager to accept her. To the side stood an equally long, six-inch thick slab with relief carvings covering the surface. From her low angle she could not see what the carvings depicted.

They set the litter gently on the floor. The coolness of the river below percolated up through her shrouds, promising to draw the heat from her back. The fourth woman entered the chamber with a large clay pot. She and another woman produced a fine brush and dipped it in the pot, soaking the fiber in some sort of red pigment. They went to work, adorning her shrouds in consecutive coats. What little coolness she had absorbed from the stone floor was swiftly stifled by the dense pigment. When her body was entirely coated, the women admired their work. One vanished for a moment and returned to present her with a death mask, its face puzzled together with many pieces of jade, and white malachite for eyes. Its expression was as blank and unremarkable as the four women attending to her burial, and she would wear this horrifically docile expression for eternity.

They placed the mask over her face. It was heavy and the jade was cold, and she saw nothing more.

Internally, she was shrieking and trashing violently about. Outwardly, she provoked no movement and no sound except a very tiny squeal somewhere at the base of her throat. It was drowned out by the constant current beneath the chamber.

They lifted her, carried her a few feet, and set her in the sarcophagus. It was cold here, hard on her back. For a few minutes she heard nothing except the low current, and she thought maybe the women had left. Something twitched. An eyelash against the mask. A flutter of movement, so tiny, but hardly insignificant. Her heart flew into a frenzy. She wriggled . . . or attempted to wriggle. Nothing happened. She blinked again, both eyelids this time. Each scrape of lashes against the jade mask seemed a revelation.

Heavier footfalls sounded, marching in and moving fast. Her heart flurried. She projected orders of movement to every inch of her body, praying any part of it would listen. She felt the heavy, inelegant heels of men entering the chamber. They moved alongside her. Stone ground against stone. The lid collapsed atop the walls of the sarcophagus, and then they began to slide it overhead.

Another twitch.

A revelation.

The little finger of her left hand.

Her eyes shot wide beneath the mask, but she saw nothing. She felt herself rocking from side to side. Merely an inch or two of movement, this way and that, but she was not imagining it. She was moving! Air seeped down her throat. A steadier, thicker stream than before. She exhaled, intending a scream. A pathetic moan flooded the sarcophagus as the lid slid into place, and puffs of air blasted her ears on either side. The current of the river was muted, but she felt it flowing beneath her.

Her right hand spasmed. The fingers splayed, shooting out like knives, and she shredded through the cotton. Her freed hand struck the backside of the lid. Pain exploded from her knuckles, splintering into her wrist. She tried to lift her arm higher, to reach up and remove the infernal mask, but her arm was weak and the sarcophagus too constricted.

No other part of her would budge. Already she felt the air thinning. She tried again to summon a scream. Maybe the men had not yet left, or maybe her cry would echo up the stairway. But nothing emerged. She had only one hand, and there was only one thing she could do with it.

She beat her fist against the lid until the skin of her knuckles burst and blood dribbled down, and she persisted until nearly every bone in her hand turned to powder, and she imagined there was nothing left but a lump of meat sprouting twisted fingers.

And still she could not scream.

She did the only thing within her power. She smeared blood across the backside of the lid, grinding raw flesh and shattered bone over coarse stone. She knew what she had to do, though she knew not why. She painted a symbol, sweeping her arm gracefully and ignoring the shrieking protests of dying flesh. It was the first thing that came to her mind. A symbol from the past, or maybe the future. A symbol that belonged to another woman. The woman who presently shared her mind from a distant future, linked by blood and bone. She painted a symbol of pain and terror, of grinning death, burning scarlet against a boundless sea of shadows.

VIRGO

Kate had never run from anything in her life, but she ran from this, and she felt no shame in doing so. It was easy to ignore pain, or to accept pain as a motivator, but she could not abide this intangible, perplexing dread. The other woman called to her from the distance, reaching to her and pleading with a pulverized hand swathed in blood, fingers splayed and twitching like the legs of a spider recently crumpled underfoot, not yet aware that it was dead. Twin shards of white watched her from within broken fragments of green flesh that reflected Kate's terror many times over. She fled, and when she looked back the other woman was lost in a swirling haze of ache and rage.

She shut her eyes.

She heard waves crashing over the sand. She moved to

and fro with the tide, toward the beach and away again, over and over. Her heartbeat gradually slowed to a steady, manageable rate.

She opened her eyes, expecting to find a blue sky, but she was lost in darkness. The only light came from tiny pinpoints in the great black veil above. She reached up to touch the brightest, but she could not see her hand. She had no hands. She had no legs. She had no torso. There was no light to give her form. She was nothing but a pair of eyes floating in the void. She could do nothing but draw imaginary lines between the white dots. She drew a woman. A kind woman with her head angled to her right, casually observing her celestial canvas. She drew half-lidded eyes and neatly-pursed lips with just a hint of an upward curl, enjoying some private joke that wasn't quite hilarious, but worth a smile nevertheless. She drew curly hair that tumbled gracefully about a heart-shaped face, tickling plump round cheeks. She drew a flowing dress of translucent fabric, which the night winds pressed against ample curves. And finally, she drew angelic wings, sprouting from the woman's shoulder blades and framing her body.

Kate blinked rapidly until nothing remained but stars.

She looked down and found her upper torso shrouded in linen bandages. Her clothes had been removed, save for an old pair of oversized tan breeches with vertical red stripes, shredded above the knees. She was tucked in a hammock stretched between two stilts. Palm trees swayed gently all about her, pointy leaves encroaching on her peripheral vision. She glanced about and found the wall of a hut on her left, with a small window. A dark-skinned older man with a white beard watched her from within, his eyes orange in the light of the many candles lining the windowsill. "Who are you?" she croaked, and was shocked by the ragged quality of her voice.

"I am Malik, the one saved your life," he replied. His accent was thick and distinctly Jamaican. "So do not bark at me again." He moved away from the window.

"I'm forced to take you at your word, Malik."

"You are alive." She heard him call from somewhere within the hut. "No word is required."

There were huts everywhere, connected by rope bridges and platforms. *Ten Shells*. Someone had brought her back. *Scarlet Devil* was moored in the shoals off the northern beach. They hadn't left without her. She wondered how long she'd been asleep. She remembered only her perplexing fever dream and a few bouts of waking to the writhing agony of a thousand fingernails grinding salt into the flesh of her back, only to fade into darkness again. The pain had been too great to consciously endure. Now she felt numb. Her back was heavy and sticky, and she dared not sit up. She wriggled slightly as a test. The skin felt taut and stiff. A giant scab. There was a distant pain, but it barely registered. She suspected it would become much less distant if she shifted more than an inch, but she wasn't ready to test that theory.

A cool breeze caressed the sweat rolling down her brow. She shivered. Her body felt weak and brittle. She wondered how much she had eaten and who had been feeding her. She didn't care for the notion of someone putting his fingers in her mouth. Somewhere, she heard Jacqueline Teach's intolerable giggles.

A tall shadow strolled up the bridge connecting the platforms. Old wooden rungs creaked beneath his heavy footfalls. "Hello, Red," Corso called as he stepped onto the platform. He stopped and wobbled slightly. "I have my sea legs, but I'll never master these damned bridges." He took a swig from a giant bottle of rum. It spilled down the sides of his mouth.

"How long?" Kate asked, dreading the answer.

"A fortnight."

"Jesus." Her back had started to tingle. She recalled a stern voice instructing her not to scratch.

"Aye. Happily, the island has a fine surgeon. Nursed you back from a murderous fever. You were lost in a raving delirium. Nothing you said made any sense. Do you remember anything?"

"I was somewhere else," she said, struggling to recall the particulars of her fever dreams. The harder she concentrated, the more distant it all became. "I was *someone* else."

"A delusion."

"It did not seem so. It seemed so real. It seemed a memory. Someone else's memory from long ago. I can't explain it." She closed her eyes for a moment and saw shards of green littered across the backs of her eyelids.

Corso was unmoved. "It will seem less real, in time. After another night's rest, you will have forgotten entirely, eh?"

"No. I don't believe I will have." She couldn't help but wonder how long it had taken the woman in the coffin to die. Minutes? Hours? Days? Somehow, she knew it hadn't been quick.

Corso smiled, slapping a palm to his thigh. "Best not dwell on it. You've more pressing concerns than dreams."

She shifted uncomfortably. "How bad is it?"

Corso moved closer, looking down on her. What little she could see of his brutish yet kind face was filled with pity. "It's not pretty. She did you good. Most of your back is raw meat. The old man in there, he warded off infection. Used a feather to paint you with an ointment. Laid linen over the wound. Over and over. Scraped away the dead skin with a scalpel to keep 'bad humors' from mustering beneath it, so he said. Quite a thing to watch. Drew the juice from maguey leaves, smeared it all over you. Wonderful plant. You know, the one with the tart fruit that blackens your fingers and mouth? Delicious. I've eaten more than my share in the last two weeks, I can tell you. Shit myself something fierce. I remember the first time I tasted—" He paused, cleared his throat. "Sorry. Getting away from myself. Anyway, then he wrapped you up in all this. Not the first dressing, mind you. Had to take it off and reapply your medicine many times over. You fought every single time, of course. You begged us not to bury you. Said you were still alive and you'd come back and kill us all." He laughed, then scowled with concern. "You must have rolled over in your sleep. You're not meant to be on your back."

She tried to shrug. "Yet here I find myself, on my back."

"Did Teach tell you beforehand . . . what she was putting on you?"

"I know what it is. I felt it."

"Wouldn't walk around shirtless ever again, unless you keep your front to everyone."

"That won't be a problem."

He cracked a smile. "I expect not."

She tried not to groan, but she couldn't mask her discomfort. A thousand pinpricks danced up her back, like tiny spiders with hot needles for feet. The groan became a cry.

She recalled tufts of red tumbling from her head, collecting on a deck. Fury clinched her chest, sweltering in the gap between her lungs. "Oh god. My hair. Is it horrible?"

"You look like a boy." He waved a hand suddenly. "A

pretty boy." He frowned, shook his head. "It's quite vexing. My words are shit. I'm sorry."

She reached up and cautiously touched her hair. She drew a shortened lock into her vision. Even in the night it was red. Her hand trembled. "Not so bad."

"My daughter kept her hair that length." Multiple emotions altered his face in the span of a second, concluding with sad resignation. He cleared his throat. "Jesus, Kate, you're worried about your hair?"

Kate tried to laugh, but a stabbing pain shot through her lungs instead. She clutched the bandages around her chest. "Throat's dry."

Corso handed her the jug. She took three hefty swallows and set it at her side. "Thanks. Find yourself another."

"Won't be too hard. The tavern is well stocked."

She looked at her ship. Its stern was facing the island, and there was a faint glow emanating from the captain's cabin. She looked around, but did not see *Persephone*. Maybe it was obstructed from view somewhere behind the surgeon's hut. "Where's Jacqueline Teach?"

Corso's grimace returned. "Took her ship and departed in a hurry."

"And she left me here."

"Aye." Corso moved to a stack of crates and retrieved a dark red lump of clothing. "She was kind enough to return this." He shook out the coat, displaying it for her. The death's head buttons grinned at her condescendingly.

Kate grunted. "Bitch."

Corso set the coat aside. He worked his jaw for a moment, as though he wanted to say something more, but he kept it to himself. Whatever it was, she was certain she didn't want to hear it.

She raised a hand and stared at the scabbed bite marks in her palm, where she had squeezed the mandible too hard. "Don't suppose I had a jawbone in my hand when I was returned?"

Corso frowned. "I think I would have remembered that."

"That's why she let me keep the coat. It's a message. She's going after it, and she wants me to know."

"Going after what?"

"We found something down there."

"What?"

"Numbers carved in the back of a dead man's teeth. Co-ordinates, I think."

"Treasure, then?"

"I don't know. Probably nothing."

"Don't suppose you remember these coordinates?"

Kate smiled thinly. "You know I do."

"We'll be going after her, then?"

"She's not worth the trouble. If there's treasure to be found, let Jacqueline get her hands dirty. I'll find her even-tually, and I'll make good on a promise I should have made good on years ago."

Corso nodded while staring forlornly at the jug of rum. She handed it to him. Her arm shook from the weight. She struggled to steady it, but the wobbling increased until she looked ridiculous. Corso took the jug and spared her further embarrassment. "You just need time," he said with a reassur-ing and completely unconvincing smile.

"Corso," she said, locking eyes with him, "who is running my ship?"

He took a swig. The mouth of the bottle popped as he pulled it away from his lips. "You already know the answer."

"Hawkes."

"Hawkes. Teach left her whores behind. Most are there."
He pointed to *Scarlet Devil*. "Crew is well rested."

"Explains why they're still here."

"They won't be for long. They've spent much on these strumpets."

"And my share?"

"Dwindling, on account of you not being conscious enough to object, and sure to perish in your sleep."

"I'm shocked I haven't awoken to a dagger in my gullet."

"You have friends who keep watch."

"Thank you, Corso."

"Didn't say I was one of 'em."

"You're here, aren't you?"

"Might be, might not. Mayhap you're dead and I'm naught but an apparition."

She squirmed with a grunt. "If I were dead, I wouldn't be in this much pain."

"True enough."

She looked again to the stars, but she could find no trace of the woman above. She tried to reform her, connecting the dots, but managed only to trace a skeletal shape vaguely resembling a human. Bones.

"Corso," she said, not looking at him. "What is it like to lose a daughter?" There was no delicate way to ask, and she knew he would not balk at her bluntness.

"Hard to describe, and I'm no poet."

She found something in the stars. Maybe an eye. "Try. Please."

He sighed heavily. "Imagine cutting your heart in twain and forging a new person from the better half, seeing everything you wish you could be blossom within that person, minus the faults and failings. It's a type of pride, I suppose, but a selfless pride. You become secondary. Everything you once thought so important seems silly. You see a thousand futures for this person, and reserve naught for yourself, save for how she might favor you in the coming years. You want to be better, you want her to look up to you rather than down, but you've already given the best part of yourself to her. You don't matter anymore. She is all that matters. And then she's taken from you, and all those possibilities vanish in a horrible instant, and you're left with half a heart. The black half. You can never be who you were. Nothing remains but sorrow and rage."

Kate looked at him. Tears had carved white lines down his dirty cheeks. "I think that's the worst thing I've ever heard."

"You are wise to have guarded your belly."

"Wasn't a choice. I am incapable."

"Then you are fortunate."

Kate wasn't sure she agreed with him, but this was no time for debate. "She holds me responsible for her daughter's death."

"Ah. Did you kill the girl yourself?"

"No."

"Then you are not responsible."

"No. But she has nothing else, and I fear rage has smothered sorrow."

Corso took a final swig, corked the rum, and set the jug at Kate's hip. "Then she is a dangerous woman." He swiveled in the direction from which he had approached, his bulky figure swaying with the palm trees. "Head's swimming. Think I'll have myself a nap on the beach."

She reached out to grasp his shirt, and a deep, grinding heat raked across her back. "Before you do," she said with a pained grunt, "would you fetch Gabe? Assuming he isn't mortified to look at me." She'd been afraid to ask about Gabe. Had he been beside himself all this time, or had he written her off completely? She wasn't sure she wanted to know. And she wasn't sure she wanted an "I told you so," which he was certain to provide.

Corso kept his back to her, angling his head only slightly. "Ah, you haven't been told, then."

"Told what?"

A long pause. "Gabe is the reason you're here. After the battle, he offered himself to her in exchange for you. Jacqueline Teach has him now, the poor bastard."

DUEL

It was a musty little playhouse that smelled of damp wood, rusty metal, and whale oil. The roof was rotting from water damage in one corner, pattering droplets on a roped-off section of soiled seats. On the stage, perched upon the stunted bow of a little ship, a pirate was easily wooing a pretty young woman with blonde hair, while two wooden slats cut and painted to resemble waves slid left and right independently of one another in the background. The insipid girl wasn't putting up much of a fuss. Instead, she was swooning and playing hard-to-get, but Katherine knew it was all an act. Katherine asked her mother what was wrong with the girl in the play. Why was her voice so high-pitched and why was she so smitten with the pirate, who had done nothing to merit her affections? Mother, looking so beautiful and ageless in a yellow dress, said there was nothing wrong with the girl, for the pirate was a tall and dashing fellow, oh-so-chivalrous, and any woman should be lucky to attract *that* kind of man. Mother was enjoying the play more than Katherine, who found it intolerable. She didn't care for any of the characters. She prayed they were all dead by the end. When the dashing pirate put his sword through a vile man's torso, there was no blood, and Katherine giggled when she realized the dying actor was pinching the blade between his arm and side. That's so stupid, she told her mother. It's not real. Mother started to laugh, but when she turned her head, her doting expression faltered, her dimples vanished, and her beauty was lost in a pallid terror that instantly drained the blood from her face, until she was pale as a wraith. She stood and practically fell on her daughter. Katherine swatted at her mother's probing hands. No, stop it, Katherine cried. What are you doing? Her mother pushed her hands away and reached out to her, touching her ear. Suddenly, for no reason at all, the theatergoers bolted, stumbling over chairs and each other, casting terrified glances over their shoulders. Katherine wasn't sure why, but she wished death on all of them. A slow death. She wanted them all to burn, screaming like the cowards they were. Mother grasped Katherine's ears and peeled away her face, and Katherine glimpsed the woman's horror through the eyeholes of her own skin. Mother turned the face around, displaying it for her. It was not flesh, but green, cracked stone, polished and gleaming, with white eyes and black pupils where holes had been not a second prior. The tendons strained in Mother's neck as she opened her mouth to scream, but there was no sound. She dropped the mask and it shattered into a hundred green pieces at

Katherine's little feet. The eyes remained level and set perfectly apart amid chaotic fragments, staring up at her.

She awoke to the night sky yet again, but she could not find the woman above. The dream, or memory, or whatever it was lingered like a foul scent, and she knew if she sat around any longer she would have no choice but to ponder its meaning.

"Where do you think you are going?" the doctor demanded as she struggled out of the hammock. The severity of his fatherly tone might have drawn a laugh if not for the pain. Her legs trembled when she set her heels on the wooden platform. She stood up and nearly fell forward. The doctor made no attempt to steady her. He simply stood there with his arms crossed, reproaching her with a scowl that creased his weathered dark skin in the flickering light of the torches. "You are in no condition."

"I'm going to get my ship back," she informed him as she unfolded the clean black shirt and dark brown breeches Corso had brought her a few nights back, freshly made by the mercer she had pressganged from Bartholomew Roberts' crew.

He laughed. "And I am Poseidon."

"I'll be back for you," she said.

He scoffed. "Have your lover apply the bandages. My hands ache."

My lover. She tried not to think about how many pieces of Gabe were left, assuming he was alive. It was more likely *she* would be applying *his* bandages than the other way around. Their final words had been spoken in anger, but few of their words had ever been kind.

"My ship needs a surgeon," she said. "The last one perished."

205

"How did he die?"

"A knife in the belly. Entirely unearned."

Malik leaned sideways and spat between a gap in the planks. "I must decline. My place is here."

She shook her head. "I think not. I shall call on you after I reclaim my ship. I suggest you take this time to gather your effects."

Malik continued to laugh, his belly convulsing.

"You think I'm joking," she realized aloud, a little stunned. *Has my voice lost its power?*

"What if I told you I have children who will miss me?"

She looked around. "Do you?"

"No."

"Didn't think so. I certainly would have noticed the little buggers scurrying about."

"But if I did, would you pressgang me still?"

She considered the question. "If your hypothetical children could not fend for themselves, no I would not."

"Then you have a code."

She shrugged one shoulder, but even so casual a motion swept fire up her back. She tried not to show it. "Of a sort."

"Does it help you sleep at night?"

"Anyone who cannot sleep, guilty conscience or otherwise, likely spends a generous portion of their day in an overly restful state."

The doctor made a face and a dismissive noise. "Your words come easily, but you are a craven witch."

"I am not craven," she replied with an irrepressible smirk that foiled her mock offense. She struggled against the tautness of her bandages and the agony of her wound as she pulled the shirt over her head. There was no resistance from her hair against the collar, which was strange. She slipped into the breeches, ignoring the lazy protests of her unused legs, and stuffed her feet into a pair of tall boots, wincing at her cramping toes when she shoved them through the tight throats.

Malik moved closer, but she warded him off with a glare. "They told me you were a captain," he said.

"I am."

"I do not see a captain. I see an animal that has chewed through its own limb to escape a trap."

Another flurry of fire ran up and down her back. She suspected she had reopened the wound just by dressing herself. She grimaced, hoping she looked suitably unpleasant. "You'll know what I am soon enough."

Malik's crow's-feet stretched nearly to his temples as his eyes narrowed into a hard glare. "A dead woman, I think. Your wound is not healed. My work is for nothing."

"We'll see." She tested her boots, pacing a bit. "Don't go anywhere."

"You truly intend to take me with you?"

"Aye."

"Then I pray you are killed."

She spread her arms and tried to smile. "You had your chance."

"I am not a murderer." He angrily thumped his heart with a fist for emphasis.

"Not yet."

She retreated from the torchlight of the doctor's hut and started across the nearest bridge into the darkness. The bandages agitated the giant scab across her back with every step. Every tingle of discomfort helped shape a picture of the horned skull and crossbones, grinning at her sadistically. She increased her pace, as if she might outrun the devil, but it matched her speed. She slid her hands along the rope lining the bridge and gazed skyward, searching for the woman in the stars, but the stars were as indecipherable as the strange patterns she had glimpsed on the walls of the pyramid she had visited in her dream.

On the northern edge of the island, a longboat awaited at the end of a long jetty comprised of smooth wet rocks stacked by the island inhabitants. Corso stood within, supporting himself on an oar as he watched her uncertainly. Her legs nearly buckled when she hopped carelessly into the boat, and Corso almost reached for her, but she held up a hand to halt him. "It's only pain, Corso. I can do this."

"You don't have to," he replied. "Hawkes might linger another day or two."

"And he might not."

"Your wound—"

"Will finish healing on the way to our destination."

"You're going after Teach, then." He pretended to be struck suddenly with a thought. "Or was it treasure? Or was it Gabe? I forget."

"You're not the forgetful type. I never said." She tapped his oar as she moved past him. "Start rowing."

"You are not well, Red."

"You're right."

"It's plain on your face."

"Good."

Corso rowed silently across the still water as Kate stood at the bow, watching her ship grow larger. All lanterns on deck were lit, with men perched along the rail laughing and manhandling strumpets. One of the Castillo brothers, she couldn't tell which from this distance, noticed the incoming boat and stood, shoving his strumpet away.

She made the trek up the ladder herself, fire raking her back with every upward heave as the scab cracked and split. The pain only augmented her pace. She couldn't hold back a loud gasp as she neared the final rungs. The shirt clung to her back. Sweat trickled from her armpits and down her sides as she reached the bulwark, but her head was cooled by the soft breeze that rolled over the ship as she stepped onboard. The pirates stared at her in shock. The strumpets giggled, unimpressed. "Where's Hawkes?" she demanded.

Domingo—she could see the scar on his chin clearly now—pointed at the cabin door. "He's taken up residence." He hesitated before he added: "Capitán."

She nodded and moved toward the cabin. The crew gave her a wide berth while eyeballing her skeptically.

"How is she not dead?" she heard someone whisper.

"Dunno," said another.

"No way anyone comes back from that."

"She *looks* dead."

"Jesus!" one man exclaimed when he saw her back.

She felt heavy footfalls close on her heels. She stopped and turned, warding off Corso with a lazy wave. His face was pale, frightened. "Your back, Red . . . it's bleeding."

"How bad?"

"The whole of it. It's . . ."

She closed her eyes and saw the grinning devil hemorrhaging blood, black as oil through her clean black shirt. She smiled, embracing her terrible state.

"I have to check you for weapons," said Ives as he blocked her path to the cabin door. His arms were folded, his stringy biceps clenched. His underbite worked this way and that and he swept a strand of perpetually wet black hair from his vision.

"I think not," said Corso, returning to Kate's side.

She set a hand on Corso's shoulder. "It's fine." She faced Ives, smiled. "Go ahead."

Ives took his time sliding his hands up and down her body, embracing her like a tender lover as he patted her back, hunching on his knees and taking particular care with her inner thighs. His thumb nudged her modesty. He stood at last and stepped aside, allowing her passage with an exaggerated sweep of his arm. He shuddered when he noticed spots of blood on his hands. "What? What is this?"

She ignored him and opened the door, stepping into the cabin.

All three candles burned in the candelabra at the center of the table. The drawers of her cabinet were open with clothes spilling out and strewn haphazardly across the deck. The air was musty with the scent of meat, spirits, and sex. The cabin appeared empty, but she heard moans of passion behind the curtain at the far end. Before she got halfway around the table, the curtain swung wide, and Hawkes stepped out, bare-naked, half-erect, and smiling pleasantly. She smirked at his manhood. In truth, it was larger than she might have expected. If Hawkes was surprised to see her, he was the only one who didn't show it. Behind him were two strumpets, one stalky and large-breasted with a fake red wig, the other a painfully skinny blonde with a pointy face and an insipid smile. The faux-redhead flourished her fingers at Kate in some ridiculous mockery of a greeting. Hawkes left the curtain open, so Kate could see the women he'd brought into her bed. He retrieved a woman's silk robe that had been draped over a chair and slipped into it. "Your hair is shorter than mine," he said, and paused, angling one ear toward her. "Nothing?" He lifted his nose and adopted a contemptuous upper-class accent. "No obvious retorts at the expense of my masculinity?"

She shook her head. "I'm not here to trade quips with a dead man."

"Ah. I suppose you'll be wanting your ship back." He took a seat, putting his back to the strumpets.

"The strumpets should leave while they still can," Kate suggested, aiming a thumb over her shoulder at the door.

The blonde immediately started collecting her garments, holding them to her tiny breasts. She skittered past Kate, keeping her head low, and carefully closed the door behind her as she exited. The stalky woman in the wig remained. "Cunt," she said, though Kate couldn't be certain if she was referring to her or the strumpet who had fled.

Kate took a seat opposite Hawkes and said nothing. Her back screamed in protest as she leaned into the stiff cushion and felt the coarse fabric bite into raw flesh, but she kept a strict face.

Hawkes' blue eyes studied her closely. "You're in pain."

She said nothing.

"Perhaps wine would ease your suffering."

"I'll need something stiffer. It's in the bottom drawer of my cabinet."

He walked to the cabinet and opened the bottom drawer, tossing clothes aside until he discovered a small round bottle with a skull and crossbones in red wax. Its contents were as black as coffee. "A private stock, eh?" He returned to his chair, uncorked the bottle and filled a dirty goblet, leaning forward and offering it to her across the table. When she did not take it, he set the glass down before her and settled back into his chair. "I must apologize for the sorry state of the cabin. I didn't have time to clean."

She said nothing.

"Unfortunately, you've been gone so long, I'm afraid I've become rather acclimated."

She said nothing.

"I think I'd like to keep it," he concluded, slapping his legs with both hands.

She said nothing.

He stared, gauging her. "Pistols at dawn, then? And when those fail, cutlasses?"

"There will be no duel."

He grinned, nearly laughing, and then covered his mouth apologetically. He glanced over his shoulder at the woman who loitered in the bed. She tittered in return. "Let's not be hasty. A duel is the only chance you have. You're sitting at the wrong end of the table." He reached beneath the table. She heard something click. He lifted the small pistol she had planted there long ago, setting it on the table within his own reach but far from hers, unless she made a sloppy lunge for it. "I've been here a while. I've removed your hidden daggers and guns, save this one."

She did not look at the pistol. She picked up the goblet of black rum and took a sip. It was a private stock she had acquired in Havana the year prior, stronger than it was succulent. It was so strong that she had intended to make a punch out of it rather than drink it straight. For now, it was exactly what she needed. It warmed her stomach immediately, sending pleasant tingles up her back.

Hawkes continued to stare at her, trying to cloak his bewilderment with an easy smirk. It wasn't working. "If not a duel, then I must claim this ship as my own."

"You shall never have this ship."

"I have it now."

"Not for long."

"Then we must duel."

"There will be no duel."

Hawkes could no longer restrain himself. He threw back his head and cackled laughter. The whore behind him joined in, matching his high-pitched squeal, and the pair were like scrawny wolves howling at the moon, confident in their dominion of this little world.

Kate took a hefty swig, stood up, leaned sideways to avoid the candelabra, and spit the alcohol across the table. It splattered Hawkes' face and chest in a thick brown stream, darkening his silk robe and drenching the table before him. He blinked the sting of rum out of his eyes. His hand fell to the pistol, but he halted as it occurred to him she hadn't threatened his life. His narrow shoulders eased of tension as he licked the rum from his lips. "Strong stuff," he remarked, releasing the gun and letting his hand slide into his lap. "I will take this as initiation of contest. A slap of the glove, so to speak. The duel will be at first light. That will give you a few hours to prepare."

"I needed but a moment," Kate replied, and thrust out a hand, tipping the candelabra. The two candles on the shorter prongs toppled uselessly and rolled toward opposite ends of the table, but the middle candle touched the pool of rum, spreading a ring of flame with a soft hiss. The fire leapt from the table onto Hawkes' robe, scaling his chest and latching onto his rum-drenched face. Fiery fingers parted his lips and crawled inside, feeding off the volatile fluid in his mouth and swiftly blackening his tongue as he shrieked and slapped at his face. "Here," Kate said as she rounded the table and picked up the bottle by the neck. "Help yourself to the rest." She shattered it over his crown, her arm shuddering on impact. Rum and blood spilled down his skull, igniting explosively. Hair and flesh became one, his nose shriveled, his eyes dried and popped, and soon he was nothing but a flaming head and a flailing body. He toppled from his chair and made terrible sounds that weren't quite screams as he jerked about like a spastic puppet whose puppeteer had suffered a stroke mid-theater. Kate retrieved the pistol from the table and aimed it at the flaming ball where Hawkes' head had been. She drew back the hammer with her other hand and held the barrel steady.

The urge to put an end to Hawkes' misery passed. After he stopped moving, she ripped the curtain from its hoops and laid it over him and stepped on the smoldering cloth until the fire was thoroughly snuffed out.

"You stupid slag!" the strumpet finally blurted, after coming to her senses. "You stupid, stupid slag!" She stretched her arm for something at the bedside table, probably a weapon, but Kate didn't bother confirming. Kate aimed the pistol to her right without looking and fired at the figure in her peripheral vision. The strumpet's red wig flew off as her head snapped back and loudly shattered one of the panes of the stern gallery.

Corso crashed through the door a moment later with Ives in tow. Both had their cutlasses drawn. Kate tossed the pistol on the table and moved through the smoke that billowed from the heap beneath the curtain. "What happened here?!" Ives demanded, mouth agape in outrage.

"Looks like your man lost a duel," Corso replied.

Others crowded the doorway behind Ives, struggling to see past him. Domingo coughed from the smoke.

"This was no duel, and there will be no duels," Kate informed them. "There will be no votes. There will be no whispers of mutiny carelessly dismissed with impunity. We go where I say we go and that's the end of it. Those who decide to stay aboard for our next venture may find themselves wealthy and happily retired." At that, the men outside reacted with gasps and whispers. "Any man who takes issue with this is welcome to disembark. I won't hear any belly-aching when we are underway. This is my ship, bought and paid for, and it belongs to no man."

She hooked a finger, beckoning Ives to her side. He moved past Corso, who watched him closely. Ives rounded the table and stared at the heap beneath it. Kate ripped the curtain away, revealing a blackened husk. Hawkes' face was an eyeless mass of charred flesh and teeth. His cooked lips had peeled back from his teeth in a macabre grin. He was thoroughly dead. "Is this going to be a problem for you, Ives?"

Ives' stringy black hair had fallen over his long face, concealing whatever dark expression he wore beneath it. After a moment, he lifted his head, swept the hair from his face, and looked at her. "Can't change it, can I?"

"Evidently not. You could, however, seek vengeance."

"What's the point?" His thin lips twitched into something that might have been a smile. "You can't seem to die."

She set a hand on the nearest chair to keep from falling over. She wanted nothing more than to drink herself into a coma and quiet the demon gnawing at her back, but dawn was fast approaching, and she could not afford to take her eyes off the crew until they were well underway. "We depart at first light." She pointed at Corso. "Fetch the island doctor. Malik, I believe his name was. Older man of a positively woeful demeanor. I require his services, and I made him a promise, and I won't have it spreading that Kate Warlowe is not a woman of her word."

Corso plugged his nose, recoiling at the stench of Hawkes' smoldering corpse. "Supposing this Malik doesn't wish to join?"

She shrugged. "Shoot him in the shin and toss him over your shoulder. He's a surgeon, he'll know what to do."

III

THE ISLAND

ARRIVAL

Due to the usual setbacks, it was nearly a month before a lookout called, "Island! Three points off the lee bow!" They had finally arrived at the uncharted coordinates, and as Kate squinted at the three volcanic peaks towering over the island, she was overtaken by a dreadful certainty: Gabe was dead.

She could conceive no reason for Jacqueline Teach to keep him alive, and given Jacqueline's persistent hatred for Kate, she had every reason to kill him. So she allowed herself to mourn him in her typical fashion, by putting herself to work, splicing ropes, cleaning the deck, and socializing with her men. For the most part she no longer enjoyed their company, feigning interest in their activities while keeping a close watch on them. She maintained a strict sobriety so as never to lower her guard, despite the pain of her healing wounds. Where once she had assumed a comradery, she now saw creatures of thirst who would turn on her in an instant if her promise of fortune proved false. It was clear to her, now more than ever, that they were a means to an end, and always had been. She saw the doubt in their black eyes and she heard their whispers below decks. They would not give her another chance. If there was nothing to be found on this island, they would take her ship and leave her on its beach with a pistol and a single shot, if she was lucky. The murder of Hawkes had bought her one more venture with few questions asked, but her dissolution of the ship's democracy would not endure beyond that.

The ship's new doctor had begrudgingly tended to her back while generally refusing to speak. She had attempted conversation every time, but his jaw usually remained tightly-clamped, eyes locked on the task. She would find him most often on the quarterdeck, gazing aft, and she would wonder what of his old life he could possibly be missing. "I might have spared you this life, if you'd given me one good reason not to pressgang you," she had told him. "My refusal was reason enough," was all he would say in return.

Her wounds had stopped bleeding, but the scars were a mess, and whenever she reached back to feel the rubbery skin, she shuddered. The scar felt like an extra layer, as though someone else's dead skin had been grafted onto her back. The memory of fire returned spontaneously throughout every day, manifesting as pain and twisting her poise. By the end of the month she had learned to live with it, to pretend she felt nothing, despite the fiery teeth gnawing at her sanity. In quieter moments, huddled away in her cabin in the middle of the night with no Gabe to comfort her, when the pain was at its worst and she thrashed violently about the bed like a child lost in the throes of a tantrum, sheets saturated in her own sweat, she wondered if it would never cease. Her hair had gained three-quarters of an inch, teasing her neck. She had evened it out with a trim, using a hand mirror she had taken from a merchant ship years past. There was no way to conceal her mangled ear, but most of the men had learned to stop ogling it after the first few days.

As she stared at the island, she felt nothing. Not pain, not sadness, not anger, not fear, not greed. The trees were bright and lush, rolling over mountainous terrain. The late after-noon sky was a deep blue and the sun was nearing the horizon, but light seemed not to touch the three peaks, which remained shadowed and indistinct. She recognized the peaks instantly. Their configuration was unmistakable. She was in the right place.

"Reef the mains and clew up the gallants," she instructed Corso, who immediately set the men to work. "We'll circle her first, but keep a distance," she told Granger as they neared the eastern beach. "This water hides teeth." She indicated the sharp rocks jutting from the water, several clusters, some revealed only between the swells of the turbulent water that rocked the ship. She leaned over the port rail of the quarterdeck and squinted down at the im-penetrable black, wondering what dangers lurked down there waiting to tear open the keel. How many others had made that mistake?

The sun was setting in the west by the time they reached the northern tip of the island, where the trees were densely-packed and there were no beaches, only steep crags for the surf to break upon in a violent white foam. Kate urged her men onward, despite their eagerness to disembark. The western side was all rolling hills and impenetrable trees, not a hint of sandy beach or a clear path through the jungle. And scattered everywhere were more of those sharp rocks protruding from the sea. *This island defends itself*, Kate thought.

By the time they reached the southern end, the sun was gone and the muted blue veil of twilight had fallen over the sea. The three peaks were dark sentinels standing vigilant as specks of light materialized one-by-one from the dimming sky, and soon the peaks were nothing but pyramidal voids where stars should have been. The perimeter of the island curved into a broad bay where the shore was lined with an inviting beach, sands glowing white with no moon yet shining. Unlike the eastern beach, the water was calm here, stars pristine and barely wavering in its glassy surface, with only a few clusters of rocks to avoid. And there, careened upon the beach, was *Persephone*, a dark husk angled at a sharp ninety degrees, her mainmast aimed at the highest peak like an accusatory index finger, and for the first time Kate felt something approaching trepidation. The lookout called unnecessarily from above. Kate had already descended to the main deck and moved between two cannons along the port bulwark. The men fell in around her, muttering absently. "Looks abandoned," said Corso, gazing through a spyglass. "Should we heave to and drop anchor?"

"Nay. We continue around that bend."

"Captain?"

"This doesn't smell right. We're exposed. We'll anchor further up, out of sight, and approach by land."

"What's your worry?" Ives interjected, squeezing between Corso and Kate. "Teach's men would be no match for us."

"Do you see any men? I don't. I'd sooner avoid whatever

fate befell them. This ship stays out of sight and out of reach."

"Seems a waste of time."

"Red's got a bad feeling," Corso told Ives. "How many times has she been right?"

Ives shrugged. "Hard to know. Only know when she's wrong."

Corso smiled. "You're getting smarter by the day, Ives."

They sailed around the long, high ridge extending along the eastern end of the beach and discovered on the opposite side a forest of mangrove trees crowding the mouth of an inlet. "This will do," said Kate. She moored the ship just out of reach of the mangroves and took extra precautions in the event of an attack. "I want every inch of this hull greased so no interlopers can scale it, and the crew always in arms. Lookouts and sentinels keep a proper watch all hours for boats or swimmers. I want a man in a boat at the anchor buoy, ready to cut the cable, and a picket boat about the ship all hours of the night, one man rowing and the other keeping watch. Rig a boarding net from main shrouds to fore. Small arms and great guns at the ready, starboard and port, and swivels loaded with case shot."

"You think that's necessary, Capitán?" Domingo asked.

"I hope not," she replied.

"Awful lot of work," Ives said.

"Not for you, Ives. You're coming with me so I can keep an eye on you."

She took a longboat into the mangroves with the small compliment of Corso, Ives, Joseph, Duncan, Harry Harmless, and the Castillos. The trees seemed to be floating atop the water, suspended on ropey stalks like oversized bushes, huge and dark shapes gliding past in the night while the boat seemingly remained still as the Castillos rowed. The mangroves grew more and more crowded the further in they rowed, and soon the Castillos were knocking their oars on the tangled maze of branches and roots. Kate maneuvered the branches out of her face, leaning right and left while ignoring severe protests from the taut skin of her back. Ives swatted at branches with affronted grunts and curses, as though he was being deliberately attacked. Corso merely stood in place at the stern with a dark look, watching the *Scarlet Devil* vanish beyond the cluster of mangroves that enclosed behind them like a mouth. The branches arced overhead, merging like fingers to form a canopy, and everyone hunched down through the tunnel. The world went pitch-black for a time, and they were forced to stop for a moment to let their eyes adapt. Everything was silent and black, as it was before the world had been forged. Kate felt as though she was floating through empty space, consciousness freed of her body. Eventually a dim, colorless texture of roots and leaves came into view on all sides, and Kate looked down to find she had hands once again. When the Castillos started rowing, stars winked on and off through narrow openings above.

The watery forest opened into a river, where the mangroves had thicker trunks and were wider spread, allowing for a clear, unblocked passage. Ives sat back and plucked leaves from his hair, sighing heavily in relief. "Glad we're out of that."

The longboat moved silently upriver for what seemed an hour, until the boat was met with resistance where the water became too shallow and muddy. Thin little leaves pointing straight up out of the water caressed the hull. Eventually the boat stopped completely, and the Castillos raised their oars to find them caked in mud. "We walk from here," Kate said.

They disembarked, sinking their boots into the shallow swamp, and they dragged the boat toward the muddy western bank. The Castillos placed the oars inside the boat, and Domingo drew forth a rope and tied it to a tree, not that the boat was likely to drift in the thick mud. Kate removed her troublesome coat, folded it, and set it on a thwart. She threw a leather sling over her shoulders with two brace of small pistols hanging in holsters from her chest, in addition to the flintlock holstered at one hip and a cutlass at the other.

"You think your five guns will be enough?" Corso teased. The rest were carrying two.

"Until someone invents one that can fire more than a single shot," she replied.

Corso frowned as he thought about that. "Not possible."

"I'd settle for a pistol what shoots where I point it," Duncan lamented.

"They're awful weighty, too," said Harry Harmless with a protracted sigh. "Me arms get tired."

The heels of her boots made sucking noises with every step, until the ground inclined and hardened. She unsheathed her cutlass and hacked at wayward branches, cleaving westward while the men followed quietly.

Soon she was sweating profusely, her black shirt hanging heavy on her shoulders and clinging to her stomach. For the first time she was thankful for her shortened hair, which allowed the humid breeze to cool the sweat on the back of her neck. Her thighs were aching by the time she reached the top of a narrow ridge and glimpsed the ocean and the southern beach, where *Persephone* was careened. She glanced southeast and found *Scarlet Devil* just outside the mangroves, little shapes moving about the deck attending to the precautionary tasks she had assigned.

They moved northwest along the ridge until they found a rocky path downward, into a lush jungle where the ground gradually transitioned from hardened dirt to soft white sands. Giant palm fronds rustled gently high above, the air was cool, and there was a feathery mist rolling over the ground, giving off a dreamlike radiance in the night. The anguish of the past month was forgotten, and for a lovely instant Kate thought everything was perfect, before she remembered she was here to confirm the death of her lover, kill the woman who had wronged her, and search for treasure that probably didn't exist. They curved southwest along a little stream and then plunged south. The ground sloped downward most of the way, sometimes precipitously, and they were forced to take their steps carefully, until the ground levelled off and the trees grew sparse.

Kate glimpsed the angled masts of *Persephone* once again, now pointing straight over her head toward the three peaks in the far north. Its angled starboard keel was warmed by a soft orange glow at the base. Kate held up a hand to halt her men and crouched in the sand just behind the perimeter of trees that separated the jungle from the beach. Corso knelt beside her and handed her his spyglass. She extended the brass tube and brought the lens to her eye, training the scope on the beach until she found the source of the light. Two dark shapes were crouched over a campfire beneath the keel.

Kate handed the spyglass back to Corso, who had a look for himself. He continued to scan the horizon, from far right to far left. "Shouldn't be a problem," he concluded. "Can't spot anyone else. It's just those two."

"Queer," Ives murmured. "Where'd everybody go?"

"To look for their treasure," Kate replied.

"Should've found it by now," said Harry Harmless.

"True," said Corso, looking at Kate. "I'd wager they got here at least a fortnight before us, what with you recovering from your wounds and all."

"Maybe they're dead," said Domingo.

"We ain't never that lucky," said Duncan.

"Let's kill them," said Ives.

"We'll never know what happened here if we kill them," said Kate.

"I'll only kill one."

"No way to approach without alerting them," said Joseph.

"Could have, if we'd moored in that bay like I said," Ives grumbled. "They can't see 'round their own hull."

Kate stood and readied her cutlass with one hand and drew a flintlock with the other. "Wait here. All of you." She started forward before they could stop her. Their hushed cries of protest faded as she marched straight down the beach toward the firelight. It was a long walk and her feet sunk deep into the soft sands with every step. A cool breeze glanced off the water and over the beach. The two men did not react as she approached. Their eyes were likely blind to the darkness beyond the fire. She walked within five paces and aimed her pistol at the man on the left, who was hunched over the fire with a pan, frying an egg. It smelled delicious. The other man was blocked by the fire. The man on the left looked up, and she recognized him but couldn't quite place him. He blinked, sweeping dreadlocks out of his face. After a moment, she said, "Israel Hands?"

"Warlowe?"

The man beyond the fire stood and rounded it. She shifted her pistol his way. She nearly dropped the weapon when she saw his face. He was skinnier than before, with dirty, tattered clothes hanging from a narrow frame. His cheeks had sunken slightly, and the hollows of his eyes seemed deeper. He appeared otherwise unharmed. A flood of relief warmed her blood. She might have cried, if she knew how. "You're alive."

"*You're* alive," Gabe said, moving toward her.

She returned the pistol to Hands before she could lose herself in the moment. "No ill intent," he insisted.

"No ill intent? You helped Jacqueline Teach betray me and set my back ablaze."

Hands lowered his head and chewed on his lip. "That's one interpretation of events."

"That's what happened." Kate looked to Gabe. "Who else is here?"

"It's just the two of us," he answered. She didn't like the way he was looking at her. There was sympathy in his up-turned brow. It did not suit him. And then she remembered her shortened hair, and how dreadful she must have looked.

"You're sure?"

He nodded. "Very sure. It's been a week since Teach and Dumaka and the rest of the crew went into the jungle. Only one man came back, but he didn't live long."

"What happened to him?"

"Not sure. He was cut all over, bleeding terribly. Said something about 'shadows' and died right there where you're standing before we could find out what happened to everyone else. We took this out of his chest." He held up a long shard of black glass. The light of the fire twisted and danced in the reflective surface.

"Why didn't you leave?"

He aimed a thumb over his shoulder at the ship towering over them. "We couldn't get this thing back in the water. No tide. Only the two of us." He suddenly looked to the sea. "Where's our ship? We need to get out of here."

"We're not going anywhere," she said.

Gabe frowned. "You don't understand—"

Kate raised a silencing hand as something occurred to her. "Wait. Why are you alive?"

Hands looked from Gabe to Kate and back again. He cleared his throat awkwardly.

Gabe ran his right hand through his hair, which was much longer than hers now. He brought his left hand around from his back and opened it for her, palm downward. His two smallest fingers were missing, severed cleanly below the knuckles. The skin had been stretched over the wounds and sewed shut.

Kate was unimpressed. "That's it?"

Gabe flinched as though remembering the pain. "That's not enough?"

"No!" she nearly screamed. "I thought she'd—"

"Kill me? No. She wanted to take a piece of me at a time. One piece each day."

"You were with her longer than two days, Gabe."

"It was that or . . ." He trailed off, eyes darting sideways, avoiding hers.

"That or what?" She knew what was coming.

"She said if I slept with her, it would stop." The words flowed with an infuriatingly casual haste. "Every night I slept with her was a night I didn't lose something."

Hands cleared his throat again.

Kate looked at Gabe's diminished left hand, the heat of the fire maddening her cheeks. "Did she tell you that imme-

229

diately?"

"Aye."

"And judging by the scant amount of fingers missing, you lasted two nights."

"Aye."

"So, she branded me and bedded you. I almost died, Gabe."

"You surely would have, had I not traded myself for you."

"You flatter yourself. She never wanted me dead. She wanted me to suffer." She indicated him with the point of her cutlass. "This was all part of her game."

"You're angry."

"I'm not."

Hands cleared his throat a third time, and Kate jerked the pistol at his way. "Do that again and it will be the last sound you ever make."

He scrunched up his face. "You've developed an ill temperament since last we met."

"It was a short meeting. I don't believe you've had opportunity to properly gauge my temperament."

He returned his gaze sullenly to the sand, dreads falling over his face so that all she saw was his bearded chin. "You're very hyperbolic right now. That's all I'm going to say. Very hyperbolic."

Gabe abandoned the sympathetic act, which she now realized was not in regard to her hair. "What was I supposed to do, Kate? She wouldn't have stopped short of my fingers."

"It's a shame she didn't start with your cock." The words fell out of her mouth before she could manage them.

He considered that for a moment, shook his head. "No. That would defeat the purpose."

She was tired of this. She turned, placed two fingers in

either side of her mouth, and whistled at the jungle. The seven men emerged and sprinted across. "It's safe," she called when they were halfway down the beach. They fell in around the fire, keeping their guns and swords drawn. Duncan was the last to arrive, waddling across the sand on stubby legs and wheezing for air when he caught up.

"Gabriel!" Domingo exclaimed.

"You're alive, my friend!" said Joseph.

"Happy surprise, this," said Corso with a warm smile.

Gabe smiled at everyone except Ives. "Where's Hawkes?"

"Dead," Domingo replied eagerly, grinning. "Capitán Kate lit him on fire. Very nasty."

"That's what I do to people who anger me," Kate said, looking at Gabe. "And, oh look, you've built a fire. Saves me the trouble."

Gabe forced a chuckle.

Ives spat in the sand.

"Why is this one still alive?" Corso asked, aiming his pistol at Hands.

"I haven't concluded what should be done with him yet," Kate said.

Hands stood slowly, careful not to make any sudden movements. "Jacqueline Teach paid me well, but she's likely dead."

"What does that make you?" Corso asked.

"Whatever you need me to be," Hands replied with a humble bow.

"What if we need you to be dead?" Kate wondered, taking two steps toward him. "What if I find myself with a pressing need to murder someone?"

Hands dropped the act instantly, his sunburned face twisting. "Then you had better shoot me in the back." He turned his back to her, facing the hull of his former ship while she contemplated heeding his advice.

Gabe stepped forward. "He's not so bad, really. No need to kill him."

Kate shot a glare his way. "As much as I value your judgment, you're returning to *Scarlet Devil*."

"We all are, I hope."

The heat of the fire was becoming too much to bear. "I won't let the solitary reason I've travelled this many leagues be the retrieval of a man who shared the bed of my mortal enemy, thank you."

"You must kill her, obviously," Gabe replied amicably. "But there will be another time for that."

"There's also the treasure to consider," said Corso. "That's why we're here, right? The *treasure*?" He stressed the final word through grated teeth.

Kate said nothing.

"Aye! The treasure!" Ives agreed.

Gabe laughed. "You really think there's anything worth taking? Teach and her men never returned from that jungle. There's nothing in there but death."

Kate rolled her eyes. "Jacqueline is a simpleton."

"Who bested you," Hands remarked over his shoulder.

"Tell me, Israel," Kate said, closing in on him, "did it not make you jealous? That she took Jenkins into her bed?"

"No. Truth be told, I am relieved to be quit of her. She's a madwoman."

"If this place is so dangerous," said Corso, "how is it you two lived this long?"

Gabe gave Kate a wide berth as he navigated past and retreated out of the light of the fire, behind the group. "Because we kept to the beach."

"Couldn't have been all that bad," Harry Harmless said as he lifted a jug from a crate full of rum.

"Where'd you find them eggs?" Duncan asked, pointing at a basket packed with what Kate had mistaken for rocks.

"Leatherbacks," Hands said.

"But don't they bury those so as no one can find them?"

Hands smiled shrewdly. "It's the start of their nesting season. You look for a big sand-angel, but that's just a decoy to throw off predators. You'll find the eggs a few meters off."

"I didn't know that," Corso admitted.

"Everyone knows that," said Ives.

Gabe was trying to herd the group away from the fire. No one was budging. "I'd rather not push our good fortune. Let's go."

Kate pointed at Duncan. "You. Escort Gabe back to the ship."

"Why me?" Duncan protested.

Gabe laughed. "You want a dwarf to lead me back? Can he see over the bushes?"

Duncan's one beady eye registered offense. "I'm not a dwarf. I'm stumpy, is all."

Harry Harmless looked Duncan up and down. "I always took you for one."

"Well, I isn't. The girth of me belly makes for an unfavorable illusion."

"Gabe has a point," Kate said. "Domingo, you'll take him back."

Domingo folded his arms. "I will stay beside my brother. I must not take no for an answer."

"Touching, but no."

"Very well."

"The rest of us will camp here," Kate continued, hoping

to avoid any further interruptions. "We'll cook ourselves some eggs and trek into the jungle at first light. Did Teach leave any weapons here?"

Gabe pointed at some crates tucked beneath the keel. "Pistols and grenadoes."

"Excellent."

"What about me?" Hands asked with a grimace, dreading the answer.

"You're coming with us."

"I'd rather not. There are snakes in the jungle."

"It's that or I kill you right here."

"I see." He glared at her. "It seems there are snakes everywhere."

Gabe shuffled back into the light. "If you're determined to go, Kate, I'm going with you."

"I don't need looking after."

"Really?" He looked to the others for support, but no one wanted to get involved. "I watched through a spyglass as she lit you on fire. You stood up and I saw the devil on your back, bright as the sun. You made a sound I can't describe and wouldn't want to if I could. Four men had to hold me in place while your flesh turned black, to keep me from diving over the bulwark right then and there."

Kate snorted. "That's dramatic." She looked to the others. "Is it true?"

The Castillos shrugged. Joseph and Harry Harmless were busy examining the basket of eggs. Ives uncorked the rum and sniffed at it. "Don't rightly remember," said Duncan.

Corso was staring into the fire. "It was one man holding him in place."

"I was a little out of my mind at the time, so forgive me if

I misremember every little detail," Gabe said. "The last I saw of you, when these men dragged your lifeless body from *Persephone* and into a longboat, smoke was trailing from your back. I was almost certain you were dead, but I gave myself over to Teach on the slim chance you weren't. And maybe if you were dead . . . maybe I didn't want to be alive anymore either."

She smiled sweetly, but felt nothing. "Romantic suicidal notions which you rescinded a mere two fingers later."

"I could have lied about what happened."

"Right now you're wishing you had."

A twitchy, scathing smirk materialized. It did no favors for his slimmer face, which was not as fetching as she recalled. "All I know is you'd be dead had I not done what I did."

"Then we're even on that score," she replied coldly with a steady chin. "I need someone to look after *Scarlet Devil*. We raided a ship with livestock on our way here. You look as though you could use the meat."

Gabe shook his head. "No."

Kate thrust her cutlass into the sand between them, letting it wobble. "This is no longer a democracy."

"It's not a democracy," Salvador parroted, and then glanced around uncertainly.

"What's a democracy?" Ives asked with a curled lip, never ashamed to disclose his ignorance.

"We had those in Nassau," said Harry Harmless. "Kept us up all night with their squawking."

"It ain't a bird, you idiot," said Duncan.

"Well, what is it then?"

Salvador looked down with a contrite expression, as though sympathy for the sand would give him the answer.

235

"It's what we was,"—Duncan interlocked his fingers in a ball, and then opened both hands and spread his arms as if simulating an explosion— "but we isn't no more."

Kate clasped a hand over the pommel of the cutlass to cease its wobbling. "It worked fine until you idiots elected a captain who would've run my ship aground first chance he got."

Gabe's laugh was bitter. "So, what are you now, our queen? Can we even call ourselves pirates anymore?"

She slowly drew the cutlass from the sand. "Call yourselves what you like. We change or we die. The world is water, and it wears away all that is solid. We too must be fluid."

Gabe was biting his lip, wrestling against contradiction. He failed. "But, you're still the captain. Nothing really changed."

She aimed her cutlass at him, arm rigid with righteousness. "Shut up, Gabe."

JUNGLE

The sky was violet with salmon hues bordering the east and black clouds encroaching from the west when Kate woke the seven men. She had slept an hour, maybe two, tossing and turning in the sand with her back constantly antagonizing her. Before her injury, she had loved few things more than spending a night on a beach, but now the grains of sand that slipped beneath her shirt were a terror on her skin. She dreamt of fire and water, of burning flesh being extinguished and steam rising in a vast hole deep in the earth, the blue sky far above with the slender outline of a woman eclipsing the sun at the circumference, looking down on her and laughing.

The men cooked half of the eggs and washed them down with rum, and everyone was lightly inebriated and happily sated by the time she ordered them to pack up. Ives filled a sack with a dozen grenadoes from the crates and slung it over his shoulder. Harry Harmless, Duncan, and Salvador took two extra pistols each, swapped out the dulled flints on those that needed replacing, and primed the pistols from their ammunition pouches. Joseph sharpened his cutlass, declining an extra pistol when Duncan offered. Israel Hands primed a musket with a cartridge from a cartouche box, and then he spent a good while polishing it with a cloth. "That'll do you no good in the jungle," Corso said. Hands ignored him while picking sand from the weapon's many crevices, his expression hard and diligent behind dreadlocks dangling over his face. When he was done, he strapped the musket to his back and belted the cartouche box to his hip.

The first sliver of the morning sun peeked over the eastern ridge as they started into the jungle. Kate took a last look at the *Persephone*, black against the grey ocean. She had considered setting it on fire, on the off-chance Jacqueline and some of her men might return, but something held her back. She had ordered Gabe to circle back in *Scarlet Devil* and keep a close watch on the southern beach while she was gone. She warned him to stay away from dark waters of the eastern beach.

They moved northward into the jungle, through the palm trees. The dark silhouettes of small monkeys watched them from above. Corso and Salvador gathered fallen coconuts, tossing away those that had cracked on impact. Hummingbirds with green mohawks zipped past, pausing briefly to acknowledge their new visitors. A big iguana resting atop a boulder in a rare spot of sunlight angled one eyeball at them, but refused to move even as they passed within two feet. The ground inclined sharply for a time, and they climbed up rocks and fallen trees covered in moss. Harry Harmless made the mistake of scrambling hastily over a trunk, boasting about how fast he was, lost his footing and struck his jaw on a boulder, giving his chin an exaggerated purple swelling.

They were drenched in sweat when the ground finally levelled off, and they entered a grove of tall ceiba trees supported by huge, twisting buttress roots that Kate and the men had to move around and climb over.

After a few hundred careful paces, the trees opened to a rolling green meadow spotted with colorful flowers. In the center was the husk of some old stone monument, clearly man-made. Kate hurried across the field, not waiting for the others. The long grass dampened her breeches as she moved through. She stepped on a cracked bed of stone, which encircled the monument like a giant plate. The pillar was severed a third of the way up, the long upper half lying toppled to one side. A once-intricate carving had been weathered down, and now only soft indentations remained. Three faces were stacked at the top of the fallen pillar. Two male faces had been dulled to an impassive obscurity, and the third at the top was mostly chipped away above a feminine mouth. Kate touched the base, and the dark grey stone was cold despite the warmth of the sun beating down on it.

Something prompted her gaze west. The dark clouds were rolling in, and soon the sun would be gone. She turned to the group as they approached and said, "We'll rest here for a spell. It will be raining soon."

"Feel like it already is," said Corso as he freed himself of his coat. He peeled the shirt from his skin and fanned himself.

"Least it won't be so hot," said Duncan.

"There's that," Kate agreed. She pointed at Corso's coat. "Hand me that, would you?"

He tossed it over. "Won't be needing it."

She removed her leather harness and wrapped the four pistols in the coat to prevent them from getting wet. She circumvented the fallen monument and took a seat in the column of shade cast from the lower half. Corso joined her with a bottle of rum and two coconuts, offering her one. She struck it open with her cutlass and drank some of the juice, fully aware of Salvador and Harry Harmless ogling her chest as she tossed back her head. She separated the two halves of the coconut, uncorked the bottle and poured rum inside to mingle with the remaining juice. She let it sit there for a moment while she leaned back against the cold stone of the fallen monument. She ran her fingers through her short hair and massaged her scalp. Her eyelids grew heavy, and she closed them for what seemed but an instant.

"Do you have any idea where you're going?"

She opened her eyes. Hands stood over her. She didn't remember falling asleep. "Aye," she said, blinking. She pointed at the tallest peak. "That way."

He crouched before her and gestured at the bottle of rum. "May I?"

"No," said Corso, snatching the bottle and taking a large swig.

Hands wrinkled his hooked nose, frustrated. "What is it you're expecting to find out here, Kate?"

"Maybe you can help me with that." She rubbed her eyes, which only seemed to make her more tired. "What was Jacqueline expecting to find? Don't tell me she didn't confide her true motives. She came here in a hurry to . . . what, exactly? Investigate a rumor?"

"So did you. When you were able."

She tried not to think about Gabe and Jacqueline's naked bodies entangled in the sheets. "I was obliged to follow. She stole a friend."

Hands studied her for a moment. "That's not why you're here."

The sky darkened. The column of shadow was lost against the cracked stone that surrounded the monument. The first raindrop tapped Kate's head, traversing easily through her shortened hair and cooling her scalp. "You're evading. I know why I'm here. Why is Jacqueline here?"

Hands blinked as rain pattered his forehead. "Not for treasure. Far as I know, there's no treasure to be had. Not the shiny kind, anyway. She's here to find a man."

Corso chuckled. "She came all this way for that? Men come to her, I should think."

Hands' eyes irritably flickered Corso's way. "Not that kind of man. A man of some import. A man who has eluded the Crown."

Kate picked up one half of coconut and sipped at the sweetened rum. "We've all eluded the Crown. What makes this man so special?"

"Woodes Rogers has placed a bounty on him, but he's done so in secret. He's informed all the right people. The kind of people who have no true loyalty to the Crown. People who are one ill-choice from being . . ." He glanced apprehensively at Corso and thought better of finishing his sentence.

"People like us?" Kate finished for him.

"Yes. People like you."

She laughed. "I always knew Rogers was little more than a pirate hiding behind the Crown. I told him as much when he held me in his custody."

Hands nodded. "He doesn't want George the Second to know what he's planning."

"And what is he planning?"

He shrugged. "I don't know. All I know is Rogers wants this man as some kind of leverage over the new king, and he's prepared to offer a considerable sum to retrieve him. Alive."

Corso leaned forward. "How considerable?"

Hands cleared his throat and glanced about in a conspiratorial manner, but none of the others were listening; they were too busy sheltering their weapons to keep the powder from getting wet. "As I understand it, the kind of sum a person might purchase vast quantities of land and retire with."

The rain was falling consistently now, pattering the stone. Kate finished her rum and tossed the coconut aside. "If his debts are so great, where would Rogers get that kind of money?"

"All those pirates he captured years past," Hands explained. "He confiscated a portion of whatever he found in their holds. Including a sizable stash of silver bars. Before his death, George the First suspected Rogers was holding back, and he hoped to teach him a lesson, but Rogers kept it quiet, even as he endured confinement. He couldn't exactly buy his freedom with silver he wasn't meant to have in the first place."

"And how did Jacqueline come across this information? I can't picture Woodes Rogers confiding in Blackbeard's daughter, let alone from across the sea."

"Through me," Hands said.

Kate reached forward suddenly, seizing him by the collar.

Fire swept up her back as she drew him toward her. She let the grief of her wound percolate her voice. "Do you know what I do to British spies who sell out pirates?"

He innocently raised his hands. "I assure you, I'm a simple seaman who was approached by one of Rogers' agents in Bristol. I was minding my own business, enjoying my chowder while reading the shipping news, as is my custom on Sunday mornings, when an unfamiliar man with a humorless temperament took the seat opposite me. He told me to relay the news only to parties who would not associate themselves with the Crown, and he made sure I caught his drift. Said if the information got back to King George, he'd find me and open my throat. Normally that kind of threat would amuse me, but when this man spoke, I knew he was serious. I kept the information to myself until I fell in with Teach's daughter."

Kate released him and sat back, shaking her head in disgust. "I helped her. She feigned a casual interest, but I was helping her this whole time."

He nodded slowly. "Rogers has been looking for your coat for some time. He's sent all manner of shady sorts your way. No doubt you've encountered a few."

"Bartholomew Roberts," she replied grimly.

"A man who was dead, as England tells it."

"He may well have been." She thought back on the odd pairing of Roberts and Sterling. The Bartholomew Roberts she had met had been nothing more than a silent beast, enraged by the death of the man who spoke for him. "He is dead now, sincerely. I saw to it. History won't know the difference."

"That's the way you like it, I expect."

She inclined her head. "Perhaps you're less stupid than

you look."

Hands looked north, toward the peaks, which were now obscured by clouds. "Jacqueline had no idea the clue to this place was under her nose all this time, thanks to her father. Not that any good came from it. If she's alive, she would've come back by now. There are people here, I tell you. Gabe and I, we heard strange things one night, from the jungle. Like birds, but not birds. We snuffed out our fire and slept in the ship that night, and I swear we heard things scraping on the hull, like they knew we were inside and they were taunting us. Gabe said it was just crabs, but he knew better."

Corso shot Kate an amused glance. "Or maybe it was crabs."

Hands scanned the jungle perimeter. "They're probably watching us now."

"The crabs?"

He glared at Corso. "I hope you're right."

Kate opened her palm. The scabs were gone, but the faint indents of teeth remained. "This man of import . . . what is his name?"

"He goes by the name of Armitage, though I doubt that's his true name."

She closed her eyes and saw the indistinct man from her dream. A tall shadow with a pale white face and a scar sealing his right eye. "Armitage," she said. "Ash spoke of him."

"He's likely dead by now," said Hands. "I told Jacqueline as much, but she wouldn't listen."

"The man was probably never here in the first place," said Corso. "This is all for nothing."

"He's here," said Kate. "Or he was."

Hands tossed his head, flinging the heavy, wet dreads out of his eyes. "How can you know that?"

Because I saw him, she almost said, but she knew they would only think her insane. "You'll have to take my word on it."

"Seeing as you'll kill me if I do anything other than take you at your word, I suppose I must."

She winced from the protests of her back as she stood. "I might kill you either way, Israel. I haven't decided yet."

He blinked up at her through the thickening rainfall. "Then I pray you will take my transparency into consideration when you make your decision."

"Maybe I will." She picked up Corso's coat with her pistols inside and tucked it under one arm. "Or maybe I'll flip a coin."

"That would be imprudent."

"I am a woman of imprudence."

She gathered up the men and they continued north into the jungle. The rain was pouring in thick sheets, but the dense jungle canopy sheltered them somewhat. The ground sloped and they carefully made their way down moss-covered rocks as the world around them plunged into deepening shades of green and brown, with fleeting glimpses of ashen sky through rare gaps in the trees. Streams of mud gushed through deep fissures in the uneven terrain. The air was crisp with the scent of wet vegetation and earth.

They descended over a hundred feet down a winding stream that cut a path through the rocks, leading them into a canyon so deeply removed from the light it appeared to be twilight, though it was nearing midday. Here there were giant leaves and blue and purple flora. The trees were taller and their trunks thicker, struggling to reach the light somewhere above. Those that had failed had become black and hollow stumps blanketed in moss. The bark that littered the bed of the canyon was dark and wet, giving off a musty scent. A river ran through the throat of the canyon, ten feet across at its broadest point. Crystalline waters swept under the trunk of a fallen tree and washed over smooth rocks. Kate dropped to her knees at the riverbank and dipped her hands in the surprisingly cold water. A little fish darted away from her fingers, its scales flashing silver. She splashed her face and was momentarily invigorated. She craned her neck and saw only slivers of dull grey through the canopy. Rainwater collected in the leaves above, bowing the branches and eventually spilling downward in large droplets. Kate looked to the branches for dark shapes, but if there were any monkeys here they were keeping quiet and out of sight. There was only the patter of rain and the constant flow of rushing water. A green frog hopped away from Kate's feet, bounding over the water and touching down on a floating leaf. She smiled. The world of cities and ships and trade and conquest seemed so very far from this primordial place. Down here it was hard to believe a civilized world had ever existed.

Harry Harmless ruined the moment. "Crikey, this hurts," he exclaimed as he crouched beside her and splashed water on his swollen jaw, rubbing at it furiously.

"Best watch your footing or you'll crack the back of your skull next time," Corso warned.

"What is that?" Salvador blurted suddenly, sprinting upriver. He halted before the fallen tree and peered over it, struggling to see around the bend where the canyon walls hooked northeast. He looked back, eyes wide with alarm. "Did anyone else see that?"

Corso looked at the others. "No."

But Salvador did not wait for confirmation or denial. He

scrambled over the tree and slid down the opposite side, and soon he was lost from view.

"Do we go after him?" Joseph wondered.

Kate remained where she was. "He'll run out of breath eventually."

Ives unsheathed his sword and tapped his thigh with the blade. "Said he saw something."

Corso shrugged one shoulder. "An animal would be my wager."

Hands gazed upriver while bending forward to rub his sore leg. "Not wise to chase animals in their environment. This is not our land. We're just, uh, uh . . ."

"Visitors?" Kate suggested with an arched eyebrow.

"Yes," Hands said. He frowned. "That's weird."

"What's weird?"

"It's an easy word, is all. Visitors. Strange thing to forget."

Corso laughed. "You've been sleeping on a beach too long, mate."

"It was probably a jaguar," said Joseph.

"Don't think islands got those," said Duncan as he waddled down the final cluster of rocks and finally joined them beside the river. He set his hands on his knees and wheezed.

Joseph didn't appear convinced. "Are you sure about that?"

Duncan took a deep breath. "Heard they was mainland cats."

"Aye," Harry Harmless agreed, "but they can jump a long ways."

"Hell with cats," said Duncan. "They isn't natural creatures."

Hands approached the fallen tree and stood on his toes. "I do not believe the Spaniard is coming back."

247

Ives spat in the river. "Spaniards got no sense of direction."

Kate's eyelids began to feel heavy as she gazed into the clear water. She wanted to spread out on the bank and let the moist, cool air caress her skin while the rushing water sang her to sleep. She forced herself up. "We had better get moving," she said.

Duncan opened his arms in protest as everyone followed Kate upriver. "I just got here, didn't I?"

They followed the river through the canyon for what felt like a mile, but found no trace of Salvador. The jungle grew darker. Thunder sounded, rolling over the tops of the swaying trees. Wind shrieked through the branches. The canyon hooked northeast and then north again. Eventually it hooked sharply northwest. They left the river and continued north along steadily-inclining ground, over big rocks and through a forest of tall pine trees. The ground levelled off and the trees grew sparse, the canopy opening to menacing grey skies where the rain fell freely. They trekked onward through a field of bushes yielding black berries spotted with purple. "Don't eat those," Kate warned.

Corso's thumb and forefinger halted just above a particularly plump berry. "Poisonous?"

"That's one word for it." She urged them to keep moving, waving her hand to the back of the group. Duncan was, of course, far behind.

Hands increased his pace, falling in alongside her and adjusting the musket on his back. "How is it you know so much about this island?"

Kate drew her cutlass and hacked through a stubborn thicket. "I've seen these berries before. I've seen what they can do."

"Where? I've never seen them."

In a dream, she didn't say. "Help yourself to a bite if you don't believe me."

"Duncan!" Harry Harmless blurted.

Kate turned to see Duncan cramming as many berries into his mouth as he could fit. His cheeks were plump, his mouth stained black. "Whut?" he mumbled through a black and purple glob, juices dribbling down his chin.

"Captain told us not to." Harry favored Kate with a thumbs-up to let her know he could handle this. "It's not a democracy, remember?"

Duncan defiantly stuffed two more berries in his mouth and struggled to chew as his face turned red, his one beady eye glaring fiercely at Harry. "Me belly recognizes no form of government, matriarchal or elsewise."

Harry licked his lips. "Well, what's it taste like, anyhows?"

"Tastes like a pig's dick, but that ain't the point!" Duncan shot back angrily, sputtering little chunks of berry all over himself. "Famished, I is! Running after all o' you in this damnable weather. Up hills and rocks, scraping me paws and gashing up me knees. It's madness! After all that, I won't be told what I can and can't put down me gull—" The little man's body instantly went rigid and he toppled forward with the grace of a plank, crushing the bush before him.

"He's had it," Ives declared without closer inspection.

"Goddammit," Kate muttered.

She trudged back through the bushes and crouched beside him, placing two fingers beneath his nose. Rain hammered his face and collected in the hollows of his eyes, but he did not so much as blink. She shoved her fingers in his gaping mouth and scooped out the remaining glob of chewed berries so he wouldn't choke. She shut his jaw to keep the rain out. "He's alive, but I'll understand if no one wants to carry him."

"I will carry him," said Joseph. He easily scooped up the little man and flung him over his shoulder.

"Stronger than you look," Ives observed.

"He is not so heavy."

They continued into the jungle, where they once again found shelter from the rain, but the ground was treacherously muddy. Despite the added weight of Duncan, Joseph kept up and silently navigated the mud without incident, easily stepping over cracks and avoiding slippery rocks. After another hour or so they came to a steep crag that vanished into the low cloud layer, and they had no choice but to head east along the base of the rocky wall. Soon they came upon the yawning mouth of a cave cut into the crag.

"Maybe your Spaniard is in there," Hands offered.

"Could be anywhere," Corso said. "Don't know what he was thinking."

Kate looked to the darkening clouds. "Sun will be setting soon. Don't think we'll find a better spot to camp."

"I am not going in there," Harry Harmless said.

"Fine. You can stand watch."

Kate went inside first, sidestepping worn-down stalagmites and dodging sharper, low-hanging stalactites. A little stream trickled down the middle of the cave's smooth floor toward the entrance. She delved twenty paces before she stopped and stared into the impenetrable darkness. "Hello!" she called, and her raspy voice echoed down a long passage. The howl of the wind rushing through the tunnel answered back, bringing with it a bracing chill that cut straight through her clothes. "We should gather some firewood," she told the others.

Firelight filled the cave at dusk, projecting exaggerated, warped shadows of stalagmites over the glistening walls, dancing like natives performing a ritual. They cooked some of the remaining turtle eggs and opened a few of the coconuts Ives had thrown in his bag to mingle with the grenadoes, and afterward they passed around a bottle of rum. Joseph and Harry Harmless were framed in dark blue at the mouth of the cave, engaged in a game of dice. Duncan was spread flat near one wall, his chest barely rising and falling. Kate, Corso, and Ives sat close to the fire.

Israel Hands was perched on a rock, his musket running up between his legs with the barrel resting on one shoulder. "What do you suppose that statue was? No one's talking about that statue we saw earlier."

"What statue?" Corso said.

"The broken one."

"There are people here," Kate said. "Or there *were*. Isn't that obvious by now? Natives. They built it."

Corso looked at the ground and rubbed the back of his head with a perplexed scowl. "I don't remember a statue."

"It was hard to miss," Hands replied with a derisive titter. "We stopped there."

Corso shook his head slightly. "I remember . . . rocks."

"A few more years and that's all they'll be," said Kate.

Corso smiled, but when he looked at her she glimpsed an uncertainty in his eyes that made her wonder if she had something on her face. He seemed on the verge of saying something, but he kept it to himself.

"Where do you suppose Salvador got off to?" Ives asked.

"I don't know," Kate said. "Domingo is going to kill me if I don't bring his brother back in one piece."

"Well, if he's got hisself in trouble, I'm not going out of my way to save him anytime soon." Ives took a swig of rum and offered it to Hands.

Kate snatched the bottle before Hands could partake. She took a sip and set it at her side. "You're a good friend, Ives."

"Spaniard isn't my friend. Hawkes was my friend."

"So, you *are* angry about that."

He feigned indifference as he stared into the fire. "Didn't need to burn him, is all. Burning's a hard way to go."

The rough fabric of Kate's shirt aggravated the raw skin of her back as she shifted her weight. "I know."

Ives looked at her with narrow, glassy eyes. Drunkenness had boosted his nerve. "Sometimes I think you enjoy it."

"Enjoy what?"

"Murder."

"Sometimes I do," she admitted. "Sometimes I don't. I did not enjoy killing that girl you meant to rape, but I enjoyed killing your friend. I enjoyed his surprise. The recognition that I had bested him. I had wanted to kill him for a long time, truth be told, but until that moment he hadn't given me proper cause to do so. I knew he'd give me a reason eventually. Whenever he spoke to me, whenever he smiled at me while picturing me naked, I saw a man who did not know he was dead. And after I killed him, I found myself content." She met Ives' hard glare. "Are you saying you've never enjoyed it?"

He blinked and returned his eyes to the fire. "I'm a man. It's different for me."

Kate laughed. "Well, you're right about that."

His gaunt face seemed to grow longer as he struggled for a response. He pointed. "Your heart is as ugly as your ear,

252

woman."

"Could be worse. Could be my entire face."

He stood, flustered. "Was that a slight?"

She smiled. "Yes. That was a slight. I was insinuating your face is hideous."

Hands moved his musket from one shoulder to the other. All this talk of murder was clearly making him uncomfortable. "Is that how you see me, Captain Warlowe? A man who does not know he is dead? Because it will greatly disappoint my daughter if I am not returned to her in one piece."

Kate snorted. "You don't have a daughter, Israel."

"In fact I do."

"How old is she?"

"She is eight." He chewed on his lower lip and looked at a stalactite. "No, she would be nine now. I've been gone a long—"

"I don't believe you." She was tired of men trying to appeal to her maternal instincts.

He leaned forward on his musket, hands gripping the barrel. "How would you know one way or the other?"

"I wouldn't," she admitted. "I've never had a child, and truthfully I don't really want one. I wouldn't know a damn thing about it." She placed a hand on Corso's shoulder. "But he would."

Corso withered slightly under her touch, shifting his eyes tentatively her way. "What do you mean? Why would I know?"

She frowned at him. "Because you were a father."

"If I am, someone forgot to tell me."

Kate squeezed his shoulder. "Corso, what is the matter with you? You had a daughter. You told me as much."

"You're mistaken." He was trying not to look at her, but his eyes sporadically locked with hers, and she didn't like what she saw there. Or rather, what she *didn't* see there. "You have me mistaken for someone else."

"I don't think I'd misremember something like—"

Corso swept her hand from his shoulder and stood. The fire sent shadows slithering over his face, contorting his kind features with confusion and mounting dread. He raised his hands defensively and backed steadily into the darkness of the cave. "I must beg your pardon," he said, "but I have no idea who you are. I don't know who any of you are."

"Corso," she said, standing, "be careful."

Corso continued to back away, his features darkening, feet lightly shuffling on the smooth bedrock. And then there was another sound, distant, from within the cave somewhere behind him. He paused, features half-shaded. Kate thought she heard a whisper, but it was not from Corso. It might have been the wind washing up the tunnel, but she felt no breeze now.

"What is that?" Ives said, pointing past Corso. "Oh, Jesus, what is that?"

Kate squinted. "I don't see any—"

A sliver of fire shot downward from above Corso's head, splitting his skull down to his nostrils with a tremendous *crack*. Tremors racked his body from top to bottom, like a man possessed. The weapon was wrenched from his head by some unseen force, fire dancing in shards of sharpened black glass. Corso's eyes spread absurdly far apart, staring two separate directions. When his legs finally buckled and his knees smacked the ground, brains oozed out of the cleft in his skull. He remained there on his knees for a moment, trembling and sputtering nonsense through the gore washing over his lips. He collapsed forward.

A shadow stood in Corso's place, black eyes gleaming in the firelight.

SHADOWS

There was no time to mourn the loss of her friend, let alone contemplate unseen forces that had robbed him of his mind before his abrupt demise. Nor could she bear the sight of addled brains slavering from the chasm in his skull. She had seen too many friends reduced to nothing more than their clammy, blushing innerworkings, all traces of humanity lost in a stew of bone and carnage. Corso was yet another in a long ledger, and she had grown accustomed to filing that ledger away. It seemed wrong to discard him so hastily, but she hadn't the time for anything more. Maybe later. If there was a later.

There was, however, time enough for vengeance. With little forethought, she snapped the pistol from her hip and fired into the darkness. The report echoed down the tunnel, but the shadow stood impervious. She lobbed the pistol and heard it clatter uselessly against the rock somewhere in the deep recesses from which the interloper had materialized.

"You missed," Ives noted unnecessarily.

"I don't believe I did," Kate replied. She'd heard the shot hit something wet, and her nostrils picked up the distinctive scent of steel burning through flesh.

"I won't miss," Ives said. He stretched his arm, aimed his pistol carefully, with one eye squeezed shut and his tongue curled over his upper lip, and fired. The shadow seemed a black void that swallowed all light, and possibly gunshot. Ives looked at the smoking pistol, mystified. "Something wrong with these pistols."

"I'll take care of this," Hands said. He crouched, resting an elbow on one raised knee, and aimed his musket. The report was deafening. The shadow remained upright and maddeningly still in the dark. "That's not probable," Hands muttered, staring at his musket.

Kate inched backwards, glancing at Corso's folded coat near the fire and wondering if the guns packed inside would make any difference. "I think you mean impossible."

"No, I mean it's a thing that cannot happen."

Kate looked to the sack of grenadoes, where Duncan was resting comfortably, oblivious to the horrors of the waking world. She knew if she lit a grenado in here she was just as likely to kill herself along with any attackers, but maybe the threat would be enough to ward them off. She hesitated nonetheless. The grenadoes could wait until she'd exhausted all options. *No need to blow myself up quite yet.*

"What's happening in there?" Harry Harmless called.

Kate turned, raising a hand. "Just stay back!"

"What is that?" Harry said, hunching forward and squinting. "Is it a man?"

"Shut up and kill it," Ives shouted.

Before he could aim his pistol, Harry's body jolted sharply. He swiveled sideways and Kate saw a spear sticking out of his back. Harry wobbled this way and that, like a drunken man attempting to stand for the first time in an hour. His knees buckled him into a casual crouch, and he let out a little yelp when he saw a jagged black tip protruding from his chest. "How'd that get there?" he wondered. His body lost any semblance of rigidity, folding in on itself like a worm.

Joseph screamed and darted away from the cave, making a mad dash for the jungle. "Back to the ship!" he cried. "Back to the shiiiiii—" His voice faded into the distance.

"Joseph, get back here!" Kate called, but it was no use. That spear had to have come from somewhere, and Joseph was running straight toward it. She pivoted to face the more immediate problem.

From the dark of the cave the shadow lumbered toward them. The light revealed a horrifying golem of a man who seemed to have been forged of pure muscle and dipped in the deep, wet rummages of the earth. His impossibly dark flesh ran with tiny cracks, like scales. His black chest was broad and powerful. He wore nothing more than a tattered loincloth and a small headdress of limp feathers. He was shorter than most men, but strongly built. If he had a face, it was indecipherable in the gloom, but his eyes ensnared the fire. In one hand he brandished a club lined with razor-sharp obsidian shards, in the other a spear. He raised the spear, aiming the obsidian tip at Kate.

"Hands, Ives," she said without looking back at them, "make for the exit."

"But there's more of them out there," Hands protested.

"I know. You'll go right. Ives, go left. I'll go straight into the jungle."

Ives grasped her suddenly by the arms and spun her around to face him. "What are you doing?!" she demanded, but his eyes were swirling with terror. "Let go of me!"

Finally, his eyes locked with hers, boiling with righteous indictment. "This is your fault."

She almost laughed. "What?"

He squeezed her arms and shook her violently. "You brought us here, you red bitch."

"Remove your hands!"

Ives shoved her to the ground, prostrating her before the thing that had murdered Corso. "Take her, devil!" he cried. "Take the woman! You can have her anyway you like! She's yours! She's the one brought us here! We wanted no part in it!"

"Jesus, man!" she heard Hands protest.

But Ives couldn't be reasoned with. "She will kill us all!"

The shadow hurtled the spear. It sailed over Kate's head and plunged into Ives' belly. He clutched the wooden shaft and stretched his gaunt face into a silent shriek as he fell on his ass near the fire.

The shadow took two paces toward Kate, staring down at her with eyes of fire. She thrust a hand in protest, slapping pathetically at his foot. Her fingers sunk into cold, wet flesh, and she retracted her hand in disgust. Her fingers came away slimy with mud. She glimpsed brown flesh where she had touched him. She craned her neck, following the man's stout legs upward. The firelight shimmered in the mud he had caked himself with, from head to toe. It was dry in patches, cracking from movement. Blood oozed from a

259

small hole in the center of his chest, pouring down his belly in a steady stream. At least one of their shots had struck him, but he seemed undaunted.

The shadow lifted the war club over its head. Obsidian shards scraped the top of the cave. Kate pressed both palms flat against the smooth bedrock and pushed herself to her feet. She retreated just as the club swept past her face. Three of the shards shattered into tinier pieces where the club forcefully impacted the ground just inches from Kate's feet.

Hands took up Duncan's cutlass and made for the exit.

Kate nearly tripped over Ives' legs in her haste to follow. She stopped there, looking down at him. He held the spear with one hand and reached for her with the other, struggling to speak. "It's . . . the . . . Devil."

She seized the spear, wrenching it this way and that, wriggling it out of him.

"NO," he shrieked in terror and agony. "DON'T TAKE IT OUT!! YOU'LL KILL—"

"I know," she assured him with a smile. She heaved the spear upward, lifting Ives into a writhing arch. He fell limp as the obsidian tip slid free, pursued by a brief, sputtering geyser of blood. His eyes went dull immediately. She spat at his corpse, wishing she'd killed him a long time ago, but every man played his part, and maybe he had inadvertently saved her life.

She returned her attention to the shadow, which was lumbering toward her, hefting the club for another attack. She reared back and thrust the spear with everything she had, fire licking her back from either the campfire or the scar, or both. The spear struck the dead center of his chest, halting his advance. The club tumbled from his grasp as he shambled backwards. Burning eyes regarded her with some-

260

thing that might have been respect. And then the fire was gone, and he fell in a black heap.

Kate smirked down at Ives. "That wasn't the Devil, you fool. It was only a man."

She started for the exit, but froze in her tracks when she saw what was waiting for her. Three silhouettes stood there, framed by the jungle. The tallest stood in the center, with a full-feathered headdress and an elaborate beaded necklace. Unlike the others, he was not painted in mud. His skin was a pale contrast, white as a ghost even by the warm ambience of firelight. His eyes were red-orange, like twin suns against a pallid sky. His skin was running with cracks, flaking like a snake from head to foot. He held a war club in one hand and a decapitated head in the other, both dribbling blood. He tossed the head forward, flexing the lithe muscles of his arm. It rolled down the cave, stopping just short of Kate's feet. Salvador's confused face gawked up at her. *There you are, you poor fool.*

She dove for the sack next to Duncan, who was still slumbering through the chaos. Her elbow landed on his chest, causing his lips to sputter a puff of air, but he did not wake. She tore open the sack and withdrew two grenadoes. The two men flanking the pale man entered the cave. She returned to the fire and dipped both fuses in the flames. "Stay back," she warned, displaying the sizzling fuses. "You know what this is?"

The shadows halted briefly, and then started forward again. She tossed the grenadoes at their feet. The pale one swiftly backed away as the steel canisters clattered toward him. He trained his red eyes on Kate as he retreated from the cave, while the other two remained, staring dumbly at the bizarre contraptions at their feet. They looked at each other. Kate ran into the darkness and flung herself to the ground, covering her head. Her ears were impacted by a tremendous force, constricting walls of air, but she didn't hear the blast. Heat blasted her back, ripping her shirt from her breeches and hiking it up about her upper torso. A tremor rolled under her and the bedrock cracked, propelling her upward. Little pebbles rained down around her, drumming her bare back and terrorizing her scar. A long stalactite impaled the ground a few inches from her face. She rolled out of the way before a second hit the spot where she'd been cowering, crumbling on impact. Tiny embers billowed into the cave. Dust wafted over the campfire but couldn't quite snuff it out. The mouth of the cave had collapsed on at least two of the interlopers, crushing and mangling them beyond recognition. Only twisted limbs and pulverized bits of skull and teeth remained, and the many crevices in the rubble shed tears of blood.

She sat up, heaving violently. Dust crept down her throat with every hoarse breath. She gripped her chest and held her breath, willing herself not to cough again. Little stars danced before her, twirling all about. Gradually they faded one by one. When the urge to cough passed, she let the air in through her nostrils, and she felt her heart decelerating to a manageable rate. She pulled her shirt down, hastily stuffing it back into her breeches. The scar seemed to shriek with every movement, and she imagined the red devil's skeletal jawbone coming unhinged and its elongated fangs spread wide in agony as she curled forward. She regimented the pain to the back of her mind, where it would accompany the friends she had lost, including Corso.

She crawled over to Duncan. Astonishingly, he was still asleep and unhurt, apart from a few scrapes and scuffs on his arms and forehead. She saw no point in attempting to wake a man who had slept through an explosion, and she couldn't muster much sympathy. If he perished in his sleep, he'd be the lucky one.

The campfire dimmed as steady streams of dirt and little pebbles sifted from fissures in the ceiling. Kate found Corso's coat and rolled it open, catching two of the pistols and letting the others clatter to the ground. She dropped the coat and closed her eyes, preparing herself to venture deeper into the cave. She knew there had to be another exit, due to the wind she had felt earlier.

A cold, wet hand fell upon her shoulder. She stiffened. Another hand fell on the opposite shoulder. And then another on her back. And another. She turned swiftly, but they seized her wrists, bending her arms awkwardly until pain shot through her wrists. Her fingers opened and the two pistols fell away. She prayed it would be over as quickly for her as it had been for the others. Their muddy fingers fumbled at her arms and legs, digging painfully into her ribs and groping areas no man should touch without permission. They elevated her nearly to the ceiling and carried her through toothy columns of stalactites into the darkness.

Beady eyes gazed down at her from above, swaying this way and that. She reached for them, and there came a collective screech, shrill and deafening, and the little creatures fell from their perches. Their rubbery wings assaulted her face, fluttering against her cheeks. She raised her hands to shield herself and felt coarse fur and needle-like teeth. They swept about her in a reverential hurricane, before swarming away, toward the fire, where the exit should have been. She craned her neck to watch them swirl about the fire with nowhere else to go. And there, beyond the swarm of bats, standing before the collapsed rubble, she saw a slender young woman with short blonde hair and pale wet skin. Her clothes hung off her in ragged shreds, baring one breast. Only one eye remained, watching Kate impassively. Her right eye had been carved out, leaving nothing but a black socket that trickled green fluids down her cheek, into her mouth.

The fire flared and the bats scattered. The girl vanished somewhere beyond the flames.

Kate's frenzied screams reverberated off the warped walls, assailing her ears. Deeper and deeper they took her, marching her into the black depths of the earth, until her voice broke and she heard only the wretched, desperate rasps of a dead woman.

IMPOSTER

When she regained consciousness, she saw tall trees swaying in the wind, leaves shimmering in low orange light. Heat blistered her cheeks as she was carried down a long, winding road walled by flaring torches. Four pairs of hands held her legs and supported her back. She could only discern vague impressions of the men who carried her. Their stony faces were expressionless, their jaws hard and set, ashen eyes aimed forward, never blinking. They had long, stringy black hair which seemed to merge with their shoulders. The mud had dried to form a second skin that gave off the musty scent of rotten earth. She could not bear to look at them for long.

The skeletal remains of buildings came into view through the dense foliage, broken limestone walls strewn with traces of red and white paint, entangled in thick vines. Eyes watched her from within the hollowed structures, dozens of twin pinpoints, lambent in the dark. In those dark spaces she saw creatures who had mistaken themselves for humans, however briefly, and now the earth sought to reclaim its resources and those who dwelled within.

The road straightened and the trees opened wide. They carried her through the ruins of what had once been a great city, down a thoroughfare once so heavily traversed that the ground had become hard and barren, but diligent weeds poked through here and there. The bare heels of the men beneath her sloshed steadily through muddy puddles, never losing their footing. Most of the stone incense burners that lined the walkway had been decapitated, but a few heads remained. Smoke billowed from sizzling torch fire in the rain. Dilapidated structures on her left ascended into darkness, too many to count and haphazardly placed, as though they had been built hastily and without foresight to accommodate a rapidly growing civilization. Huts scaled the steep eastern slope on her right, as in her dream, but now they were dirty and listing, and many had collapsed. Each oval hut stood atop a stone base and was topped with a domed roof of dried palm leaves. Silhouetted figures stood within the open doorways, all of them bulky and clearly male. *Where are all their women?* she wondered.

As they carried her further into the city, the buildings on her left grew dense and large, and soon she was carried past a two-hundred-foot-long rectangular complex. It stood atop a thirty-foot sloped platform. Red walls burned with torchlight, illuminating the heavily decorated frieze that ran along the building's upper half. Sculpted serpents navigated the mosaic façade, slithering in square tessellations from one end to the other. Bas-reliefs showcasing various figures decorated the wide columns that supported a patio along the front. A grand stairway of some thirty steps led up to the middle of the structure, where a narrow, triangular corridor, three times as tall as a man, cut through to the other side, but she could see only darkness beyond. Someone had taken great care in designing this place, and she could only assume it was a palace.

Not long after the palace, she was carried through the same pair of jaguar statues she had seen in her dream. One had misplaced its head, while the other stood oblivious to its twin's decapitation. Its yawning mouth threatened to devour some distant enemy. Its fangs had been worn down and its features had been dulled, but it was more menacing by torchlight than it had been by day, through the eyes of the other woman.

The four men carried her down the steps into a sunken courtyard, where thick vines reached through cracks in the limestone, glistening with sap and dew, like the tentacles of a kraken bursting forth. She imagined the ground as nothing more than a thin plate that might break apart at any moment, depositing all above into the sea to be consumed by ancient monstrosities that prowled underwater caverns running through the globe, where they saw darkness as lustrously as daylight, through stalked eyes that had adapted over the centuries as they patiently awaited the world's end. Her stomach reeled at the dizzying contemplation and its brief but potent veracity, and she squeezed shut her eyes and held her breath as a curdled blend of coconut, rum, and eggs ascended her throat in a nauseating bubble. Tears burned the seams of her eyelids. Though she would've been happy to rain vomit on the men beneath her, she did not wish to soil herself in the process.

"Where are you taking me?" she demanded, after the nausea subsided. The men carrying her remained silent. She wondered if they could talk, and briefly, absurdly, if they were even alive.

They halted in the middle of the courtyard and eased her down onto the uneven stone, in a sitting position. Two departed, leaving the other two to guard her. One was tall and bulky, with a white band painted across his eyes, slashing through the mud that caked his face, and a necklace of jade beads interspersed with long, pointy teeth, probably from a large cat. Three giant claw marks traversed his torso, all the way to his groin. The other warrior was short and sinewed muscle, with a golden band across his eyes and blotches of yellow puzzling his muddy upper torso like the spots of a leopard.

She tried to stand, but their strong hands gripped her shoulders and forced her to her knees, and she was reminded of Dumaka pressing her against the deck. *Dumaka. Is this where you and your mistress met your end? I do hope it was unpleasant.*

She looked up, squinting through darkness and stinging rain. Lightning flashed, illuminating what was left of the city in stark monochrome. There should have been three pyramids standing tall before her, but she saw only the east pyramid, bordered by rows of torches that stood like reverential disciples. Its stepped foundation gleamed crimson in the rain as though rinsed in blood. The other two pyramids had been reduced to large mounds of rubble, obliterated by some unimaginable cataclysm and overtaken by jungle. A bolt of lightning struck the tallest peak, and she glimpsed a man standing in the ruins of what had been the central pyramid, his long shadow extending across the courtyard. Darkness fell. The downpour increased, hammering the top of Kate's head and matting her short hair against her temples. She swallowed, and a knife of pain slid down her throat. The hands on her shoulders tensed, fearing her retreat, but she had no intention of fleeing.

The man sidled easily over the rubble, balancing himself on a long staff. He dropped effortlessly from the pile into the courtyard and started toward her. Lightning flashed again as he edged closer, and for an instant she saw him in full. "Tz'uul," she heard herself mutter instinctively, in a voice she did not recognize. She could not remember what it meant. The two warriors looked down at her, their eyes momentarily vivacious. Their curiosity faded just as quickly, and the dull cloud of deathlike stupor returned.

The white man stopped before her and clacked his staff twice against the limestone. The amber iris of his lone eye ensnared the torchlight like a ring of fire and regarded her with unguarded marvel, while the orb of his right eye bulged against a seam of crudely-sealed skin set deep within the crevice of an old saber wound, striving to break free of its fleshy prison. "One woman was promised, yet two have arrived." His tone was as flat and harsh as it had been in her dream, lacking any discernible emotion. He spoke as one risen from the dead, with no warmth in his veins.

"Armitage," she growled, briefly forgetting the hands on her shoulders and trying to stand. Her knees lifted an inch from the ground before smacking it again, hard. She grit her teeth and muttered a curse. Muddy fingers clutched her shoulders.

The white man's broad, ugly face formed many creases as he frowned. She could not determine his precise age, but he couldn't have been less than fifty. His skin was darker than before, with sunspots riddling the top of his forehead. His short black hair, which was now streaked white at the temples, stood on end with an uneven cut, giving him the appearance of a madman. As before, he was swathed in black, but his long coat was old and tattered. His boots were perforated, revealing filthy, battered toes. No longer did he carry a pistol, just a rusty old cutlass. He wore no shirt beneath the coat, baring a broad chest covered in scars. A large medallion dangled from his neck, etched with the beautiful face of a proud woman with high cheekbones, a wide nose, and full lips. Blank orbs lacking irises or pupils were set within almond-shaped eyelids.

Kate craned her neck to meet his lackadaisical gaze, blinking rain out of her eyes. "Where is Jacqueline Teach? Is she alive?"

Armitage nodded slowly. "She is. For now. It appears one of you is an imposter."

"I make no claim to be anyone other than who I am," Kate replied, writhing angrily against the impervious claws of her captors.

"And who are you?"

"I am Kate Warlowe, captain of the *Scarlet Devil*."

"A woman captain?" His bulky jaw worked from side to side. "You've brought a ship."

She smiled shrewdly. "I assure you, it's well out of reach." She prayed Gabe had followed her strict instructions. If she was gone too long, he might do something stupid. *As he did with Jacqueline Teach.*

"Your accent . . . you hail from . . ."—he struggled with the name— "London."

"Aye."

His eye glazed with rumination. "I think maybe I did too."

"Can't you remember?"

He looked up, past Kate. "Not always. It's all so long ago, and this place has a way of fogging up the things that don't matter."

She saw Corso briefly, smiling kindly from across the table in her cabin, raising his mug in toast. "A friend of mine forgot something very important just before he died."

Armitage gripped his staff and ground it against the limestone. "It only seemed important until he forgot it. How can something be important if you don't remember it?" His voice trailed midsentence, as though he had realized he was dreaming. His eye drifted over Kate's head.

She looked around. Lightning flashed, and she saw dozens of shadows on either side of her peripheral vision, gathering in the courtyard. A fleeting glimpse of short and robust figures, and inquisitive, dirty faces, interspersed here and there with taller white men, dressed in the tattered rags of sailors. At the center of the crowd towered a black man, taller than all the rest. She recognized him immediately. She strained against her captors ineffectually, projecting her fury at him, but he wasn't looking at her. He wasn't looking at anything, really. Something was missing in his eyes. His scarred chest hardly moved.

"I know that man," she growled. "The negro."

Armitage's eye perused the crowd until he found Dumaka. "Ah, yes. He arrived with the others. Weeks ago, I think. Is he a friend?"

"Of a sort." *One I will happily murder.*

"Not anymore, I'm afraid. I doubt he will recognize you."

"What is this place?" she demanded. "Who leads these

people? Where is the king?"

"I govern these people," he replied with sudden conviction. "The remaining son of Ix Chak Sahkil resides in the jungle. He believes himself the demon Zipacna."

"Sure."

"He has lost his mind and left the burden of leadership to me."

"I've seen him. He wears a great headdress and does not slather himself in mud. There's something wrong with his skin."

"Zipacna was said to resemble a scaled caiman. His brother gave him the name. A mockery of his condition."

Kate opened her palm and looked at the faint toothmarks. "The brother who deserted?"

"Yes. We do not speak of him or his treachery."

A treachery you shared in, she did not say.

Armitage clacked his staff twice, like a judge with a mallet. "The prince's warriors have brought you before me, which was no doubt by his order."

She looked to the gathering natives, wondering if the frightening pale warrior was among them, but she saw only shadows beyond hammering sheets of rain. "Why does he not come forward? I lobbed a grenado his way but I do not believe I killed him. He was quicker than the others." She wondered if the prince had hunted down Israel Hands and Joseph in a fit of rage over the death of his warriors. As if decapitating poor Salvador hadn't been enough. And what of Duncan? Was he still sleeping soundly in his cave? Would he ever wake? *Perhaps he's the lucky one.*

"The prince fears this place." Armitage possibly shared a little of that fear, but his voice remained measured and impassive. "He believes his mother will return."

"Return?" She looked from left to right. She felt of the heat of the natives as they shuffled closer. A low energy coursed beneath her knees, through the limestone, from the soft patter of their footfalls. The leftovers of *Persephone's* crew moved in tandem, as though they had never been pirates. Dumaka moved with them, never so much as glancing her way. It was impossible to despise him any longer. There was nothing left to despise. *Or maybe it's all an act*, she reminded herself.

Armitage's lone eye rolled apprehensively over the gatherers. "They all believe it. I would kill you now, if I could, but they would kill me in turn."

"You'd kill me?" She might have laughed if her throat didn't pain her so. "But we just met."

"Women are unnecessarily complicated creatures. You do not belong here. I tried explaining this to them."

"Where are the rest of your women?"

His brow creased with a passing uncertainty. "Dead from plague, around the time when the pyramids were felled by quaking earth." He hesitated, as though struggling to recall the particulars. "Many cycles ago, I couldn't tell you the precise number. Many crops were lost. Entire fields burned, struck by lightning. We now live off fruit and fish and monkeys and . . . other things. The maize is gone. There is a little corn left." The edges of his mouth bent into a scowl. "I won't miss the corn when it's gone. It's murder on my gums. I've lost two molars."

Kate narrowed her eyes distrustfully. "A plague killed all the women?"

"And some of the men."

"But mostly the women?"

"Mostly the women." Armitage chewed on one side of

his mouth.

"You don't think that's a little strange?"

The glare of his one eye was fierce enough for two. "No. Not really. Women are ill-suited for this world."

Kate indicated the red pyramid with a jut of her chin while keeping her eyes on Armitage. "Yet the queen's pyramid remains."

Armitage turned, regarding the red pyramid as though for the first time. "How do you know that is the *queen's* pyramid?"

"She's buried there. Do these people know what you did? Do they know you helped murder her?"

He lifted his staff and clacked it against the limestone in a conclusive manner. "They wanted her dead as much as I. She muddied their race and they blamed her for all their woes, as primitives tend to do when things go wrong." He set both hands atop his staff and scrutinized her. "You're a pirate, are you not? You possess an officious haughtiness, but I cannot believe the Crown appointed a woman to rank of captain."

"Aye. I am a pirate, for lack of a better term."

"Then you know how quickly the tides can turn when a crew smells failure." Armitage's eye narrowed skeptically. "Wait a minute. How do you know so much, anyway?"

"Perhaps I am the woman they've been waiting for."

"Or perhaps you're just very perceptive."

"She's a liar!" came a female voice she recognized all too well. "I know this woman!" exclaimed Jacqueline Teach from between the stone jaguars. The natives and the white men who had once been *Persephone's* crew gasped and fell to their knees, lowering their heads. She scuttled down the walkway into the courtyard and moved between Kate and

274

Armitage. She was wearing a white dress embroidered with red and orange beads, tucked into a brown skirt with red stripes that slanted sharply into a V. The dress would have clung to most women, but it hung loose on Jacqueline's bony frame, wet and translucent in the rain. Her wrists and ankles were shackled in metallic cuffs ornamented with many various beads. Her face was painfully gaunt, with sharp cheekbones and eyes ringed in dark circles.

Jacqueline pointed a shaky finger at Kate's nose. Her wrist was skeletal. "She is a liar." Thunder rolled over the mountains, and Jacqueline let out a yelp. She quickly composed herself, lips quirking into a little smile that did not suit her.

"Hello, Jacqueline," Kate said, managing a level tone despite the rage seething deep within, beseeching swift and brutal vengeance. She fantasized springing forth and seizing the bitch's head and twisting until her scrawny neck gave way. "What are you wearing? You look positively absurd."

Jacqueline glanced downward, touching her dress. "This is the dress of a queen." She didn't seem so sure.

Kate forced a laugh, although it came out as more of a guttural grunt. "And why are you wearing queenly garb?"

"I am Ish . . . Ishi . . . Cha . . ." Jacqueline withered and turned sheepishly to Armitage. "What the bloody hell was it?"

"Ix Chak Sahkil," he answered, deadpan.

"I'm her. Reborn." She returned her attention to Kate, straightening her posture and lifting a quivering chin. "I just didn't know it." A flash of lightning exposed feral desperation in her sleep-starved blue eyes. She looked to the sky, waiting, and when the thunder rolled overhead, she leaned close to Kate, mashing cheek against cheek, and hissed in her ear, "They're going to kill us both." She pulled away and smiled nervously at Armitage, adjusting her ill-fitting dress with an awkward shimmy of her hips.

"Just one of us, I think," Kate said.

Jacqueline tried to cut Kate off with a stern shake of her head, and then feigned ignorance. "What are you talking about?" There was not the slightest hint of acknowledgement for what had transpired between them on *Persephone*, nor did she seem surprised to see Kate alive. Kate wondered if Jacqueline remembered what she had done. She seemed, at present, concerned only with her own mortality.

Kate nodded at Armitage. "This woman is the imposter, and I can prove it."

"Words!" blurted Jacqueline. "Meaningless words."

Armitage circumvented Jacqueline. She reached for him and he slapped her hand away. "How?" he said to Kate.

"I demand audience with your queen."

"Don't listen to her," Jacqueline urged with a nervous jitter. "She's quite mad. Just look at her. A sane woman would never shear her hair so short."

"You did this to me," Kate reminded her evenly. "And far worse."

Armitage looked to Jacqueline, who returned a less-than-convincing expression of open-mouthed, doe-eyed flabbergast. "Whaaaat? No!"

Armitage's broad shoulders settled as his expression turned dour. "I'm afraid I cannot ignore two omens." And then, under his breath, he muttered, "These brown fuckers won't let me."

"You can and you should," Jacqueline implored. "I know her."

Armitage looked from one woman to the next. "Is that

true?"

"Aye," said Kate. "We're old friends."

"As friendly as women can be," he replied mirthlessly. He snapped his fingers at the warriors flanking Kate, and they promptly released their grips.

Kate stood, flexing her sore legs and ignoring the taut protests of her scar as she stretched her back. "Take me to the queen's tomb, and I'll prove to you I was summoned here."

Jacqueline seized Armitage's arm, clinging to him. "She's lying. The bitch will say anything."

Armitage glanced at her incredulously. "If she's lying, we'll know soon enough. Either way, Chaac demands a sacrifice."

"The queen?" Kate asked. She wondered how a dead queen could be making demands.

"No." Armitage raised a hand to the heavens and spoke words he plainly didn't believe. "The god of rain. Chaac."

Kate licked rainwater from her lips. "Seems you're good on that score."

Armitage offered a resigned shrug. "These people love their sacrifices." He gestured at the two mud warriors. "This is Black Macaw, and that's his little brother, Yellow Jaguar. If either of you try anything, they'll kill you. Let's go see the queen and see what she has to say about this." And again, under his breath, he muttered, "Nothing, I wager."

Jacqueline stuck close to Armitage as he led them across the courtyard, clacking his staff all the way to the red pyramid, where torches flared of ethereal intensity and billowed smoky red columns in the rain. At the foot of the stairway was a large stone sculpture of a woman reclining on her back, with her hands about a dark-stained plate receptacle that sat on her stomach. She was nude, apart from wrist and ankle cuffs. Her serene yet vaguely inauspicious face, angled ninety degrees to the south on a slender neck, bore the same features as the medallion Armitage wore from his neck. Her relaxed pose reminded Kate of the otters she had witnessed during a visit to Chesapeake Bay, cracking open clamshells on their bellies. They were the most adorable creatures she had ever seen, and she thought it queer this disconcerting statue should remind her of them. Even more disconcerting was the human-sized slab of rock laid out before the sculpture, stained in blood.

"We use this for offerings of flesh," Armitage announced, pointing at the plate with his staff.

"Yes," Kate drawled, "I surmised as much."

He led them around the sculpture and up the stairs of the stepped platform, clacking his staff upon every step. Kate's legs quickly began to ache. Halfway up, she realized how exhausted she was. Jacqueline, on the other hand, seemed invigorated by fear, easily keeping pace with Armitage. She cast nervous, impulsive glances over her shoulder repeatedly at Kate. Kate wasn't sure what was going on in the other woman's head, but she was finding her own rage lessened with every step. Jacqueline was plainly in over her head.

Near the top, Kate looked back, and in the courtyard she saw the shadows of the villagers gathering about the reclining sculpture, their heads angled upward expectantly. She estimated five dozen, including the remnants of *Persephone's* crew. Were there so few left alive? Perhaps there were hundreds more hiding in the huts and ruins, afraid to venture forth. Dumaka, standing tall amidst the crowd, matched eyes with her at last, but she glimpsed no trace of recognition. Perhaps there was a vague curiosity, a slight crease in his brow, but it faded quickly.

The top of the platform was lined with more flaring torches, bordering a tall temple glowing orange from within. Kate took a moment to bend forward with her hands on her thighs until the burning subsided. She righted herself and craned her neck, blinking against the hammering rain. The mansard roof supported a tall roof comb that vanished into the cloud above. She felt suddenly lightheaded and was forced to close her eyes for a moment. She followed Armitage and Jacqueline through the portico, between two giant pillars that bore the heads of feathered serpents, and into the outer vaulted room. Black Macaw plodded after her, panting heavily.

The interior was humid and smoky with incense, but Kate was glad to be out of the rain. She paused to peruse the faded network of hieroglyphs covering the walls. Serpents, giant birds, men on thrones, strange contraptions, rows of slaves, and extravagantly garbed men and women who seemed to be enjoying themselves in some fantastical underground world. Entire sections had been scraped away, possibly on purpose. She wondered if history had been intentionally expurgated.

A wall separating the outer room from the inner ran through the middle of the temple, bearing a stone tablet carved with a towering tree decked in jewels and spreading two long branches to resemble the shape of a Christian cross. Etched at the top of the tree was a giant quetzal bird, plump and comfortably nesting. Smoke rolled up the tablet from incense burners at its base, obscuring the details. "Keep moving," Armitage said, clacking his staff twice.

He led them through a low archway into the inner vaulted room, where there was a large square hole in the floor, with a stone slab of equal size displaced beside it. A vaulted stairway led down into black. Armitage skirted the hole and removed a torch from a sconce along the back wall. He motioned for all to follow and descended the steps. Jacqueline pursued quickly, as if close proximity would prove her loyalty. Kate remained still, watching torchlight flicker off the glyphed walls in the passage below, until Black Macaw nudged her into movement.

The passage down into the belly of the pyramid was narrow and steep, and Kate's sore legs quivered with every step. Her every breath and grunt was annoyingly amplified. She plugged her nose at the sudden stench of earth and decay, not from the tomb below, but from the warriors at her back. "Must they dress themselves in mud?" Her raspy voice assaulted her ears as it echoed off the walls.

"They believe they are the first men," Armitage answered from the steps below, his voice loud and harsh. "Molded of mud by the forefather gods. They await the return of Ix Chak Sahkil, who will make them flesh again."

"Makes sense," she quipped.

"Not really," he replied casually, oblivious to her sarcasm. "They're quite insane."

"They don't understand English, I take it."

"Christ, no. I made the mistake of teaching the queen our language. I preferred when I couldn't understand a word she said. Truthfully, she didn't give me much choice. She would've killed me if I'd declined."

"Probably she should have."

He came to a halt and swiveled with an inquisitive eyebrow. "Why do you say that?"

She stared down at him. "Because you helped murder her."

He blinked. "That's a good point."

"I should think you'd be against her return."

"I must humor their beliefs."

Kate had never given credence to mermaids or giant sea serpents or ships crewed by ghosts. She had balked openly at the superstitious natures of sailors, dismissing their wide-eyed warnings with sarcastic retorts and, if she was deep in her cups, derisive laughter. But she could not account for precognitive knowledge of a place she had never visited, of a woman she could not possibly have known, and a man she was certain she had never met until tonight. The dream had seemed so vivid, and now it had been all but confirmed as genuine. There was more to this island than a rational mind could grasp, and she wasn't about to try. "The fact that the other two pyramids fell doesn't concern you just a little?"

Armitage paused to consider her rhetorical query. He raised a finger as though he was about to present an intelligent counterpoint, and said, "No more talking."

They continued downward in silence. The stairs opened into a small chamber, which led to another set of stairs leading toward the center of the pyramid. Armitage's torchlight wavered halfway down. He halted for a moment, watching the flame until it flared again. A low rumble became louder and louder as they descended. The walls seemed to be trembling, and little trickles of water slid down here and there, like tears. Patches of moss clung to the ceiling. "We should go back," Jacqueline said, but her voice was tiny and meek.

At the bottom they entered a thirty-foot-long chamber Kate remembered all too well. The walls, which ran twenty feet up and slanted into a corbelled arch, were covered with black glyphs and red murals. She slid a hand along the cold limestone and felt a low current channeling through it. It was damp in here, and the flow of the river somewhere beneath was much louder than she recalled.

The sarcophagus waited at the end of the room, topped with a thick stone slab with a relief carving of, presumably, the woman inside. She was painted primarily in red, clothed in a regal gown with a massive headdress, sitting upon her throne in the underworld, flanked by green, feathered serpents, with a magnificent black jaguar lounging at her feet staring off to the left, its whiskers curling into an extravagant mustachio. In the small space beneath the inclined wall beyond the sarcophagus, the stone floor had cracked and broken through to a sliver of darkness, like a mouth, about as long and wide as a child, from which the sound of rushing water emanated. A thick layer of moss had spread across the shattered stone from the lips of the crevice, with one wayward strand of green reaching out and touching the head of the sarcophagus.

"Well," said Armitage, setting his staff against a wall and looking around. "What now?" He bellowed every word to be heard over the raucous current that overpowered all other noise in the tomb.

Kate snapped her fingers at Black Macaw and Yellow Jaguar, who had remained at the entrance, studying the ceiling with transient curiosity. "I'll need their strength."

Armitage squinted his lone eye. "You wish to open the tomb?"

"Is that a problem?"

"It might be."

"You're not afraid of a dead woman, are you?"

Armitage relented instantly. "You two. Open the coffin."

Jacqueline's head swiveled all about as she tried to take in everything at once. She looked thoroughly out of place, even in her queenly attire.

The warriors plodded around Armitage and positioned themselves to the left of the sarcophagus. They curled their fingers beneath the stone slab and heaved with what seemed a minimal effort. The sarcophagus released a distinctly human exhalation of air, along with a sour stench not unlike foul breath. Kate inhaled through her mouth until it passed.

The warriors hefted the stone slab and let it slide carelessly over the opposite end. It hit the ground, resting lopsided at the edge of the sarcophagus. Kate moved forward, looking down. The interior was swathed in a powdery red pigment. The queen's shrouds had been ripped open, possibly by her own hands, exposing her crimson skeleton. Her legs were sprawled at awkward angles, as though she had thrashed herself to death. Her hands covered her ribcage, the bony fingers of the right twisted and broken. Jade animals and little human figures were scattered about the interior. The skull was covered by a death mask puzzled together from many pieces of jade, with red pigment collecting in the many seams like little rivers of blood running through canals of green earth. The eyes were white with empty black irises that saw nothing and everything.

Armitage shuffled to Kate's side and sighed. "This seems a wasted effort."

Kate pointed at the coffin lid. "Turn it over."

Yellow Jaguar looked to Armitage for his endorsement. Armitage shrugged. The warriors moved around the sarcophagus, gripped the lid, and gracelessly flipped it over against the wall, where it came to a rest at a ninety-degree angle. The warriors stared at whatever had been revealed, blocking the view until Armitage beckoned them. They moved out of the way, standing behind him. "What is that?" Armitage asked, and for the first time he sounded truly interested. On the underside of the lid, a crude death's head with horns had been scrawled in blood, long since dried and permanently stained into the pockmarked stone. Two humerus bones crisscrossed beneath the grinning skull.

Kate looked to Armitage, who returned a blank stare. She smirked confidently over her shoulder to Jacqueline, who was slowly backing away as a terrifying comprehension took hold. "Wait," was all she could say.

Kate took three paces forward, until the toes of her boots tapped the base of the sarcophagus. The torch in Armitage's hand cast her shadow over the scant remains of Ix Chak Sahkil, but the white eyes of the jade mask were no less potent in the dark. She grasped the tails of her shirt, lifting it high over her head and stretching taut the rubbery tissue of her scar, sensing its sinister outline. She heard a gasp, the sound of knees collapsing against stone, and the urgent pattering of feet.

When she turned around, Armitage's face was creased with stupefaction, the mud-covered warriors were kneeling on either side of him with their heads bowed in reverence, and Jacqueline Teach had already broken into a mad flight for the stairs.

SACRIFICE

Jacqueline didn't make it far. Black Macaw and Yellow Jaguar returned her kicking and shrieking to the tomb, where they stripped her naked. Kate caught glimpse of her wash-boarded ribs and stick-like thighs before averting her eyes. Armitage collected the dress and skirt from the ground and offered it to Kate. "This belongs to you," he said, but the skepticism lingered in his eye. "For now." His eye drifted furtively toward her bare breasts.

She declined with a smile, pushed the dress away, and put her shirt back on, tucking it into her breeches and tightening the laces. "No thank you. Let her wear it. There's no sense to be parading her around naked."

Puzzlement bunched his brow. "But, it's yours now. It will guarantee your safety. It would be wise to—"

"I may have been summoned here by your queen," she said, jabbing a finger at the bones in the sarcophagus, "but I am not *her*."

Armitage retrieved his staff and gripped the top with both hands as he leaned toward her, whispering conspiratorially while angling an apprehensive eye at the warriors, who were watching Kate closely now. "How did you arrange this?"

"Arrange this?" She laughed. "I was brought here. I hadn't time to open that coffin, and how would I muster the strength even if I had? I'm not even sure how these two brutes managed it. You smelled the foul air that came out of that thing. Evidently it has been sealed for some time."

He remained skeptical. "When they discover you are a fraud, they will remove your heart while you are still breathing."

She frowned, struggling to picture it. "Is that possible?"

"You'd be surprised."

"I'm too tired to be intimidated, sir. You'll find me in a more coercible state once I've had a proper night's rest." She prayed he was convinced. The sooner she was renewed, the sooner she might come up with a sensible plan for extracting Armitage from this place and ransoming him to Woodes Rogers. At present, she had no idea how she would accomplish this without the aid of Hands and Joseph, assuming they were alive.

Armitage wasted no time, urging them back up the stairs. He emerged from the temple and confidently bellowed declarations in the same alien tongue Kate had heard in her dream. No longer could she comprehend the words. The language was harsh and wrong coming from him, and he often hesitated to recall the proper word, but after each pause his voice grew in strength to compensate for his lack of mastery. She heard the name "Ix Chak Sahkil" several times throughout the course of his speech. He took her hand and held it aloft, and the gatherers in the courtyard cheered as resoundingly as their miniscule number could muster, except for the former pirates, who remained stone-faced. But then the rain abruptly ceased, and the crowd fell silent.

The warriors held a squirming Jacqueline in place, spreading her arms apart and allowing all below to feast their eyes on her nakedness. Kate couldn't bear to look at her. She implored Armitage to cover her up, but he merely smirked at her unexpected concern and said, "We have little time to waste."

"What's the hurry?" she wondered.

"Chaac demands sacrifice."

"Oh, right. We mustn't upset Chaac."

Armitage nodded, impervious to her sarcasm. "We have an imposter to deal with."

Kate groaned and slumped forward. She realized how girlish she must have looked, but she was too exhausted to care. Her entire body ached. She hadn't slept since the beach, unless falling unconscious in the cave counted. "Can it wait? My legs will have no more of this."

"I'm afraid it can't." He raised a hand skyward. "The rain has stopped. Already they take it as an ill omen. It will be dawn soon. Follow."

Armitage led them down the stairs, through the small crowd, and northeast out of the village to a heavily forested path through the crevice between the northern and eastern mountain, where dozens of spectating monkeys lined the tree branches, shadows with lambent eyes. They occasionally chittered and hooted, but most remained silent and curious.

Much of the trek was uphill along a winding path sporadically choked with boulders that had rolled down the steep mountain crags to collect in narrower passages. Armitage made no attempt to help Kate as he sprinted nimbly up the slick, moss-topped rocks with the agility of a younger man, balancing himself on his staff, not that she would have accepted his hand had he offered. Behind her, she heard Jacqueline stumbling and moaning as the two warriors urged her forward with grunts and prods. The ache in Kate's thighs subsided to a distant numbness, and the chill of the wet morning air reinvigorated her. Her body seemed to have passed the point of needing sleep, preparing itself for a new day, but she knew she would pay for it in the afternoon.

It seemed two hours before the crevice opened and they emerged on the opposite side of the mountains. The ground levelled off and soon began a blessed decline, and through an opening in the trees Kate saw the curved upper edge of the island maybe a mile off, and the dark grey plane of the ocean stretching toward infinity, blotted with the first pale light of dawn showing through sparse breaks in the cloud cover, and she desired nothing more than to be off this godforsaken spit of land.

They passed under trees bearing giant orange and red fruits that reminded Kate of passionfruit. "Those are juicy and delicious," Armitage said. "Don't eat them."

Kate retracted her hand from the nearest. "Are they anything like the berries my crew found in a meadow?"

"No. These just make you shit. A lot." He frowned. "What berries?"

"They cause paralysis."

"I don't know anything about that."

"You used them on the queen."

"I don't remember that." Before she could object, he paused to raise a finger. "I'm not suggesting you're a liar. It sounds like something I'd do. I just don't remember it."

Jacqueline continued to whimper the entire way, until Armitage struck her so hard across the face that her head snapped around and she slumped unconscious in the grips of the two warriors. "We'll stop here for a spell," he decided. The warriors set Jacqueline's limp, naked body between the gnarled buttress roots of an old ceiba tree and stood watch on either side of her.

Kate didn't feel like stopping. She knew better than to crouch and get comfortable. She worried her legs might not want to move again, and if she closed her eyes even for a moment she would not wake. She stood in place, swaying in a dreamlike state of weightless vigor, with inexplicable vitality coursing through her veins like a drug. A little trickle of sweat rolled down one temple. It was going to be a hot day.

Armitage dug inside his jacket, feeling about his hips, and produced a dried gourd with a little rope around the throat. He offered it to Kate and shook it to let her hear the water inside. She took the gourd and removed the corncob that served as a cork, drinking greedily from it. Water streamed down her chin and soaked her shirt. She recorked the gourd and handed it back to him without a hint of gratitude.

She turned around and stared at the procession of two dozen or so natives that had shadowed them all the way from the village to witness whatever gruesome ceremony Armitage intended. They had kept an apprehensive distance. They shied from her direct gaze whenever she looked at them. Most were short, underfed, and sickly, sparsely clothed in old rags. Some had painted their faces and bodies with the same red pigment that had stained the bones of their queen. Many had pierced their noses with bones and stretched their ears with giant plugs. She couldn't imagine why anyone would intentionally mutilate their body in such a fashion, when hers had been mutilated twice against her will. There were no children among them. The oldest were middle-aged and the youngest appeared to be teenagers. Their almond-shaped eyes yielded little expectation or hope, only trepidation and uncertainty. A final generation, waiting to die.

None of the former pirates had tagged along, except Dumaka, whose hard face remained passionless. His bare, scarred chest was slick with sweat. He stood among them like a towering shadow, neither shepherd nor sheep. If he pondered his existence, he gave as little sign as a tree. As much as she wanted to despise him, she couldn't help but feel sorry for him. Vengeance was out of the question now. Death would be a kindness.

"I'm hungry," said Armitage, patting his belly.

"What about poor Chaac?" Kate quipped, against her better judgment. She was starving.

"Chaac will wait." And under his breath, he muttered, "I was eager to be quit of the city."

"I could help you with that permanently," she suggested.

His eye narrowed. "With your ship, you mean?" He allowed a wry smile. "No, I think not. Neither of us is leaving here anytime soon."

"Why not?"

"Because this is where we belong."

"Care to elaborate?"

He inhaled deeply. "No."

She could think of no good reason for him to want to remain here, governing a people whose religious views he clearly didn't share. *Who are you, Armitage, and why would King George put a bounty on your head?* What leverage could this man possibly hold over a King? She scrutinized him, but found nothing exceptional. Apart from the slash that had robbed him of an eye, he was one of the least noteworthy men she had ever seen.

Armitage snapped his fingers at the warriors. Black Macaw vanished immediately into the jungle. There came a high-pitched shriek, abruptly cut short. And then another. A moment later, the foliage bristled, and he materialized with two dead monkeys dangling from one hand, his war club in the other, matted with black fur and blood. He offered the monkeys to Armitage and grunted. Armitage appraised the dead animals, and then gave the warrior a curt nod, shooing him away. Yellow Jaguar gathered fallen branches and arranged them in a pile. He produced flint rocks from a small pouch and clacked them together repeatedly, sparking a fire and blowing on the flames until it spread throughout the center of the pile. Black Macaw skinned the monkeys with an obsidian knife while Kate watched with equal parts revulsion and fascination. When he was done, he shoved twigs through their little bodies and suspended them over the fire. A peculiar yet succulent aroma filled the air, and Kate's stomach growled in anticipation as she watched the pink meat slowly turning dark over the fire, dribbling juices that sizzled in the flames.

When the monkeys were thoroughly cooked, Black Macaw handed one to Armitage and kept the other. He tore off a leg and handed it to Kate, shaking his arm impatiently until she took it. She eagerly sank her teeth into it, squeezing shut her eyelids as she worked through the tough, stringy meat. It was a little overcooked, and the taste reminded her of dry pork, which she'd never been all that fond of. She prodded the warrior's arm with her monkey leg. "You wouldn't happen to have any salt, would you? Maybe some rum to wash this down?" He glowered at her as if he understood she was mocking him, eyes narrowing to slits within the white band. "Suppose not," she concluded, and gnawed off another chunk.

Armitage smirked as he tore apart his meal. "You're sure you don't want to put on the dress? They'll be more susceptible to instruction if they believe you are their queen reincarnate."

"No, thank you," she replied. "I'd rather not offer you another look at my bosom, or anything else, for that matter."

He feigned offense. "That is not my intent."

"Really? And here I thought you aimed to make me your queen." She smiled coyly. *I have plans for you as well.*

"I have no interest in the fairer sex."

"You might have fooled me. You were gawking at my breasts in the tomb."

"Breasts are peculiar obstructions, difficult to disregard." He peeled away a strip of meat, stuffed it in his mouth, and walked away. He settled near a large tree, leaning against the trunk while facing the ocean and eating.

Kate watched him while chewing at her monkey leg. When she was done, she tossed the bone aside and rubbed her hands on her breeches. Her loins burned suddenly. "I need to make water," she called over to Armitage.

"Don't wander far. These woods are dangerous."

"No shit." She descended east into the jungle, navigating thick trees, dense bushes, and down a little creek, until she discovered a lowland forest of lush ferns, where she was satisfied no one could spy on her. The leaves were pleasingly soft, with tiny furs that caressed her skin as she descended amongst them. She slid her breeches down and crouched, relieving herself with immense satisfaction while absently regarding the dirt beneath her feet. A face gazed back at her, barely a shade lighter than the dark soil. She brushed the dirt away with her fingers, revealing a little clay figurine holding two tiny babies. The blank face disclosed no gender, but the chest had large mounds for breasts. It was wearing a tall square headdress with feathers etched in the clay, and its broad head was flanked by giant ears with plugs through the lobes.

The crack of a twig snapped her to attention. She thought she saw movement beyond the ferns further down the creek. She dropped the figurine, pulled up her breeches, and slunk forward on hands and knees to investigate. She came to a toppled trunk and peeked her head cautiously over it. On the other side, atop a small stepped platform of white limestone bathed in a column of sunlight, two dark figures flanked a white figure who was hunched upon a square stone in the center of the platform. His fissured skin was as blinding as a dry salt flat in the midday sun. The lofty feathers of his headdress were stiff and crimson, matching his bloodshot red and orange eyes. The multi-colored beads of his necklace glinted in the sunlight. *Zipacna*, she realized in horror. His skirt had been removed and he was tending to his impressive nether region with a white knife, which appeared to be forged of a long thin bone, while the other two watched intently. Before him, smoke wafted from a round stone pot with faces carved along the outer perimeter. He pinched the foreskin of his penis and inserted the knife through it, his dour expression never changing. The warrior on the left crouched beside him to catch the blood on a parchment, and then folded the paper and tossed it into the fire. The smoke billowed and red embers ascended along the black plume. Zipacna's red and orange eyes burned through the smoke, fixing on her.

Kate ducked behind the trunk, shuddering violently. She crawled away, never looking back, despite the dreadful certainty Zipacna had spotted her and was stalking her through the ferns, intent to ravage her with his blood-soaked manhood. She kept her head low the rest of the way back and struggled to disregard what she had witnessed.

"You took too long," Armitage said when she returned. He was almost through with his meal, plucking the last remnants of meat from a ribcage.

"I saw something," Kate said, still in shock.

He nodded, unsurprised. "I'm sure you did."

"It was—"

"I don't want to know." Armitage tossed the bones away and licked his fingers, gazing off into the distance.

"You look dead, Kate," Jacqueline Teach murmured. One arm was draped over a root of the ceiba tree. Her bloodshot eyes were half-lidded, and she slurred her words as if drunk. "How are you still standing?"

Kate kept her gaze level, avoiding the woman's skeletal, pale body. "Why wouldn't I be?"

"After everything, you stand there as though nothing has happened."

"You mean after you set my back ablaze?"

Jacqueline looked down at herself. Her ribs protruded

painfully with every shuddering breath. "I was so angry."

"You give them exactly what they want." Kate stepped forward, anger renewed.

"Them?"

Kate flung a hand, indicating Armitage. She lowered her voice to a hiss. "*Them*. Men. They want us to believe we are weak. They want us disjointed and alone, because deep down they know we are stronger. We always have been, and they hate us for it. They're happy to watch us squabble and destroy one another over petty trifles. And you, you treacherous beast, you feed them exactly what they crave, and you compel me to do the same. I have never crossed a man so fickle and dangerous as the woman before me."

Jacqueline's slender chest trembled slightly, a chuckle stopping short at the base of her throat. "Not so deadly now." She managed a smile. "But you won't forget me, will you, Kate?"

"How can I? You've ensured I will take you everywhere I go for the rest of my days." Kate shifted her stance, wanting to scratch at her back, but not in front of Jacqueline.

Jacqueline licked her pale lips. "I gave you what you needed to survive this place. Had I not, you would be dead. I don't know how you did what you did in that tomb." She shook her head at the incongruity of it all, eyes briefly widening to reveal steely, haunted irises. "But you couldn't have done it without me."

Kate made a dismissive gesture and turned to leave. "I don't believe I could survive any more of your favors."

"Why won't you ask her name?"

Kate halted. "Whose name?"

"You know very well who." Jacqueline's voice was suddenly sharp with indictment, cutting the air between them like a knife. "Don't play the fool, Kate. You're anything but. I'm not asking much."

"You deserve nothing."

Kate marched toward Armitage. "We're wasting time," she told him. "The sooner this is done, the better."

Armitage looked up from his half-eaten monkey, surprised by her sudden resolve. He gestured to the warriors and followed her, tossing the monkey carcass aside. The procession of natives loitered a moment, muttering to one another uncertainly, and eventually followed, keeping their distance.

The path narrowed again as the jungle foliage and trees grew densely-packed, and eventually gave to treacherous, rocky slopes. The clouds parted, and the sun was beating down by midday, rays striping through the canopy to cook the soil. Kate's fatigue returned as the humid air stifled her breath. She felt the meat churning in her stomach, refusing to move on. Sweat streamed down her sweltering forehead and into her eyes. Her ankles grew stiff and her feet sore as she maneuvered carefully down large boulders, mossy slopes, and tangled webs of vines and weeds.

She stopped feeling sorry for herself after she looked back to see Jacqueline stumbling down a cluster of rocks, with the warriors holding her upright by the armpits. Tiny lacerations covered her legs, and her bare feet were clotted in blood. When she saw Kate staring at her, she cast her head down in shame and covered her breasts, but the warriors seized her wrists and pried her arms apart. She took a deep breath, straightened her back, and lifted her chin. Her eyes locked with Kate's, and a stubborn pride toughened her face. She tried to plant herself in place, thrusting out a foot and bracing herself against a boulder, despite her captors urging her forward. Yellow Jaguar drove a fist into her belly, doubling her over his shoulder. Her face shook and her cheeks turned red as she fought for a breath that wouldn't come. Kate thought she would die then and there, but she had always underestimated Jacqueline's tenacity. After what seemed a minute, Jacqueline started to cough and gasp hoarsely. They continued dragging her down the slope, not waiting for her to recover.

I should be savoring this, Kate realized, shocked that she wasn't. She forced herself to picture Jacqueline severing Gabe's fingers, one at a time, and showing them to him, before he settled on what she had to admit was the wisest choice. She imagined Jacqueline straddling him eagerly, while he lay motionless and stone-faced beneath her, determined not to enjoy himself, despite the betrayal of his easily-flattered loins.

Today you die, Jacqueline, she decided. *A death long overdue.*

It was another two hours down the snaking path before the trees opened on a slim strip of flat land where the jungle had been cleared away, which ended abruptly at the rim of a massive hole that seemed to have been punched into the earth by a god. Standing at the edge of the precipice was Zipacna, brandishing his giant club. She felt heat radiating from his cracked skin like the rage of a dying star. Beside him was a tall, thick stake that had been driven into the ground. Its lower half was stained in blood.

Dread took form in Kate's stomach like a rapidly expanding parasite, clawing its way up to her chest and throat. She considered retreating into the jungle, but doubted she would get very far. Instead, she pointed brazenly at the prince. "That *thing* cut off my friend's head!"

Armitage absently rubbed his nose and then studied the tip of his thumb. "Was your friend a Spaniard?"

"What does that have to do with anything?"

He stared at her as though she was an idiot. "Zipacna does not like Spaniards." He motioned for her to follow. "He will not harm you."

She summoned her courage and followed Armitage as he approached the prince. Zipacna stared at her, angling his head like a dog listening to a curious sound. Dried blood stained his legs and bare feet. She wondered how he was still standing after what she had witnessed in the jungle. If he was in any pain, he didn't show it.

She avoided his red eyes and inched toward the hole, leaning forward. It was nearly two-hundred feet in diameter and one-hundred-and-twenty feet deep, an almost perfect cylinder with sheer limestone walls patched in moss. Vegetation spilled over the upper rim on all sides, clinging to the walls, and long vines stretched from the opening all the way down to the vibrant blue pool at the bottom, alongside thin white waterfalls. The midafternoon sun cast the curved shadow of the western rim midway across the water below, like the dark edge of a waxing moon. Kate backed away for fear the ground might give way and hurtle her into the bowels of the earth. She turned away, unable to look at it any longer, and saw the faces of the villagers watching from the jungle, where they lingered, refusing to come any further, including Dumaka, who seemed bound to them despite the indifference in his eyes.

"Bring her," Armitage said, and the warriors dragged Jacqueline forward. They turned her around and pressed her back to the stake, drawing her hands behind her and fastening them with an old leather strap, while the prince's horrible red and orange eyes hungrily scaled her body from bottom to top. When the warriors were finished, they moved behind Kate.

Armitage withdrew a long obsidian knife from his coat. Fear mounted in Jacqueline's eyes as she watched the knife pass from Armitage to Zipacna, who set his war club on the ground. She began to squirm against her binds, wriggling her body ineffectually. Zipacna stepped before her and placed the tip of the blade against her chest. He pressed it into her skin. Jacqueline screamed as he started to carve, his wrist twitching like an artist with a paintbrush.

Kate felt her fingernails digging into her palms. She looked down at the dirt and closed her eyes. For an instant, she saw Eira Roberts turning away from her to face the blue ocean, the last thing Eira would ever see. It had been quick for her, at least. Kate wondered if the girl had heard the crack of her pistol in the split-second before her world went dark. She'd pushed Eira from her mind until now, as she had done with so many others. It did no good to dwell on the dead. Deservingly or not, the deed was done and there was no undoing it.

She opened her eyes and forced herself to look. *This is not the same.* Eira had been young and impulsive, too young to pay so steep a price. Jacqueline, on the other hand, had betrayed her many times over. *You've earned this, my dear.*

Zipacna finished his carvings, and Jacqueline was left bleeding and moaning, with three little hieroglyphs drawn across her breasts, streaming rivulets of blood down her belly. Zipacna handed the knife back to Armitage, who accepted it with a grimace. He looked at Kate. "If you've anything you wish to say to this woman, now would be the time."

"What are you going to do?" Kate asked.

"W-what are y-you going to d-do?" Jacqueline parroted, trembling in pain and terror. Her eyes darted wildly for an exit, or someone to come to her rescue. Kate had witnessed that last-minute desperation too many times. There were no exits, and no one ever came.

"It is best that the entrails are exposed," Armitage answered, "so Chaac may consume her from within." He rolled his eye. "Or so they say." He took a deep breath. "Anyway." He returned his attention to Jacqueline, placing the knife between her legs.

He's going to open her from the bottom up. A bubble ascended her throat, and she tasted half-digested monkey meat. Her saliva turned metallic. She tightened her stomach and held her breath.

Jacqueline opened her mouth, but the shriek lodged in her throat. Zipacna's red gaze fell to the black thicket between Jacqueline's thighs. He licked his cracked lips. Beneath his loincloth he was visibly aroused.

The two warriors were breathing heavily on either side of Kate. She could almost hear their rapidly thudding heartbeats and the blood pumping through their veins down to their loins. She heard the villagers chanting softly in the jungle behind her. Armitage's arm tensed as he prepared to do the deed. Jacqueline finally let out a pathetic squeal, but Armitage pressed his other hand over her mouth to shut her up. Her giant round eyes locked with Kate's.

"Fortune smiles," Kate proclaimed on a sudden exhalation.

Armitage paused. "It does?"

She stepped forward and raised a finger that begged consideration of a proposal. "As it happens, I once promised to remove this woman's entrails for her. I should very much like the honor, seeing as I won't get a second chance."

Armitage let out a heavy breath and lowered the knife. "Fine. Yes. Good. I hate this part. The smell."

"I've grown accustomed to it," she replied. "Give me that."

Armitage flipped the knife over and offered the leather-wrapped hilt to Kate. He stepped aside. The weapon was surprisingly light. The notched blade glinted wickedly in the sun. Zipacna glared fiercely at her as she approached, letting out a low hiss. She forced herself to meet his gaze, and for the first time she took note of his features, which were curiously familiar. His nose was not broad like the others, but distinctly long and pointed, with a straight bridge she usually found attractive in other men. The bone of his brow was strong and prominent, and his black eyebrows thick and sharply-arched. Within deep-set eyes, orange swirls vivified predominantly red irises. If not for his flaking white snake-skin, he might have been handsome. Kate looked away, refusing to see any beauty in him.

She aimed the tip of the blade at Jacqueline's shuddering belly and inched forward. The tip pierced her skin, drawing a thin trickle of blood that ran down into her navel. Her cheeks quaked as she lifted her chin, trying so hard to re-main proud. She met Kate's eyes and forced a smile. Her lips parted, but Kate spoke first. "What was your daughter's name?"

Jacqueline's broad shoulders slumped as the fear drained from her face. She spoke the name with relief. "Adaline."

Kate smiled. "Pretty."

Kate faced the prince, keeping her smile, and drove the black glass into his throat.

XIBALBA

"WHAT HAVE YOU DONE??" Armitage roared, while the villagers shrieked and scattered into the jungle.

The blade slid easily from Zipacna's throat, and Kate's chest was doused in the warm arterial spray that followed. The blood seeped into her shirt, molding the black fabric to her breasts. The prince's strange eyes held hers, toiling with hate and confusion and something else she didn't quite understand. Maybe relief. His eyes rolled up in their sockets to reveal red veins strewn against white. The gush of blood sputtered and ran down his trembling front, painting him red. His legs buckled and he collapsed in a heap.

Kate heard the intense patter of footsteps moving toward her with a purpose. She pirouetted and flung out her arm, projecting the knife. Yellow Jaguar could only gawk at the incredulity as it spiraled through the air and skewered his sternum. His feet and arms flew forward while his body was punched backwards. He landed on his back, clutching the knife and unleashing a dreadful howl.

Black Macaw charged. Kate dropped beside the heap of Zipacna, recovered his club, and hefted the heavy thing with all her might. The tall warrior was within three paces as she swung it in a wide arc. He lifted an arm to shield himself. The club connected with a tremendous crack, bowing his forearm like rubber and splattering her with flakes of mud. The impact sent him gyrating away like a rebuked dancer saving face and moving on to his next target. Shreds of his skin clung to the glass shards embedded in the club.

Armitage was staring, frozen in place, with his arms outstretched in a pleading gesture. "Stop," was all he could say. "Stop this!"

Kate tossed the club aside and glanced at Jacqueline, who was watching her with an odd tranquility, a little smile teasing the edges of her lips. Kate moved behind her, heels dangling over the edge of the precipice, and frantically unfastened the leather straps. Jacqueline almost collapsed, but threw out a foot to steady herself. "Run!" Kate implored. "Run south and don't stop until you reach the mangroves!"

Jacqueline nodded and wasted no time, forcing her clumsy legs into a sprint.

Black Macaw turned around, his right arm hanging flaccid and purple. He lifted the war club in his good hand and charged again, crushing past Jacqueline. She was thrown off her feet into a wild somersault, landing on her rear near Armitage, who promptly kicked her in the face. She rolled away and curled into a fetal position while he pummeled her back with his boot. He suspended his foot over her head for a final blow, but she rolled out of the way just before his heel impacted the dirt. She scrambled to her feet, sparing a final glance at Kate before she disappeared into the jungle.

Kate hunched behind the stake as Black Macaw threw himself against it. The base splintered, tipping toward the precipice. Kate wrapped herself about it. She struggled to maintain her grip, but the stake was listing and her fingers were sliding. She looked down and saw a leaning silhouette at the curved shadow's rim in the water far below.

Black Macaw drew back and swung his club.

"NO!" Armitage protested, throwing himself forward too late.

She saw the club coming and instinctively released her grip before her arms could be pulverized. The club hit the stake as she tumbled away, raining splinters down after her. Black Macaw steadily shrunk as he roared down at her, deprived of his victim.

Rippled limestone walls sped upward. Kate feebly threw out a hand, her fingers grazing wet mossy patches but unable to grasp anything solid. Just when she thought she might fall forever, her back slapped the water.

The impact forced shut her eyes for only a split-second, or so she thought.

When she opened her eyes, stars littered the dark sky above, blurred through her waking vision like smudges of chalk on a slate, and bordered by a black perimeter. She was floating on her back in the warm water, feet suspended somewhere beneath her. She listened for sounds, but heard nothing beyond the constant flow of the waterfalls streaming from above. She checked herself for wounds and was surprisingly unscathed, as far as she could tell, apart from a scraped palm.

She waited in the water, gazing up at the edge from which she had tumbled, and listening for voices while the fine mist of the falls rolled over her in translucent curtains. After a few minutes, she concluded everyone had gone, probably to pursue Jacqueline. She wondered if the girl made it. Maybe Jacqueline would meet up with Israel Hands. *Or maybe they've already caught her and tortured her to death.*

"Well, this was pointless," she announced to no one, slapping the water with her palm. The scar along her back ached in reply.

Wasting no time, she rolled up her wet sleeves and urged herself into a paddle, toward the nearest vine. She grabbed hold, testing her weight, but her hands slipped too easily. There were too few notches to support her all the way up to the foliage spilling over the rim above. So, she swam for the curved wall. When she reached it, she felt around for something to grasp. The limestone was cold to the touch. She tested the notches until she found one large enough to support her. She placed her toes on a small outcropping beneath the water and climbed up. She continued until she was halfway up, carefully feeling around and testing her weight each time before pulling herself up. There were many crevices in the ripples of the limestone to offer leverage. She kept her eyes focused on the dark perimeter above rather than looking down. If she fell, at least she'd only hit water. Two feet above her was a sturdy vine that hadn't yet reached the water, but was close enough to the wall to help her the rest of the way. She heaved toward it, reaching up. Her fingers grazed the vine.

She heard a low hiss beneath the constant flow of the nearest waterfall, but it wasn't water. She looked to the crevice before her and saw something uncoiling itself within. It shot forward before she could react. She glimpsed a pair of needlelike fangs and a forked tongue, just before it latched onto her scalp. A sharp sting lanced through her skull, confounding all rational thought. She instinctively released her grip on the wall and clasped her hands to her face, grabbing the snake and tearing it off. She felt its fangs rip from her forehead, spilling warm blood and venom into her eyes. She got a look at it as she started to fall. It appeared jet-black in the night, with a yellow stripe running down its underside. She hurled it at the wall. It hissed back at her in protest before smacking the limestone, straightening its body in shock, and tumbling out of sight. She flailed her arms as she fell, grasping madly for the vine above, but it was too far out of reach. The intense sting clouded her sight. The vine blurred as she fell away from it. The world was totally dark by the time she hit the water.

She floated in a void, empty and hopeless, as the poison spread like wildfire through her veins. The sting was soon traded for a heavy throb, and soon the throb blossomed into the worst headache she'd ever suffered, pulsating within her skull like a second heart, pressuring her sinuses and pinching her optic nerves. She raised a hand, but she was unable to see her fingers even as she wriggled them desperately. She lingered in the black with nothing but pain to accompany her. She stared upward in hopes the constellation Virgo would blink into her vision, one star at a time, but the woman in the sky did not penetrate the void, not this time. She waited and waited, while anguish swept through her head and fire through her arms and legs in maddening torrents. *Am I dead? Is this what eternity is? Darkness and pain?*

An hour passed. Or a minute. Or a second. Time was

meaningless, for she had no breath to gauge its passing. The pain reached its peak, and then each wave was less than the last, and eventually she felt only a dull numbness in her head. The heat retreated from her veins, until she felt nothing in her limbs, as if they had vanished entirely. A distant, constant white noise infiltrated her ears, growing louder. She felt her chest expanding and contracting. Her arms and legs tingled back into existence, but the world remained black and without form.

When she raised her hand again, a web of indigo flurried across her fingertips. She looked down. Far beneath the dim glassy surface of the water, the rocky bed was colored in undulating curtains of the ethereal. She jerked involuntarily in the water when she realized what littered the lakebed were not rocks, but hundreds of grinning skulls resting amidst ribcages and various other bones. There was not one complete skeleton, all had been broken apart and stirred into a disjointed soup. They were small, smaller even than the men she had encountered in the village, but not small enough to be children. She blinked, unable to comprehend what she was seeing as blue light danced over the remains. She traced the source of the shimmering columns to a cavernous opening in the southern wall of the rock, just beneath the surface of the water. The opening was wide, curving downward at the edges, like a frowning mouth.

She looked up. The wall she had attempted to climb gradually came into view. The stars dimly winked into existence, but they had lost their potency. The world above seemed so far away. She looked to the cave, contemplating the source of the light and how far in it might be. The snake's venom had become intoxicating, churning densely in her skull like too much rum. *Perhaps it will not be much different than drowning*. She had drowned once, only to be revived by a man with a special talent that mystified most, and the euphoric high that washed over her now was not entirely different from the sensation she had experienced after the gagging throes of agony.

She blinked, eyelids slowly sliding shut and slowly opening again. It seemed to take forever. Time stretched across the surface of the water like a soft breeze grazing a calm sea. Her skin started to tingle. Schools of tiny fish nipped at the fine hair along her arms, their translucent skin revealing frail skeletons. Bulbous black orbs, thinly-ringed in gold and silver, sprouted from their little skulls. They sucked tenderly yet greedily at her skin. She swished her arms about, and the fish darted away with surprising speed. She rolled down her sleeves to keep them away. She considered trying to climb the wall again, but doubted she'd have the strength to make it more than halfway, and there had to be more snakes waiting up there.

I'll be dead within the hour, whatever I do, she reminded herself as she looked to the mysterious and strangely inviting cavern beneath the water. *Might as well*. She took a deep breath, curled forward and dunked her head in the warm water. The snakebite stung only for a second, and a little cloud of blood formed about her head, dissipating swiftly. She kicked out her legs and propelled herself toward the cavern, while the carpet of skulls observed her from below with scathing delight. The fish followed her much of the way to keep an eye on their future meal, but they scattered suddenly when she passed under the wall, as though hitting an invisible barrier.

She swam into the haze of blue light, through a labyrinth of stalactites, over pockmarked boulders and a long bed of soft sand, which kicked up a cloud when she swished her feet close to the ground. She swam through a maze of long roots twisting down and around and up again into the earth. The cavern was blurry and confusing, but her breath seemed infinite, as it does in a dream. She latched onto stalactites and roots to pull herself through. She ran her hands over the rock formations, noticing seashells fossilized in the limestone. The cavern narrowed into a thin channel, and she glimpsed a blurry orb somewhere at the end of it. The blue light faded for a moment, obscured behind a rock, and her chest tightened in alarm, but then it returned, swathing her in its cool radiance, and she breathed a sigh of relief, bubbles rolling up her face, and she inhaled without thinking, because there was no way this was anything more than a dream, and she let the water flood her lungs.

She tried for another breath, but something was lodged in her throat. Her lungs clenched and hardened. Panic struck her all at once. She flung her arms and legs, dashing them on the rocks and roots, propelling herself forward into a concentrated patch of blue light. She flailed madly, clutching her chest and listening to the sounds of her own convulsions, fingers rending at her chest.

Ten feet above, she saw a circle of water reflecting everything below, as though someone had placed a mirror in the rock. She dashed for it, fighting through convulsions and the immense pressure that shot through her skull from one temple to the next. Something white and stick-like materialized through the mirror. It broke into five digits and wriggled like a spider, and she realized it was a hand, swishing about in search of something. With no other options, she strained for the hand. Jagged nails dug into her wrists, and she was suddenly wrenched upward, through the mirror. She was helped up onto a flat slab of limestone by small, clammy hands. She choked globs of water all over herself while the stranger patted her back. She convulsed on her hands and knees, eyes squeezed shut, until her head seemed ready to burst like a grape. When at last breath returned to her lungs, she looked up to greet her savior.

A corpse smiled sweetly back at her, oblivious to its desecrated flesh. Short blonde hair appeared white and silvery in the blue light that shimmered off the close walls of the air pocket. Green fluids trickled down a snowy white cheek. A tiny white crab lurked within the hollow socket where the corpse's right eye had once been, teasing the light with its pincers. The crab thought better of emerging, and hastily retreated to its den, but Kate could still see it moving around in there. The corpse's nostrils were black and shriveled like burnt parchment. The dead girl's pale, fissured lips peeled from rotten teeth.

"Eira," Kate croaked as she massaged her chest. "You're not real."

The corpse looked down and studied its pale hands for confirmation of its veracity. The little crab nearly tumbled from the open eye socket, grasping the rim with a pincer and scurrying back up into the safety of darkness.

Kate took in her surroundings as she retrieved her breath, keeping the apparition at arm's-length. The little chamber was virtually spherical, a bubble of pitted limestone, with thin roots descending from the ceiling and nearly touching Kate's head. Blue light filled the little chamber from the opening below. "Where in God's name is that unearthly light coming from?"

The corpse raised a hand, watching curiously as the webs of light danced along its palm. Thankfully, it seemed unable to speak. Kate had never held much interest in conversing with the dead.

Just beyond the dead thing was a dark passage that cut through the rock in a sharp sliver that had probably been caused by an earthquake. Kate couldn't be sure how far it went.

The corpse stared her inquisitively, jaw slowly unhinging into a comically dumb, gawking expression, and Kate's fear of the thing subsided. When she realized the dead girl was looking at her forehead, Kate touched the welt where the snake had bitten her. It ached as she pressed it. "Snake venom," she murmured to herself. "It's causing me to hallucinate."

A sticklike hand shot out, grasping Kate's arm and squeezing painfully, and the fear returned in a smothering torrent. The little crab swayed in the eye socket as the corpse sternly shook its partially hollow head. A slimy morsel of brain matter drizzled out, rolling down its cheek and collecting on its soiled breeches. The corpse's lips moved, but nothing emerged except a sour whiff of putrefied fish and seaweed. Kate grasped the dead thing's arm, struggling to free herself of its grip. Its clammy skin was slick with a layer of green film, like a sponge left too long in the sink, and green fluid leaked from the pores. She swallowed her fear and leaned forward, refusing to be intimidated by the dead, and smiled in the other's rotten face. "You're going to tell me the way out."

The thing that resembled Eira tilted its head and smiled. It released Kate and pointed down at the blue hole from which it had pulled her up.

"You want me to drown."

The corpse shook its head, but a little smile played at the

edges of those terrible lips.

Kate pointed at the dark passage. "Where does that go?"

The corpse cast a casual glance over its shoulder, as if it had forgotten. The crab scuttled deeper into the hollow. The remaining eye held Kate's gaze for too long.

"You don't want me going that way," Kate concluded. "That's the way out, isn't it?" She smiled confidently and stood without waiting for confirmation, avoiding the roots as she circumvented the dead girl. "Begging your pardon, but you're not much for discourse."

The thing remained where it was, facing the spot where Kate had been, with its hands placed neatly in its lap. Kate looked at the back of its skull, finding the small hole where the shot had entered. A tiny white pincer poked out, snipping at tendrils of blood-matted hair to clear a path. The crab had made its way through. Kate shuddered and turned away.

A sound trickled from the dead thing's mouth, low at first, and then building in pitch and regularity. It was giggling. The crab scuttled out of the hole and slid down her hair, abandoning its cranial sanctuary.

Kate increased her pace and slid into the crevice, which was just wide enough for her body as she turned sideways. She shimmied down the passage, dragging her shoulder blades and breasts along the cold, flat rock. Infuriating giggles pursued her as the walls steadily tapered, constricting her torso. A cool breeze prickled the flesh along her arms. She angled her head into the darkness, calling to it, but she heard nothing in return. She let out all her breath and pushed onward, awkwardly sliding sideways as the space thinned until the walls touched either side of her head. She carefully leveraged her feet over rocks that had collected along the ground, one atop the other. The last thing she needed right now was a twisted ankle. She did not stop, and soon she could scarcely take in breath. Pain knotted in her forehead as she raked the wound over the rocky wall. It seemed twenty steps before the dead thing's giggles faded behind her.

She drew in her chest and stomach, flattening herself as best she could. Her head grew paradoxically light from lack of air and heavy with the renewed throb of the snake bite. Her saliva turned rusty, seeping down her throat and into her belly. She felt sick, but this was not the place to empty her stomach.

She made the mistake of taking in air, and found herself jammed between the walls with her head locked sideways and one foot wedged in a cluster of rocks. Panic clouded her mind yet again, overtaking the throbbing and nausea. Her back ran cold, every inch of the scar flattened against the rock, crying out in protest. Her arms hung uselessly at her sides.

She closed her eyes and let the icy needles of fear pass through her, taking very shallow breaths. Warm light crept through the seams of her eyelids, glancing off the rippled walls from somewhere at the end of the passage. She carefully lifted her foot, freeing it from the rocks. She exhaled sharply and slid with a scream toward the light, knowing that if the walls compressed even a hair further, she would never get out.

Oh, God. Please.

Something wet and cold teased her neck, tracing a slimy film. Two fingers, index and middle. She heard a brief giggle of excitement cut short, like a child realizing the cookie jar isn't meant for her. And then, a low hiss of barely contained fury. Tingles of fear crawled up her back. Adrenaline quickened her heart and urged her through the slim gap. Despite the protests of her breasts and shoulder blades, she inhaled sharply and made herself fit, notching forward. The walls opened a few inches, allowing her to swing her head around and get a look at whatever was behind her, brushing the tip of her nose across the rock. She knew what she would find before she saw it.

The thing that wore Eira's skin was there, squeezing through the space behind her, reaching greedily for her. Its lips spread into a wide, mirthless grin as it dragged its cheeks along the rock, contorting itself to fit through. The friction of the walls peeled away the tattered rags, like a snake shedding dead skin, revealing a body that was scarcely more than a thin sheet of flesh stretched over a skeleton, shorn away at the hips, ribs, and shoulders, exposing spindles of grey muscle and juts of bone.

It's not real, Kate told herself. *That's not her. She's not there. Nothing is there.*

Nevertheless, she scrambled for the warm light, palms flat on the rocks as she slid sideways. She heard the thing panting in pursuit. Terror surged through her, manipulating her limbs into movement like a marionette dancing frantically on the strings of a spastic puppeteer. Her scalp felt tight against her skull, icy cold yet blotted with hot patches.

It's not real. Eira is dead, rotting at the bottom of the sea.

The air turned sour, breath warmed the lobe of her remaining ear, and Eira was real.

ASCENT

The dead girl's fingers probed her ribs and grasped at her buttocks, fumbling for purchase. Kate screamed through clenched teeth and shoved herself forward. One final push. She wouldn't have the strength for another. If the walls narrowed again there would be no going forward, and retreating the way she came was out of the question. The thing in pursuit would be happy to welcome her into its desecrated arms and confine her there. A companion to rot alongside, pinched between a crack in the bowels of the earth, forever.

The walls yawned suddenly, like the jowls of a leviathan waking from its slumber, and Kate was deposited into yellow light on her hands and knees. When she looked back, twin pinpoints glared at her from the black slit in the rock, unable to proceed further. The dead thing made a low, guttural sound of dismay. The eyes dwindled and blinked out, like candleflame deprived of oxygen.

Kate collapsed onto her back and massaged her chest, rubbing her sore breasts. The rubbery second skin of the giant scar ached against the slab of flat, wet rock. She felt moss beneath her fingertips, slick and warm. The air was oppressively humid. An angry vapor roiled in yellow rays of light. She gazed upward, struggling to comprehend what she was looking at, but her head felt foggy and dense. She ran the back of her hand over her forehead, and it came away smeared in a milky green discharge. She curled forward and placed her palms flat on the ground to shove herself up. She swayed in place, staring up in disbelief.

Over one-hundred feet up, the source of the light streamed from an opening in the rocky ceiling, down a huge column of coiling roots that stretched all the way to a large emerald pool in the center of the massive cavern. It might've been the corded arm of some great wooden god that had come to rest beneath the earth, reaching for the sun in its final throes of death. Wayward roots ran along the domed ceiling, spreading from the hole and forging a path through stalactites and rock, curving down along the walls. A few were suspended in midair, grasping at nothing.

As immense as the cavern was, she found herself gazing longingly at the patches of moss lining the rim, where the water didn't reach, wide and lush enough to accommodate her entire body if she wanted to rest. *If I stop, I die*, she told herself.

She stepped into the warm water, which was shallow at first, but sloped steadily as she neared the base of the roots. After ten paces, the water reached her waist and tickled her navel. She leapt forward and swam the rest of the way, wondering if the pool connected to the other channels, including the one she had been swimming through before Eira—or, the thing that *resembled* Eira—had pulled her up.

She reached the roots and climbed onto them, finding them thick and sturdy, with plenty of hand and footholds in the many crevices between the thick stalks. The wood was warm to the touch and sticky with sap. She embraced the roots, but her arms only encompassed a tenth of the huge, entwining column. Warmth flowed into her chest and limbs, invigorating her. She closed her eyes for a moment and entertained the notion of being drawn into the roots, her skin hardening into impenetrable wood, and some explorer finding a wooden woman within the giant tendrils a century or two later. The thought did not frighten her.

She started the climb.

A glorious ache seemed to expel the poison from her arms and legs as she made her ascent. The warmth radiating off the roots cleared her head, imbuing her with the tree's vigor and life. Yellow light caressed her face, growing warmer with every upward heave. Sweat broke out along her arms, sliding down her straining muscles. The rubbery skin of the death's head scar rippled fretfully along her back, kneaded by distended muscles beneath. Halfway up, she paused to have a look at the pool below. It was so much smaller now. She licked her lips and continued up, eager to be quit of the underworld. She sliced her palm on a protruding splinter, but felt no pain, and she left a trail of red handprints the rest of the way up.

When she was within five feet of the dome, the stalks began to bend outward, forcing her to slant perilously over the great precipice, and she was momentarily paralyzed by a sweeping vertigo. Her arms trembled, dripping sweat. Her eyes felt as though they were growing too large for their sockets. She clutched the roots and closed her eyes, grinding her fingernails into the wood and taking long breaths as her body imbibed the tree's heat.

Just as her courage returned, a twig snapped from somewhere above. For a mortifying instant, she thought the roots were giving way. The yellow light dimmed. She looked up to see the silhouette of a man's head peering down on her. She could see nothing of his features, just the outline of unkempt curly black hair and broad shoulders. He was shaking. "You there," she called, discarding caution. If the mystery man proved dangerous, she'd deal with that problem soon enough, but getting above ground was her first priority. She freed her bloodied hand and reached for him. "I could use a hand." Straining from plummeting to her death, her words manifested as primal grunts, barely intelligible.

The man darted from the entrance. Yellow light blinded her as it glanced off the wet leaves above. Without forethought, she raised a hand to shield her eyes and nearly slipped from her perch. She grabbed hold with both hands, tearing loose a brittle stem and dangling precariously as she watched it spiral downward for what seemed a minute before it impacted the shallow perimeter of the pool with a little splash.

She swallowed her fear and clutched the largest, sturdiest stalk, wrenching upward with whatever energy remained. Her back shrieked in fiery dissent, but she let the pain drive her forward. Her feet hastily scrambled for purchase in the many footholds as she made her way up. It helped to pretend the tree had fallen on its side and she was merely crawling over it, not dangling for her life. She reached for the hole, which cut through dirt and rock, and she seized one of many large vines twisting out of the soil. She kicked off the roots and threw herself upward into the slender passage, scaling the latticework of vines and spreading arms and legs to brace herself within the twisted duct where the earth had given way, with nothing beneath her but a sheer drop. She tried not to think about the dome, or why it hadn't collapsed entirely, but she prayed whatever magic supported it did not fade within the next few minutes. She kept her eyes on the leaves above rather than looking down. She stretched an arm skyward. Sweat rolled down her temples, pattering her shoulders like so many drops of rain. One hand burst free, fingers expanding in the warmth of the sun. She felt around until her fingers discovered another vine along the surface. She tested its leverage with three sharp tugs, and pulled herself up with one final heave. She exploded to the surface and opened her arms, seizing the ground and pulling herself onto one side. She rolled onto her back, between two massive buttress roots, and soaked up what little sun remained as it neared the western horizon.

The tree's gargantuan size was humbling, but she was distracted by something attached to the trunk. A pale hand, amputated at the wrist and trailing dried blood, was pinned to the trunk by some sort of long white nail. Curiosity superseded the desire for rest, and she forced herself up. She wobbled about, setting a hand on one of the buttress roots to keep from falling over. On closer inspection, the nail appeared to be bone. *A stingray spine*, she realized. The palm of the hand had been pressed flat against the tree, and the spine had been driven directly into the center of a cross that was branded in the skin.

Something snapped in the distance. Another twig. She spun around to see a tall, powerfully built figure with curly black hair rolling down the long slope descending from the tree. He was plainly dressed in the casual garb of a sailor, sleeves and breeches rolled up, and barefooted. He came to a halt at the bottom, deftly sprang to his feet, and fled into the jungle without looking back. "Wait!" she called, but he did not return. She gripped the stingray spine and wrenched it free of the trunk. The hand remained in place, glued to the tree by blood and sap. She stuck the sharp spine down her breeches and started downward, carefully skirting the hole and scurrying down the hill, dancing over a dense network of roots and vines and boulders. Her thighs burned and her right knee was threatening to give out, but she couldn't afford to rest until she was off this cursed island and safely aboard her ship.

"Who are you?!" she called into the jungle, but the jungle did not answer. Branches swayed back into place where the man had plunged through them. She reached the base of the hill, spared a final glance over her shoulder at the giant tree for reaffirmation of its existence, and continued into the jungle.

She followed the path of swaying branches and footprints until she came to an expansive, impossibly green field of tall grass bending in the wind as sherbet hues brimmed the western horizon. None of this looked familiar, but she suspected she was on the eastern end of the island, near the beach where the jagged rocks would have torn through her ship's hull had she sailed any closer. A monkey—or what she *hoped* was a monkey—loosed a chilling howl some-where behind her. She spotted the black-haired man bolting into the jungle on the opposite end of the field. She bent forward to set her hands on her knees and catch her breath, waiting for the sharp pains in her chest to subside before she persisted onward.

When she recovered, she followed a zigzagging little stream across the field and continued into the jungle on the other side, where the trees were oppressively thick and dark, blotting out any trace of the fading sky. She stepped awkwardly on a rock and twisted her leg, and her right knee seemed to explode, dropping her on the spot. The throbbing agony endured for several minutes. She sat there cradling herself in the dark, listening for sounds that weren't there. No animals. No trickling water. No rustling leaves. Nothing.

When the pain dwindled to something more manageable, she struggled to her feet and tested the lame knee, hissing as she placed pressure on that leg. She limped onward the rest of the way, through a long, silent darkness.

The jungle broke upon an inky black sky sprinkled with stars more vibrant and plentiful than she had ever known, even during her many years in long stretches of sea, far removed from the fires of civilization. She stepped onto a plate of hardened volcanic ground which encompassed a large field, its rippled surface allowing for no trees or shrubbery. Perhaps the central peak had erupted long ago, and its streaming lava had pooled here. In the center was a dark stone pillar, much like the one she and her men had encountered on the trek from the southern beach, but this one stood tall and unbroken. She limped around to get a look at the other side, glimpsing the prominent profile of a king carved in the stone, wearing a crown of three skulls that blossomed feathers at the top. A long tree ascended his extravagantly-patterned robe, touching his chin. The branches extended about him, gracing the heads of the giant, blocky serpents on either side.

But she instantly forgot the imposing monument when she saw what the king's blank eyes looked upon. It was a scene she would take to her grave. A native woman in a white dress hiked up to her hips straddled a naked man atop a rectangular stone altar, chanting in the strange language of her people. Her hand was inside his chest, plunging through a bloody cavity beneath the sternum, while he gawked at her in horror, unable to scream. He had the same curly black hair as the man she had been pursuing. The woman withdrew his beating heart, clenched in a fist. Severed valves squirted blood in every direction, splashing his mortified face and the woman's chest, molding her dress in deep red against full breasts and hard nipples. The man's head fell back, and his body shuddered one final time. His chest constricted, flesh fading to a ghostly shade and sinking into his ribs as blood bubbled out of the cavity and poured down his sides. The woman arched her back and presented the heart to the heavens, letting the blood dribble on the quetzal feathers of her headdress and down her face, into her eyes and mouth. She let out a final moan of pleasure and dismounted the dead man, revealing the erection she had been perched upon, which stood firm even in death. His fluids dribbled down her inner thighs. She unfolded her brown and red-striped skirt down to her knees, smudging it with blood as she smoothed the creases. Kate was drawn to the woman's navel, which brandished a large medallion engraved with a proud man's face, crowned with a jaguar head. She looked from the medallion to the monument. The likeness was identical to the man carved in the giant pillar. *A king*, she guessed. *This woman's father.*

The native woman froze when she spotted Kate and tilted her head, unafraid. The woman placed the heart upon the altar, next to the dead man's leg, and stepped forward, studying Kate from top to bottom. "Tu'ux a taal?"

"I don't understand." Kate briefly considered fleeing into the jungle, but something told her this woman meant her no harm, despite what she had just witnessed. She reached down and grasped the stingray spine protruding from the front of her breeches, just in case. The woman's eyes descended to the weapon for a moment, but her brown eyes appeared unconcerned behind the red band of paint that slashed horizontally from temple to temple. Her face was broad and exotic, with luscious lips that Kate imagined any man would consider himself lucky to drink from. Every move was casual and confident, yet her posture was refined and proud, and even barefoot she stood a few inches taller than Kate. Her skin was dark in the night, sheened in sweat and blood that glittered of infinite crimson starlight. She was no older than Kate, possibly years younger.

She was one of the most beautiful creatures Kate had ever seen, and she knew she was facing a queen. *The* queen. Ix Chak Sahkil. The woman whose mind she had entered from across leagues of time. But she was so young now—not to mention, *alive*. Kate resisted an absurd urge to prostrate herself before her.

None of this made any sense. It had to be a dream. Perhaps she had surrendered to exhaustion in the cave, and she was down there still, comatose and dying of the snake's venom while the corpse of Eira lovingly caressed her new plaything. *Eira.* That had not been Eira. Whatever it was, the fear had given her motivation to keep moving. "It was you," Kate concluded.

The queen cocked her head, confused.

"You led me here. The light in the water. Eira. You dug around in my mind and you found her and you used her to push me forward. It was all you." But this was a younger queen who had not yet encountered the man who called himself Armitage, and had not yet been taught English. This woman had no inkling of the sad fate she had just sealed for herself and her people. Not yet.

The queen moved to Kate's left and touched her sleeve, rubbing the fabric between thumb and forefinger. She looked at the dead man's shirt and breeches scattered beside the altar, perhaps connecting the materials.

Kate grabbed the woman's thick wrists, clutching her metal cuffs and shaking her. "Why did you bring me here? What did you want me to do? Warn you? Stop you? I cannot change what you've done." Kate released her and pointed at the dead man on the altar. "His blood is not the answer. You were stronger without it." *But he's already in you*, she didn't say, even though the woman clearly didn't understand her words.

Kate lowered her head in frustration. She was so tired. Everything hurt. She wanted this to be over. She wanted to sleep. Nothing made sense here, but she knew she'd been led here for a reason. Her eyes fell to the stingray spine in her breeches. She touched the brittle bone and looked up suddenly. "Am I meant to kill you, is that it?" She looked at the queen's stomach, shielded by the metal face of a dead king. Even now the Spaniard's seed was quickening within her. Kate drew the stingray spine from her breeches, clutching it firmly, until her knuckles turned as white as the bone in her grip. She aimed the needlelike tip at the queen's belly, just above the medallion. The queen stared indifferently at the weapon, undaunted. Kate opened her fingers, letting the spine fall. It broke into three pieces against the stone ground. "What difference would it make?"

The queen circled, fascinated yet confounded by this alien creature before her. Her bare feet made no sound upon the volcanic rock. She moved behind Kate and softly laid her hands on her lower back, sliding them upward. Her fingers curled, gripping Kate's shirt and sliding the tails out of her breeches. Kate stiffened as the queen's fingers slipped beneath the shirt and up the rubbery skin of the scar. She felt the pressure of the other woman's fingers, but nothing else. The skin had lost all sensation. The ache ran deeper, as with the water cutting through the subterranean channels beneath the island. The queen gasped at the breadth of the wound. Her hands slid around Kate's sides, to her stomach, drawing her into an embrace from behind, pressing Kate's back against her chest. The other woman's warmth radiated into her core, but she did not feel invigorated. An uncertainty was bleeding into her gut, curdling everything within. The woman's large breasts mashed against her shoulder blades. Her chin rested on Kate's shoulder. One hand ascended to cup a breast, squeezing gently. The other descended into Kate's breeches, fingers winding through the curly hair between her legs. Two fingers slipped into her, while she thumbed a nipple with her other hand. Her movements built in urgency and aggression. Her teeth sank into Kate's neck.

Kate shouted a protest, curling forward and spreading her arms wide. Heat exploded from her back, billowing her shirt. The woman cried out in shock as she was hurtled away, landing hard on the rock. Kate turned to face her. The queen raised trembling hands to shield herself while pleading in her strange language. Her arms had been scalded an angry red, smoldering in the night. Steam wafted from the fabric of her dress. The face in the medallion distorted beyond recognition as its features melted into searing metal. The queen's jaw fell open, elongating her pretty face into a caricature of terror, and the deafening scream that followed shook the ground until the volcanic rock fractured between the two women. The crack extended from the queen's feet to Kate's, expelling a fine red mist from the depths.

RETURN

She shuddered into consciousness to find herself huddled in the embrace of massive buttress roots. The sky was gloomy with clouds, the air fresh and brisk, beading her arms in morning dew. A bright green lizard made its way down one of the roots, scampering over her fingers without acknowledging the disparity between human and tree.

She wondered how long she had been unconscious. She prayed it had been no longer than one night. When she stretched, everything hurt. Daggers pierced her lungs when she inhaled, so she resorted to shallow breaths. Her mouth was dry and her tongue stuck to the roof of her mouth. A headache pinched her sinuses. Fortunately, the drunken nausea of the snake bite had vanished and all that remained were the effects of a potent hangover. The welt on her forehead had subsided and no longer oozed pus, but was sore to the touch. Perhaps the snake hadn't injected as much venom as she'd thought. Perhaps its venom was merely hallucinogenic. Perhaps the tree had healed her. She winced through a chuckle at the absurd notion. Whatever the case, she was not dead.

She threw back her head to take in the great tree, resting her short hair against its smooth bark. There was no trace of the severed hand that had been nailed to the trunk, or the trail of blood that had crusted its bark. A quick glance confirmed the hole from which she had crawled was only three feet away. She couldn't look at it long, for fear something might materialize from the black and drag her back to the depths. Though the warmth of the roots was a comfort, the tree was synonymous with the world below, and she was eager to be quit of this place.

Standing was not as difficult as she expected, but her left knee plagued her as she descended the hill. She hobbled west through the jungle, and when her ears picked up a distinct sound she quickened her pace, shoving through huge fronds until she came upon crystalline water rushing southward over smooth boulders as silver fish leapt upstream in impressive arcs. She assumed the river ran south all the way to the marshlands where she and her men had come ashore after boating through the mangrove forest. There had been an aqueduct cutting through the ancient city, and this river had to be connected to it.

She followed the water north along the western bank, toward the three peaks. The clouds roiled like a witch's brew, moving so quickly it seemed time had lost all leniency, and she felt her pace increasing along with them, propelling her inexorably toward her final destination. Thunder agitated the heavens, charging the moist ether with a hot, electric current that prickled the fine hair along her arms. There was no breeze to offer respite. The maddening hum of countless insects overtook the sporadic chirping of birds and chattering of monkeys. The world renounced its vibrancy, giving to shades of silver and black. The trees, once so lush and welcoming, became dark, oppressive barriers that promised no shelter. Wisps of fog sifted along many crevices of the three mountains like ghostly fingers. The central summit vanished into a passionless grey.

A white bolt struck the top of a tall tree, crackling down its trunk and quaking the earth. The bolt held there a fraction of a second longer than lightning should, searing a serrated arc into her retinas.

Kate blinked . . .

The island was gone, submerged in a crimson sea that stretched infinite leagues in every direction. An orange mist rolled patiently over unrippled, blood-red water. She found herself standing on the bow of a ship. There was no wind to impregnate the sails. Above it all, the flag of England drooped pitifully. She lowered her gaze, and there, at the foot of the mainmast, was Armitage, on his knees with his arms outstretched and hands cupped, offering something. She took three steps forward. He held a heart, rapidly beating. It was the only sound. Each pulse impacted her ears like a drum. He mouthed words she could not hear. Blood bubbled from his mouth, down his chin. At first, she thought he was offering her the heart, but his lone eye was fixed on something just past her. She turned. A woman stood at the foot of the bow, features hidden in mist. She wore a long, black dress.

Kate blinked . . .

The tree's trunk burst into flame midway down, and the blaze billowed into the branches and leaves. The upper half of the tree listed as fire enveloped its top. Its trunk creaked noisily, until it splintered and crashed to the ground ten paces before Kate, extinguishing its leaves in the river. She moved forward and set her hands on its smoldering, blackened husk, channeling heat through her fingertips. She climbed over and continued forward, glaring at the thundering heavens, which had made evident their intent to thwart her.

She followed the snaking river through the jungle. After an hour or more, she paused to bowl her hands in the river and splash her head, letting the cool water stream into her shirt. She bowled her hands again and brought the water to her lips, drinking slowly at first, and then greedily. Her throat protested less with each swallow. A hummingbird zipped up to investigate her, darting about her head. She was smirking at the little bird's green mohawk when the clack of a musket's hammer stiffened her back.

"You there," came a familiar voice as the hot metal ring of the barrel pressed the base of her skull. "Turn slowly."

She raised her hands and did as instructed, pivoting slowly. She smiled when she saw his face. "Israel," she exhaled.

Israel Hands' vivid green eyes betrayed no sign of recognition, only fear. The frazzled coils of his beard were stained along the chin, as if he'd torn into someone's throat with his teeth. His dreadlocks were caked in mud, and his shirt was no longer white. His cheeks were ruddy and flaked from sunburn. After a moment, he blinked. The barrel wavered. "Kate?"

"I thought you'd forgotten," she said with a sigh of relief.

He lowered his musket. "This place has my mind all

fogged up. Ever since we left the beach. I think we were safer there. Wasn't until you came along and took us inland things started going foggy."

"My mind has never been clearer," she assured him.

He appraised her with a quick glance up and down. "Are you certain? You look terrible."

"I imagine so." She pointed at the Spanish rapier sheathed at his hip. "You still have your sword."

He touched the hilt. "I still have my sword." He seemed a bit surprised by that fact.

She allowed herself a smile. "I love you."

"Really?" One eye narrowed. "You wanted to kill me, before."

"Well, right now I love you because I need your sword."

"I suppose honesty is a more valuable trait than emotional constancy."

She presented an open palm. "Less talking, more sword."

He unsheathed the weapon and offered it hilt-first. She tested its balance and found it extremely light. The polished blade mirrored the heavens, elongating the clouds. She shoved the sword through her belt.

"That's not a cutlass," Hands warned. "It's a thrusting weapon. You can't go slashing and cutting with it. It's a gentleman's weapon. For a gentle*man*. Not a gentlewoman. There's no such thing, far as I—"

"I know how to use a rapier," she said with a roll of her eyes. In truth, she couldn't remember if she'd ever handled a rapier, but she kept that to herself. "I need you to follow me, Israel."

He shook his head. "I'm going back to the ship."

"If you were going back to the ship, you'd be there by now."

"I lost my way. I've walked from one end of the island to the other, I think. North and south, east and west. It's easy to lose your way here." Lines formed along his brow. "It's downright improbable."

"Not if we follow the river."

"A fair point," he said, setting the musket on his shoulder and starting south.

"Hands!"

He halted. His broad shoulders settled, but he did not turn. "What?"

"I need your help."

He laughed. "For what? There's no treasure to be found here."

She closed her eyes and saw Armitage offering her his heart on the deck of a strange ship. "There is. I've met him."

Hands turned with a skeptical smirk. "Armitage? I don't think he's—"

"He's here," she promised.

Hands sighed. "We should go back to the ship and fetch more men. We had too few when we left the beach and we have fewer now."

"More men to surrender their wits to this place? I think not."

He jabbed his temple with a thumb. "I've kept my wits. Mostly. Maybe I get a little confused sometimes, but I know who I am. I am Israel . . ."—his eyelids fluttered desperately, and for an instant she thought he wouldn't remember—"Hands."

She couldn't help but stare at him. The man had managed to maintain a semblance of his identity, which was more than she could say for most men who had ventured deep into this island. "It's possible I underestimated you."

A scowl twisted his sun-ravaged cheeks. "Possible?"

She felt her teeth gnashing. Nothing came less naturally than offering a compliment, but she needed him. "You are stronger than I thought."

Hands took a few paces toward her. "You're only offering sugar because you need my help."

"Yes," she admitted, "but, it happens to be the truth."

"I suppose that will do," he muttered. "Flattery has always been my weakness, notably when offered by an attractive woman, though I must say, you smell as though you crawled out of a cow's asshole."

She sniffed herself. He wasn't wrong. "Pardon me a moment." She splashed into the river and soaked herself in the water, dropping to her knees and letting the current push her clothes against her body. She ran her hands through her hair, and her palms came away covered in dirt and blood. She dunked her head many times, while Hands watched with an arched brow. The laces of her shirt came undone and revealed her breasts, and Hands turned away at once. She refastened the laces as she strolled out of the water.

"Have you encountered Joseph?" she asked.

Hands turned around, glancing at her chest to make sure she was decent. "The negro? Haven't seen him."

"What about Duncan? The little one."

"Figured he died in the cave."

"He was there when I was taken."

"I saw the cave collapse. If he's still in there, he's dead."

"Or sleeping," she replied with a mirthless chuckle. "And Jacqueline? Have you spotted her running south like a chicken with its head lopped off?"

He looked down. "I was stirred by womanly screams last night, can't be certain when. Hours before dawn. I tracked the screams to a grove. The mud people were already on her. They carried her north." He pointed at the three peaks. "That way."

She sighed. *Oh, Jacqueline, you couldn't do one simple thing and not get captured. You're the worst.*

Hands rummaged his fingers through his dreadlocks in a bout of frustration. "Who are these people?!"

"It doesn't matter," Kate replied. "All that matters is we retrieve the man who leads them. We don't want to disappoint Woodes Rogers, now do we?"

They continued the rest of the way in silence. As they neared the village, they passed a broken dam where the aqueduct spilled carelessly into the river. The clouds dropped rain without warning, in unrelenting sheets. Hands produced a red sash and sheltered the lock of his musket. They followed along the eastern rim of the aqueduct to a rope bridge that stretched across the water and led into the remains of the city, meeting up with the main thoroughfare.

Rain loudly hammered the dilapidated structures. A building crumbled inward as water streamed through it. A man screamed from within and a teenager fled the collapsing walls and ran out into the street. Hands instinctively took aim. The teenager was practically naked, save for a loincloth. Blood poured from a gash in his scalp. Kate set a hand on the barrel of Hands' musket and pushed it downward. The teenager prostrated himself before her and muttered what sounded like apologies, concluding with, "Ix Chak Sahkil." He fumbled her boots and she kicked him away. He bolted into the jungle.

Kate and Hands continued up the thoroughfare. No torches or incense burned. Kate swept her gaze from west to east, waiting for men to emerge from the ruins and huts, but no one did. She glimpsed no movement in the dark interiors.

The palace seemed smaller by day, less imposing than it had been at night. All torches were extinguished. Kate drew the rapier from her belt and started up the grand stairway, wincing through the burn of her thighs and the throb of her knee. Hands fell in line after a moment's hesitation. They halted at the top of the platform to take in the long complex, as rain curtained over the frieze and the snakes seemed to move through the mosaic. She glanced over her shoulder to make sure Hands was still at her back. He nodded. She stepped into the huge triangular corridor, out of the rain. She gazed at the dark, vaulted ceiling, listening to the echoes of her heels as rain cascaded beyond the exit at the far end, like the backside of a waterfall at the end of a cave. The corridor was maybe fifty paces across, but she halted midway when she heard voices. She stood in the dark, straining to listen through the incessant rainfall. She heard a man's voice, and maybe a woman's sobs, coming from somewhere beyond.

She halted at the exit, just before the wall of rain, and looked down upon a large garden with trim grass, four ceiba trees in the four corners, and two square fountains on the far sides. A stone pathway led from the palace to a large round limestone plate atop a stone mound in the center of the garden. The plate funneled slightly toward a cistern drain in the center.

Armitage stood upon the outer rim of the plate, with Jacqueline on her knees before him, while Black Macaw watched. Jacqueline was naked and streaked in red, her arms and limbs a mosaic of deep, crisscrossing slashes. Blood matted the black hair between her legs, coursing down her inner thighs and streaming into the cistern, diluted by rainwater. Armitage was grasping her left breast as he worked a jagged obsidian dagger through it, sawing downward. Jacqueline's face was beyond agony, lost somewhere behind a veil of white skin. When Armitage withdrew the dagger, the breast flopped away from an open circle of gore, dangling from pink tendrils of fat, blood vessels, and threads of skin. He tore it free, jolting her forward, and placed it upon her head, so that the nipple pointed to the sky, and he contemplated his work as would a hatter who has crafted a cap he's not entirely proud of. Thick red rivulets streamed into her flat black hair and down her passionless, gaunt face. Armitage plucked the mutilated breast from her head and lobbed it into the cistern. "It's been so long, I'd forgotten," he remarked to Black Macaw, "it's easier from the bottom up." He placed the dagger beneath her remaining breast and said, "One more, and you will be a woman no more."

Kate stepped out of the palace and into the rain. "Israel, I've changed my mind." She aimed her sword at Armitage. "I'm afraid I must murder this man."

COLLAPSE

As Kate Warlowe plunged silently toward Armitage, a furious gust swept over the garden, tearing at her clothes and skewing needles of rain into her eyes, as if the elements meant to lock her in place. She blinked through the sting of the rain and the throb of her left knee and charged forward, arm and rapier levelled as one.

Black Macaw spotted her before Armitage realized anything was amiss. The mud-shrouded warrior hefted his war club and moved to intercept. One blow from that club would shatter the thin blade of her rapier.

She was about to surrender her resolve and retreat when thunder cracked, but not from the sky. Black Macaw's shoulder exploded blood and bone, spinning him in place. His necklace snapped, spilling jade beads and teeth down his front. The club slipped from his hand. He dropped to one knee and slapped a hand to his shoulder, fitting a flap of skin back in its place. He slouched for a moment, took a breath that expanded his scarred chest, and stood. His eyes burned through the white band painted across his face, but not for Kate. He retrieved the club with his working arm and bellowed a high-pitched cry, charging down the mound and flying past Kate. She looked back to see Hands drop to his knees and scramble to reload his smoking musket. She briefly entertained helping him, but she couldn't afford to turn her back on Armitage.

She surged forward until she reached the foot of the mound, where she halted and put her weight on her good leg. Armitage drew his rusty cutlass and gazed down at her from the cistern. The tails of his long black coat billowed in the wind. The medallion no longer hung from his neck. His eye narrowed to a fine slit. "How are you alive?"

She lingered at the foot of the mound. "I had help."

His thin lips twitched. "From who?"

"Your rightful queen. She led me to the surface." The notion sounded crazy enough in her head, let alone spoken aloud. She couldn't explain it, but she knew it to be true.

Armitage allowed a single chuckle. "Either that or you have fortune on your side. And you wasted your one chance to escape this island?"

She trained the tip of the rapier on his heart. "There's a man who will pay a great deal of money for you."

His eye faltered a moment. "What man?"

"It doesn't matter anymore. I don't care how much you're worth. I've changed my mind. You need to die. There's nothing for it."

He looked back, probably at Jacqueline, but Kate

couldn't see her from her low angle. "Can you believe this woman?" he remarked. He returned his diminished gaze to Kate. "I've forgotten many things in my time here, save one. No one has bested me in combat."

She tapped her temple. "Someone took your eye."

"And I took his life in return. I can't recall his face, or who he was, but I know that much."

"Large talk," she taunted. She needed him to come to her. He would easily take off her head if she rushed up the mound in her weakened state. "Yet you remain up there, knowing you have the advantage. Are you afraid to face a woman on level ground?"

He hesitated. "When this is over, I promise you I will be the last *man* standing." He smirked at his own jest and suddenly propelled himself forward.

Before he made it off the cistern, a bolt of lightning arced soundlessly from one end of the sky to the other, and Jacqueline Teach shot up to frame herself against it, naked and striped in crimson like a red and white tiger, pouncing at Armitage with what little life remained. She managed to snag an ankle midair. It was enough. Armitage's leg flew out from under him and his knee hit the rim of the cistern, and Kate heard bones fragmenting on impact. He spun, carried forward on his own momentum, and hit the slope like a sack of rotten fruit, rolling all the way down. Kate took a step back, anticipating his recovery once he reached the bottom. Sure enough, he clumsily sprang to his feet, but he screamed when his shattered knee refused to support his weight. As his legs went flimsy, he thrust his sword at Kate, but only managed to fall on his face with his arm stupidly outstretched. She placed a heel on the blade, which nearly vanished in the heavy grass. Armitage tugged at the hilt, frothing and snarling like an animal with its limb wedged in a trap. Kate shoved the rapier through his wrist, pinning him to the ground. His shriek was warbled and pitiful. Thunder boomed at last, rolling through the clouds in the direction the bolt had travelled.

Kate left the rapier there and easily snatched the rusty cutlass from his hand. She doubted the blade would have held up in a fair fight, but it would be enough to end a life. She lifted it high, freezing in that pose, waiting for him to look up. And he did, and his elongated expression of mortal terror was exquisite.

The next bolt nearly threw her off her feet. It shot directly into the cistern, and though she could not see it strike from her angle, she heard and felt it electrify the water in the reservoir below. The ground tremored, driving up rocks and roots along the mound. She beheld the giant bolt, suspended in time. The lids of her eyes shielded her retinas before she could be blinded.

Again she found herself aboard a ship adrift in a sea of red wine spilled over glass, a blistering mist encroaching on all quarters. Armitage was hunched before the mainmast, cupping a rapidly thudding heart and hastily murmuring words she could not hear. A hand fell on her shoulder, pale and skeletal, but she was not afraid. She turned, knowing who she would find. Shadows cloaked the woman's face, but Kate did not need to see her to know who she was, who she had been, and who she would be.

Her eyes opened. The bolt was gone.

Armitage whimpered like a child at her feet, his scarred face red and bloated. He fumbled at the rapier's blade and managed only to slice his fingers.

Kate looked back to see how Hands was faring, and she

wasn't disappointed. He had overpowered Black Macaw and was presently beating the warrior's face in with the butt of his musket. Black Macaw's hands fell to his sides after several blows, but Hands wasn't ready to let up, and kept pounding until he ground Macaw's face into a muddy stew of flesh, bone, and brains. He stood rigid and swept back his wet dreadlocks, surmising his work.

Armitage reclaimed Kate's attention by grasping pathetically at her boot with a bloody hand. "Please don't . . . please don't kill me."

When she looked down at him, a memory returned to her. Hundreds of skulls scattered over rippled sand, shimmering in blue light. Small. Feminine. "You killed them," she said, surprised she hadn't figured it out sooner.

His eye squeezed shut. "God, it hurts. Take it out."

"You killed them," she repeated.

He opened his eye and blinked up at her through the rain. "Who?"

"The women. I saw their bones at the bottom of the pit, in the water. They didn't die from a plague. You sacrificed them. All of them. Why?"

"I . . . I can't remember."

"Maybe pain will help." She leaned on the rapier's hilt, savoring his scream.

"Wait!" he cried, and she eased off the sword. His brow bunched as he struggled to recall. "She was . . . speaking through them. Their words became a pestilence. There *was* a plague. It claimed many men, but the women endured."

Kate resisted a laugh. "I thought you didn't believe such nonsense?"

He tried to roll onto his back, but twisted his impaled arm and hissed. "The prince did. Zipacna. He believed his mother was trying to return in the body of another, but none of the women were strong enough to accommodate her spirit. She needed someone of great strength. None of them were strong. She drove them mad one by one. Many turned to murder, killing their husbands in their sleep." He frowned through a flood of pain and recollection. "Her memory was enough to poison their minds. The prince believed their deaths a necessity, to silence his mother's evil once and for all. Even those who remained lucid were sacrificed to the pit, for fear the queen's spirit would seek them out. I merely served the prince's will. But he went mad, took to the jungle, and left his kingdom to me before he could accept his role as king."

She made a sad face. "And then a pair of women arrived to spoil your quaint little paradise."

He nodded feverishly, and she glimpsed something she had glimpsed in too many men at the business end of her blade. Talking was keeping him alive, and he desired every breath. "One woman was an obvious imposter who had to be punished, the other . . . harder to dismiss."

She smirked. "That must have been terribly frustrating."

His face was so red and puffy, she was reminded of an overly ripe tomato. The white streaks in his hair seemed to be spreading. "They believed you were the one. Strong enough to nurture the queen's spirit without going mad."

Kate could still feel the queen's fingers probing her crotch and squeezing her breast. "Well, there's the paradox. I was strong enough to resist her."

"Nonetheless, I would've made you a queen, and these superstitious brown shits would have been satisfied that their queen had returned to release them of their curse, and you and I could have ruled to—"

"Oh, do shut up." She slapped his cheek with the flat side of the blade, leaving an angry welt. "You would've murdered me at the first opportunity."

He raised his other hand. "No. Please. Please don't kill me. I'm not meant to die here. Not like this."

"You're right," she concluded with a dismayed sigh. "As much as I would love to put this blade through your face, you are not mine to kill."

When he realized she was serious, his silly face eased of fear, if not agony. But the fear returned when she reared for another strike. The cutlass descended faster than rain, clashing with the rapier and showering chips of rust as it followed the thin blade down to Armitage's wrist, separating flesh and bone. He retracted a blood-squirting stump and threw back his head for a cry that would no doubt have surpassed the last, were it not for her boot crushing his jaw and dropping him unconscious in the wet grass.

"See if you can stop the bleeding," she told Hands as he approached.

"I thought you were going to kill him," he said, looking relieved that she hadn't.

She stepped on Armitage's severed hand and drew the rapier from the wrist. She plucked the hand from the grass. "So did I."

Hands tore off one of his sleeves and kneeled to bind the wound. "What stopped you?"

She looked to the sky, anticipating another bolt, but it didn't come. "His days are numbered. Might as well secure the bounty first."

Kate ascended the mound, dreading what she would find up there. Steam rose out of the drain in the center of the stone plate. Jacqueline was on her back, placid blue eyes taking in the sky, with one hand over the circle of gore where her breast had been removed. Kate wasn't sure if Jacqueline was alive, but the pool of blood draining from her body into the cistern told her she would be dead soon enough. There were too many cuts to count. The dying woman's eyes shifted as Kate kneeled beside her. "Is he dead?"

"Not yet," Kate replied. She lifted Jacqueline's hand to have a look at Armitage's work. She shuddered. "Jesus."

"It doesn't matter," Jacqueline said. "He did worse down there."

Kate avoided looking. "I'm sorry."

"It's what I deserve for . . . what I did to you."

Kate couldn't think of anything to say. She placed Armitage's severed hand in Jacqueline's and smiled. Jacqueline's fingers tightened, and blood dribbled from the shorn wrist. "Small comfort," Kate said.

Jacqueline looked at her. "Why did you save me before? You were safe. Armitage—"

"Armitage is nothing," Kate said. "You were many terrible things, Jacqueline, but many terrible things are better than nothing."

Jacqueline smiled faintly, fighting to keep her eyes open. "Adaline is waiting for me. I know it."

Thunder tore through the clouds. Kate looked northeast, where the temple of the red pyramid peaked over the palace. She looked at Jacqueline, whose eyes were beginning to close, each breath shallower than the last. Kate placed one arm beneath Jacqueline's legs and the other at her back, fighting through the protests of her left knee and lifting her. "What are you . . . doing?" Jacqueline asked, her voice barely a whisper.

"I'm not going to leave you out here."

"You should."

"I agree," Kate said. "But I'm not going to."

Hands watched as Kate descended the mound and carried Jacqueline across the garden. She mounted the steps into the triangular corridor of the palace. When she limped out the front of the building, dozens of natives were waiting with blank expressions in the thoroughfare. She swallowed an urge to retreat and started down the grand stairway. They spread apart as she neared, moving to the opposite sides of the road.

Her arms and legs burned as she carried Jacqueline north through the village, holding her close. Jacqueline's eyes opened briefly to gaze up at her, and fell shut again.

Kate found Dumaka alone at the base of the decapitated jaguar statue. He stared at her, his brow creasing. The rain washed over his dark face and washed away any sliver of recollection. He looked skyward, distracted by a thunderclap.

Kate passed between the twin jaguars and down into the sunken courtyard. The clouds encroached on all sides, rolling down the mountains and over the pulverized remains of the fallen pyramids, but they shied from the red pyramid, as if some intangible force held them at bay.

She shambled across the courtyard to the reclining female statue at the foot of the red pyramid. Jacqueline's arm fell limp, and she dropped Armitage's hand. Kate instinctively kneeled to retrieve it, balancing Jacqueline on her good knee to free one arm. She tossed the severed hand onto the stained plate that sat on the statue's stomach. "An offering of flesh," she quipped. The woman's stone face remained serene, but her blank eyes seemed to see all.

345

Pouring water and her throbbing knee made the climb up the steps treacherous. Her legs wobbled under the added weight of Jacqueline, skinny though she was. Kate hunched under every rumble from the dark clouds, fearing another bolt. The final three steps were the hardest. She wavered at the top, leaning back too far and nearly toppling. She angled sharply forward, using Jacqueline's weight to right herself, and forced herself to the top with a final burst of fleeting vigor. She dropped to one knee before the temple. Jacqueline's lips parted, but her murmurs were too low. Kate stood and carried her through the portico, between the pillars bearing feathered serpent heads, and into the perpetual haze of incense that choked the temple interior.

She moved through the low archway to the inner vaulted room, where she set Jacqueline down. As she took a flaring torch from the sconce along the back wall, she thought, *Who keeps these things lit?* She secured the torch in Jacqueline's lifeless arms, angling the flame away, and lifted her again. The sound of rain faded as she descended into the bowels of the pyramid, taking care not to smack Jacqueline's head on the wall, though she wasn't sure Jacqueline was still breathing.

She carried Jacqueline to burial chamber at the bottom and shook her to see if she was alive. The torch slid free, clattering against the stone floor and continuing to burn. After a few minutes, Kate was certain she was holding a dead woman. Blackbeard's dark legacy had finally come to its end, eight years after his demise.

She crossed the chamber and set Jacqueline in the open sarcophagus alongside the crimson bones of Ix Chak Sahkil, sweeping aside jade figurines. She thought she heard a voice, so she leaned close to Jacqueline's mouth, but the current of the river beneath the chamber was too loud. No breath touched her ear. "Goodbye, Jacqueline," Kate said, wiping blood and dirt from her cheeks and bringing out her faint freckles. She smoothed out her hair as best she could. Despite the ravaged state of her body, Jacqueline had never looked so peaceful. She'd been an angry thorn in Kate's side since their first meeting, but it was impossible to despise her now. "I'd forget you if I could."

As Kate placed her palms on the rim of the sarcophagus and pushed herself up, the earth trembled and the coffin sank, dipping her forward. She braced herself to keep from falling on top of Jacqueline's body. The queen's skull rolled up and struck the top of the coffin interior, shattering the death mask into jade fragments. Kate looked to the end of the chamber. The crack in the floor beyond the sarcophagus was spreading, pieces of the moss-covered stone crumbling away and splashing in the flowing water below. A fine, cool mist sprayed her cheeks as she peered into the darkness. The sarcophagus tilted toward the crack and began to slide.

Just before Kate shoved herself off, she thought she saw two red eyes glaring back at her from the world below.

And then the floor gave way, and the giant sarcophagus plunged into the water, taking the remains of Ix Chak Sahkil and Jacqueline Teach with it. The lid followed next, and the blood-drawn devil grinned as it vanished into the watery abyss.

Kate bolted for the stairway as the yawning crack chased her heels, retrieving the torch on her way. Chunks of the ceiling struck her head and shoulders as she scrambled up the rumbling stairs, ignoring what felt like a knife lodged in her left knee. She angled sharply in the space where the stairs changed course, torchlight dancing across one wall and projecting her frantic shadow across the other. The pyramid swayed midway up the second set of stairs, hurtling her sidelong and bruising her shoulder. She looked back to see the stairs falling away behind her, taking the hiero-glyphed walls with them. Her bad knee clinched as she labored upward, forcing the joint into movement and screaming through the pain.

When she reached the top, the temple was slanting sharply, the floor breaking into puzzle pieces beneath her. She pitched the torch aside and dashed out the portico just before the two pillars flanking the entrance cracked at their bases and fell toward one another, smashing the serpent heads together. She hobbled down the front of the pyramid as fast as she could without sacrificing her footing. When she glanced back, the temple had crumbled and huge pieces of debris were pursuing her, and she increased her pace. She angled right as a pulverized serpent head rolled past, and left to avoid a huge chunk of the roof. Two thirds of the way down, the steps started to crumble beneath her, and she surrendered caution and leapt down them two at a time. Her left knee exploded pain with every impact of that heel. She reached the bottom and swerved to avoid the reclining female statue, a split second before debris piled against it. The plate slid off the statue's belly, catapulting Armitage's severed hand. She never saw where it landed.

When she made it a safe distance into the courtyard, she turned to watch the pyramid fall. The heap of rubble was indistinguishable from the other two when it was over, apart from the white dust rising from it.

Kate sat down to catch her breath and massage her knee. She opened her mouth to catch rainwater, letting it slide down her parched throat. The rain ceased a moment later, and the clouds broke to reveal fragments of blue.

Feet pattered the ground somewhere behind her, and when she stood and turned, dozens of villagers were there, along with the men who had once been *Persephone's* crew, gawking at the remains of their queen's pyramid. Their faces wrestled through various emotions as they looked from the rubble to Kate, and she wondered if they would worship her or murder her. Possibly both.

She was contemplating retreating into the jungle when the first shot rang out, cracking over the limestone. The villagers turned south. Another shot. Another. And another. The villagers shrieked and scattered toward the remains of the pyramids, racing past Kate.

Gabe Jenkins and eight pirates filtered through the twin jaguars, aiming pistols and brandishing cutlasses. Kate raised her arms. "Hold fire!" A few more shots were fired before they halted. She marched across the courtyard. "I told you to stay on the ship," she said, aiming a finger at Gabe, but a relieved smile betrayed her.

"You've been gone for three days," Gabe said.

She stopped before him. "Has it been that long?"

Gabe stared at her clothes in disbelief. "You look like you've been through Hell."

She looked down, touching her shirt. There was as much blood as there was fabric. "It's not mine. You're no prize yourself."

Lack of sleep extended the lines about his eyes and the vertical crease between his brow. His long black locks hung heavy with sweat. "I lost seven men getting here. Two died fighting natives wearing mud. The other five . . . they just . . . vanished. We found one. Pieces of him, anyway."

"That tends to happen here. If you'd stayed on the ship

349

like I ordered, those men would be alive."

He made an ugly sound through his nose. "And you didn't get anybody killed?"

"I can only claim responsibility for Ives' death," she said. "The others went stupid. Duncan did himself in with some poisonous berries. Salvador ran away and got his head lopped off. Corso started forgetting things."

"What things? I haven't forgotten any—"

She crossed her arms and shifted her weight to her good leg. "What is your mother's name, Gabe?"

"Very funny," he said.

"I'm serious. What's her name?"

He laughed. "I know my mother's name, of course. It's . . ." He hesitated, frowning. "It's . . ."

She pointed south. "We're leaving. Now."

"But we just got here!"

Joseph appeared at Gabe's side, grinning broadly. Aside from a small cut on his forehead, he appeared uninjured. "I brought help!"

"Glad to see you alive, Joseph," she said. "But I didn't need help."

Gabe rolled his eyes as he shoved his pistol into his blue sash, next to his curved dagger. "You never do."

She looked back to see the last of the villagers fleeing into the jungle beyond the fallen pyramids. "I had everything in hand. They were just about to crown me their queen, I think."

Gabe scrutinized her for a moment, and when he realized she was serious, he threw back his head and howled laughter. His face turned red as his stomach convulsed. He wiped a tear from his eye and exhaled slowly to calm himself down. "So, you're good here. We'll just be on our way."

"Let's not go that far," she said, brushing shoulders with him as she moved past. She was nearly to the jaguars when she realized no one was following. She turned to find perplexed expressions. "What are you waiting for? I've secured our fortune. We have to get it back to the ship, before you fools forget your own names."

DEPARTURE

Armitage squealed as Hands and Gabe deposited him unceremoniously upon *Scarlet Devil's* main deck, as they would an oversized fish. He rolled onto his back and cradled his shortened arm. "What are you going to do to me?"

The desperate query was meant for Kate, but she was preoccupied with the sapphire sky. The storm had retreated to the western horizon, where lightning sizzled through churning grey. The sun was low in the sky, hovering above the dark clouds and soon to vanish behind them. She closed her eyes and tossed back her head for a moment, relishing the heat on her neck. She couldn't wait to crawl into her bed. There wasn't an inch of her that didn't ache.

It had taken them four hours to get back to the ship, following the main river back to the marshlands, from which they boated through the mangrove forest. They encountered no natives along the way, and the birds and monkeys were strangely silent. It was as though the island's inhabitants, human and animal, had gone into hibernation. But amid that calm, Kate had felt something stirring in the soil beneath her feet, channeling into the trees and through the current of the river, and she had urged the men forward, denying their pleas for rest until they were safely aboard *Scarlet Devil*. And as they boated through the mangroves she kept a close watch on their stern, waiting for the mud warriors to appear, but they didn't.

The crew gathered around Armitage to investigate their alleged treasure with skeptical grunts and murmurs. Granger kicked Armitage in the leg and said, "How does this wretch make me wealthy?"

"Leave him be," Kate ordered. "He's no good to us dead."

"He don't look much good alive neither."

"I won't argue that."

She found Malik near the mast, rummaging knotted fingers through his white beard, which had grown bushy. "I need you to seal this man's wound," she told him. "Cauterize it, if you must."

He scrunched up his dark, crinkled face as he stared at the sun. "A wound like that will fester."

"It won't," she assured the surgeon. "His body is stubborn." *That's the only trait he and I share.*

He shot her a defiant look. "Supposing he does not wake tomorrow?"

She took hold of his shirt and drew him close. "Don't fuck with me, Malik. This man will make us all rich, including you. But if he dies, you will follow his corpse to the depths."

The surgeon refused to break his glare. "You are a villain."

"Did I ever feign otherwise?"

He jerked away just as she released his collar, and he accidentally flung himself against the mast, smacking the back of his head. He righted himself and pushed past her in a huff, moving to starboard to attend to Armitage, but not without throwing a curse her way.

Hands greeted her with a weary nod. He'd washed the blood out of his beard and most of the dirt from his dreadlocks, but he appeared no less exhausted. "Pains me to say it, but you should scuttle *Persephone*. I saw some of my crew out there, thinking themselves natives. Wouldn't want any of them remembering what a ship is for. They're mad and dangerous now. Who knows what they would do."

Kate considered his suggestion while looking at the island. "No. We'll leave it."

He relented with a tight smile. "You're the captain."

Gabe approached. "Where to, Captain?"

Kate looked at Hands. "Israel?"

Hands pointed east. "My contact is in Tortuga. Might take some time, but she'll secure a meeting with Rogers."

"She?"

Hands nodded. "You'll like her. She's a villain."

"Tortuga it is," Kate said. "All hands, make sail and prepare to cast off! Helmsman!" She scanned about. "Where's the bloody—?" She turned to find Tolliver standing behind her. "Oh. There you are. Set your course for Tortuga." Tolliver grunted and moved for the quarterdeck.

Gabe rallied the men to heave the lines, and Kate watched with satisfaction and relief as the sails rose. The ship was off by dusk, under full sail and a strong wind.

The first stars appeared as Kate stood atop the quarter-deck, looking aft as the island diminished on the horizon, barely distinguishable from the wall of clouds beyond it, until lightning touched the sea and cast it in silhouette. Gabe joined her, carrying a bundle under his arm. "Armitage is secure in the brig."

"Good," she said. "Keep him well fed."

"Malik is down there with him, watching over his patient," he added with a chuckle, "pretending not to care."

"Good." Her vigor had all but fled. Every blink was a struggle to reopen her eyes.

He pointed at her forehead. "What happened here?"

"Snake bit me."

"A snake bit you."

She looked around, feigning puzzlement. "We're above deck, yet there's an echo."

"Was it poisonous?"

"It set my blood boiling, so I'd expect so."

One eyebrow lifted incredulously. "What are you made of, Kate?"

"Flesh and bone, same as you. And it all hurts. I intend to sleep for a year."

Gabe removed the heap from under his arm and handed it to her. "Found this in the longboat when Domingo and I returned to the ship."

She unfolded the bundle and stared at it. Silver skulls grinned back from a bloody canvas. She crumpled the coat and tossed it over the rail. It opened midair, sleeves outspread, and landed on its back, bobbing in the wake of the ship. She lost sight of it a moment later. "I'll buy a new one in Tortuga."

Gabe casually laid arms on the rail beside her, giving her

a view of his diminished left hand. He flexed the three fingers that remained and retracted them, cracking his knuckles. "Domingo wasn't happy to hear about his brother."

"I should think not," she replied lethargically.

"He blames you."

"Of course he does." She was too tired for sorrow or regret.

Gabe turned his back to the ocean and leaned against the rail, folding his arms. He cleared his throat. "We need to talk about Jacqueline."

"No we don't. She's dead. Nothing to talk about."

He lowered his head, but his eyes remained on hers. "Well, *I* need to talk about Jacqueline."

She waved a hand. "Talk to someone else."

"Sure," he said, pushing himself off the rail. "I'll have a chat with Corso. He's a good listener. Oh, wait, he's dead."

She was too exhausted to be baited. And maybe she simply didn't care enough to bicker with him anymore. "Then talk to no one."

"You're still mad," he concluded.

She sighed and started for the stairway. "I'm not mad. I'm just tired."

"So am I," he said, following.

She pivoted and held out a hand. "What are you doing?"

"I'm coming with you."

"No, you're not."

"I thought you weren't mad."

"I'm not, but that doesn't mean I want you taking up space in my bed."

He scratched furiously at the thick stubble darkening his chin, scowling. "I see. Will you be all right in there, on your own?"

For whatever reason, she saw herself in a yellow dress, bending over the gunwale of her husband's merchant ship, gazing at her distorted reflection in the water. She'd been on her way to the New World. To America. A woman with another name. A memory from another lifetime. "It occurs to me I've been on my own my entire life, whether there's a man at my side or not."

Gabe opened his arms in a nonchalant gesture, but could not conceal the fact that he was pleading. "It doesn't have to be that way."

"I wasn't lamenting, Gabe." She offered a deceptively amicable smile. "Will you be all right out here, on your own?"

She departed before he could muster a retort.

The captain's cabin smelled of scorched flesh. Hawkes' stench had lingered in the seams of the wood, but she hadn't noticed until being removed from it for a few days. She unlaced her blood-encrusted shirt and lifted it over her head, tossing it onto the table. She kicked off her boots and slid down her breeches, hobbling on her right foot toward the bed. She sat at one corner of the bed and studied her cuts and bruises. Her left knee had swelled to a purple knob, painful to the touch. She crawled naked into the sheets and mashed her face into the pillow.

It seemed less than an hour before she woke to the drip-drip-dripping of water. She sat up and groggily scanned her quarters, spotting no dark shapes in the gloom, but the dripping persisted. Leaning over the bed, she found no puddles. Something snagged her eye, hanging from the deckhead, long and sharp and white, like a giant tooth. Water streamed down its smooth surface and dangled from the pointed tip in expanding drops before pattering the deck at the foot of the bed. Her vision gradually focused, if not her mind.

She plopped back onto the pillow and closed her eyes, dismissing the manifestation of her weary, troubled mind. The drip-drip-dripping went on, but increased suddenly in urgency, and the pattering made a different sound now . . . *spongier*, as if the drops were impacting something softer than the deck.

Under the creaks and groans of the old ship, there came a low whisper. She dismissed it as one of the men in the decks below, but when the whisper grew, it sounded feminine. Kate opened her eyes expecting to see something at the foot of the bed, but nothing was there. All of this seemed vaguely familiar. The pattering stopped abruptly. She looked up. The stalactite remained, with an expanding drop dangling from its tip. It held there a moment, its tail extending. The tail snapped, and she followed the drop downward. The droplet broke upon dead flesh and rolled down between burning red eyes. A hand extended over the bed. White fingers curled inward, save the index, which aimed a silent accusation.

Kate rolled sideways and snatched the book at her bed-side table—"A General History of the Robberies and Murders of the Most Notorious Pyrates, by Captain Charles Johnson"—and launched it at the apparition, screaming, "Let me sleep, devil!" The book hit the globe beside the table, toppling it.

Kate stared into the darkness for a long while. When she was confident the ghost was not coming back, she turned to face the stern gallery. She removed a slat of wood from the broken pane and peered out at the glassy black water, parted in a V by the ship's wake. The light of a thin moon danced along the waves in bone-white slivers.

She spotted something sharp and black peaking over the dark blue of the horizon. The sails of a ship, perhaps. Or maybe just a blot in her weary vision. She lost sight of it in the gloom.

IV

FINAL COMMERCE

TORTUGA

The devil's teeth gnawed at her back as she took in Tortuga from the balcony of her room on the third floor. The scar had been tormenting her in the three months since departing the uncharted island, with increasing fervor over the past week, and she knew something was coming.

The beak of a leather tricorn hat dipped angrily between her eyes. Her hair had grown a few inches, teasing her shoulders only when she sharply angled her head. Already the thick red tresses ran wavy, ending in windblown furls that gave her a hawkish appearance. After a lifetime of untamable locks, she rather fancied this length. Her attire had evolved as well. She wore a long black jacket with burgundy trim and brass buttons, a close-fitting waistcoat of deep wine damask brocade, a slanted belt over a bright red sash trailing long tails down one leg, tight black trousers that disclosed the shape of her legs, and low-heeled black boots laced up the front.

She stretched her gaze to the harbor, where ships crowded the old docks, and several more were anchored further out in the water, their lanterns flickering softly in the night. Beyond the harbor was the black wall of Hispaniola, curving off in either direction. She looked from east to west, to the vast dark blue on either side. She hadn't left Tortuga since arriving, and she was bored with the stillness of land. *Soon*, she told herself as she watched two men disembark from an unremarkable three-masted ship at the foot of the longest pier and make their way through the town.

The deck's wooden railing groaned as she leaned against it to peer down at the two men. The Windward Cutlass was an old structure perched over three-hundred feet above sea level along a steep hillside, supported by thick stilts. A winding road cut through tall trees and huge rocks, all the way to the front entrance of the tavern. The bottom floor was a large, open-air hall, bustling with drunken merriment all hours of the night, and she could hear them down there now, dancing and singing. Lodging took up the second and third floors, and the rooms on the backside offered a breathtaking overlook of Cayona, the town below. Cayona was nestled within the lowlands on the southern end of the island, a cluster of weatherworn buildings that varied in accommodation and class. The finest of the structures were quite beautiful, having been constructed by wealthy farmers from the prior century. The worst were barely a step above huts, with palm-thatched roofs. All were falling into disrepair, as the island's population had dwindled since banning pirates. But the local governor had abandoned his post long ago, and Tortuga had seen a small resurgence in not-so-honest merchants, smugglers, pirates, and other shady types over the past few years. The air was a pleasant mélange of livestock, brine, and the fresh, sweet scent of the lofty trees that covered most of the island's mountainous terrain, spreading a latticework of roots over giant rocks.

Kate lost sight of the two men as they started up the road to the tavern. She returned to her room and presented Armitage with a smug smile. He muffled a curse through his gag and struggled in the chair he was bound to by the waist and legs. She laughed as he wobbled back and forth. "I cannot wait to be rid of you," she said, though in truth she would miss taunting him.

His eye flashed of anger, but his resolve quickly surrendered to weariness. Over the past three months she had kept him just barely alive with one helping of bread and water a day. The streaks in his hair had spread, infesting the remainder of his hair with grey. He had lost much of his bulk, and his beard was long and scraggly.

He muffled something derogatory. She moved close and removed the gag from his mouth. He tried to bite her fingers, but she withdrew her hand just before his teeth clacked. "I will kill you," he huffed.

"No you won't."

He lowered his head, knowing it was true. He took a deep breath and looked at her. The anger was gone. Only fear remained. "You know what's coming."

"Yes." She stuffed the gag back in his mouth. "But it's not coming for me."

There was a rap on the door. "Come in," she called, while gripping the flintlock pistol at her hip.

Israel Hands stepped in, glancing at Armitage. He was

one of only eighteen men who had remained at her side since reaching Tortuga. The rest had joined other crews, disillusioned at the sight of Armitage and skeptical of Kate's assurances. Malik, having saved Armitage's life, had stormed off as soon as the ship was moored, offering his services to the local infirmary. Domingo was gone too, cursing Kate for the death of his brother. She made no attempt to stop them. The angrily departed were of no concern to her. The fewer the crew, the bigger the reward for those who had remained at her side.

"Rogers is coming," Hands announced. "I'm sure you noticed his ship."

"Right on schedule."

Hands nodded. "Viera keeps her promises. She's waiting in the hall."

"Stay with Armitage." She gave him a hard look. "If I don't return within the hour, and you hear a fight, you know what to do."

Hands nodded again.

Kate descended a creaky spiral staircase into the smoky chaos of the tavern hall, where her ears were assaulted by an endless stream of laughter. Her mouth watered at the mingling aromas of ale, roasting pigeon, and a wild boar sizzling on a spit. She passed a trough in one corner, where a young sailor with bright red cheeks rode a giant, disgruntled hog while drinking from two mugs as his friends cheered him on. Eventually he toppled into the mud and laughed himself silly.

Kate slid through the crowd, between long tables and benches. A band of three sat atop an elevated stage, enjoying a drinking break. A colorful parrot observed the drunken occupants from a chandelier, squawking endlessly about "pieces of eight" and "doubloons."

The scant remnants of her crew were scattered about, mingling with other pirates. Joseph raised his mug to her. She spotted Gabe at a round table in a dark corner, with two men she didn't recognize. He nodded to her and indicatively jutted his chin. She followed his gesture to the front entrance, and there stood Woodes Rogers and a man she didn't recognize, both dressed inconspicuously, probably trying to pass as merchants.

The innkeeper, Viera Silver, moved to intercept Rogers and his cronies. She collected their weapons and deposited them in a barrel, and then took Rogers' arm in hers and led him to a table. After seating Rogers and his companion at a round table near the fireplace, she crossed the room, slinking through rowdy drunkards in a purple dress that bore her petite shoulders and ample cleavage. Viera was a slender, beautiful black woman with a seductively dubious gaze many years removed from her exotic, youthful face, as though she had pilfered the eyes of an older woman. Her long black hair was frizzy and hectic. Briolette drops of purple amethyst dangled from each ear. As she passed through the long benches, a drunken man reached for her with wriggling fingers. She avoided him with a casual sidestep and an impassive glance to let him know he was but a minor obstacle in her path.

The edges of Viera's full lips curved slightly as she approached Kate. It couldn't be qualified as a smile, but it was more than she offered most. "The man you have been waiting for is here." Her tone was low and silky, with traces of a Jamaican accent. "Did you note his attire?"

"I did."

Viera leaned close for a whisper. "No one knows he is

here."

The beautiful innkeeper's hot breath on Kate's remaining ear stirred an inexplicable flutter in her belly. "What are you suggesting?" She knew the answer before it was whispered.

"We should kill him now."

Kate glanced about at the tavern occupants, finding men here and there who might not have been as drunk as they appeared. "Do you trust everyone in this room, Viera?"

Viera gave Kate a withering look. She had a way of leaning back her head and casting half-lidded eyes down upon anyone she spoke to, no matter their height. Kate stood an inch taller, but she often felt shorter when facing Viera directly. "Do you think me a fool?"

"Quite the opposite," Kate assured her.

"This island once belonged to the buccaneers," Viera informed her sharply, her breasts swelling as her breath intensified. "When my husband returns from his business, we could retake it with your help. Rebuild Fort de Rocher and defend this place. There is no shortage of fruit and livestock."

Kate touched Viera's wrist. "There will be a time for that. In my experience it's best only to kill a man no one will miss."

Viera's vaguely judgmental eyes held hers. "And this stops you every time?"

"Not always," Kate admitted.

"You think Rogers has spies here?"

"I'd be disappointed in him if he didn't. He's a keen man. He wouldn't have made it this far on chance."

Viera did not bother scanning for potential spies. "I have men too."

"And I'll signal if I need your men."

"If?"

Kate looked at Rogers, who was perusing the crowd with a curious look, possibly taking note of secret associates. "He's not here for a fight. Even if some of these are his men, he will not risk losing his prize over a scuffle."

Viera's body swiveled. "If you say so, Captain. Follow me."

"You don't have to call me that," Kate said.

Viera threw an impassive glance over a petite shoulder. "As you wish, Kate."

Rogers nodded curtly as the innkeeper led Kate to him. He didn't bother to stand. British propriety would only betray his disguise. Or perhaps he didn't consider her a woman. Viera slid out the chair opposite Rogers and offered it to Kate with a smooth gesture. Kate didn't sit right away, pausing to surmise the man before her, who scarcely resembled the man she had encountered several years prior. He was much slimmer now, without the double chin or large gut she remembered, but he wasn't necessarily healthy. His skin was sickly-pale. Dark circles undercut his eyes. There were gaps in his bushy black eyebrows where he had plucked at them too often. The musket ball wound that cratered his left cheek was even more prominent. He wore a frumpy brown frock coat with gold frogging along the breast, tan breeches with white stockings, and gold-buckled shoes.

"It has been a long time," Rogers said. "What in God's name happened to your hair?"

Kate ignored the question and nodded at his younger companion. "Who's this, then?"

The other man's bright green eyes snapped to attention. He was a little too pretty, with a sharp jaw, gleaming white teeth, a trim beard, and sandy-blonde hair. He wore varying shades of grey over a slim frame. He couldn't have been much older than Kate. Before he could stand to introduce himself, Rogers placed a hand on his shoulder and said, "Later."

Kate and Rogers traded a long stare.

"Care for a drink?" Viera asked.

"Nothing for me," said Kate.

Rogers broke the stare to smile at the innkeeper. "Brandy and orange juice."

Viera's half-lidded eyes dodged his, finding something of greater interest on the other side of the room. "We do not carry oranges."

"Brandy, then."

Kate sputtered a laugh. "You're not very good at this merchant disguise, are you, Woodes?"

Rogers worked his jaw in frustration. "Ale."

Viera flicked a speck of nothing from thumb and forefinger. "Would you like anything to eat?"

"I hear pigeon is plentiful here."

"We have more of this bird than we know what to do with."

Rogers raised a finger. "Then you shall have one less pigeon to worry about."

"We are saved," Viera replied, deadpan.

Rogers' younger companion raised a hand. "Nothing for me."

Viera's eyeline briefly flickered his way, as if noticing him for the first time. "It is a good thing, then, that I forgot to ask." She turned her back to both men and casually drew a finger across her long neck, glancing at Kate as she did it.

Rogers' gaze descended as he watched Viera leave.

"Stunning woman. I should like to meet her husband."

Viera didn't speak much of her husband, but Kate had heard rumors of the man's villainy. "So you can string him up and steal his wife?"

Rogers waved a hand. "Pirates are no longer my primary concern."

"And you believe pirates will never concern you again?"

He allowed a thin smile. "I didn't say that."

"It must frustrate you."

"What?"

"Being forced into business with a pirate, especially one who has eluded you for so long. One who slipped right out from under your nose."

Rogers shifted in his seat, throwing a sidelong glance at the man beside him. "At this moment, the business itself is all that matters."

The band began to sing in a rich baritone while strumming their instruments. *"Here's a health to the King and a lasting peace. May faction end and wealth increase. Come, let us drink while we have breath, for there's no drinking after death."*

"Where is he?" Rogers asked at last.

Rogers' handsome companion watched Kate closely, waiting for a reaction.

"And he that will this health deny, down among the dead men, down among the dead men . . ."

Kate looked up. "Upstairs. You may find him something of a disappointment. I did."

"Down, down, down, down . . ."

Rogers leaned forward, barely able to contain himself. "Is he alive?"

"Down among the dead men let him lie!"

"He's alive, but he remembers very little."

"It doesn't matter," Rogers said, sitting back. "All that matters is that he is the man I'm looking for."

"And you've brought me silver?"

"Yes, silver. More than you can spend."

"You'd be surprised what I can spend, Woodes."

"Let charming beauty's health go round, with whom celestial joys are found. And may confusion yet pursue, that selfish woman-hating crew."

Rogers stroked his jaw in contemplation, absently lifting an index finger to plug the hole of his old wound. "How did you know I brought silver?"

"Israel Hands informed me of your secret cache."

Irritation fluttered his eyelids. "It's in the hold of my ship, well-guarded. Should anyone attempt to board her—"

Kate raised a hand to cut him off. "Trade without subterfuge is within both our interests. I have no intention of taking your silver by force."

"And he who'd woman's health deny, down among the dead men, down among the dead men. Down, down, down, down. Down among the dead men let him lie!"

Rogers pulled his gaze from the band and smiled shrewdly. "Would you like me to reveal which of these men work for me?"

"Less than you'd have me believe, I'm sure."

He shrugged. "Or more."

"Like I said."

"In smiling Bacchus' joys I'll roll, deny no pleasures to my soul. Let Bacchus' health round briskly move, for Bacchus is the friend of love."

She slapped a palm on the table. "A fight will end in bloodshed and accomplish nothing. We both know this. And even if you win, Armitage will be dead by the time you find him."

"And he that would this health deny, down among the dead men, down among the dead men. Down, down, down, down. Down among the dead men let him lie!"

"I've considered all outcomes," Rogers added after pausing to regard the loud singers with a look of mild distaste.

"I doubt it," she replied with a smirk.

The silent companion had lost interest in the conversation, his eyeline diverted by Viera as she approached their table carrying two pewter mugs. She set foaming ales before Kate and Rogers. "I didn't want anything, Viera," Kate said.

"That is a sad story," Viera replied in silky monotone as she sauntered off.

Kate and Rogers sipped liberally at their ales while watching the band finish the song.

"May love and wine their rights maintain, and their united pleasures reign. While Bacchus' treasure crowns the board, we'll sing the joy that both afford. And they that won't with us comply, down among the dead men, down among the dead men . . ."

Rogers set down his mug and wiped suds from his mouth with the back of his hand. "Have you not asked yourself why I would risk so much for this man?"

"Down, down, down, down."

Kate licked suds from her lips. The ale was gritty and nearly as black as coffee. She knew better than to drink too much and too fast. "I've had three months to come up with a theory."

"Down among the dead men let them lie!" The crowd broke into applause. A drunken man fumbled his way up the stage to shake the hands of the singers.

Rogers raised the mug to his ugly face, and revealed a

crafty smile when he lowered it. His cheeks were blooming. The ale was already doing its business. Rogers was starting to enjoy himself. Kate prayed Viera hadn't poisoned his drink. "Shall I tell you the tale? You might find it difficult to believe."

Kate brought a fist to her mouth to stifle an artificial yawn. "Don't bother, I already know it."

"Armitage told you?"

"He didn't have to." She took a deep breath. "George the First despised his son, and it's not hard to see why. God only knows how many pets and young girls the little shit tortured before George had him sent him away. The son who sits on the throne presently is no true son. Not by blood, anyway. Adopted in secret. A kind-hearted, stupid man, but not a cruel man. The true heir was banished to sea and promised pain of death should he dare return to England. I imagine he started out on a merchant vessel, turned the crew against its captain, and assumed that man's role with feigned humility. Eventually he landed on an island and discovered a weakened people, easy to manipulate. He murdered their leader and usurped the throne. Meanwhile, in England, rumors abounded of the true heir's existence, but no one could prove so outlandish a theory. No one . . . save *you*, Governor Woodes Rogers, who wishes to retain his lofty title by any means. The Crown could deny everything, but what if this supposed imposter knows things no one could possibly know? I suppose it doesn't really matter either way. The mere threat would be enough to ensure you a life of governorship in the Bahamas, with as much funding as you demand, while you keep this wretch of a man imprisoned in your mansion for the rest of his days, as a kind of indemnity."

She threw caution to the wind and downed the rest of her ale, watching Rogers' expression sour over the rim of her mug. She tossed the empty mug on the table. "As I said, I had three months to develop a theory. Am I close?"

Rogers folded his arms and looked around. "Where is my pigeon? The service here is wanting."

Viera appeared a moment later and dropped a platter with a fat pigeon before him. She wandered away before he could request a fork and knife. He poked at the bird, testing its heat, and then tore off a leg. Blood dribbled all over the table. He frowned at the pink, undercooked meat. "I seem to have misplaced my appetite."

Kate stood, tired of socializing with this bore of a man. "Shall we proceed upstairs? You'll be wanting a look at the merchandise."

Rogers dropped the leg on his plate and wiped his hands on the table. He stood and said, "Lead the way." His handsome young companion in grey followed suit.

Kate summoned Gabe and Joseph with a hooked finger. Both stood and shoved through the crowd to get to her. The four men followed her up the spiral staircase to the top floor, and along the slim hallway leading to her room. She rapped her knuckles on the door, and Hands opened it a moment later. They filed through into the room. Rogers and Hands exchanged curt greetings, while Gabe kept his eyes on Rogers' silent companion and his hand on the curved dagger in his blue sash.

Kate led Rogers to Armitage, who had fallen unconscious in his chair. "He looks dead," said Rogers. "Is he dead?"

Kate slapped Armitage across the face, tossing his head to one side. Armitage blinked into consciousness and looked around. Rogers kneeled before the prisoner and seized him by the hair, looking him in the eyes while Armitage cursed unintelligibly through his gag.

"Jesus," said Rogers. "It is him."

The handsome man in grey spoke up. "How can you be sure?"

Rogers ran his finger down the saber wound that had taken Armitage's right eye. "Because I gave him this."

Kate laughed. "He told me he killed the man who did that."

"I'm afraid not."

"Nothing he says is true."

"What happened to his hand?" Rogers unfolded Armitage's sleeve and drew it back to prod at the crudely-sealed stump. Malik hadn't made it pretty, but he'd saved the man's worthless life.

"He came at me with a sword," Kate replied.

Rogers stood and habitually brushed his hands on the breast of his coat. "No matter. I must say, I'm impressed."

"Oh, I'm sure that will pass and you'll be back to hunting me in a year."

"It needn't be that way, Kate. With what I'm giving you, you could purchase a sizable plot in America. Settle down. Buy horses, cattle, and slaves. Enjoy the rest of your life."

She grinned. "You'd like that, wouldn't you?"

He raised his hands amicably. The gesture didn't suit him. "Merely a suggestion. I'd hate for us to cross paths again."

She took a step forward, bringing her nose inches from his. "Yes, you would."

Rogers pulled away and moved for the door. "Bring the prisoner to the docks at dawn. And bring as many men as you please, if you fear a trap."

"I don't."

He walked right past the man in grey and kept going, but the man in grey did not follow. "Does your friend wish to join my crew?" Kate asked.

Rogers stopped at the door and turned. "Consider him a gratuity, for your diligent work."

Gabe choked on something that might have been a laugh.

"He's not my type," Kate drawled.

"You will want to hear what he has to say." Rogers paused for a final look at the man in grey. "What you do with him . . . I leave entirely to your discretion."

Rogers gently closed the door. Kate raised an eyebrow at Gabe, who shrugged in return. "We've about two hours before dawn," she said. "Go back downstairs and enjoy yourselves until then."

Gabe and Joseph hesitated a moment, glaring at the stranger. The man in grey smiled. "I assure you, gentlemen, I intend no harm upon your dear captain."

"No, please," Gabe said, thrusting a hand at Kate, "try it and see what happens. She's never happy unless someone is trying to kill her. I would advise against aiming for the heart, though. Because—"

"Because I don't have one," Kate finished with an extravagant eyeroll. She jabbed a finger at the door. "Out. And take your invisible bag of clichés with you."

Gabe made a show of searching about for his invisible bag. "Where did I . . . where did I put it?"

"OUT."

Joseph fled. Gabe followed at an infuriatingly slow pace, pirouetting on his heel at the door and offering a little bow before he closed it.

She turned her attention to the stranger. "Now, who the fuck are you?"

The stranger moved around the bed and found a stack of books on the bedside table. He picked through them until he found the one he wanted. He displayed it with a proud smile. "I knew you'd have it. 'A General History of the Robberies and Murders of the Most Notorious Pyrates, by Captain Charles Johnson.'" He sighed. "The 'Captain' bit isn't entirely truthful, but it adds an air of authenticity, don't you think?"

A minute passed before she found her tongue. "You are the man Rogers commissioned to write that rubbish?"

He clutched the book to his heart, feigning injury. "Oh, I imagine it was rather hurtful, what with your name being excluded. That was not my decision, I assure you."

"I couldn't care less about my name. In fact, I'm pleased you omitted it. I can only imagine what you'd have conjured about me if I'd been in there."

"Conjured?" His chiseled jaw dropped.

"You invented facts where you had none. And the deaths of Edward Teach, Charles Vane, and Bartholomew Roberts were outright deviations from reality."

His eyes shot wide with excitement. "You saw them die?"

"Is this an interview?"

He started to sit on the bed, but quickly pushed himself off it. "Before we go any further, I should ask, which colloquial voice do you prefer? Nautical? For example, when answering in the affirm—"

"Be yourself," she said with growing impatience.

"I would not attempt to be anyone else."

She hoped she wasn't frowning. "Are you drunk?"

"I do not partake of spirits. They might rob me of my

senses."

Kate suddenly found the room too stuffy. She retrieved her spyglass from a little round table and walked out onto the balcony. Charles Johnson's feet shuffled in pursuit. She extended the brass tube and brought the eyepiece to her eye, following the main street of the town all the way to the docks, where she found *Scarlet Devil*. Across from her ship was the tall ship Rogers had sailed in, its crew busying themselves about the deck.

"She's a beautiful ship, your brigantine," Charles said, suddenly at her side. He grimaced. "Is it acceptable that I refer to a ship as a female? Or do you take offense?"

"Why would I?" she asked, wondering if he was mocking her.

"I heard a rumor that you reclaimed the ship that once belonged to your husband. The *Lady Katherine*, it was called. They say you murdered its second captain in cold blood. A man named Shelby. I interviewed a lad named Baldwin who told me the whole tale." He looked to her for confirmation.

She remembered it well enough. "If Captain Shelby had stepped aside, he'd be alive."

"I see. And where is that ship now? The *Lady Katherine*?"

She felt the pressure of her molars gnashing. "I sacrificed her."

"An unlucky ship, it would seem."

"I did what had to be done. Sentimentality and survival do not often coincide."

His handsome face lit up with excitement. "Oh my god. That is a fine quote. May I use it?"

The wooden railing creaked as he set his hands on it. "Mind the railing," she cautioned.

"May I?" he asked, opening a palm.

She handed him the spyglass. He brought it to his face and closed one eye as he swept it about, searching for the docks. "You remind me of Anne Bonny," he said. "I enjoyed writing her the most. I felt an odd kinship with her, though we never met. There are times, and I'd ask you not to share this with anyone, that I am convinced I was meant to be born a woman."

Kate suddenly wanted to be anywhere but here. "Well, you weren't, so you're not."

"Sometimes, when my wife is away, I steal into her wardrobe and—" The balcony railing groaned as he put too much weight on it, and he shuddered forward, nearly dropping the spyglass.

"Careful," Kate said.

He laughed off his carelessness and slapped the spyglass in her palm. "I should very much like to tell your story, Kate."

"Pity. I don't want my story told."

"Why not?"

"My story isn't over," she explained. "If you tell it prematurely, I'll have to keep a closer watch on my stern."

"You intend to return to piracy? That's absurd. With what Rogers is giving you, you could retire comfortably for the rest of your days."

"I suppose I could, but then what would I do?"

"Live your life."

"I am living my life."

Various emotions crowded his pretty face. "I'm afraid I just don't understand. You want me to walk away from here empty-handed, is that it?" He turned to face the town again, shaking his head.

"Can you do that?"

He kept his back to her, lowering his head slightly and hissing through his teeth. After a moment, he said, "Yes. I don't like it, but yes. I suppose I can."

"I'm not sure I believe you."

"I am a man of my word."

Rogers' parting words echoed in her mind: *"What you do with him . . . I leave entirely to your discretion."* She smirked at his shrewdness. Either she would accept Charles Johnson's proposal and be forced into an early retirement, or she would murder him and tie up a loose end for Rogers. Johnson, after all, knew far too much about Rogers. *I always knew you were a pirate, Woodes.*

She pulled the flintlock pistol from her sash and aimed it at the back of Charles Johnson's head, drawing back the hammer with the heel of her hand. The wooden clack would've been distinct enough to anyone who'd handled a pistol, but he seemed not to identify it. "Charles. Turn around. Look at my face and tell me what you see."

He swiveled with slumped shoulders, like a child about to be scolded. When he saw the pistol, melancholy turned to alarm. Before she could choose between pulling the trigger or frightening him into silence, he jerked himself away in surprise. His ass impacted the deck railing, splintering the balusters. The railing gave way beneath his weight with a tremendous groan. He flung an arm, managing to grab the barrel of the pistol and wrench her toward him. She shifted sideways and threw out a foot to brace herself, shakily supporting both their weight as pieces of railing fell away. His body slanted over the precipice, green eyes darting from her to the gun. Her arm trembled as the pistol started to slip through her fingers. Fire streaked across her back in the contour of a grinning skull, goading her to let go.

"Please," he said. "I won't write another word."

"You're finally telling the truth, Charles." She opened her fingers and kept her hand there in a parting salute, watching him plummet amidst a hail of twirling balusters into the trees below. The only sound he made was a little yelp when he hit the first tree, and then he was gone. The trees swayed around the spot where he fell.

Kate turned with a little smile, pleased with this unexpected turn of events—and froze when she saw Viera Silver standing in the open doorway, staring impassively. "Viera. Shit. I didn't hear you come in."

"You have much on your mind," Viera replied, her tone unreadable.

Armitage was alert and staring in horror at Kate, muttering through his gag. He wobbled back and forth in his chair. Viera's half-lidded eyes briefly considered him, but found nothing of intrigue.

Kate fumbled to conjure an explanation as the innkeeper sauntered into the room. "The . . . um . . . the deck . . . you see, it . . ."

Viera threw herself on the bed, spreading her arms and legs and staring upward. "I am disappointed," she said with a heavy sigh. "Woodes Rogers has left my tavern without a slit in his throat."

Kate let out the breath she'd been holding in and forced a tiny chuckle. She wasn't sure how much Viera had witnessed, or whether it mattered. "Rogers, yes. His time will come."

"If you say so." Viera extended a slender arm over the edge of the bed, pointing. "Who was he?"

"Who?"

"The man who broke my deck."

Kate turned to have a look for herself, as if she hadn't been directly responsible. A humid breeze swept up from below, tugging at the tails of her long black coat. Her hair shifted gently, grazing her shoulders. "He was no one."

Viera rolled out of the bed and smoothed the folds of her purple dress. She joined Kate out on the balcony, studying the broken railing. She shook her head. "This place is falling to shit."

"I'll pay for it. A few bars of silver should do it, yes?"

A mirthless chuckle sounded from deep in Viera's throat. "I like you, Kate. And not just because you are fine on the eyes."

"You do?" Kate was stunned. She hadn't been certain Viera liked *anyone*. "You shouldn't."

"I know I shouldn't." Viera plucked the tricorn hat from Kate's head and placed it on her own. It was a little big for her. She held her chin up as the hat dipped nearly to her eyebrows. Her lips crept into the faintest trace of a smile, and her seductive eyes slid Kate's way. "That's why I like you."

In the east, the night sky was turning a deep purple that mirrored the amethysts hanging from Viera's ears. "It's almost time," Kate said. "A worthless man for a fortune in silver. A fair trade, wouldn't you say?"

"I won't pretend to understand any of it," Viera admitted, closing her eyes. When those eyes weren't casting cold appraisal, she looked much younger than her thirty years. Kate found it hard to believe Viera was a year older than her. "What will you do with the money, Kate?"

Kate shrugged. "Maybe I'll take Rogers' advice and purchase land in America."

Viera furrowed her brow. "With slaves?"

"I've raided slave ships and I've seen the horrors below decks. I've done many terrible things, but I cannot abide slavery. Anyone living on my land would be free."

Viera's eyes fell on her from an angled head, filled with skepticism. "Are you saying this to impress me?"

"What?" Kate laughed. "No. Why would I—?"

"I'm teasing you," Viera informed her flatly. She prodded Kate with a sharp elbow.

"Oh."

"It sounds nice, this plan." Viera made a sound like a kiss between her front teeth and lower lip. "But you wouldn't linger there."

"I've never been good at lingering anywhere."

Viera nudged the hat with two fingers, but it slid back down to rest just above her eyes. She removed it and handed it back to its owner. "My husband does not trust land. He says it refuses to move with the tide."

Kate nodded in agreement as her eyes drifted from the forested mountains to the dwindling firelight of moldering structures huddled below. Extravagant houses, shops, a cathedral, and huts roofed in leaves. They were all rotting. She fit the hat atop her head, dipped the beak low, and said, "That's why none of this will last."

RECLAMATION

A white sun blazed across a cloudless sky, bringing a suffocating heat down upon the deck, but Woodes Rogers felt only the glorious euphoria of relief.

The young crewmen were remarkably efficient for undisciplined merchant sailors, and their course to Nassau was a straight and easy one. All were settling down to games and leisure as the sun dimmed orange and then red in the west and squashed into a rippled oval before vanishing to reform itself on the other side of the world.

In the gloom of twilight, Captain Lumley plodded up the forecastle and clapped Rogers hard on the back, jarring him out of abstraction. "We're steady at six knots, Governor."

"Don't do that again," Rogers said, giving him a fierce look.

Lumley dropped his hand and dismissed Rogers' anger with a laugh. He was a middle-aged Welshman with a scraggly beard, curly brown hair, a pointy nose, and a toothy grin that drove Rogers mad. "Do what?"

"Don't manhandle me. I am not your friend. We are business associates, nothing more."

"You're too serious, Governor. I pray you're just as serious about the other half of my payment."

"You'll get the remainder in Nassau."

"That's just fine, then, Governor. That's just fine. Worried me, it did, seeing all that silver leaving my ship. And handing it over to a woman, at that. It's enough to make a man's cock shrivel up inside him."

Rogers despised having to hire a merchant ship and suffer these simpletons. At least the captain had allowed him his cabin, after a generous stipend. "What silver?" Rogers said, staring at the man pointedly.

Lumley frowned, until realization dawned. He mimed buttoning his mouth. "The word is mum, Governor."

"I'm glad you understand," Rogers said. He turned aft and watched Lumley's boy of fourteen years ascend the shrouds. He was a handsome lad with flowing blonde locks and a strapping build. *Must get his looks from his mother*, Rogers thought. "Silence is worth more than silver, Lumley. I'd hate for anything to happen to your boy. What was his name?"

Lumley's hand found Rogers' collar, drawing him near. "Did you just threaten my son, Governor?"

"I did," Rogers replied. "I am a powerful man, Lumley. Should anything happen to me, people will come looking."

The Captain kept his grin. "Maybe I'll tell them Warlowe killed you."

Rogers groaned. *Predictable. So predictable.* If Lumley kept this up, he might find himself the victim of an unfortunate accident in Nassau's harbor. "I have men in Tortuga. They saw me leave unharmed. If I am to drown between Tortuga and Nassau, it wouldn't exactly be a difficult mystery to solve."

Lumley released his collar and broadened his grin. "No need for threats, is all."

Rogers smoothed his frock coat and smiled pleasantly. "I shall retire to your cabin for the night, Captain. I'd rather not be disturbed. It has been a long day." He knew the man was glaring at him as he moved aft, mouthing obscenities.

In the cabin, the man who called himself Armitage—Woodes had known him by another name, long ago—looked up from a dark corner. His remaining hand was chained to a locked chest packed with cannonballs. He'd tried to drag the chest but had only managed to bruise up his wrist. "This is a trap," he murmured. "Warlowe set you up. You don't believe me, but you'll see."

The wretch had been saying "This is a trap" since he'd been brought onboard, but he refused to elaborate with anything more than fearful eyes and a trembling lower lip. "I cannot believe or disbelieve what has not yet been disclosed," Rogers said as he poured himself a glass of brandy. He sliced an orange in half and squeezed the juices into the glass, mixing it with a little spoon. "Warlowe is long at our stern, and I see no sails in pursuit. I know you are the man I've been searching for, even if you don't. The trade was fair. Warlowe has what she wants, for now. I cannot possibly fathom how this might be a trap."

"You'll see," Armitage repeated. "You'll see."

"I invite you to enlighten me."

Armitage looked at the floor, his shoulders trembling. "It would sound ridiculous."

Rogers took a seat behind his desk before the stern gallery and stretched his legs. "You've been among the natives too long, I think. The jungle addles one's mind, believe me, I know. I've witnessed it firsthand, in my younger days of exploration." He sipped at the brandy, letting it warm his stomach. "You don't remember me, do you?"

Armitage looked at him from across the cabin, squinting his one eye. He shook his head. "I don't remember much before the island. I think I was someone of import. I think people were looking for me. I was running from them, when they should've been running from me. That's what I remember. I was wronged. I know I was wronged." Crow's-feet extended from his lone eye as he struggled for recollection. The crevice of the saber wound seemed to deepen, emphasized by dim candlelight. "Something was taken from me. And it was no small thing."

"A throne was taken from you," Rogers replied. "And the man who wronged you sent me to find you, long before I governed the Caribbean. To assassinate you. We dueled, you and I, and it was a good fight. You were a fierce opponent then. I daresay I feared for my life, but I persevered, as I am wont to do, and when I saw an opening, I seized it. You fled with one less eye. Fled to your little paradise, where no one could find you. And it never occurred to me you had been wronged until I was betrayed by the very same man, years later. Our dearly departed King George the First, your father. I had brought order to the Caribbean, brought an end to the pirate menace. Expulsis piratis, restitua commercia. Piracy expelled, commerce restored. And how did he repay me? I returned to Britain to find my company liquidated. The new governor refused to honor my debts, despite all I had accomplished with the funds I had borrowed. In the end, money was all that mattered. Not results. Not loyalty. I was imprisoned, and in that dank place my heart sickened with resent for the man on the throne, a man I had called a friend. He abandoned me. I contemplated ending my life."

He looked over his glass to make sure Armitage was still listening. "Through that dark fog of despair came an ambitious young writer named Charles Johnson, promising redemption. Another tool of the Crown with delusions of fame, but through this man I saw my way out. I befriended this young fool, and together we crafted stories in service of Britain's fortitude in the face of merciless reavers. Tales to dissuade anyone with romantic notions of piracy. Tales of villains larger than life, each of them meeting a gratifyingly bloody end. We left out most of those who had eluded us, those who were still reaving. Warlowe and her ilk. And it worked. The fiction became reality. Everyone believed it. Johnson didn't need to provide sources, not with a 'Captain' before his name and Woodes Rogers to qualify his facts. Again, I had served the Crown."

He took a sip of brandy and swallowed bitterly, blinking through the sting. "And one day I was released, and they told me I was to be absolved of my debts, and they sent me back here, because the pirates were returning. I had proven myself once before and I would prove myself again. 'Clean up the scraps,' they told me. So I tracked down Bartholomew Roberts, who I knew to be alive still, despite what Johnson put in his book, and I set him upon Warlowe. She had something I wanted. The key to finding you. The key to my revenge. A man whose very existence threatened to unravel an entire kingdom. I meant to find you myself, but to my everlasting surprise, Warlowe did the work for me. And now I have you. My retribution." It occurred to him he was rambling on like a madman now, but he didn't care. It felt good.

"I'm no good to you," Armitage insisted, practically whining now. "I don't know anything. I don't know what you're talking about. I don't know who you think I am, but if I am the person you say, I remember none of it."

Rogers laughed. "It doesn't matter. The threat is enough to secure my position in the Bahamas forever, and keep the funds coming from England. Warlowe figured that out. She's a sharp one. A fleeting kind of intellect that serves her only in the moment, not longstanding intelligence, but an impressive intellect for a woman."

"Are you going to take my other eye?" Armitage asked. "It's all I have left."

Rogers nearly choked on a seed of orange. "What? No, you fool. Haven't you been listening to anything I've said?"

"I'm sorry. Don't hurt me."

"I'm not going to hurt you. Jesus!" Rogers took a deep breath, cooling his blood. Brandy sometimes turned on him, intensifying his fury. "You will live comfortably for the rest of your days under my care. My wife is a fine woman. She will tend to you. Perhaps, one day, you and I shall become friends." He doubted it, but he figured he might as well give the man something to look forward to.

"Friends?" Armitage looked at him, and there was a severity in his eye that hadn't been there before. "Men like us don't have friends."

"What makes you say that?"

"Charles Johnson. Your writer friend. Where is he now?"

Rogers smiled shrewdly. So, Armitage had been listening after all. "I left him in the care of Kate Warlowe."

"Kate Warlowe." Armitage lifted his stump. "She's the one who did this."

"Aye," said Rogers, pleased that Armitage's mind wasn't entirely lost. "I took no pleasure in leaving him there, knowing his fate when he was so plainly oblivious to it." He sighed. "I'm afraid Charles became dangerously obsessed with the truth. He served his purpose, but I have no desire to see another volume of that book printed. You see, the Bahamas are mine again, and I cannot abide piracy to flourish. If Warlowe returns to piracy, I will see her at the end of a rope."

Armitage shifted his body, but it was impossible to get comfortable on the deck, chained to a chest. Rogers stood and moved to the bed and gathered two pillows under his arm. "Lean forward," he told Armitage, and he stuffed the pillows between him and the chest. Armitage leaned back and let out a long sigh. "I am sorry about your eye." Rogers returned to the desk and fell in the chair. "That was another man. A much younger man. Naïve in his loyalty. That man is gone now. He died in that prison. He paid his debts. The man you see before you now owes England nothing. They owe me everything."

Armitage placed his stump atop the chest and slumped his head, falling silent. A few minutes later, he was snoring. Rogers shook his head in disgust. Whatever brief light he had glimpsed in the man's eye was lost now. He wondered if it would ever return.

He would've preferred keeping Armitage in the brig, but he couldn't afford to take his eyes off him. He supposed he would never be able to take his eyes off Armitage again. He would have to keep him somewhere safe in the governor's mansion on Nassau, under constant guard. Armitage would never be allowed to wander into the town. Agents of the Crown could be anywhere, possibly right under Rogers' nose. He would need to watch his own men closely, learn who he could trust.

Despite the relief Rogers presently felt, he knew his life was about to become much more complicated. It was no small thing, blackmailing a fraudulent king who would do anything to maintain his lie. George the Second would seek every opportunity to eliminate Rogers' scandalous leverage over him.

He downed the remainder of his brandy before the reality of the situation could fully dawn on him. He poured another glass and downed that one as well, wincing as it burned his throat. He was asleep in his chair within the hour, with brandy swirling about his head as the ship swayed from side to side.

He dreamed of Nassau. He was wandering through the streets at night, looking for someone, but wherever he went, the lights blinked out. Silhouettes appeared at each window, snuffing out their candles. He followed a shadow as it slunk between two structures. The full moon shone down on a cobbled alleyway between two large structures. At the end of the alley stood a slender woman, framed against blue moonlight. He started toward her, calling out. She wore a tricorn hat and a long black coat, billowing in the breeze. As he came closer, he saw the face of Kate Warlowe. She was smirking at him. He fumbled about his person for a pistol or a cutlass, but he had neither. When he looked up, she was walking away, unconcerned with him. "Wait!" he called. "Stop!" She didn't seem to hear him. She rounded a corner and he followed after her, only to discover another empty alleyway.

His eyes opened to red light sifting through the stern gallery, illuminating the cabin in bloody ambience. Rogers stood and listened, but heard nothing. No voices on deck. No thumping of feet. No waves crashing against the hull. He tested his balance, pacing behind the desk. The ship was stationary.

Across the room in his corner, Armitage was alert and staring at the door. His broad face was beaded in sweat and he was trembling violently. He looked at Rogers. "She's here!" he said. "She's here!"

"Warlowe? That's impossible!"

"Not Warlowe. But she knew! She knew what was coming!"

Rogers was halfway around the desk when he heard a creaking sound. The latch lifted on the cabin door, and it gently slid open, spilling a line of red light across the deck. The line grew as the door opened to reveal the silhouette of a tall woman in a long dress. Dozens of dark shapes crowded behind her. Outside, the world was swathed in crimson. Rogers stepped before the desk. "Who are you?" he called.

She did not answer. She just stood there, motionless. He couldn't be sure if she was even breathing. He reached back to find the flintlock pistol he had placed on the desk earlier, but his fingers only found rolled charts and a compass.

The woman's legs seemed to barely move beneath her long skirts as she eased into cabin. The red ambience of the stern window illuminated her as she stepped closer, and Rogers was shocked to see the face of a pretty young woman. Her raven-black hair was long and straight. Her eyes were steely blue, nearly grey, penetrating the shades of red.

Light freckles dotted her cheeks. Her lips were as pale as her skin. Her arms were streaked with deep cuts that did not bleed but had not healed. A low-cut black dress bore her broad shoulders. Above the breasts, her chest was scarred with three strange glyphs. Her left breast, he was horrified to see, had been cleaved, and nothing remained but raw meat, trickling fluids down her dress. A necklace of jade beads hung from her neck, and at the end was a man's desecrated hand, grey and shrunken, a bone protruding from the severed wrist.

The woman's dead eyes held Rogers' for a long moment, and he found his legs rooted in place, refusing to carry him further. She did not blink. Not once. A terrible smile split her white lips. She turned the smile on Armitage, and she spoke down to him with a voice that reverberated through the cabin, with a strange accent that hinted at French and hinted at something else. "You have something that belongs to me," she said.

"God save me," Armitage whimpered. He tried to raise his hands in prayer, but one was chained to the chest, and the other was gone, hanging now from the woman's neck.

Her grin spread wide. She reached down to seize him by the throat with a slender white hand and draw him toward her. His arm stretched taut along the chain as she dragged him toward the center of the cabin. The heavy chest skidded a few inches before it hit a raised plank and wouldn't budge any further, but the woman didn't stop. Armitage let out a warbled shriek as the muscles of his arm elongated and his joints separated with loud pops. His skin peeled apart at the elbow, bones gave way, and the forearm detached with a tremendous snap of cartilage and a splash of blood.

Armitage's wail dropped Rogers to his knees, clutching

his chest as the blood froze in his veins. "Stop this," he heard himself say.

The woman shoved her hand into Armitage's wailing mouth, muffling his shrieks. His neck inflated as she drove her fist down his throat. His face turned red and his eye rolled all about, madly searching for a way out. His chest shuddered and swelled as she twisted her arm inside him. The muscles of her arm tightened. She clutched hard and pulled upward, and Rogers heard something crack inside Armitage, like the shell of a clam being pried open. The stumps of Armitage's arms spread outward. She wrenched herself out of him. Blood fountained from his mouth. The woman's arm emerged shrouded in a crimson glove. In her fist she held his rapidly thudding heart. Severed valves spurted blood through her fingers and down her dress. She turned her grin on Rogers and extended the beating heart to him. Each beat impacted him like a hammer to the chest. Armitage's flesh turned white before his face struck the deck. His eye settled on Rogers as the shrinking amber iris clouded over.

A warm, wet lump rolled down Rogers' inner thigh and weighted his breeches. He smelled the vulgar stench of his own shit a moment later. His spine gave out. The woman moved forward with startling speed and caught him by the throat before he could faint. He gazed up into her beautiful, terrible white face. "Please don't kill me." The voice that came out of him belonged to a lesser man. A coward.

"You are already dead," she said. She placed Armitage's heart in his hands. It was warm but no longer beating. "You will clamor on hands and knees through the long darkness, and at its end you will find no dawn. A pestilence is already in you, feasting on your heart and mind. And so it will be with your empire, and all empires to come."

She left him trembling in the dark, holding Armitage's heart. The door creaked shut behind her as she joined the dark figures waiting on deck. Rogers dropped the heart and struggled to his feet. He trudged forward in a drunken shamble, nearly tripping over Armitage's corpse on his way to the door.

He pushed through the door and found himself enveloped in a crimson mist. The ship had come to a dead stop in the doldrums of a blood-red sea, with not so much as a soft breeze to caress her limp sails. A score of bodies hung from the yardarms, swaying gently in the mist. Their bellies had been opened and their entrails spilled out of them, drenching the deck in blood. He recognized the pale, petrified faces of the crew. Among them was Lumley's son, his swollen purple tongue hanging out of his mouth. And at the foot of the mainmast was Captain Lumley himself, sitting with his legs splayed out before him. He cradled his own decapitated head in his lap, while blood oozed in black rivulets down the stump of his neck.

Rogers shambled past the open hatch leading to the hold and smelled death from below. He glimpsed a pile of bodies, none of them in one piece. He moved on to the starboard bulwark and fell between two cannons. He pulled himself up on the rail and stared in disbelief.

It was a galleon, as black as night, with red sails. Shadows moved about its deck, their red eyes gleaming back at him. And the woman in black stood upon the quarterdeck with her bloody hand on the helm, facing forward, long black hair trailing behind her like ink in water. Oars extended from the ship's many oar-ports, like the long legs of some giant sea-spider, and the ship plunged into the fiery mist.

And then it was gone.

Rogers collapsed to the deck on his back, watching the mist toil over the ship. He did not move again until a day later when the ship crashed into Nassau harbor, its keel sliding up over the beach. They found him huddled against the bulwark, rinsed in blood and reeking of his own shit, surrounded by death.

Plague followed, cold and slow. It swept through Nassau and claimed over half of the populace in the years that followed. Its final victim was Woodes Rogers. He died in his bed during the summer of seventeen-thirty-two, gripping his chest through a final spell of icy shivers while muttering the words carved in an oak plaque above his mantel.

"Piracy expelled, commerce restored."

Kate's journey begins here

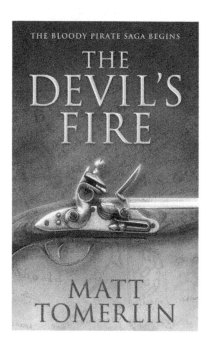

Available at Amazon.com
and bookstores

facebook.com/thedevilsfire
@MattTomerlin

TheDevilsFire.com | mtomerlin.com

Made in United States
Orlando, FL
10 November 2021

10331181R00236